The Bitter Taste of Death

In Maat's Service
Volume 3

Kathrin Brückmann

ORIGINAL TITLE: BITTER SCHMECKT DER TOD
HORI UND NACHTMIN BAND 3

ISBN-13: 978-1542641050

ISBN-10: 1542641055

MAP OF ANCIENT EGYPT

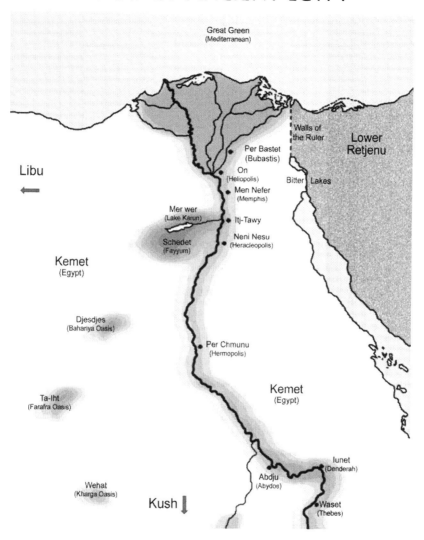

Great Green
(Mediterranean)

Walls of
the Ruler

Lower
Retjenu

Per Bastet
(Bubastis)

On
(Heliopolis)

Bitter Lakes

Men Nefer
(Memphis)

Libu

Mer wer
(Lake Karun)

Itj-Tawy

Schedet
(Fayyum)

Neni Nesu
(Heracleopolis)

Kemet
(Egypt)

Djesdjes
(Bahariya Oasis)

Per Chmunu
(Hermopolis)

Kemet
(Egypt)

Ta-Iht
(Farafra Oasis)

Iunet
(Denderah)

Wehat
(Kharga Oasis)

Kush

Abdju
(Abydos)

Waset
(Thebes)

Principal Characters

Historical persons are set in bold characters, followed by pronunciation pointers in parenthesis and the translation of the names in italics. The letter combination 'th' is pronounced like an aspirated 't'.

Senusret III. (Senusret) – *husband of goddess Ouseret*
A ruler spurred by a bird.

Hori and his family
Hori – *name of god Horus*
Has to prove someone's innocence.

Sobekemhat (Sobek-em-hat) – *Sobek is at the top*
Hori's father and the vizier, but not wise.

Nakhtmin and his family
Nakhtmin (Nakht-min) – *Min is strong*
Wants to protect his wife.

Mutnofret (Mut-nofret) – *(the goddess) Mut is beautiful*
Has a mind of her own.

On the way
Djehutihotep (Dshehuti-hotep) – *Thot is content*
A nomarch wanting to elevate himself.

Seneb – *the healthy one*
His chamberlain proud to look up at his master.

In Waset
Ouseret – *the mighty one*
Desirable nag who remains silent.

Nehesy – *Nubian*
Her father who suffers under her silence.

Meseh – *crocodile*
Basket maker, who rarely keeps silent.

Antef – *He who brings his father along*
Nomarch of Waset, for whom silence is worth gold.

Amunhotep – *Amun is content*
First prophet of Amun in Waset and too old to keep silent any longer.

Hereret – *flower* and Hapi – *name of the river god*
Silent servants in Hori and Nakhtmin's house, but only there.

Ipuwer (Ipu-wer) – *the big one from Ipu* (old name for the Min nome)
A doctor who makes Ouseret break her silence.

Merwer – *the much loved*
A tradesman on the go, who promises a lot.

Sanefer – *beautiful son*

Merwer's son who doesn't think his methods very promising.

Satnefert – *beautiful daughter*
Merwer's daughter, whose promise is lifted by his death.

Ankhes-Nit – *She lives for the goddess Neith*
His wife, who lives on his promises.

Nofru – Beauty
His servant, very promising in many regards.

Ini – *Gift*
Sells Merwer's goods and hopes for the promised reward.

Wahka – with a steady ka, Heny – *sedge*
Merwer's tenants, who keep silent at first then say too much.

Seni – *my brother*
A registrar about to regret his corruptibility.

Kawab – *Pure ka*
Prophet of Khons, corruptingly disloyal.

Bakenamun (Bak-en-Amun) – servant of Amun. Principal of the House of Life zn Waset.

Neferhotep – *beautiful and content*. Physician at the House of Life in Waset.

Amunmose – *Born by Amun*. Head of the archive.

Sarenput – *Son of the years..* Nomarch of Ta-Seti.

Senusretankh – *May Senusret live*. Principal of the hemu-netjer of Amun.

PROLOGUE

Pharaoh Senusret dropped to his knees before the golden effigy of the god. "Oh, Amun, my divine father! Don't abandon your son, grant me heirs! The Two Lands need a Horus in the egg!" he cried out. His second wife had just given birth to a dead boy; he was still in mourning. His throat tightened, but he was the king. He had to be strong. In a lower voice he continued, "Grant me peace within the Two Lands because my heart is filled with grief, and I cannot swoop down on my enemies like a falcon."

He heard feet scrape behind him, where he knew Ameny, the first prophet of the God, was waiting. When he rose and turned, his faithful companion kept his gaze averted as if such weakness demonstrated by his king troubled him. He sighed. At least he could rely on Ameny not to carry what he heard within the sacred site outside its walls. Where else but here could he put his emotions into words? However, the prayer had barely eased his pain over the loss of an heir to the throne. He dreaded having to begin his day's work.

The flapping of sandals announced the arrival of the three other prophets, who would perform the morning ritual for the god. They bowed to their ruler and stretched out their arms at knee-height. As he left the sanctum sanctorum, Amun-Ra's glistening rays caressed the hieroglyph-adorned forest of columns and him, the king of the Two Lands, as well. The sounds of the morning hymns for Amun floated through the hall. The promise of a new day soothed like balm and consoled him.

As soon as he entered the office, his secretary announced two visitors. Senusret would much rather have enjoyed the peace he'd found during his stay at the temple a little longer, but the demands of the Two Lands couldn't wait. "Who is it then, Atef? Never mind, send them in," he grumbled.

The sight of the two physicians who'd been so deeply involved in the horrible events of recent days hit him hard. His heart darkened as if a shadow entered it, a shadow of the damned. "Didn't I relieve you of your duties for a while?" he growled and impatiently waved away their reverences. "Have a seat."

With courtly elegance, Hori, the son of his vizier, glided from his bow onto the offered stool. Dark-skinned Nakhtmin moved more awkwardly, as usual. He couldn't imagine a more disparate pair than these men, albeit their diverse views had allowed them to solve two intricate mysteries. Senusret held both in high esteem and felt closer to them than to most of his trusted advisers—and he certainly couldn't blame them for what had happened. "What brings you here?"

Hori answered, "Your majesty, we beg your permission to travel to Waset."

Waset! The mere sound of the word reminded him of another pressing problem. Askance, he studied the young doctor. "What do you want in the Southern City?"

Nakhtmin's face turned a shade lighter at his sharp tone, almost the color of mud, but it was he who replied, "Um, it's because of Muti. I mean my wife. She needs to convalesce in a place where she isn't constantly reminded of her loss. And since I'm from the south…"

The grief in his words brought burning tears to Senusret's eyes again. Regretting his harsh words, he wanted to apologize, but that wouldn't befit a king. "Is Lady

Mutnofret well enough for such a journey?" he asked more softly.

"Yes, your majesty," Nakhtmin murmured.

"How is Queen Nofrethenut?" Hori inquired. "I haven't seen her for three days now, and I'm sure she's well cared for by my colleagues. However…"

"Weak. Shaken. Grieving." Senusret pressed his lips together to keep them from quivering, then he added, "On the mend, though." He sighed and considered the friends' request. He'd prefer to keep them close. Concerning the health of his wives, he trusted these two more than any other royal physician. Maybe because they belonged to the small group of people who knew exactly what happened that night. Knowing them to be at hand would calm the part of his heart that worried about his second wife. Then he could better concentrate on other problems, but he had promised the friends a vacation, and he wasn't one to renege on his word. So they'd chosen Waset—maybe not a bad thing to have them there. He smiled. "I grant you permission. Furthermore: you may use my royal rowboats." He watched them expectantly.

Hori's eyes brightened, but before he could accept, Nakhtmin said, "I believe Muti would prefer a less hurried means of transportation. She hasn't recovered yet."

Senusret knitted his eyebrows. What cheekiness! No, only concern made Nakhtmin talk so disrespectfully. They shared the same bitter fate, they had both lost a son before he could take his first breath. He splayed his hands. "The decision is yours. Boats and men are at your service. I'll have Thotnakht write up an authorization. Additionally, I'll send messengers to the nomarchs of the south to inform them of your journey, so you'll receive comfortable accommodation wherever you decide to stop."

Nakhtmin's face turned a shade darker as he stammered, "Your majesty is too kind… Thank you very much!"

Senusret waved dismissively. "However, I also have a request: Keep your eyes open on your journey and report back to me about the nomarchs' activities."

Hori's eyebrows hiked up, and he leaned closer. "Problems, your majesty?"

Instead of replying, Senusret rubbed the root of his nose. What should he, what could he reveal to the young men? He balked at burdening them with more worries since they desperately needed a break to recover. Still, he couldn't afford to pass up this chance of enlisting their sharp minds. "I currently have nobody to report to me what the powerful men in the south are up to," he replied in a general manner. No need for them to know why he wasn't kept in the loop. As his ears and eyes, they wouldn't face any danger. Just a small favor, and a harmless one, too.

"Hum, what should we watch out for?" Nakhtmin inquired.

Senusret saw his discomfort and wished he could simply send them off on a pleasure trip. However, without an informer in the powerful southern nomes he felt blind in one eye. The nomarchs' accumulation of offices challenged his own influence significantly and with growing force. Some of them had even become adepts of the divine mysteries and thus bearers of secret knowledge he'd rather have consigned to trusted people only—ones he'd selected himself. Unfortunately, the nomarch title was heritable, the only office in the Two Lands, thus he couldn't influence succession. Instead of appointing men of his trust in far parts of the country, Senusret could only strive to prevent the existing rulers from elevating themselves to kings within his kingdom.

He rubbed his temples to lessen the pressure, but his powerlessness in this matter scorned him. Some districts had even established their own calendars based on the regency of their nomarchs instead of the years of the pharaoh's rule as was custom everywhere else. Levies from the south had also dwindled, always a bad sign. Maybe he needed more people down there to keep him informed, but that wasn't easy to achieve. Without an excellent cover, nobody reached a position close to the mighty. The nomarchs were clever and cautious. If only he could kick them out of their offices! Unfortunately, the rulers of the south maintained faithful militia armies—presumably to guard the borders. And as the ruler of the Two Lands, Senusret couldn't simply invade the territories of his tributaries, not without good reason.

A cough drew his attention.

The two physicians stared at him, awaiting a response. What should he tell them? "You should watch out for signs that these powerful men appropriate things no mortals are entitled to. Maybe you'll also learn where my taxes drain away. Last but not least, I need to know who is loyal to me and whose fealty seems questionable to you."

Hori pulled a long face. "But your majesty! Actually..."

His friend placed a hand on his arm and silenced him. "We'll keep our eyes open for you, my king, but only as far as it won't hinder our recuperation. I don't want to endanger Muti or exhaust her."

Nakhtmin's objection annoyed Senusret. Quite impertinent for someone from Upper Egypt, growing up with mud between his toes! His anger vanished as quickly as it had seized him. Nakhtmin had spoken as a physician, and his patient was no less than his wife. The man's concerns were justified. He sighed. "Oh well. I can't ask for more. I wish you a safe and pleasant journey."

ON THE RIVER

Day 2 of month Wepet-renpet in Akhet, the season of inundation

Disgruntled, Hori stood in his garden, staring at the numerous sandbanks in the riverbed of the Nile, whose waters seemed to evaporate in the glaring heat. How he burned to finally travel to Waset, the city so dear to him because of the woman who lived there. However, Nakhtmin refused to set out at such low water levels when countless shallows endangered boats and passengers. His friend didn't want to cause Muti further troubles, and Hori didn't dare to ask her himself what she preferred. Nakhtmin acted protective toward her like a dam, shielded her from everything, and Hori dreaded a quarrel. Time dragged like sticky tree gum. When would the Nile finally flood? Hopefully, Nakhtmin wouldn't come up with new excuses then, like raging torrents. They had to await the time when the water gradually rose, while the continuously blowing northern winds would fill their sails and carry them south against the current. After all, when the inundation reached its peak all boat traffic came to a standstill. And in the south, the waters rose several days earlier, which meant they'd be traveling toward the high tide. Hori grinned. That prospect might convince Nakhtmin to use the pharaoh's speedboats after all.

How much he longed for Ouseret! His beloved had left for her hometown half a month earlier, and every iteru of distance separating them appeared like an enemy he needed to defeat. If only he'd learned the true reason for her hasty departure before then. He still remembered every word of the letter Nakhtmin's father-in-law had shown to him a few days ago:

To Imhotepankh, head of physicians in Itj-tawy, from Bakenamun, head of physicians in Waset, greetings. You inquired about physician Ouseret's reputation. Know this: Ouseret is the daughter of physician Nehesy, and both worked at our House of Life until recently. Then, however, a patient of Nehesy died, and he was suspected of maltreatment. I found myself forced to relieve the physician of his duties. At the Kenbet, presided over by vizier Sobekemhat, Nehesy was convicted of causing his patient's death by medical malpractice and sentenced to five years in the quarries of Kheny. Thereupon physician Ouseret—although free of blame—also left the House of Life. I hope I was able to help you with this information.

A bitter laugh escaped Hori. No wonder Ouseret shied from him when she learned who his father was: vizier Sobekemhat. Hori felt tempted to think the old man had convicted Nehesy only to spite his youngest son. He loved to put obstacles in his way and wrinkle his noble nose at Hori's endeavors, particularly when he failed. Why did the vizier have to preside in court over Ouseret's father and sentence him? Five years in the stone pits…that equaled a death sentence. Hori wanted to curse but restrained himself. The gods certainly followed a plan by letting all this happen. "Maat, is this your doing?" he whispered with hope rising in his heart.

The goddess of a just world order had guided his steps before and thus taken care that perpetrators of vicious crimes were punished. Of course, this had to be the reason! Maat herself wished him to travel to Waset and disclose the unjust verdict. The physician from Waset had to be innocent, and Hori would prove it. He closed his eyes and imagined how soft Ouseret's hard features would turn as soon as he'd freed Nehesy from the quarries. How grateful she'd be!

His own father, though… Hori noticed he was clenching his hands. Oh no, Sobekemhat wouldn't appreciate his efforts in the service of Maat. It wouldn't surprise Hori if the self-righteous vizier had been prejudiced against the accused just because he was of the same profession his unloved son had chosen—against his father's will. The more Hori thought about it, the more he grew convinced that his father had come to premature conclusions in his anger. Still, Sobekemhat's mistake was Hori's chance. If he proved Nehesy to be innocent, nothing would stand in his way to Ouseret's heart.

Hori hurried toward the gate offering passage to the neighboring estate where Nakhtmin lived. Maybe he and Muti would welcome him more enthusiastically than in the days before when they were still grieving the loss of their unborn child.

One of Nakhtmin's gardeners looked up at the sound of Hori's steps. "The master and the mistress are sitting at the riverbank," the man explained.

Hori thanked him and headed toward the Nile. Behind a lush oleander bush, he spotted the couple sitting with their arms around each other. He didn't want to intrude, but before he could retreat, Nakhtmin noticed him and waved him over. Mutnofret's smile lifted Hori's heart. Although he'd held no responsibility for the events that caused her miscarriage, he felt daunted in her presence. He greeted both more formally than usual, even bowed.

Muti pulled up her eyebrows. "Did Hori swallow a stick?" she asked her husband and rose with some difficulty since she still suffered from the after effects of the miscarriage and fever. She turned toward the house. "I was about to lie down, so you'll be undisturbed."

Nakhtmin grabbed her hand. "May the gods bless your dreams."

When her light steps faded, Hori said, "She seems almost fully recovered." He lowered himself onto the bulrush mat next to his friend.

Nakhtmin nodded. "Her body, yes. But the loss weighs heavy on her—on both of us. I wish she'd finally cry…"

"Perhaps she'll get over it soon," he said lightly but refrained from adding that they were still young and would certainly have more children soon. As a doctor, he knew all too well about the dangers of pregnancy and birth, and only half the children reached adulthood. Therefore, every budding life carried a promise with uncertain fulfillment. "With regard to the pharaoh's offer…" he began cautiously.

Nakhtmin interrupted him right away. "All right, you won. Muti says she wants to get away as fast and as far as possible. So yes, let's use the royal rowboats."

"Oh, good." Only yesterday, when they'd spoken to the king, he'd declined the offer and opted for a restful trip during which Muti could relax and recuperate. Hori grinned. Several days or even weeks on the river probably weren't what a woman would regard as restful, whether it was healthy or not. And he couldn't have abided to proceed at a snail's speed, had even considered letting them travel on their own, while he rushed ahead. "How many days until we can set out, do you think?"

Nakhtmin rolled his eyes. "You're worse than Muti's little brothers who couldn't await the last new year festivities!" he exclaimed. "The gods alone know when the waters will rise, but it can't be long now."

Hori's scalp itched. He pulled off his wig and scratched.

"Don't!" Nakhtmin called. "The wound has barely healed. If you scrape off the scab, it'll bleed again." After examining the injury with his fingers, he brushed over the stubble above Hori's forehead. "White. Like Muti's," he murmured, aggrieved.

"There is worse. The stone pits for example." Hori immediately regretted his clumsy attempt to change the subject when he saw his friend's harried expression. Of course, to him the light-colored strand in Muti's hair symbolized the loss of their child. And Hori often recalled with horror the moment when the shadow entered him. "I guess it'll remind us forever of that terrible night. I wish I could forget all about it."

Now it was Nakhtmin's turn to look guilt-stricken since he hadn't been possessed by a shadow. "I'm sorry. Let's not talk about it. What was that about stone pits?"

"That's where Ouseret's father has been sent. And the quarries are as good as a death sentence; very few survive the hard work for long—certainly not a physician whose hands are only skilled in the use of lancet and scalpel but not in splitting rock under a glaring sun. Oh, Nakhtmin, we need to hurry!"

His friend groaned. "If I trepanned your head, I'd probably find a worm screaming Ouseret's name all day and nothing else. But I do understand the need for speed. Still, neither you nor I can force the divine Hapi to swell according to our wishes. Oh, and I must tell you…I won't be available to help you this time. You'll have to clear Ouseret's father on your own. Muti needs me now."

That was a fierce blow! Nakhtmin looked determined though. Hori wouldn't be able to change his mind, so he sighed in resignation. "Oh well, I guess I'll have to deal with it on my own then."

Day 3 of month Wepet-renpet in Akhet, the season of inundation

The gods must have heard Hori's pleading. Only a day later at dawn, Nakhtmin, Muti and he boarded the royal speedboat, a slim wooden craft with a high bow ending in a carved lotus flower and an even higher stern, where carriers stowed their luggage baskets.

Ameny handed them a package, wrapped in linen and bearing a seal, over the vessel's side. "A gift for Amunhotep, the first prophet of Amun in Waset."

Muti's father had only recently ascended to the same position in Itj-tawy, but Waset was the main cult site of Amun. Therefore the first prophet of its temple held at least the same rank as Ameny in the royal residence, although the latter exerted a greater influence on the king. Hori nodded at Nakhtmin's father-in-law with appreciation. A present and a friendly message might make the powerful man look favorably upon them, an advantage if they intended to investigate at the House of Life, which belonged to the temple.

The captain commanded the men hoist the sail, while the rowers went down on one knee and grabbed the oars. The men on the shore side pushed the boat away from the pier until it glided into the waterway. Then the men on both sides dipped the oars into the water. At the command of the coxswain, they pulled in unison. The boat was propelled forward so fast that Muti barely had time to wave goodbye to her parents before they rounded a bend in the river. During the next hours, the crackling of the sail and the commands of the coxswain formed a monotonous background noise only interrupted by occasional warnings from the fellow at the bow, checking the water for shallows, which prompted the helmsman at the stern to lean into the rudder and steer the boat into deeper water.

Thanks to a fresh breeze from the north, the boat plowed through the Nile so fast spume occasionally sprayed their faces, a welcome cooling-off on such a hot day. There wasn't much space on board, and Nakhtmin had immediately claimed the shade of a structure made from bulrush mats for Muti. Hori had no choice but to settle next to his friend and roast under Ra's glistening rays.

In the beginning, they'd all been excited, particularly Mutnofret, who had never traveled far from the royal residence Itj-tawy, just like himself. "Look how far the fields extend!" she'd cry or, "A village! I wonder who lives there."

Every time, Hori had grinned. His farthest journey had taken him to the temple of Osiris near Neni Nesu, which lay about five iteru south of the residence. One iteru was the distance a boat could usually cover in one hour, but this wasn't a common boat! After only two hours, they'd passed the sanctum on the western shore, and soon after they approached the capital of the twentieth nome of Upper Egypt. Its buildings rose on the eastern shore, and the helmsman steered the boat toward the harbor.

"Are we going to stop here?" Muti asked in her excitement. "Can I take a look around the city?"

"We'll only swap the oarsmen," the coxswain announced. "His majesty ordered us to take you to Waset without delay."

The boat rocked seriously under the steps of the departing men and the fresh crew, and soon they set off again. The sight of a steady up and down of sweaty backs and their trained moves that propelled them forward so quickly lulled Hori. Rise, dip the blade in, lean back, pull the oar and sink down. The blade rises. Start over again. Hori glanced to Muti who'd dozed off with her mouth open. He nudged Nakhtmin with his elbow. "Just look. If that isn't restful!"

His friend grunted in displeasure. "I'd just fallen asleep myself."

The crew changed every two to three hours, depending on where the next stop for the speedboats was located. When the celestial body hovered right above them, the helmsman steered the craft into the shade of a waterfront grove and let the rowers rest. Grinning, Hori watched the men cheer and jump from the bow into the water. "You think it would harm our dignity as royal physicians if we did the same?" he asked Nakhtmin.

He wiped sweat from his face. "By the gods, I feel like roasted fowl." After a glance at Muti, he winked. "The guardian of my dignity is still sleeping. Let's take the risk!"

Giggling like children, they dropped their shendyts and hurried to the bow. Oh, what relief the cool floods offered. He swam a short distance lest the next man jump on his head, then lazily floated. Oh no, the current pulled him too far from the boat! With haste, he paddled back and grabbed one of the oars.

Puffing like a hippopotamus, Nakhtmin surfaced beside him. "Lovely! I could stay here for hours," he called.

That moment, Hori noticed movement between the reeds on the mostly flooded riverbank. "Better not." He pointed at the gray beast whose ears, eyes and nostrils showed above the waterline.

Nakhtmin paled. "Damn! The rowers will wake it up with their screaming and splashing."

"At least it's alone, as far as I can see." Nevertheless, he moved over to the nearest crew member and told him of the threat.

"Hippo! Hippopotamus!" the youth shouted.

The whole crew fell silent immediately. The helmsman lowered a rope at the rear so the swimmers could climb aboard there, not at the bow where the dangerous animal lurked. Nakhtmin hastily hauled himself up, obviously no longer willing to stay in the water for hours, and Hori also appreciated solid planks below his feet. Not even a crocodile took it up with an angry hippopotamus!

A few daring fellows jumped back into the river anyway, but this time from the stern.

"Muti's still asleep," Nakhtmin said with relief in his voice. "She'd give me an earful all the way from here to Waset if I jumped in again."

Hori laughed. "You're right, it's not worth risking that!"

Soon the last drops of water had dried on their heated bodies, and they donned their clothes again. A little later the boat set off once more, and in the evening they disembarked in Khemenu, the capital of the Hare nome.

After a day of doing nothing in the glaring sun, Nakhtmin felt more exhausted than after long hours of service at the House of Life. "We need to find accommodation quickly before all beds in the inns are taken," he whispered.

Hori pointed at a group of men who seemed to await someone at the pier. Judging by their high quality uniform clothing, they were servants of the nomarch's household. Next to them stood carriers with two palanquins. Nakhtmin gasped. "For us?"

"What did you think it means when the king—life, prosperity and health—allows us to use his speedboats and announces our arrival? That we'd have to take care of accommodations on our own?"

Nakhtmin bit his lower lip. He hated it when Hori acted like an arrogant know-all. As if this weren't something special for him as well. However, this wasn't the time to argue with him—in front of all these strangers—so he held out his hand to Muti and helped her up. The fact she'd been dozing pretty much all day showed him how weak she still was, even if her tongue had fully recovered, quick and sharp as before.

The servants bowed to them, one a little lower than the other. He was the one to address them. "Welcome to Khemenu. I'm Seneb, chamberlain of the nomarch and prophet Djehutihotep. Our lord is awaiting you. If you'd be so kind as to take a seat?"

Hori climbed onto one palanquin, and Nakhtmin settled next to Muti on the other. While their litters still stood next to each other, Hori murmured, "They are even sending us the chamberlain!"

Grinning to himself, Nakhtmin assumed his friend was impressed after all. Soon his jaw dropped in astonishment though. In front of a splendid temple stood a gigantic statue made of alabaster, at least four times a man's height.

"Have you ever seen such a huge statue?" Muti called. "Tell me, Seneb, who does it depict?"

The chamberlain fell back and walked beside them with a complacent smile on his face. "This is an effigy of my master Djehutihotep, and it was he who had it brought from the stone quarries in Hut Nebu for the glory of the pharaoh—life, prosperity and health—and the great god Thot, whose first prophet my lord is. Apart from that, he's also mayor of this metropolis." With that he hurried ahead again, visibly content with the impression his city made on the courtiers from the royal residence.

Looking at the statue, Nakhtmin thought the nomarch had it made mostly to his own glory. He bent close to Hori. "A man with many offices and honors is our host."

Hori nodded slowly. "Not the kind you'd want to have for an enemy."

At the nomarch's residence, not only the big man, but a magnificent banquet awaited them. Djehutihotep only offered the finest food at his table, and Nakhtmin wondered if people ate and reveled here in such a manner every day. That would explain why the tributes to the king didn't pour so copiously from this nome. The oasis wine, however, flowed like water. In the middle of the hall, almost-naked dancers gyrated to the rhythm of intoxicating music.

The nomarch was a man of advanced age—Nakhtmin estimated him to be at least fifty years old—and besides a sprawling belly he featured an impressive double chin wobbling up and down during his frequent fits of cheerfulness. "How wonderful to meet you again so soon and under much more pleasant circumstances," he told Hori, whose eyes widened in astonishment before he gave a barely noticeable nod.

When could these two have encountered each another before? Djehutihotep granted him no time to ponder the question as he turned to Muti and him, offering his welcome. But the friendliness he displayed toward their group of travelers never reached his eyes, which seemed to constantly probe them in a sinister way. As if he knew of Senusret's request to report back on the actions and behavior of the nomarchs… The ruler of the Hare nome was one of the most powerful among them, as he never tired of pointing out, since his family had held this high position for generations. Nakhtmin acted appropriately impressed but also realized their host was a very sick man. The pale skin, the sweating, all signs of heart issues and the honey disease. If he checked his urine, it would likely taste sweetish.

The sons of the fat man also indulged themselves, and why shouldn't they? The oldest would inherit his father's office and rule over the Hare nome after him, without interference of royal administration. His brothers and sisters were also well provided for. Nakhtmin sighed. Luck simply dropped into some people's laps without them having to reach out for it. Hori likewise only would have had to fulfill his father's wishes to reach power and honors without effort, but he'd stubbornly insisted on becoming a physician against the old man's will. For the first time, Nakhtmin admired his friend although he often acted like a spoiled brat.

Musing over such things, Nakhtmin spent the most part of the evening in silence, while Muti skillfully conversed with Djehutihotep and Hori talked to his physician. He couldn't think of anything worth telling these high-and-mighty folks, he the son of a minor priest from Khent-min.

Then all of a sudden, their host directed his words at him. "Now, my young friend, I heard the temple of Thot caught your attention?"

Shocked, Nakhtmin choked on his food and nodded while coughing. "Oh yes," he croaked as soon as he'd caught a breath. "A magnificent building, albeit it pales against the glory of the statue in front of it."

Pleasure showed in the nomarch's face. "Ah! Transporting the statue unharmed all the way here was an incredible undertaking, equal to none in the Two Lands. It was loaded onto a giant sled pulled by four workforces of forty-three men each."

Fortunately, Nakhtmin didn't have to fake his reaction as he called, "That truly is an unbelievable achievement! How did the men manage to pull the sled with such a heavy weight on top over such a long distance?"

Djehutihotep bent toward him and said in a conspiratorial manner, "Water. The ground below the skids needs to be kept moist, that's the secret. The sled moves easily then." He laughed jovially. "I like to tell myself that transporting the statue was the greatest achievement of my reign. The scene is depicted in my grave. Would you care to visit it before you move on? However, the site is one iteru east of Khemenu…"

Hori turned around and said with honest-sounding regret in his voice, "Unfortunately, my lord, we need to leave at dawn. However, we feel truly honored by your offer."

Nakhtmin nodded vehemently. Walking several hours to the necropolis of the nomarchs would be too strenuous for Muti.

The next moment, Hori exclaimed, "Did you just say *east* of Khemenu? Aren't your graves built in the Beautiful West?"

The powerful man smiled with some restraint. "Unfortunately, the rocks on the western shore aren't suitable for constructing grave sites—too crumbly—while east of here we've got wonderful limestone. Thot's temple is made of it as well. Thus, my ancestors started digging their graves into the rocks there, and I follow their example."

Hori shook his head in visible confusion. "Graves in the east!"

To Nakhtmin's relief, his friend didn't elaborate on what that meant for the death cult, the local weryt and the like. He was too tired to keep his eyes open much longer. "Um, forgive me, Djehutihotep. I'm really exhausted after such a long, eventful day and would really love to retire now," he started out.

A shadow crossed the ruler's face, but a hearty smile chased it away so quickly, Nakhtmin wondered if he'd only imagined it. The nomarch called, "Of course, naturally. I won't keep you any longer and wish you farewell since you're planning to leave at dawn. Safe journey!"

They thanked him politely for his exceptionally fine hospitality, and Djehutihotep beamed. "Perhaps we'll meet again soon. Seneb!"

The chamberlain appeared at his master's call. "My lord?"

"Take my guests to the rooms prepared for them."

"Certainly." He bowed and made an inviting gesture with his arm. "If you'd be so kind as to follow me, please?"

Nakhtmin rose and staggered with fatigue aided by slight intoxication, as he had to admit to himself. The wine had tasted nice, and since his mouth had been idle for most of the evening, he'd apparently imbibed more than he'd consider healthy under normal circumstances.

The next morning, Nakhtmin's head ached, Sekhmet's punishment for excessive drinking!

"Should I ask Seneb if he can provide my ailing husband with a laurel wreath?" Muti teased, while he tottered to the privy, groaning.

"Since when are you the sunut curing me?" he grumbled.

Returning, he found a chain of fresh leaves on his bed and gratefully wrapped it around his head. Soon, the cool freshness and the scent brought some relief, and a small breakfast of fruit, bread, onions and fish marinated in vinegar restored him further.

The sun had barely risen when they left the palace with only Seneb offering farewell since his master and family still slept. Hori seemed to cope better with yesterday's indulgences than he did, or had his friend been the wiser one for a change and restrained himself? Either way, Nakhtmin appreciated the cool breeze blowing away the last remains of pain and numbness.

Again, they were carried past the gigantic effigy of Djehutihotep, whose shadow seemed to cover most of Khemenu at this time of day. Then they stepped aboard the royal boat. Another day of glaring sun! Nakhtmin groaned. At the last moment, he asked one of the servants who had accompanied them for his palm frond.

Hori grinned. "Excellent idea! Can I have one, too?" he called.

The servants did their bidding, but their faces showed disapproval at their poor manners. Naturally, it was demeaning for men of importance to fan themselves, but Nakhtmin couldn't care less. Groaning, he sank back and smiled at his wife.

The corners of Muti's mouth twitched. "If you donned finest royal linen, you would still remain a peasant," she whispered. Nakhtmin pinched her side.

Hori snorted and fanned himself with vigor. "I guess that makes me a peasant, too."

She laughed out loud. "You only picked bad company, which is rubbing off on you now."

He grinned broadly. "The best company a man could wish for!" As soon as the harbor of Khemenu disappeared from their sight, he turned serious. "Well, Nakhtmin, what do you think of our high-and-mighty host?"

He pursed his lips while mulling it over. "I'm starting to understand why phar-aoh—life, prosperity and health—wished for our untainted views on the nom-arch's behavior. Too much power on too few shoulders, or so it appears to me."

"In contrast to you two loafers," Muti interrupted, "I listened carefully to what fatty revealed about himself. That statue of him—"

"Presumptuous!" Nakhtmin called. "Should a mere mortal strive for something like this? Only the king and the gods deserve such honor."

"There's more to it, my husband. The priests of Thot will bring sacrifices for the statue every day once Djehutihotep has passed on to the celestial realm."

"Well," Hori mumbled. "That clearly shows how he rates himself: equal to the gods. I'd never have expected that from someone who…um…" His hand moved to the bronze bracelet on his left upper arm.

Nakhtmin knew that it covered the ankh sign, the symbol of life carved into his skin, which had something to do with the secret ritual Hori had to perform recently. Of course, he couldn't talk about it—as usual. His chest tightened as he thought of the two ostracized persons, whose names must not be mentioned again. The former vizier of the Two Lands had abused his power to get inconvenient people out of his way or silence them. And the executed vizier's wife had been even more deviously cunning. Her shadow had haunted Hori even from the realm of the dead with her hatred. How much more dangerous did that make someone like Djehutihotep whose power was all-encompassing in this world? "At least it won't be long until he sets off to the Beautiful West," he murmured.

Hori nodded. "He didn't look well at all. His physician told me about the cures he'd administered. No matter how friendly he was, the man has no clue. The overuse of enemas will send Djehutihotep to his grave sooner than without any treatment." He shrugged. "Even better, right? The king won't have to worry about his shady activities much longer."

"Don't be too sure. His spawn is eager to follow in his footsteps," Muti cautioned. "The nomarch title being heritable only fosters fat and lazy administration in the nomes. Nobody in the Hare nome has to make an effort to win the king's favor. Nobody needs to show diligence and skill. Here only one man has to look favorably at you, and it's not the king."

Nakhtmin gasped. "Muti!" If his beloved was right, that questioned the whole order in the Black Land! But hadn't he thought along the same lines?

Hori nodded. "She's right. And who but our young king could change ancient ways—for the better?"

Muti's gaze said, 'There you go, at least one person recognizes the smartness of my heart.' Still, he'd never dare to suggest such a thing to the king, feeling too insecure in the position to which Senusret had elevated him. After all, the pharaoh had only asked them to observe, not to give instructions.

The first hours of the day passed so quickly, they barely noticed until a change of oarsmen interrupted their conversation.

"Where will we alight this evening?" Nakhtmin asked the helmsman. The wind carried a scent, which gave him a prickling sensation. It smelled of home!

Indeed, the man replied, "Khent-min, the capital of the Min nome."

His heart hammered in his chest, and his hands moistened.

Muti cried out in cheer "Oh, Nakhtmin! You have to show me where you grew up!"

He'd rather not do that. If she saw the ramshackle hut in a decrepit quarter of the city, she'd feel ashamed of him. His father had only been a hem-netjer of the lowest level. As such a minor priest of Min, he wasn't granted a large estate like the one in which Muti grew up. To distract her, he pointed at the landscape to their left and right. "Just look how far the Nile already extends here. The fields are almost completely flooded."

Shortly before they reached their destination, Nakhtmin recognized the islands rising from the water. At the knee of a long bend in the river, he saw his birthplace, which he'd left so many years ago to study in Itj-tawy. Ra's fading rays dipped the gorgeous temple of the fertility god in a glowing light. Lush palm copses surrounded the sanctum and seemed to place feathers atop.

"Oooh!" Muti cried out in wonder.

"What a view!" Hori exclaimed.

Pride welled up in Nakhtmin's heart. Perhaps his hometown wasn't as shabby and provincial as he remembered it? "Let's visit the temple tomorrow," he said excitedly. "I'll show you where—"

Hori's hard grip around his wrist silenced him. His friend shook his head ever so slightly. What was that all about? Oh, of course! He only cared to see Ouseret again as soon as possible. No matter this was supposed to be a recreational journey serving Muti's recovery, he wanted to turn it into a race. Still, he bit his lip. Not worth arguing with him. "Well, we can do that on the return trip."

Again, the nomarch received and hosted them, but to Nakhtmin's growing pride, the dignitary presented himself more modestly than pompous Djehutihotep. However, he wielded similar power, and Nakhtmin found that disconcerting in the light of their recent experiences. But they weren't here to consider the state of the empire's government. Instead, he meant to concentrate on Muti's well-being. With joy in his heart, he realized the lethargy she'd displayed since the miscarriage had lifted and made way for vivid interest in everything she saw. This journey truly was just what she needed to forget her sorrows. Early the next morning, they stepped onto the rocking planks of their craft once more.

Day 5 of month Wepet-renpet in Akhet, the season of inundation

The closer they got to their destination, the more restless Hori became.

"Sit still! You'll make us capsize!" Nakhtmin admonished him again and again.

On the evening of the third day since their departure, they arrived in Waset, also called the Southern City. Not even Nakhtmin had ever been this far south, and except for Itj-tawy, he'd never seen such a large city. Waset was gigantic! As expected, the temple of Amun dominated the sea of houses, but he also spotted many palaces and estates.

Hori stood up but had to flail his arms until he found his balance in the rocking boat. Then he gazed at the buildings. "One can clearly see this has once been the residence of kings," he called. "Just look how straight the streets are. Shouldn't be easy to get lost here."

"Yes, indeed, not a bend or dead end." Nakhtmin grinned. In Itj-tawy, some districts were a lump of crooked alleys often enough ending at a wall. After having traveled for so long, though, he understood why dynasty founder Amenemhet had moved the capital of the Two Lands farther north. News took too long to reach the outposts of the delta from Waset and vice versa.

As they approached the harbor, Hori stretched and craned his neck to search the riverbank.

"Looking for Ouseret?" Muti mocked. "She's probably awaiting you with greatest longing."

Ashamed of his glee, Nakhtmin watched Hori blush and lose all his self-confidence.

"Yes...no..." he stammered. "How'd she know? I just thought..."

"You thought she'd be sitting at the pier all day pining for you, admit it."

Hori's complexion turned even darker, and Nakhtmin thought that Muti's tongue was not only sharp but unerring. It was quite nice not to be the target of her taunts for once. But his friend had suffered enough, time to release him. "Nevertheless people are awaiting us." He pointed at a group of servants with two palanquins on the pier. Additionally, he noticed armed men carefully watching the proceedings at the harbor and felt slightly threatened.

Arrival at the Southern City

Day 5 of month Wepet-renpet in Akhet, the season of inundation

Why should Ouseret come to the harbor? She didn't even know he was coming. Disappointment dampened Hori's anticipation anyway. While he was carried through the city to the palace, he barely paid attention to his strange surroundings. When the large double gate came into sight, Muti's cry of surprise pulled him from his brooding, though.

"The ancestors of our king once resided here," Nakhtmin explained to his wife. "Thus the double gate, just like in the Great House of Itj-tawy. Look over there! That must be the temple of Amun."

Hori's head jerked around to the massive stone walls, behind which his beloved had to be. The House of Life, where she'd be working as physician, had to be located in the temple compound. If only he could go right away…

Antef, nomarch of the Waset nome, welcomed them in a manner so friendly, it calmed Hori's fluttering heart a little. The ruler was a slender man in his thirties with an intelligent, expressive face dominated by bushy eyebrows. Hori's gaze remained glued to those since they moved whenever the nomarch talked or used any facial muscle. They appeared like creatures with lives of their own.

When the nomarch learned they intended to stay awhile in the Southern City, he offered them an unoccupied house in the former government district. "First thing tomorrow, I'll send my servants over to make sure you lack nothing," he assured Muti. "Until then, I hope the modest rooms in my residence will suffice."

While servants carried their luggage into a corridor, Nakhtmin stammered his thanks, and Hori was more than content with the arrangement. As luxurious as the former palace of kings might be, he'd rather stay somewhere unobserved by the nomarch's staff. Although Antef seemed a kind and generous man, he likely wouldn't appreciate him sticking his nose in matters of local jurisdiction.

As if Antef had guessed his thoughts, he said, "Your father, the venerable vizier of the Two Lands, is doing well, I hope? It was a pleasure to host him recently, but he seemed somewhat frail."

Recently, ha! That must have been at the Kenbet, the court trial during which Ouseret's father had been convicted. And what did he mean by frail? Stiff would fit better. Hiding his emotions behind a smile, he said, "Oh sure, he's sprightly as always. My father will survive us all." If only to spite him!

Antef's chamberlain invited them to the table. Unlike in Khemenu, no banquet awaited them, which suited Hori just fine. Instead, a rich but simple meal was served, likely just the kind of food the ruler would normally eat. Nice to see modest nomarchs existed. Pomp and swank often disguised despotism and corruption.

"I've heard about the horrible events at the royal residence. Is it true that you were part of it?" Antef inquired.

Nakhtmin almost choked and cast Muti a worried glance.

"I won't dissolve into tears if someone mentions it," she snapped, pulled her hand from him and fingered the white strand above her forehead. "Really Nakhtmin…" Just in time, she remembered where they were and suppressed the rest of her reprimand.

Certainly not for long, Hori thought. His friend's constant fussing over her made it impossible for her to forget the terrible experience and truly mourn. He should try to talk some sense into him. Wait a moment, how could Antef possibly know about what happened? Then it dawned on him that the first prophet of Khonsu must have told him. The high priest of the moon god had been one of those attending the ritual to ban the shadows of the damned. The blabbermouth shouldn't have gabbed about it! Hori's breath caught. No, he couldn't have done that! No adept would dare. The secret knowledge needed safeguarding. And the rest that wasn't secret... He sighed. Of course, news traveled. "Mutnofret and I were victims of the curse," he confirmed. "And like her majesty queen Nofrethenut, she lost the child she carried. This journey primarily serves our recuperation." That would hopefully satisfy the man's curiosity. Now that Hori had made it clear how uncomfortable the topic made them, he should have the decency to back off.

Antef studied him intently but dropped the subject.

Hori congratulated himself on the idea to present himself as ailing as well. That gave him a plausible reason to be in Waset. One thing the remark had shown clearly: Though Waset was far from the royal residence, the nomarch didn't live under a rock and appeared to place great importance on being informed about everything. Maybe he wouldn't tolerate Hori snooping around, so it was better to keep him in the dark for now. Naturally, Antef would make a great ally smoothing the path for them, opening doors, but Hori couldn't be sure yet if the man was trustworthy. Too bad the king had announced their arrival. He'd have preferred to move unnoticed, at least in the beginning.

"...soldiers at the pier and in the streets," Nakhtmin was saying. "Do you feel threatened?"

Hori perked up. He hadn't noticed any of that.

Antef's eyebrows danced to his affable smile. "Oh, no, young friend, those are just my militia troops. They keep law and order in the city. But yes...occasionally we have to deal with robbing Bedouins, although they don't come this far since my people guard the borders. The soldiers serve to protect the general public."

Protect or monitor? Pondering the question, Hori pursed his lips. Although Antef seemed friendly and obliging, he apparently possessed sharp teeth. Woe to everyone who endangered the man's position!

Hori sighed in despair. Militia patrolling the city? That might make his task more difficult.

Day 6 of month Wepet-renpet in Akhet, the season of inundation

The next day, while Muti inspected the interior of the large estate Antef had provided for them, Hori took his friend aside in the garden. "Listen, you shouldn't display your concerns about your wife so much. I noticed whenever you make a fuss about her like a mother-duck over her ducklings, she's reminded of what happened. Give her time. The distraction will help heal her wounds."

In quick succession, Nakhtmin's face showed anger, confusion and finally realization. He sighed. "You're probably right. By Sekhmet's arrows, she seems to cope better than I do!"

Hori averted his gaze when Nakhtmin wiped tears from his eyes with angry moves. "You'll see, once she meets Ouseret again, the two will quack like ducks,

23

while we can find out if the patient of Ouseret's father really died because of the treatment he received. I believe she meant to prove he died of natural causes when she studied the papyri at the House of Life in Itj-tawy, trying to show her father didn't do anything wrong and couldn't possibly have healed the man."

Nakhtmin stared at him. "Say, can you ever think of anything else but this woman?" he called. "I'm sick of hearing her name, seriously!" With that, he stomped off.

That wasn't fair! Hadn't he just tried to help the couple get over their grief? After all, he knew how much a loss like that hurt since Ouseret... Oh! He ran after his friend. "Nakhtmin! You're right, I can't think of anything else." Mortified, he lowered his gaze.

The corners of Nakhtmin's mouth twitched. "It's all right. You're in love, that's normal. Beautiful house, isn't it? I wonder why nobody lives here."

He shrugged. "I guess many of the magistrates and officials moved with the king to the new residence when Amenemhet founded Itj-tawy. I have seen quite a few deteriorating buildings on the way. A residence without pharaoh is like a body without the breath of life."

"You may be right, but this house is younger and the garden well-kept. The former inhabitants can't be gone for long."

Before his friend could slide back into his grief, Hori said, "It's ideal for us. I've been worried Antef might watch our every step, but here we are on our own."

Nakhtmin snorted. "That's what you think. The nomarch has provided us with a cook and two servants, a man and a woman—want me to continue?" Although Hori shook his head, he added, "Then there are soldiers everywhere..."

On the way coming here, Hori had also noticed them. They always strolled through the streets in pairs, seemingly at leisure, but their gazes were alert. In Waset barely anything could happen without the ruler learning about it soon.

"Anyway, I'd bet a gold deben that they'll report everything we do to their master. We better take caution in whose presence we talk about Nehesy and the search for the true reason of his patient's demise."

Damn, his friend could think on his feet. "At least their assignments will keep them confined to the house; they won't be able to follow us when we're out and about," he replied rather lamely. Then Nakhtmin's exact words sank in and his heart leapt with joy. "Did you just say 'we'? Does that mean you'll help me investigate?"

An elbow connected with his ribs. "You'd be lost without me."

Indeed, he would!

That same day, Muti yielded to his urging and composed a message to Ouseret, which Hori accepted with trembling fingers. "I'll drop it off at the House of Life for you," he cried and hurried into the bathroom.

He'd love to throw himself at the feet of his beloved, but both his friends advised against it. That alone might not have kept him from doing it, but he remembered all too well her appalled reaction: "The vizier of the Two Lands is your father?" Under these circumstances, she'd likely be anything but happy to see him. However, if he ran into her at the House of Life by pure chance...

He thoroughly cleaned himself, then let Hapi, the servant of Antef, shave all hair from his body and dressed in a freshly laundered shendyt, as was appropriate for a visit to the temple. In good spirits, he set out. Maybe he could find out today what exactly Nehesy had been accused of. Medical malpractice—who'd ever heard of such a verdict? That sounded like the man was suspected of intentionally causing his patient's death without anyone being able to prove it. Hori was convinced every other judge in the Two Lands would have acquitted him, not Sobekemhat though. Wasn't it Hori's personal responsibility to undo his father's misjudgment? The goddess of a just world order must have brought him and Ouseret together, so he'd learn about Nehesy's fate.

These straight streets were really great. Without losing his way once, Hori reached his destination and passed through the impressive pylon of the Amun temple into a vast courtyard. Of course, he could have used the direct entrance to the House of Life for the ailing in need of medical care, but he wanted to walk over as much of the ground Ouseret's elegant steps had graced as possible. Hori squinted at the blinding white wall of limestone painted with colorful murals of scenes from the life of the god. The yard was completely deserted. He headed for a second, almost as mighty pylon, behind which he suspected lay another courtyard surrounded by the actual temple and the buildings of the House of Life. Far from it! This yard also lead to a gatehouse made of stone. The compound was much larger than the sanctum in Itj-tawy, but then Waset was the main cult site of the god also called the hidden one, and hidden he truly was.

To his right rose a building of breathtaking beauty, plain but with perfect proportions. Seven steps led to a stone baldachin resting on columns and arching over the divine bark, which was mounted there on a pedestal. Curious, Hori stepped closer and read the inscriptions. This was the Sed festival chapel of Osiris Senusret, the first of this name. Awestruck, Hori touched the velvety stone of a pillar covered with inscriptions and depictions of the gods. Not daring to climb the steps, he circled the building and found another stairway on the opposite side and entered. Although made of stone, the building was airy and flooded with light. A true artist must have created this!

"Hr-hrm!"

The ostentatious clearing of a throat had to be directed at him. Hori turned and stood before an older hem-netjer giving him a stern look.

"What are you doing here? Who are you? I don't know you." His gaze slid over Hori's attire and got stuck at the amulet with the udjat eye, which marked him as a physician. A smile spread over his face. "Oh, a doctor! So you must be looking for the House of Life?"

"Right you are," he replied. "I'm Hori, physician of the pharaoh—life, prosperity and health—and since yesterday a guest of nomarch Antef." The next moment he regretted having revealed his name and everything else. Now Antef would find out that he'd come here. Well, no harm done. What was more natural for a traveling physician than to visit other Houses of Life?

The smile on the priests face deepened, but he didn't bow. That meant he held a high rank. "I'm Senusretankh, the principal of the hemu-netjer of Amun. I've already been informed of your and your colleague's arrival. Welcome."

"Oh." Baffled, Hori followed the friendly man. Now he realized secrecy would have been futile and might have raised suspicion. After passing through another pylon and the adjoining third courtyard, he finally found himself in front of the temple buildings.

"The House of Life is behind that gate over there," Senusretankh explained.

Hori nodded and wanted to take his leave when he remembered something. "Oh, my colleague Nakhtmin is the son-in-law of the first prophet of Amun Ameny and bears gifts for the venerable Amunhotep. When do you think the prophet will be able to receive him?"

Senusretankh smiled again. "My master will be eager to hear the latest news from the royal residence. I'm sure he won't let the chance slip to host a dinner in your honor. I'll send you a message."

Hori forced a pleased expression although he felt no inclination to waste time on social obligations. "You'll find us in the Street of Palm Fronds. Antef has assigned us an estate there."

The principal nodded. "I know which one it must be. The family who used to live there recently fell out of favor."

"Ah, well, I don't want to keep you any longer Senusretankh. Thank you for showing me the way. We'll meet again soon, I'm sure."

"See you soon, Hori, son of Sobekemhat."

Hori closed his eyes in agony. Secrecy would really have been in vain if that man even knew who his father was.

In the shadowy corridors of the House of Life, he encountered a servant carrying a stack of linen cloths and stopped him. Without thinking, he blurted, "Can you tell me where to find physician Ouseret?"

The man bowed reverentially while eying him from down there with curiosity. "Are you the royal physician from Itj-tawy? You'll certainly want to call on the principal of doctors first."

Hori cursed himself for his clumsiness. Having a servant teach him etiquette was quite embarrassing. Fortunately, it was so gloomy here, his burning cheeks wouldn't show. "Of course I want to do that. Take me to him. Um, that is, if he has time to receive me," he stuttered. At least he hadn't mentioned Muti's message for Ouseret to this curious fellow. If the head of physicians was carved of similarly unyielding wood as his counterpart Imhotepankh in Itj-tawy, he might demand to see the message first. More heat rose to his head. He should have brought a gift to win the man's favor, which he'd need if he meant to question people here. And he hadn't even thought of getting a recommendation from the House of Life in Itj-tawy. But Imhotepankh wouldn't have had flattering things to say about him anyway...

"Follow me, please," the servant said and marched ahead. "You'll find venerable Bakenamun behind this door."

Sandals flapping, he left. Hori closed his eyes for a moment to brace himself, then knocked.

"Come on in, come on in!"

He entered the generous room filled with fresh air and daylight. To keep flies out, only a thin linen scarf covered the doorway leading outside. Through the veil he could make out lush greenery, likely a part of the garden of Amun. Behind an imposing desk of black wood with white marquetry—ebony and ivory!—sat a short round man, who studied Hori as closely as he eyed him. Then a hearty smile spread over his face. He jumped up and came around the desk, almost pushing over a servant who'd been fanning him with a palm frond. Then he spread out his arms as if to embrace his visitor. "Ah, welcome, welcome! You must be one of the royal physicians."

Surprised, Hori returned the smile and bowed. "You're right, wise principal Bakenamun! I'm Hori."

"Incredible!" Eagerly, he rearranged a stool for Hori and told his servant to bring refreshments. "Sit down. You must be thirsty, being used to a different climate and all. Incredible! The vizier's son!"

Hori lowered himself and made a dismissive gesture. "Oh please, don't go to any troubles on my account. I don't mean to occupy your precious time for long."

Bakenamun hauled his vast backside back into his recliner, causing it to creak in protest. "No troubles, no troubles at all. How are things in the royal residence? We hear so little, this far south... Ah, there we go, food and drink, there we go. Help yourself, try the pomegranates. Have you ever seen such large and juicy fruit? Yes, they prosper admirably here. Admirably!"

While Hori enjoyed the red pulp, Bakenamun ran his mouth without pause. Hori already wondered if he'd ever get a word in. However, a man so talkative would likely also spill everything he knew about the scandal in his own house if he skillfully guided him toward the topic.

He was licking juice from his fingers when Bakenamun's tongue took a turn down the right path. "It's so horrible what happened. The Horus in the egg...horrible! Did you and your colleague Nakhtmin really help ban the shadows?"

"You seem well informed here in the south," he replied in surprise. "Yes, it's true, but let's not talk about it! The memories are too harrowing. Nakhtmin and I came here to recover from those terrifying events. His wife, the daughter of Ameny, also lost her unborn child during that night of horror. And I..." He touched the bracelet on his left upper arm, which covered the ankh sign marking him as an adept of Osiris. Although Bakenamun wasn't an adept, he likely knew what such a mark implied.

"Say no more! I understand, I understand."

Hori nodded gravely. "These things are not for human ears. You should be glad to remain ignorant."

Bakenamun shuddered, though probably with pleasure like someone jumping into cold water on a hot day. "Ah! The king must count himself lucky to have servants like you! Very lucky. Whatever we can do in the Southern City to sweeten your stay, just name it!" As if only to himself, he murmured, "The savior of the Two Lands here with me in my office!" He clapped his hands. "Say, where has Antef set you up? Maybe you'd be more comfortable in my estate since there's so much coming and going in the palace..."

Hori suppressed a grin. The principal obviously regarded him as some precious jewelry he was eager to show off to his friends. "Don't worry, venerable Bakenamun, but thank you for your concern. Antef has provided us with an abandoned estate in the Street of Palm Fronds, offering every comfort we can wish for, in addition to peace and seclusion." He paused as a shadow flitted over the man's face. Had he offended him?

"The Street of Palm Fronds, hm. I know which one that is."

The second person today, who immediately seemed to guess which house. Strange. The street was fairly long with many buildings lining it.

"Would you like me to show you around?" the head of physicians interrupted his thoughts. "This isn't Itj-tawy, but our House of Life is one of the oldest and largest in the Two Lands."

Hori forced a pleased smile. "I'd much appreciate that, but I don't want you to neglect your duties on—"

"Say no more! It's an honor! An honor!"

Sighing, Hori accepted his lot. He'd have preferred to meet Ouseret alone. However, showing up with her supervisor might have its benefits—she couldn't simply send him away then. Unfortunately, Bakenamun seemed to think Hori had never seen a storage room from the inside before since he explained in much detail how they kept herbs, rinds, honey, wine, linen for bandages and many other things. After this lengthy lecture, he opened a heavy door behind which a doctor stood bent over a long table, preparing a balm. Shelves reaching to the ceiling were stuffed with repositories of all sorts and bushels of herbs.

"By the way, this is our Neferhotep," Bakenamun said and granted the older man a fatherly smile, causing him to return a curt nod before he tossed dried herbs into a mortar and cut off further words with heavy pounding.

Hori sneezed when the rising dust entered his nose. They left the storage room and entered a yard surrounded by colonnades. Here the ailing received treatment. Whenever they crossed the path of another physician, the principal introduced them to each other with great enthusiasm, but no matter how hard Hori tried, he couldn't spot Ouseret. Likely she worked in one of the rooms, taking care of a wealthy patient.

"Um, may I take a look into the treatment rooms?" he finally asked.

"Oh sure, sure. Let me see which one isn't occupied at the moment. We don't want to disturb the sick."

Hori suppressed a groan. That wouldn't get him anywhere. "Oh, of course. Let's just forget about it. I'm sure they don't look much different from ours." He laughed, but even to his own ears it sounded fake. He'd better take the direct approach. "I was hoping to see physician Ouseret. We met in Itj-tawy a little while ago when she treated my injury. I wanted to thank her again for her thorough care."

His companion's face turned to stone. "Ouseret? She isn't in Itj-tawy any longer?"

These words struck Hori like a blow to the chest. He couldn't breathe. His beloved wasn't here? When he finally managed to inhale again, he wanted to scream, 'No, thanks to you blabbering to Imhotepankh about her father's case!' But what good would it do to alienate the man? Besides, if Bakenamun believed Ouseret was still in the residence although she'd boarded a boat heading south weeks ago, what could possibly have happened? Fear clamped around his heart. Did she have an accident on the way? Had she fallen prey to murderous robbers? Something like that must have happened or else she'd be here. All his hope evaporated; the sun dimmed its light, and red shadows flitted across his eyes. What would the Two

Lands come to if she didn't breathe within them any longer? He staggered.

"Are you unwell?" Bakenamun asked with concern.

"The heat," Hori croaked. "I should rest awhile. Thank you so much for your hospitality. I'm sure we'll meet again." He turned on his heels, left the baffled principal standing there and hurried toward the other door leading from the House of Life. Outside in the shadow of the high wall, he leaned against the doorpost and gasped in sudden pain. If only he hadn't come here to receive such devastating news! Then his beloved could still walk the earth in his imagination, his agony bittersweet, not sharp as a thousand blades.

"Ssst," someone hissed beside him.

Confused, he looked around and spotted nose and eyes of a man peering through the narrow crack between door and frame. The next moment a chubby fellow slithered outside with stealth as if nobody was supposed to see him. "You're looking for Ouseret?"

Numb, Hori nodded. He'd seen the man earlier, treating people in the yard. So he was a physician.

"You'll find her in the Street of Basket Makers. She has a room in the house of Meseh and his wife."

"But..." Before he could find out more, the doctor had vanished into the House of Life. Hori struggled to wrap his mind around what he'd just heard. "Ouseret...is alive...?" he mumbled then cried, "Ouseret is alive!"

A woman hurrying past cast a curious glance back at him, and in his joy, he wanted to embrace her and dance with her, but he restrained himself. Ouseret lived—the sky had turned blue again, and the air tasted sweet.

Nakhtmin sprawled on the bed and let his thoughts wander, while Muti got them settled in.

"You can leave, girl, take the rest of the day off." With a contented smile, Muti closed the lid of the chest in which Hereret, their temporary servant, had stowed their clothes. With her foot, she pushed the travel baskets into one corner. "All in place. We can rest now," she said after the young woman had left the room, then she lay down next to him.

Rest how? His friend had set off like a hunting dog tracking his quarry and they wouldn't get any peace until he'd dragged them all into this new investigation, even Muti, although she was still so weak. Doofus that he was, he'd promised to help!

Nakhtmin placed an arm around her hip and pulled her close. "I wish Hori hadn't come along," he lamented. "Because of him we had to travel in such a rushed manner. Because of him we have to answer curious questions that only stir up unpleasant memories. I'd have preferred to take you to Khent-min at our own speed, or somewhere else where nobody knew us or what happened."

She drew away from him, her lazy satisfaction blown away. "And I wish you'd stop handling me as if I were fragile! By the gods, I even wish I'd left you at home and traveled with Hori alone, instead of—" She bit her lip.

Nakhtmin froze. "With me, you wanted to say? When did I become so aggravating to you that you can't stand my presence?" His heart pounded dully in his chest.

He turned away from her so he wouldn't have to see the scorn in her eyes. Or was it contempt?

Heavy silence filled the room, tenacious like syrup. Why didn't she contradict him? If only he'd followed Hori's advice and not gone on about the past again! When he turned around, silent agony distorted her mouth.

"Oh darling!" He embraced her, and she relaxed into uninhibited sobbing. "I'm so sorry," he whispered in her hair. "I'm such an idiot. I'm truly sorry."

"These questions—you must learn to bear them," she said later. "If I can do it, you should, too. You haven't suffered half of what I've gone through. We lost a child. That happens every day thousands of times in the Two Lands. We'll have another child, because we have each other. Let's not rummage around in the horrors of the past, I beg you."

Softly, he kissed the tip of her nose. "It's because I can only imagine what you must have gone through…" And he'd been attending to queen Nofrethenut during the dark hours when she suffered the same fate. "…I want to protect you. Oh, my Muti, fearing for your life devastated me!"

With tears glistening in her eyes, she managed the most enchanting smile. "Well, you can relax now. I'm here, and so are you. Let's enjoy that."

If only he could take such a light-hearted view. But he certainly didn't want to fight again. "Give me some lenience. I'm only a little boy from Upper Egypt."

She hiked up her eyebrows. "Is that so? Little? Let's see how small my Upper Egyptian brat is." She parted the folds of his shendyt.

"Muti!" he cried in mock indignation.

They still lay snuggled up against each other when the door flung open and Hori stormed in. "She's alive! Ouseret is alive!"

Nakhtmin rolled his eyes—that woman again—and Muti snapped, "Why shouldn't she?"

Looking confused, Hori wiped his forehead. "Of course, you don't know!" And then he told them what happened at the Amun temple and what he found out, his voice cracking occasionally. "I'm telling you, Bakenamun is his own echo. He constantly repeats what he just said and his mouth never stops."

Nakhtmin cackled. "Sounds familiar to me."

"Shut up! At least I've found her." Proud, he folded his arms.

Nakhtmin stared at him, but Muti posed the question, "And? What did she say to my invitation? When will she come?"

His usually so self-confident friend squirmed. "Um, ah, hrm."

Muti studied him doubtfully then said to Nakhtmin. "He speaks in tongues, my husband. Do you understand what he's saying?"

"No." Nakhtmin shook his head. "I really don't." He had to muster all his self-control or he'd crack up laughing.

"Oh you two! This is a serious matter! I couldn't possibly…How would I have…? Ugh." Sweat pearled on his forehead.

Nakhtmin released a whimper. "He didn't dare, hehehe."

His wife placed one fist on her hip. "Hey, it takes a lot of courage to knock on the door of a basket maker, and in a foreign city, too! Everyone knows how dangerous those are."

"Hahahahaha, stop it!" Nakhtmin couldn't keep a grip on himself when he saw

Hori's angry look. But as soon as his friend fled from the room and slammed the door behind him, he dashed after him into the garden. Grabbing his shoulder from behind, he said, "Listen…"

Hori shook with rage. His back and his shoulders were stiff with tension. "You have no idea how I despaired, believing something horrible must have happened to her. I thought I'd lost her forever! Can you imagine what anguish struck me down?"

Nakhtmin removed his hand. "Damn, yes, I can. How do you think I felt when Muti's life was at stake? Recently and even before that when she was attacked by…"

Hori's shoulders drooped, and he turned around. "Of course. Sorry, I wasn't thinking. But you had no right to mock me, laugh at my misery!" he retorted, scorn flaring up again.

Feeling guilty, Nakhtmin gnawed his lower lip. "It's just…we've talked it all over, and I think we've found our way back to each other. Everything will be like before. It's such a great sensation, bubbly like air in the water, if you get my meaning."

Hori sighed. "I guess so." He nudged Nakhtmin's shoulder. "I'm glad for you. Will you now help me find my happiness? I mean it's one thing to 'accidentally' run into Ouseret at the House of Life, but something completely different to knock on her door after everything that's passed between us."

"Of course." Nakhtmin clamped his mouth shut as if to suppress another fit of laughter.

Muti, wrapped in her light linen dress again, approached them. "So, which of you will brave that dangerous basket maker?"

That sufficed to crack him up. Cackling and giggling he sank onto the lawn holding his belly.

Muti's foot in a sandal nudged him playfully, which only made him laugh more. "Once my husband has regained sanity, maybe he'll accompany his wife to the district where the basket makers live," she said loud enough to drown out his whinnies. "That is, if he gets a grip before sundown."

A short time later, Nakhtmin walked with his wife through the streets of Waset and asked, "Why do you think Ouseret didn't return to the House of Life? Why does she hide at a…" His mouth twitched. "A…"

"Basket maker?" Muti supplied with an evil smile.

The vehemence of Nakhtmin's laughter made people ambling toward them keep their distance and cast them suspicious glances. Gasping, he covered his hurting ribs. "That word! Never say it again!"

"Tut, tut," she uttered in mock concern. "That'll pose a problem since Ouseret lives at a b—"

"Dear gods!" he gasped. "Have mercy, I can't take more."

To his tremendous relief, they'd almost reached their destination. After asking two people for directions to Meseh's house, they stood before the basket maker, who'd opened the door himself. The nice looking man of medium age pulled his mouth into a grin as wide as a reptile's, which might account for his name meaning crocodile. Only a very sharp look from Muti—worthy of her mother Isis—kept him from bursting out in laughter again.

When they inquired about the tall female physician, Meseh's brow furrowed and his face closed up. "Ouseret? Yes, she lives here with me and my wife. What do you want from her?"

Muti's gaze condemned Nakhtmin to silence, which he preferred anyway. She told the basket maker of her friendship with the woman.

His face lit up. "Then you must be lady Mutnofret from the royal residence! Of course, Ouseret has told us about you. Unfortunately, she isn't here but out shopping with my wife at the market. Why don't you come in? My house is yours."

"See! Dangerous," Muti hissed as she slipped through the door right behind Nakhtmin.

Faking a coughing fit, he croaked, "Choked!"

"Wait, I'll get you a mug of water. Or should we open a jug of beer to celebrate? My wife would scold me if such high-ranking guests had to... Have a seat." He scurried into the adjoining room and rummaged audibly. "Here it is! Freshly brewed, my wife knows all about it." He placed two jars on the mat on which Nakhtmin and Muti had settled and removed the linen cloths serving as lids. However, when they reached for them, he cried, "Wait, I'll sift it...not necessary? Hehe. Well, then, to your health!" He fetched a jar for himself and handed out reed straws from which to drink. That way they wouldn't swallow the dregs of fermented bread.

Nakhtmin sucked and took a big gulp. "Ah, that's nice. Your wife certainly knows how to make a good brew."

Meseh beamed and looked even more like a crocodile.

"We expected to find Ouseret at the House of Life," Muti said. "But someone there told us she now lives with you." She left the unspoken question hovering in the room.

The basket maker shook his head, looking downcast. "A difficult matter. When she returned from Itj-tawy, her family's house had been confiscated, so she no longer had a home. I met her by pure chance the day she was standing in front of the gate to the estate and didn't know where to turn, poor little thing."

This time, Nakhtmin really choked on the beer. Calling imposing Ouseret a poor little thing was quite the joke. Muti kicked his shin covertly.

Meseh didn't seem to notice. "You should know she treated my wife when she was ailing for several weeks without expecting any reward in exchange, which I simply couldn't have afforded. We lead a very simple life...and since my son's room isn't used now—he married recently—well, I invited her to move in with us until she's managed to prove her father's inno—oh!" He slapped a hand over his mouth and stared at them in shock.

Muti grabbed his other hand. "Don't worry, we know about it."

Nakhtmin nodded eagerly. "That's the reason why we are here, among other things. We want to help Ouseret and her father."

Meseh clapped his hands. "I'm so happy to hear that! She's a good child, Ouseret is! If you ask me, Merwer's son, this Sanefer, he doesn't deserve her as his wife after accusing her father in such harsh words! No reason to bawl her eyes out, right?"

Surprised, Nakhtmin stared at him then at Muti, who looked just as astonished.

"Sanefer?" he echoed. Who called his child 'beautiful son'? That man was probably a pompous pansy. He already disliked the fellow. And the other thing—that was hard to believe in many ways. Ouseret didn't seem the type to bawl her eyes out over anyone. She appeared so self-confident and strong, like he'd never be. Besides, he'd really thought she liked Hori. Last but not least: If she'd been promised to a man, why had she told neither Hori nor Muti?

"Oh dear, me and my running mouth…my wife always scolds me for my rambling, always!"

Nakhtmin got the impression everyone here liked to echo their own words when they talked, just like Hori had mentioned. Maybe that was part of the local dialect in addition to the drawl. "Maybe you could tell us a little more about it?" he encouraged.

Distressed, Meseh wagged his head. "You should know, Merwer is the man whose death Ouseret's father has been accused of causing. She was engaged to his son Sanefer for several inundations now, but Merwer refused to provide him with the means to set up his own household, year after year."

"And that's supposed to be the reason why Nehesy would have killed Merwer? That sounds like a…flimsy pretext, not a valid cause for harboring such rancor against someone."

Meseh shrugged, and the arrival of the women spared him an answer. Mutnofret rose, still a little clumsy, and approached the taller one. "Ouseret! I'm so glad to see you again!" She wanted to hug her, but the physician's drawn face dissuaded her.

"Mutnofret? What are you doing here?" Ouseret sounded disgruntled. "And Nakhtmin." Her gaze flitted about the room.

Nakhtmin stood as well. "Looking for Hori? He too is in Waset, but Muti and I came to visit you without him first. He didn't want to ambush you, if you know what I mean."

She lowered her head gracefully. "I appreciate that." Her hand clasped the handle of the basket so fiercely the knuckles turned white.

Strange how she seemed even more a foreign creature here in her hometown than back when she was staying with them. She radiated less attractiveness, too, or was it simply her tension that made her seem so different?

"Wife, our guests are Mutnofret and Nakhtmin from the royal residence," Meseh introduced them although his wife would have guessed that much already.

She was about to bow when Muti touched her shoulder and said, "Don't. We are friends."

Meseh's wife nodded. "Then you're welcome, very welcome in our home! By the merciful Isis, husband, what can we offer them? Nothing in the house but onions, bread and a skinny fish."

"Oh, we don't want to impose on you," Muti interjected. "Actually, we meant to ask Ouseret if she'd like to spend the evening with us. The nomarch has provided us with an estate as well as servants, and I'm sure they'll prepare a feast for us tonight."

"Such noble folks," Meseh's wife whispered. "So noble! Ouseret, you must go with them. Go, child. When will you get another chance like that? Go with them and enjoy the company of your friends."

Ouseret's features tightened. "You are my friends as well, and who could be kinder and more generous than you? But I'll go with them."

"Doesn't sound too excited," Nakhtmin murmured in Muti's ear.

"Well, we did kind of ambush her," she replied in a low voice, "And you know what she's like."

Soon after, the three of them strolled down the Street of Basket Makers. Nakhtmin rambled on and on about their journey and the reception they received in Khemenu, only to fill the uncomfortable silence. What was wrong with this woman? Close-lipped like a clam. Hori would find her hard to crack, and he wasn't looking forward to the ensuing lamentations. Two men of the local militia headed toward them, and they had to walk single file to make room for them. The soldiers made no attempt to give them more space.

"Why did you come?" Ouseret suddenly asked. Then she hissed, "What...?" Clenching her fists, she took several deep breaths. "What are you doing here? Such noble folks, tut!"

"I thought you'd like to see us again," Muti replied demurely.

Nakhtmin could see the hurt in her face and couldn't stand it any longer. Who did Ouseret think she was? The queen of Waset? "Horrible things happened in the residence after you left. Maybe you heard? The shadows of the damned crossed the river. The Horus in the egg—dead. Muti also lost our child!" His outburst ended in a dry sob.

Ouseret halted. "What did you say?" At long last her stony face broke open. "Oh, Muti, I'm so sorry!" She hugged her.

"We had to get away from Itj-tawy, away from the memories," Muti mumbled.

"Yes, yes, of course! I understand."

"She almost died as well," Nakhtmin cried out, still not mollified. "She needs to recuperate, therefore this vacation. And she wished to see you again."

Ouseret closed her lids for a moment and chewed her lower lip. Content that he'd managed to make her feel guilty, Nakhtmin marched on. "It's right ahead, the house at the corner on the Street of Palm F—" The aghast look on Ouseret's face made his voice catch in his throat.

"Oh, I know the place," she blurted. Her eyes glistened with tears. "That's where I was born."

REVELATIONS

Hori sat at the top of the estate's roof on the lookout for his friends. What took them so long? Had the physician at the House of Life lied to him, and Ouseret didn't live at the basket maker's house? With fierce determination, he battled his anxiety she might not want to see him again. After all, she'd trampled his declaration of love and his proposal under her feet... He frowned. Never before did he have to work so hard to win a woman's favor although she was in desperate need of support and therefore should have jumped at the chance to select a man with connections, offering protection against her enemies. She'd probably realize that soon. And once he'd cleared her father of all allegations, she'd sink into his arms in gratitude.

His sparking confidence waned. What if all that didn't make a difference? She'd rejected his generously offered hospitality although Imhotepankh, the nasty principal of doctors, had chased her from the House of Life. She'd rather fled the city. Was he so...loathsome to her? He sighed. Ouseret was another mystery he'd have to solve.

At long last, he saw three figures turning into the street. The sight of the slender and tall woman made his heart pick up its beat. Just a few steps from the gate, they stopped. Why didn't they come in? Instead, they talked and talked. He bent forward. Every fiber of his body screamed Ouseret, Ouseret! He almost toppled over and down to the terrace of the floor below!

Finally, they walked to the gate. Hori jumped up, hurried down the stairs and ran toward them. He met them on the garden path leading to the house, but the cheer on his lips faded when Ouseret froze then jerked back from him. She seemed about to turn and walk away.

"First, listen to what we have to tell you," Muti urged and grabbed her hand.

Ouseret's full lips curled. "I believe everything's been said between Hori and me." She freed herself of Muti's grasp. "It was a mistake to come with you."

Hori felt like a beetle squashed under her sandal. Still, they had one last chance to make her stay: try to achieve the one thing Ouseret should wish for the most. "We know about it. We know what happened to your father and why you went to Itj-tawy," he blurted and stepped closer.

Hissing like a cat, she stepped back. "You know nothing, you spoiled little brat, son of a corrupt courtier!"

Her words cracked down on him like whiplashes. He staggered. His friends also looked horrified by Ouseret's behavior. Nevertheless Muti grabbed her arm again. "I understand that this is a bit much for you to take. Still, I want you to come inside with me. We'll talk, only you and I, while those two remain in the garden. I promise you won't see them again until you want to. All right?"

Hori spotted their servant Hapi hurrying toward them and signaled for him to stay away. He didn't want the man to become witness to his rejection.

Still undecided, Ouseret huffed, but then she followed Nakhtmin's wife into the house, which felt like victory to Hori. Nakhtmin, however, groaned. "Dear gods! I really don't know what makes her so special to you. She makes a hedgehog look like a cuddly animal. Come on; let's sit by the river where it's cooler."

They walked to the wall at the waterfront, and Nakhtmin opened the gate lead-ing to the jetty. Hori glanced back at the house and detected the women sitting on the terrace. Then a moving figure caught his gaze. Annoying Hapi headed toward them.

"Don't you have anything to do inside, like wait on the women?"

"Hereret is taking care of that, master. You don't need anything?"

"Only peace and quiet," Nakhtmin replied.

Reluctantly, Hapi turned around, and Hori followed his friend onto the pier after closing the gate behind them. They settled on the wooden planks.

"Strange, Muti gave the girl the rest of the day off. Why is she still here?" Nakhtmin wondered. "Um, listen, Hori. I have to tell you something."

His apparent unease caused Hori to expect the worst. "Spit it out!"

Nakhtmin sighed. "Ouseret is engaged—or used to be."

He jumped up as if bit by a scorpion. "What are you saying?"

His friend pulled him down again. "We went to this...pfff..." He released a gig-gle, and Hori wanted to shake him.

"...Basket maker, but Ouseret was running errands with his wife, so we waited. Meseh told us that Ouseret is or was engaged to a certain Sanefer. He wasn't very clear about the current state of affairs."

"Impossible!" Hori screamed. "She'd have told me!" Or not? Why should she have done that? He buried his face in his hands. "Oh, Ouseret!" he mumbled dully. Had he already lost her to another man before they even met? Just because she'd passed the age when girls usually married, he'd assumed she was still saving her-self for the right one: him! But what man who laid eyes on her wouldn't want her? How stupid of him to believe she'd still be available! If her heart already belonged to someone else... He felt Nakhtmin's hand on his back.

"That's not everything," he said. "Her fiancé Sanefer is the son of a certain Merwer, and that was the patient Ouseret's father allegedly killed by a wrong dos-age of his medicine. Supposedly, because for years Merwer refused to give his son the means to settle down with Ouseret."

Hori looked up. "What a despicable man! What father would act like this toward his son?" Well, he wouldn't put such behavior beyond his own father, but thanks to the pharaoh, Hori already had his own household. He snorted. "In Nehesy's place, I'd have lost patience as well, having to watch my daughter suffer. Ha, wrong dosage... I'm starting to understand why my father suspected something far worse during the trial. Let's call it by its true name: poisoning." He rose.

"Where are you going?"

"Inside, of course. I have to tell her that I understand. That I know what must have happened. That I won't pursue her favor any longer." Never mind his break-ing heart, Ouseret loved Sanefer. Sanefer loved Ouseret. His own declarations of love must have been highly loathsome to her. Oh, why hadn't she told him?

Nakhtmin grabbed his shendyt to hold him back. "Don't you dare!"

"Hey, let go! What are you doing?" He pulled on the cloth but couldn't free himself.

"You want to tell her now you're convinced of her father's guilt as well? Oh, I'm sure that will comfort her," his friend scoffed, and Hori deflated. "Besides, I won't let you turn my wife into a liar. She promised Ouseret that she won't have to face us unless she wants to. And there's something else you don't know yet: This estate is Ouseret's parental home."

He released a crude curse. Had he called Seth's scorn onto himself, or why did the gods throw such obstacles in his way? "All right, I'll stay," he said and sighed.

Only now did Nakhtmin let go of him, and he sank back onto the wooden planks.

"By the way, it seems Sanefer left her because of this affair. Meseh insinuated that Ouseret bawled her eyes out because of him."

"Oh?" With new interest, he lifted his head. "What an idiot! Now he should have the means. I wouldn't hesitate a moment."

Nakhtmin laughed out loud. "Not you, of course. You don't love your father. But what if, let's say, Ouseret's father killed me? How'd you feel about that? Could you marry the woman whose father committed such a crime?"

Hori chewed on his lower lip. "Ouseret is not her father. Who says she's responsible for what he did?"

"Well, thanks a lot. Always good to know where one stands," Nakhtmin cried and turned away sulking.

Hori groaned. These days he always said the wrong thing, it appeared. Well, no wonder he could hardly think about anything but Ouseret. However, his infatuation with her could turn out his greatest obstacle in solving the mystery. "You also think he could have done it, right? I mean Nehesy." Damn, he'd thought it would be easy to prove Merwer died of natural causes or that his death had been someone else's doing, simply because Nehesy had no reason to kill his patient. Albeit the doctor must have harbored a grudge against Merwer. Oddly enough, the man still picked Nehesy as his physician although there might have been misgivings. "Only Ouseret can tell us what really happened," he squeezed out between clenched teeth.

"Come on, let's walk a bit," Nakhtmin suggested. "I've hardly seen anything of the beautiful garden yet." He turned to the door in the river wall. "Brooding is futile until we learn more."

Hori appreciated Nakhtmin's prudence. He'd almost ruined everything by barging into the house, spouting nonsense. Strolling past bushes and under trees toward the pond, he imagined Ouseret's caring hand behind every flower. Why hadn't he noticed earlier how unique and beautiful everything was here? He plucked a blue flower and inhaled its scent. The beginning of a poem he'd heard a long time ago came to his mind, and in his thoughts, he tweaked the lines to fit Ouseret as the addressee:

You are my first sister,
You are like the garden,
which you planted with flowers
and all sweet-smelling herbs.

Then he cried out, "If only she'd let us help her!"

Dusk approached then darkness encroached until they only stumbled and staggered through the garden. Nakhtmin was hungry and thirsty and seriously tired of listening to Hori's love-stricken sighs. Didn't he realize how hopeless his case was? A wicked thought sneaked into his heart: wouldn't it be better for his friend if Ouseret's father remained a convict? Sanefer obviously had turned away from her because—

"Nakhtmin? Hori? Where are you?" Muti's call interrupted his silent monologue.

About time! Together they broke through the bushes like water buffaloes, Hori spurred by his hunger for Ouseret, not food. Dear gods! Hopefully, Antef's servants hadn't heard what the women had discussed. Nakhtmin had seen them leave the estate at dusk, heading home, he assumed. The meal they'd prepared would be cold by now. What a shame.

When the four of them finally sat around the low table, he dug in greedily. Instead of chairs, they sat on cushions, which seemed to be custom everywhere in this household. On the terrace, they were placed on mats. Muti also ate with a healthy appetite, but Ouseret and Hori only nibbled on the roasted duck or munched a plum. The palm wine seemed more appealing to Hori—which he might dearly regret in the morning, Nakhtmin thought. To slow him down, he placed a warning hand on his arm. "You'll need your wits tonight," he murmured, and Hori nodded.

Muti announced, "I guaranteed Ouseret that she's still as safe under this roof as when it belonged to her family. Nobody will hurt her here, trouble her or condemn her." She cast a sharp glance at Hori. "She agreed to tell her side of the story because I promised we'd help prove her father's innocence."

Nakhtmin suppressed a groan. How could Muti make such a promise when Hori and he were pretty much convinced of Nehesy's guilt? He cleared his throat. "I promise we'll do everything in our power to reveal the truth," he said with emphasis.

His friend nodded eagerly. "You don't need to fear me either. No matter what we uncover, I only mean to help you."

Ouseret's lids fluttered for a moment, but she still sat rigid and upright like a queen. At Muti's encouraging nod, she sighed and relaxed her shoulders. Then her dark, velvety voice sounded. "Where to start?"

"How about at the beginning," Nakhtmin suggested. She obviously wasn't used to talking about herself.

"My story...well, the beginning." Her gaze flew over the terrace, grazed palm trees, acacias and sycamores. "In this house, we once were happy...but not for long. My lock of youth hadn't been cut off yet when my mother died of a consuming disease. During that time, my wish to become a physician like my father was born."

Nakhtmin nodded. That explained a few things. Although the temple schools were open to women, only few daughters of noble families considered going for another profession than running their husband's household. In poorer families, women often had to earn their keep out of necessity, not passion for the work as Nakhtmin knew from experience.

"I eagerly learned to read and write and accompanied Father when he visited patients in their homes. Quite often he was called to Merwer, a man who'd gained wealth through his trade business and could afford to summon a sunu to his house." Ouseret took a sip from her mug.

"Um, what ailed Merwer that he needed your father's services so often and over such a long time?" Hori asked her, his fingers kneading a lump of bread into a ball.

Ouseret stared at Hori as if surprised to see him here. "Chronic joint pains, headaches, clogged metu, itchy skin, intestinal worms, take your pick. The man basically suffered from everything and anything."

That made Nakhtmin prick his ears. "You're saying he *believed* he suffered from all kinds of diseases?" That sounded familiar. Like the woman who used to come to the House of Life every day for treatment. It took him awhile to realize she simply was lonely after her husband and children had left for the Beautiful West. More than medicine, she needed a comforting hand and someone who listened to her. But that couldn't have been the reason in Merwer's case. Still...very interesting.

Now she stared at him in surprise rather than irritation. "You might be right. We were never quite sure. At least the joint pains were ailing him for real—every year around harvest time they afflicted him—and that's what Father mostly treated. Swathes for the swollen joints and a concoction abating the disease from inside. Naturally, I met his children during those visits. Sanefer and Satnefert were about my age."

"He didn't put too much thought into naming them, I guess," Muti mocked and drew an angry look from Ouseret.

Nakhtmin glanced at Hori, who'd flinched and now rolled his bread ball over the table with determination. At least he restrained himself.

"The one truly languishing in Merwer's house," Ouseret continued as if Muti hadn't said anything, "was his wife. I soon realized she was suffering from a consuming illness similar to what my mother had although for a long time she wouldn't admit it and kept up the house work as if she were healthy and strong. Father often sneaked a restorative remedy in for her."

"Why the secrecy?" Nakhtmin asked the question written on Hori and Muti's faces. It amused him how easy it was for Ouseret to intimidate these two usually so strong and self-confident people.

Her dark shoulders rose in a gesture of helplessness. "I really don't know. Hm, I never asked Father and never even thought about it before. It was just the way things were. Father often called her a poor soul, although Merwer seemed a good husband, always friendly to her and to everyone else. He gave me sweets or pretty little things he'd brought from his trading trips."

Strange. Nakhtmin had imagined Merwer as an unpleasant fellow after what he'd heard about him. Had the fact that Nehesy—or someone else—killed him led him to form a dire picture of the man? Or was it Merwer's refusal to let his son set up his own household?

"Tell us more about the children," Muti prompted demurely. The answer to that question obviously interested Hori even more. His restless messing with the bread ball ceased abruptly.

As if to make up for the sudden inactivity, Ouseret started kneading the seam of her dress. In a barely audible voice she said, "We liked each other, got along well."

Nakhtmin observed Hori directing a gaze at Ouseret that seemed to pierce her in search of the truth deep inside her heart.

To like each other was a reasonable if not very fulfilling basis for marriage. Hori seemed to have picked up the same trace since his face brightened with the flame of hope. Nakhtmin had to suppress a groan.

Now Ouseret pushed out her chin in defiance. "I wanted a husband, and Sanefer was young and pleasant. I trusted him. So our fathers agreed on our wedding."

Again a peculiar choice of words. Was Ouseret even aware of what she'd just revealed? She wanted to marry the man because she could trust him. She really didn't open up much. Nakhtmin knew nobody more inaccessible than Ouseret. What miracle had Sanefer performed to win her trust? Or was it the other way round, and she couldn't trust anyone anymore because he'd disappointed her so much? "But you didn't set up your own household for a long time?" he prompted.

Her eyebrows hiked up in surprise. "How do…? Oh, Meseh, the blabbermouth. No," she sighed. "We were in no hurry." She noticed Muti's incredulous look and quickly added, "Merwer's financial situation was always too precarious when Sanefer asked him for the means to buy a house. We understood."

"I thought the trader had been quite wealthy?" Hori wondered.

Again the dark shoulders rose in a fairly indifferent gesture. "He was, but he…hm… He invested his funds in large enterprises, trade trips to the oases mostly, but also to the Nile island Abu where he purchased ivory and ebony. Far too often, his caravans didn't return, or a ship sank. Then everything he'd spent on donkeys, carriers or wares was lost."

Showing keen interest, Hori leaned forward. "Um, if he lost more than he won, how could he have been wealthy? That doesn't make sense. How did he finance the next trip if the previous one didn't return profit?"

She drew back from his proximity and snapped, "How am I supposed to know? Wasn't my business!" She continued softer, "However, he was a man with many cows in his stable as he liked to say."

"Oh, he also owned land and farmed it?" Muti cried out in astonishment.

Nakhtmin giggled. "That's a saying here in the south, meaning he didn't put all his eggs in one basket." Duh, farming again. Muti was right to call him a country yokel. "Um, he always had several enterprises going and never invested all he had in one undertaking."

"Ah," she replied.

"Actually," Ouseret interjected, "he also tried farming with a new kind of grain from foreign lands, just before he…perished. He expected great profit from white grain brought to the Two Lands by traders from far east. Because he'd been praising the exceptional taste with such enthusiasm, Father…" She swallowed with difficulty. "Father gave him money in exchange for a share in his profits, so Merwer could buy more, enough to plant a field."

"But then it would have been stupid of Nehesy to kill the man who owed him!" Nakhtmin exclaimed. "What happened with the grains?"

Ouseret snorted. "Nothing. At harvest time, when Father expected to get his gold back, Merwer confessed that he didn't have it. The grains, sowed shortly after the Nile floodings, sprouted just fine, but then the plants dried up. Father had been well aware that he might lose his investment, and unfortunately he did."

"Hm." Nakhtmin pursed his lips in thought and glanced at Hori. Judging by his drawn face, he seemed to think along the same lines: another reason for Nehesy to kill his patient. He would have been raving mad at anyone dragging him into such a shady deal. Merwer must have known long before the harvest time the seed had withered, but hadn't told his partner. "And Sanefer? He can't have been happy when the wedding was postponed over and over again," he said in hopes of finding a more convenient suspect in Hori's rival.

The question made Ouseret squirm. Did she mean to protect the young man she loved or had once loved? "No, he wasn't happy, but…already too caught up in his father's business, he even accompanied the freight boats heading north without getting paid for it. He was gone for the major part of the year. And I had finished my studies and graduated as a physician. There…simply was no hurry." She splayed the fingers of both hands and looked at them. "Soon after, Merwer suffered his first attack of joint pains of the year, and Father gave him the same highly effective medication as before: blue lotus, incense and colocynth."

Hori nodded. "That should certainly help. The right dosage is essential though, or else…oh."

"Exactly." Ouseret ground her teeth. "But father didn't do anything wrong, I vouch for that. He couldn't! Merwer must have taken more than Father recommended. However, the vizier didn't believe him, acted as if Father had made the medicine too strong on purpose to take revenge. He couldn't prove that though. Ghastly, ghastly man!" Her eyes filled with hatred, and she scowled at Hori as if he were responsible for his father's actions. Then she sighed and rose. "Now you know the whole story. I'll leave."

Nakhtmin thought to himself they still knew very little about the whole affair. How had Sanefer lost her trust? Did Merwer's symptoms fit with colocynth poisoning? Who had the means to give him more than he should, and for what reason? "Wait, Ouseret, I'll walk you home," he said. "At night the streets are dangerous."

She snorted. "Antef's soldiers provide protection. However, your company won't be a nuisance."

Oh, that woman! He almost took back his offer then simply shrugged. Maybe he'd manage to get more out of her, and the walk back would help clear his mind.

First Steps in the Investigation

Day 7 of month Wepet-renpet in Akhet, the season of inundation

The northern winds fanning his body, Hori lay awake on the roof when his friend returned. No way could he have fallen asleep with so much for his heart to mull over. Had Nakhtmin teased more out of Ouseret? Hearing his friends whisper to each other, he decided not to disturb them although his nagging thoughts wouldn't let him find sleep until dawn approached. Then the first rays of the sun tickling his nose jerked him awake. After tossing and turning for a while, he gave up.

He sneaked down the stairs one floor to find a fresh shendyt. In the corridor, he encountered Hereret and smiled at her. "Nothing invigorates a man like the sight of a flower in the morning," he said alluding to her name with secret pride in having taken Nakhtmin's advice to heart. These days he memorized his servants' names.

Cupping her mouth with her hand, she giggled shyly. "Oh, master!" She passed him and brushed his still bare hips as if by accident.

His body reacted although he didn't want to, and he really didn't. So he hurried into his room and slammed the door before she could see his erection and draw wrong conclusions. He certainly didn't need to stumble into the same trap as back home with his own maid who'd fallen in love with him and caused him quite some trouble when she got pregnant. However, she too had lost her unborn child to the shadows...

Shendyt under his arm, he entered the bathroom downstairs. After relieving himself into the sand-filled receptacle, he climbed into the knee-high basin and let Hapi pour fresh water over him, which flowed into a hole near the wall and drained into a bin outside. The gardeners would use it to water the plants.

While Hapi pumped more water from the well inside the house, Hori dried himself with a linen towel and spread scented balm on his limbs. Then the servant shaved him, and just in case he wanted to enter the temple, Hori had him take care of his scalp as well. Hereret handed him his thoroughly combed wig and tied his shendyt with a belt. Last but not least, she lined his eyes with black eye makeup. Now he felt prepared to face Ouseret again. One glance into the bronze mirror told him he could take it up with any Sanefer.

Steps approached from behind, and Hori recognized Nakhtmin's dark figure. For a greeting, he only grunted and lowered himself onto the privy.

"Slept well?" Hori called.

"Mhm, yes, just not enough," Nakhtmin grumbled.

"A cold shower will perk you up, right, Hapi?" Laughing, he left the bathroom and headed for the garden, where Hereret had set the breakfast table in the shade of a vine-covered pergola. The girl was still lurking nearby to serve them, but Hori sent her into the house. He wanted to discuss their next steps with his friends without being overheard. The maid obeyed reluctantly.

Soon after, Muti and Nakhtmin joined him.

"So," he urged. "What are we going to do today to clear Ouseret's father of all suspicion?"

His friend groaned. "Hori! Let me wake up first!"

42

He ignored him. "I think we should find out where Merwer lived and talk to the neighbors, hear what they have to say about the family."

"Sounds very inconspicuous," Muti quipped. "If all three of us show up there questioning people, I'm sure nobody will wonder why we take such an interest."

Hori felt struck down with a cudgel, but she was right. They had to sneak up on Merwer's family somehow. Under a pretext! He snapped his fingers. "We'll go to the store! If Merwer dealt in precious goods, he must have had a shop where he sold his wares. And I guess his son is running it now."

"Sanefer?" Muti displayed an evil grin.

Harrumph! "Yes. Sanefer, the beautiful son. Such a silly name! What if one of us goes there pretending to shop for something special...and asks if they deliver to Itj-tawy. Should be easy to strike up a conversation."

"That might work," Nakhtmin mumbled.

"You'll have to do without me. Ouseret offered to show me the city today. Only me!" She glared at Hori.

What a shame! He'd have preferred to spend the day with his beloved than with tedious investigations. But she'd made it pretty clear, yesterday, how unbearable his presence was for her. "I respect Ouseret's wish to not come near me," he said stiffly. "That'll change once I..."

Nakhtmin stared at him in disbelief, and his wife burst out in laughter. "Once you've proven Nehesy's innocence? I think you're forgetting something. Nothing will be in Ouseret and Sanefer's way then," she jeered.

"Oh! You...you...!" He jumped up and fled to the pond. Could she be right? He simply had to convince Ouseret he was the better man for her, not one to let her down because of some malicious accusation. After all, she hadn't moved into Sanefer's house yet, and she didn't exactly seem happy. Right, if everything was fine between her and her fiancé, why did she live at the basket maker's place and not with him? And why had she not returned to serve at the House of Life? She'd arrived several days before Hori in Waset, but principal Bakenamun still thought her in the residence. Or had she been banned from this House of Life as well after her father had been convicted? Old Imhotepankh in Itj-tawy hadn't hesitated to kick her out the moment he'd learned about it.

Nakhtmin stepped up to him. "Seriously, Hori, you have to tear this foolish love from your heart. She wants to move into another man's house."

"Does she? Why then hasn't she done so already?" Forget Ouseret? That would mean giving up on life itself. Then he might just as well spend the rest of his miserable existence in the weryt since without her, there was no light and no air in his world. He narrowed his eyes. "She told you something last night, right? Spit it out!"

Laying a placating hand on his shoulder, he said, "She said nothing. We talked about mutual acquaintances in the residence and about...that thing. About Muti." He sighed. "We don't know what happened between Sanefer and Ouseret. Whatever it was, you must realize that she doesn't like you. It was more than obvious last night. She avoids you, flees your proximity."

"But...if I save her father..."

"Don't mistake gratitude for love. And how could she feel grateful toward you, knowing what you expect from her in return? You're like a trader offering her dates in exchange for a jug of beer."

Tears burned in Hori's eyes. "But dates are worth more than beer!"

Nakhtmin shook his head and pulled an aggrieved face. "What good will it do you if her jug is empty? She has no beer for you. She gave it to Sanefer."

Hori felt as empty as Ouseret's jug.

Walking beside an unusually silent Hori, Nakhtmin didn't have to ask many people until someone pointed them in the right direction. The edifice in which the trader Merwer offered his goods was located at the edge of Waset's market place. It didn't amount to more than adobe walls and a roof made of braided bulrush, one of many such market stands rimming the place. Toward the market, the shop was open, no wall. A wooden awning propped up with two poles provided shade but could also be lowered to serve as a gate to lock up the shed. Under the awning stood a table with a selection of products on display.

"That's it," he told Hori. "Do you see the man inside? That could be Sanefer." He had to raise his voice to be heard over the shouts of the marketeers.

"Fish, fresh from the Nile! Buy my fish!"

"Onions, fresh onions!"

"A new basket in exchange for this coarse shendyt? You must have spent too much time under Ra's rays!"

A striking number of armed men strolled around among the stands. Hori mumbled something unintelligible and stared at the man behind the sales counter. He wouldn't be of much use right now. Nakhtmin sighed and acted as if he perused the offerings of other traders—meat, vegetables, milk, earthenwares as well as other household commodities—and gradually sneaked closer to the stands with luxury goods. In front of a perfume maker's display he stopped.

"What can I please you with, noble lord?" the shopkeeper asked eagerly. His small dark eyes appraised the quality of his shendyt and jewelry.

"Oh, I don't know," Nakhtmin said reluctantly. "I'm looking for a present for my wife, but it should be something special. We're visiting Waset for the first time, and the gift is supposed to remind her of this trip."

The man clapped his hands. "I've got just the right thing for you!" He grabbed Nakhtmin's wrist and tried to pull him inside.

Overwhelming scents tickled his nose. Ouch, how stupid of him. He wanted to move on, but the trader was persistent like a fly.

Now his shop neighbor joined them. "Don't listen to him! I can offer you jewelry worthy of a queen. What do you want with his stinking stuff? In the sun, his salves melt and turn into rancid fat. A woman's heart, however, rejoices at the sight of such jewels." He grabbed Nakhtmin's other hand.

They tore at him from both sides until Hori finally jerked out of his lethargy and thundered, "Enough! How dare you! Touching a royal physician. You, riffraff!"

To Nakhtmin's relief both immediately let go of him and before they could grasp what a big fish was slipping from their nets, Hori pulled him away. Now they stood almost right before Sanefer's shop. Behind them, the jeweler and the perfume maker still quarreled and accused each other of hawking poor-quality products and stealing each other's customers. The shouts and particularly Hori's exclamation had drawn general attention to them. The presumed Sanefer now also stood in front of his table to see what all the ruckus was about. So they ran straight into him. By accident, or had Hori guided their steps that way on purpose?

"Pardon me, noble lords, I'm so sorry! I didn't mean to stand in your way!" the young man cried out. "Royal physicians from the residence, indeed. You've come to the right place. Nobody in Waset offers a greater selection of exotic treasures than I do." He stepped aside and waved his arm toward the shop. In a conspiratorial murmur, he added, "Sahut resin from the Sekhet-Hemat oasis, leopard furs from lands south of the Nile, bracelets of carved ivory. Come on in, come on in, and see for yourselves!"

Nakhtmin feigned interest. "I'm looking for a present for a lady of high rank. Something special."

"My lord! I can show you jewelry, turquoise from the mining land Biau set into the bones of the gods, as bright as the moon..."

"You have silver jewelry? My wife loves silver!" Nakhtmin cried, thinking it was time to display some enthusiasm. Hori and he followed the young man into the dark interior.

The shopkeeper bowed assiduously, almost subserviently. Nakhtmin furrowed his brow. A little too submissive for a man of wealth—as far as they knew. Apart from that, he seemed quite likeable, no matter how much he wanted to dislike him out of loyalty to Hori. At least he wasn't as sleazy in his advances as the salve maker.

"I'm your servant and will show you what we've got."

Servant? Nakhtmin almost laughed out loud. Only a hired salesman. How silly of them not to consider that possibility. Now they had to wriggle their way out of here without spending a month's wages in Sanefer's shop. Displaying indecision he fingered the proffered pectoral. "Oh, I don't know...I've seen similar things in the residence," he said, mimicking Hori's most conceited tone. "Which dealer do you work for? Looks like he also sells his goods in Itj-tawy. What do you think, my friend?" He nudged Hori, who gave him a blank stare.

The salesman nodded eagerly. "Sure, sure. My master Merwer...that is, I mean, Sanefer..."

Now Hori also seemed to realize he wasn't looking at his rival since his face brightened a little.

"My master also delivers his wares to the residence, but I have it on good authority..." He lowered his voice. "A new delivery of ostrich feathers has arrived from Kush just now. Unfortunately, I don't have them in the shop yet. Would that be something to intrigue your wife? I could make provisions for you to visit my master at his estate where he also stores his wares. I'm sure he'd open his treasure chamber for special customers like you."

Before Nakhtmin could respond, Hori exclaimed in ostentatious excitement, "Oh that would be magnificent! Your master Merwer—that was his name, right...?"

Looking sad, the youth shook his head. "No, Sanefer. Merwer was his father. He died recently. What a tragic loss! Tragic! We're still aggrieved. There's never been a finer man than Merwer! Lending his ear to anyone, always offering good advice and support. He even promised to let me have a share of the profits if I kept up selling so much. Then I could finally..." He fell silent, a longing look on his face

45

reminiscent of Hori's yearning expression.

Nakhtmin exchanged a quick glance with his friend. Merwer had given the young man hope, and now he expected a dream to come true. Most likely, a woman played a role in it. Nakhtmin smiled understandingly. "Oh, the son will surely honor his father's promise to you?" he quickly probed. "The son of *such* a man, raised by such a *generous* hand, can't possibly be anything but kind toward his fellow human beings."

The salesman lowered his gaze and shoved his feet through the dust. "I'm sure," he mumbled. "Someday he will."

Hori warbled, "But my good man! Such a promise is a legacy! Remind your new master in a timely manner."

Without much hope in his eyes, the youth looked at them. "Thank you for your advice, my lords. I will do as you say."

Nakhtmin pitied the employee. It was obvious that Sanefer didn't mean to keep his father's promise, and the youngster didn't dare to say anything bad about his new master.

"Merwer, Merwer," Hori said. "The name sounds quite familiar. My father—he's the vizier of the Two Lands—may have mentioned it recently in connection with some tragic event. I remember because the man who caused his death was a physician like me. I guess that must have been someone else of the same name."

Oh, how clever of Hori! Nakhtmin cast him an admiring glance.

The salesman's eagerness flared up again. "Not at all, that was him! What a coincidence! And you're such noble people!" He bowed and bowed until Hori placed a hand on his shoulder. Then he sighed. "My poor master! He died because this physician, Nehesy is his name, made his medicine too strong. The vizier himself came to the city to chair the trial. If you asked me, the charlatan got what he deserved. My poor master! How cruelly he'd been treated!"

Nakhtmin and Hori feigned appropriate dismay.

"Did you *see* your master perish? With your own eyes?" Nakhtmin whispered, holding one hand over his mouth like a village gossip.

Now the youth dropped all restraints. "Oh yes, I visited him at his sickbed. My poor master was often ailing, and his afflictions were as exotic as the wares his donkeys carried into the Southern City. Nobody was able to heal him. But my master trusted this Nehesy, who managed to ease his pains. He summoned the doctor to his house, even let him participate in his enterprises, agreed to his son marrying the physician's daughter—pah!" He spit out in disgust. "Well, that's none of my business. Still, my master must have suspected something since he kept postponing the wedding. Nevertheless, he still consulted Nehesy. If only he hadn't! I found my master in cramps on bloody linen, lying in his excrement, unable to give me instructions. The next day, he was dead!"

Hori nodded thoughtfully and said in an unctuous voice, "That must have been horrible for you. And still you stand here, doing your duty. Good man!" He removed a copper deben from his wrist and handed it to the salesman. "Sacrifice a jug of wine for your master when he's arrived at his habitation in the Beautiful West."

Speechless for a moment, the man bowed again and again. "Thank you, many thanks!"

Nakhtmin grinned to himself. Among common people 'Sacrificing a jug for your master' usually meant drinking it yourself, and this fellow would likely do exactly that. "Now, with regard to Sanefer's ostrich feathers, you wanted to tell us more about how we can meet Sanefer to inspect them," he reminded the man.

"Oh, right, I'll tell my master that you'd like to see his storage rooms. When would it suit you?"

"As soon as possible," Hori said, not giving Nakhtmin time to consider the answer.

He kicked Hori against his ankle, hoping to silence him. After all, they shouldn't appear too eager in case the copper deben hadn't completely fogged up the servant's mind. The youth shouldn't start wondering after they left. "What my esteemed colleague means is that our stay in the Southern City will come to an end soon. Do you think your master can receive us tomorrow afternoon?"

"Definitely!" the salesman cried with enthusiasm. "I'll let him know this evening. And since my new master is still busy sorting out his father's bequest, he'll be at home. For two royal physicians, one of them son of the vizier of the Two Lands, he'll certainly make time."

Visibly pleased, Hori said farewell. Nakhtmin however remembered just in time to ask, "And where do we find Sanefer's estate?"

"Oh, of course! It's a short distance outside the city at the riverbanks. Just head north on the road along the Nile, then you can't go wrong. It's the last building before the fields begin."

Outside and out of earshot, Hori said, "Well done!"

Nakhtmin smiled. "You too. Great idea to flaunt your father. Now we have a solid reason to visit Sanefer. Albeit the boy in there didn't tell us much we didn't know already. At least he confirmed it all. Unfortunately, it really looks like Merwer was kindness incarnate."

"Yes, that's what Ouseret already told us. Why does that bother you?"

"Think about it, Hori. If everyone loved him, nobody had a reason to harm him, except..."

"Oh, damn!"

OFFICERS AND PROPHETS

Day 7 of month Wepet-renpet in Akhet, the season of inundation

Back at the estate, Hapi awaited them with a message. "A servant of the first prophet Amunhotep dropped this an hour ago," he said. His gaze had a furtive quality, Hori thought. The fellow probably couldn't read but seemed keen to learn the content of the letter.

Hori took the message written on fine papyrus and skimmed it. "Amunhotep invites us to dinner."

"Oh, great," Nakhtmin said. "I meant to visit the man anyway and take him Ameny's gifts."

Hori noticed Hapi's pricked ears. Dear gods, harmless courtesy calls couldn't be of interest to the nomarch! Nevertheless, he felt uncomfortable being spied on so inconspicuously although he didn't plan to do anything untoward. "Is the lady Mutnofret back yet?" he asked. When Hapi negated, he suggested to Nakhtmin, "Let's wait for her in the garden." Out there it would be easier to avoid prying eyes and ears. Even better if he sent the man away. "Oh, Hapi, please go to the Amun temple and inform the first prophet that we are happy to accept his invitation." He guided his friend to a spot where they'd see the servants approach and made sure nobody was around before he said, "We need to talk to Ouseret again before we visit Sanefer."

Nakhtmin had made himself comfortable in the shade of a sycamore and blinked at him lazily. "Why?"

"Remember what the salesman said: Merwer had cramps and the linen was bloody. Since nobody mentioned a wound, his excrement must have been bloody. Shouldn't we foremost find out the cause of his death before we poke around some more? Maybe Ouseret is right, and the wealthy man succumbed to one of his illnesses."

His friend snorted. "You'd take any chance to see her again! Do you really think Nehesy would have been convicted if that had been a viable option? Then every physician in the Two Lands would be scared out of his wits for fear one of his patients might die. I imagine your father would have realized that. The pharaoh—life, prosperity and health—would have replaced him already if he couldn't trust his vizier in legal matters."

No, Sobekemhat wasn't stupid but stubborn. Could his anger at Hori and his choice of profession extend to all physicians? Unfathomable that the pharaoh's highest officer harbored such prejudices and yielded to them. Deep in thought, Hori plucked a sycamore fig from the tree, whose low branches brushed his shoulders. "True, the symptoms fit with colocynth poisoning," he admitted and listed them, "In small dosages, it helps against chronic joint pains, clogged metu, a wheezing lung and ulcers. In too high dosage, however, it causes cramps, bloody dysentery, clouded consciousness and finally death. But to die from it, Merwer would have had to eat more than one fruit."

"Maybe he confused them with watermelons. That happens, as you know."

Incredulous, Hori lifted his eyebrows. "Children might do that, yes, but only until they taste the first bite. Have you ever tried a colocynth? It's bitter! And the pulp is much lighter than the reddish color of melon. No, I think we can discard that possibility unless Merwer had really peculiar preferences."

"Right, I haven't thought this through. But the same holds true for Nehesy's medicine, and no doctor would make such a mistake in measuring and use a whole colocynth and more for a remedy. Let's consider the other ingredients. Blue lotus calms and eases pain. Hm, I don't expect the lotus served him to increase his lust like it does for the concubines in the harem. That also tastes bitter and too high a dose makes the tongue slur and the eyes see things that aren't there."

Hori waved dismissively. "Right, we can disregard the lotus. That leaves incense, a precious substance. Helps with inflammations and pain, so it's perfect for chronic joint aches. Even in high dosage, it's not poisonous. So, if there wasn't anything else in Merwer's medicine, the colocynth must have been the culprit. The symptoms fit as well."

"Still, I wouldn't completely abandon Ouseret's suspicion it might have been a deadly disease. There are afflictions showing similar effects. Ulcers in the metu, for example." Before Hori could contradict him, he recognized his error. "No, that would have been recognized much earlier. The man hadn't been that sick. He'd have been confined to his bed long before the bleeding of the metu started, and apparently that wasn't the case until he took Nehesy's medicine."

Although they hadn't come up anything new, Hori now saw clearer. Unfortunately, so far everything incriminated Ouseret's father, whose innocence he wanted to prove. He summarized, "So, Merwer most likely has been poisoned but not necessarily by Nehesy." He paced under the tree. "Let's assume he did not do it. Could it have been an accident? Confusing the colocynth with watermelons is possible but not probable because of the bitter taste. Merwer might have been plagued by more severe pain than usual and decided to take more of the remedy than his physician had recommended. In that case, Nehesy would have needed to prepare a really large portion to provide a deadly amount of colocynth—against medical best practice since the concoction would have gone bad before his patient could take it all in the prescribed quantity. No, Nehesy wouldn't have prepared so much. And if Merwer consumed everything available to him—against his doctor's advice—he would probably have gotten sick but not died." He glanced to Nakhtmin for agreement, but his friend had closed his eyes and breathed evenly. Fallen asleep, tut, tut. What should he do now? He was far too agitated for a nap, so he decided to roam the city on his own.

He told Hapi, who had just returned from his errand and was lurking near the door, what he was up to and left the estate. Beyond its walls, he turned around and looked back. Hard to imagine it had once been Ouseret's home... The full impact hit him like a fist to his stomach. Her father had fallen out of favor, been dispossessed—and now they spent their vacation here! How did that make Ouseret feel when she heard about it? She might have thought he'd arranged for exactly that accommodation. In any case, this coincidence didn't help ease her anger at him. Upset, he kicked a stone out of his way, then a sensation of helplessness seized him. Why did she scorn him so? Only because of his father? By now she should have realized he meant to help her and didn't care what Sobekemhat thought. Shouldn't she feel glad for anyone willing to prover her father's innocence? And still she only reluctantly opened up to them—without giving away too much about herself, of course. It almost felt like she was afraid of what Nakhtmin and he might find out. Was it possible she knew her father had committed the crime? No, it couldn't hurt Nehesy now if they found solid proof of his guilt. His heart skipped a beat, his feet wavered. Not only Nehesy had a reason to wish Merwer dead but Ouseret as well!

Dumbstruck Hori just stood there for a while, then he staggered toward a park where he sat down in the shade. The scene unfolded before his eyes: beautiful Ouseret so in love with Sanefer, but his father keeps pushing out their wedding, month after month, year after year. Then Nehesy loses his savings in one of Merwer's enterprises. Her father is ruined, her beloved so close and still unreachable. How could she not despair? All of a sudden a chance presents itself to her. As a physician, she knows the dangers of the drugs Nehesy prepares. It's so easy for her to add a lethal dose of the poison. She either ground the seeds of the fruits herself or stole powder at the House of Life. Oblivious, the father administers the medicine to his patient... Hold on, maybe Nehesy did suspect something. He might have taken the blame without objection to protect his daughter.

A far too convincing scenario for his liking. Hori couldn't tell which pained him more: that he might have fallen in love with a murderess or that she killed out of love for Sanefer. How deep her feelings for the man had to be! And wouldn't Sanefer know or at least suspect what happened? Otherwise the couple would have married after the period of mourning, which should be over by now. When exactly had Merwer died? Couldn't have been too long ago, definitely some time before Ouseret came to the residence. Hori felt like he'd known her for half his life, but not much time had passed since she tended to his head wound. He quickly calculated. His father returned from Waset and Nehesy's trial at the end of the first decade of the previous month. So that was about forty days ago. Merwer's death might have occurred quite some time earlier since the kenbet chaired by the vizier didn't convene very often. Come to think of it, why was he even needed? Antef had enough judges at hand who could have tried Nehesy, and that included himself and the prophets of the significant deities. He'd need to mull that over some more.

For now, he concentrated on the passage of time again. Likely, it took awhile until Merwer's family realized their husband and father had not died of natural causes. How long would it have taken for Nehesy to get accused and arrested? The embalming procedure took seventy days, and with the following funeral, the period of mourning ended. Maybe Merwer's body was still in the local weryt, the embalming compound. He might be able to examine him...no, they wouldn't give him access to the isolated compound, not without the king's orders and permission from the principal of the weryt in Itj-tawy. Besides, the organs must have been removed from Merwer's body already. Triple-horned cattle that he was, he'd forgotten to ask Ouseret what day the man died!

He recalled yesterday's conversation with her. Ouseret hadn't seemed like a woman looking forward to her wedding. If that was possible at all, she'd appeared even more downcast here than back in Itj-tawy. Maybe the trader's son really broke up with her as, according to Nakhtmin, Meseh had insinuated, and that distressed her. If Sanefer suspected her, it made perfect sense for him to close his heart to her—more sense than him reneging on their betrothal because of what her father did! He didn't really buy into that no matter what Nakhtmin might say.

So many questions! If only he'd been at the trial, then he'd know a little more. He glanced around. Numerous officials lounged in the park, dozing through the hot midday hours. Judging by their attire, they were mostly scribes. An idea sparked. There had to be a record of the court session at the nomarch's palace. How could he get his hands on it?

When folks started heading back to their work places, he followed them into the corridors of the administrative department of the former royal palace. One after the other, the men with the scribe wigs disappeared behind doors, which all looked the same. Where was the archive? Resignedly, he asked an errand boy hurrying past. He pointed him in the right direction.

Hori's heart thumped as dully against his ribs as his fist did against the wooden door. Nobody called him in, so he simply entered and found himself at the start of a suite of adjoining rooms. The individual rooms were divided by an endless number of shelves, as far as his eyes could reach. In the diamond-shaped trays rested scrolls over scrolls.

A man sitting on the floor and copying a document in the faint light of a bulrush lamp looked up at him. "What can I do for you...um...my lord?"

Now he was glad he'd put so much effort into his attire this morning. "Greetings. Is this where you store transcripts of the kenbet?"

"In these rooms everything worth keeping is kept," the scribe twanged.

Hori assumed that meant yes. A rustling noise came from behind the wooden shelf; they weren't alone. "May I take a look at the records of the last trial chaired by the vizier of the Two Lands?"

The man shrugged and barked, "Seni! Can you get this man what he's looking for?"

A gaunt little man with a bent back and haggard shoulders emerged from behind the shelf. "The last kenbet, you said? Right away, right away."

To Hori's relief nobody asked if he was entitled to read the transcript, but he had no idea if such information was secret and only for eyes of authorized persons. For a while, only rustling sounded from one of the rooms farther away, then Seni returned with a scroll. "Here it is."

Hori reached for it, but Seni pressed the document against his skinny chest and shook his head. "No record may leave this room."

By Thot! He should have known. Hori rubbed his neck. "Um, may I read it in your presence?"

The two men exchanged doubtful looks, then the scribe nodded. Seni sighed and began unrolling the papyrus. Hori's eye widened. It seemed to go on forever.

"That long?" He'd never be able to memorize it! Skimming the lines, he could tell that plenty of witnesses had given statements. Just to learn their names seemed a tremendous step forward. He scratched his scalp under the wig. The air was rather stuffy in here. "Phew, um, could someone make a copy for me? I'd pay a good price for it." He unclasped his expensive collar and dangled it in front of Seni's nose.

Greed flashed in the man's eyes, then he blinked several times and held out a hand. His colleague, however, eyed Hori with distrust, and before Seni's fingers could clamp around the precious garment, he called, "Stop! On whose orders should this document be copied? Know the following: We cannot simply give such a record to anyone."

Hori broke into sweat. And he was so close to his goal! Now only one thing could help him. "On orders of Sobekemhat, the vizier of the Two Lands, who is my father."

Stupefied, the two clerks gaped at him, while he imitated the pompous tone of the scribe still sitting on the floor, "Know the following: This is a matter of great urgency. The noble vizier needs this copy for the archive in the royal residence because somebody misplaced his record."

The scribe snorted. "So typical! Nothing but sloppiness at the residence. My fingers and toes wouldn't suffice to count the times we had to make copies for those slovenly slobs. I've heard about you, my lord, you are the royal physician from the residence. Seni will finish duplicating it for you by the day after tomorrow, noble lord."

Baffled, Hori nodded then grinned. For once, there were benefits to everyone knowing about them. The fellow didn't question if he really was who he claimed to be. Highly content with this result, he wanted to put the collar around his neck again, but Seni cleared his throat ostentatiously. His outstretched right hand wiggled its fingers. The vizier's son or not, he wouldn't get it for free. Hori sighed. He should have mentioned his old man earlier, but he still didn't feel comfortable having lied so bluntly. Hopefully, his overly generous bribe also guaranteed their discretion.

Nakhtmin had slept longer than usual. However, he didn't feel rested but even drowsier than before. He wasn't the only one. The whole garden seemed weighed down by the midday glare of the sun. Merely a light breeze drifted over from the river, carrying the scent of mud. He wasn't used to such a hot climate anymore. Just think how miserably cold he'd felt after moving north!

Hori wasn't to be seen anywhere and Muti apparently hadn't returned yet. Or were they in the house? Hard to imagine in this heat. He took a look inside anyway. Nobody there but Hapi.

"If you're looking for the other master, he's gone into town."

"Thanks," Nakhtmin mumbled. He couldn't hold it against him although a nap would have done Hori good. The proximity of his beloved obviously made him restless. Nakhtmin blinked up at the sky to estimate the time of day—still awhile until the evening meal, too long to sit around idly all by himself before they'd pay a visit to prophet Amunhotep, whose duties would keep him at the temple until sundown. Maybe he should also explore the city. Hori and he had seen quite some pretty things in the morning at the market. What had started out as a pretext not only seemed like a good idea now but an outright necessity: find a little treasure to make Muti's heart rejoice. He climbed the stairs to the upper story and packed a few small but valuable items he could exchange into a bag: figure-shaped pearls of colorfully glazed faience, currently very popular in the residence, magic spells against all kinds of ailments he'd written on strips of papyrus and amulets from the temple of Amun in Itj-tawy, which Ameny had given them to take along for such purposes.

Passing through the gate of the estate, he almost ran into a palanquin crossing his path. Carried by four servants, a man curiously peered out between the curtains. Nakhtmin gave a curt nod and started to move on when the stranger addressed him. "Greetings. I didn't know someone had moved into Nehesy's place. I'm Kawab, and my house is down the street a few steps. Oh, you're also a physician?"

Nakhtmin smiled noncommittally and nodded. "We're only staying in Waset for a short while as guests of the nomarch. He set us up here. Have a nice day, neighbor, hm, priest Kawab." A clean-shaven head and crescent amulets, this had to be a hem-netjer of the god Khonsu and a high-ranking one, too, since he could afford a house in this area. Maybe even a prophet? Apparently, not everyone here took his duties as seriously as the high priests in the residence, who performed the morning and evening rituals for the god themselves.

Instead of signaling his bearers to move on, Kawab leaned toward him. "Oh, one of the physicians of the pharaoh—life, prosperity and health! I was hoping to be introduced to you. Are you the son of the vizier or the son-in-law of Ameny, the first prophet of Amun?"

"Excuse my poor manners, I should have introduced myself." How embarrassing. The lapse made his cheeks burn. "I'm Nakhtmin. Ameny is my wife's father."

Kawab beamed. "Brilliant, just brilliant! The whole city talks about you. We so rarely have dignitaries from the royal residence here. My friends will be so envious when they hear I've been talking to you. Would it be impudent to...I mean it would be such an honor... Can I convince you to be my guest? Oh, you already have plans, I'm sure..."

Nakhtmin tried to hide his annoyance. He wasn't some kind of hunting trophy to show off! Indeed, people in this city were different from those in the residence. About to decline, he wondered if this priest might be able to tell them something relevant about Nehesy. As neighbors, they must have known each other, and Kawab seemed quite talkative. "No, I just wanted to take a look around the city, but I can just as well do that tomorrow. I'd be happy to accompany you."

The priest clapped his soft hands in joy. "They say you and your friend accomplished a great feat. Banning the shadows is no trifle!"

"How do you know? The king himself ordered absolute..." His voice trailed off. Rather silly to believe such an event could be kept secret.

Kawab actually giggled. "As second prophet of Khonsu, I'd have had to be blind and deaf not to realize what was going on when my colleague was summoned to the residence with utmost urgency after he'd just returned from there. No need to worry, however, we know how to keep a secret."

Yeah, right, he sure looked the part. Nevertheless, Nakhtmin nodded.

"Ah, here we are, there it is. Come on in, come on in." Kawab waved invitingly toward a gate, which opened as if of its own accord to let the priest and his entourage enter. The carriers lowered the palanquin so their master could climb out effortlessly. Nakhtmin followed him through a lush garden to an assembly of seats in the shade of a pergola. There Kawab clapped again, this time however to summon a maid. "Bring us refreshments. Wine or beer?"

"Beer," Nakhtmin said since his head was still a bit heavy after the extended nap. Wine would make him far too drowsy. "Or could you get me some juice?"

The dark-skinned girl whispered, "There's none prepared, my lord."

Kawab's expression promised she'd regret this as soon as his guest had left.

Nakhtmin felt sorry for uttering a special request not so easy to comply with right away. Nobody kept fruit juice at hand. In this heat, it would ferment in no time unless kept in earthen jars to cool them. "Never mind, beer will suit me just as well," he said.

"I'll squeeze some fruit for you, lord."

When the girl a little later placed a jug of pomegranate juice in front him and poured some, he thanked her. "I really appreciate that you made it fresh for me."

Casting a timid glance at her master, her face turned a shade darker. Then she scurried away.

Although he'd acted so affable toward Nakhtmin, Kawab seemed to lead his household with stern discipline. Well, nothing of his concern, though it wasn't something that endeared his host to him. He lifted his mug. "To your health!"

Kawab followed suit with his wine.

Glancing around, Nakhtmin noticed the poor girl still stood within hearing distance lest she miss a request. Maybe this should concern him after all and he could do something for her? "Your maid is very obliging. You must be treating her really well, so nobody lures her away from you. I'd be happy to have such a girl in my service."

The prophet furrowed his brow. "If you lust for her, feel free to enjoy her."

Heat shot into his face. "Oh...I didn't mean...I'm not like that!" He composed himself. "I'm happily married!"

Kawab looked as if to say, 'So what?' Then a cunning expression of understanding and complicity conquered his face. "Your wife doesn't need to know."

Nakhtmin felt nauseous. Inside, he shook himself. The prophet reminded him of the cat king, a brothel owner in Itj-tawy. Doesn't need to know? Nakhtmin could never trust him even if he were tempted. Such knowledge would give the man nice leverage. Leverage to achieve what? Likely, Kawab didn't care, just collected levers for whenever they might come in handy. The man was disgusting, and he should get out of here straight away. "Um, thank you for your hospitality, but I should..."

Kawab's moist, bloated paw fell heavily onto his hand. "Oh, please! You have to tell me all about the shadows. And of course, you must stay for dinner!"

"I...no. Dinner? That's impossible. My wife..." If he didn't stop stuttering right now, Kawab would walk all over him! Where was Hori when he needed him! He'd know how to handle such an obnoxious fellow. Of course! Nakhtmin suppressed a smug smile, straightened his back and mimicked Hori's expression when he said, 'What happens in the weryt stays in the weryt.' "With regard to the shadows—I'm really sorry, Kawab, but I must not speak of them. The king himself—life, prosperity and health—and the gods command silence since such knowledge is secret for a good reason and only available to very few people. Personally, I'd have preferred to never learn anything about them."

"Oh," Kawab huffed. "Too bad. I'd hoped my friends—" Too late, he noticed his lapse, but struggled on. "Never mind. Then tell me, what news do you bring from the residence? Is the royal family well?"

Nakhtmin stared at him in disbelief. How could the king be well after the Horus in the egg, his much longed-for heir, had been born dead? How could his wives, who were still in mourning? He loathed feeding this blabbermouth and satisfying his lust for the suffering of others. "Hm, yes, all were fine when I left. I will tell the king about your kind concern and give him your best wishes." Couldn't hurt to boast about his connection to the palace although Hori was closer to Senusret. Nakhtmin relaxed. Since he wouldn't be able to shake the man off soon, he might as well make the best of it. "You mentioned a certain Nehesy, in whose house we're staying. Others have mentioned the name before. It sounded like he's been involved in some scandal...?"

In exaggerated dismay, Kawab slapped his hands together. Right away, the girl appeared from the shadows of the bushes. "Master...?"

"What?" The prophet glared at her in irritation. "No, you can take yourself away. And don't you dare eavesdrop on us!" Then he turned back to Nakhtmin. "Yes, indeed, this matter arrested quite some attention. You must have heard about it in Itj-tawy, haven't you?"

He made a noncommittal gesture. "We had our own problems at the time. A physician, right?"

In his eagerness, Kawab leaned close and huffed. "A physician who ferries his patients directly to the Beautiful West with his own hands. I'd call him a ferryman of the dead. To think how friendly he'd always acted, kissing up to the rich and powerful so they'd trust him. Even I enlisted his services! It's a miracle I'm sitting in front of you today."

"You must enjoy the protection of the gods," murmured Nakhtmin trying to sound deeply moved. "A physician killing the sick? That's against Maat! An abomination. Tell me, who did he murder?" He waved a fly from his face and refilled his glass. "The juice is really refreshing."

In a gesture of helplessness, Kawab turned his palms up. "A rich man called Merwer."

Feigning disbelief, Nakhtmin exclaimed, "Unfathomable! Nehesy must have had a good reason for committing such a crime. This Merwer was an evil person, right?" Shaking his head, he leaned back and looked at him expectantly.

"Not at all, Merwer was a kind and really generous man, who honored the gods with bountiful donations. Particularly the temple of Amun benefited from his generosity." To Kawab's chagrin, it seemed, although Amun was the most important god in Waset. "Well, people say Nehesy entrusted Merwer with several gold deben to invest in his enterprises, but they turned out a failure."

"Ah." Nakhtmin hid his disappointment. Ouseret had told them almost exactly the same. Didn't look like he might learn anything new here. Now he regretted not having wandered off into the city.

Downcast, Kawab shook his shaved head. "I'd never have expected Nehesy to commit such a heinous crime, my neighbor and frequent guest in my house. I'd have lent him any amount if he'd asked. If only he'd asked..."

Nakhtmin didn't find it surprising that Nehesy had preferred murder to owing such a sleazy fellow. Hold on, what was he thinking? They were supposed to prove Nehesy's innocence! "You mentioned enterprises. What kind of business did the man run?" Apart from bribing priests—for what purpose? So they'd overlooked things that were a little dodgy? Maybe they should find out more about the temple donations. And Amunhotep's invitation gave them a perfect opportunity.

Kawab rolled his lower lip between thumb and forefinger. "Mh, this and that. Mostly trade trips south, I think. He appeared quite successful in that field, although I've heard about a few officials at the nomarch's court sponsoring his endeavors in hopes of a nice profit and losing most of their investments."

Nakhtmin pricked his ears. "So, Nehesy wasn't the only one. I'm surprised Merwer still found people providing means for him if luck fled him so often." That smelled fishy. Merwer's store was full of precious goods, and presumably there was also a well-stocked storage. Why didn't he pay off his partners if he was an honest trader?

"Oh, some folks doubled their investment or even tripled it. However, it's risky. Ships capsize, wares spoil, caravans get robbed…"

"Yeees," Nakhtmin said with little conviction. At least they'd gained a whole bunch of new suspects they should check out. Merwer must have been the kind of man to sell a heap of dung to a fly as the saying went. That might have been his downfall. Unfortunately, it still looked like Nehesy's twofold grudge must have upset him the most among Merwer's business partners. Apart from the lost gold, there was his daughter. The trader had agreed to her wedding his son, then didn't follow through but stood in the couple's way. But what did Nakhtmin know? Other people might have despaired far more because of their losses. But what if Merwer did cheat people and someone found out? That could enrage a man enough to take revenge. They had to identify all those he might have bamboozled. "Can you tell me who also lost their stakes in Merwer's enterprises?"

Kawab narrowed his eyes at him. "Why does that interest you? Nehesy has been convicted. He did it."

Damn, he hadn't been subtle enough. "Good to know. It's just that I find it hard to believe a colleague of mine could do something like that," he said lamely.

Kawab snorted. "Only a physician could have done it, if not Nehesy than another colleague of yours. I attended the kenbet as judge." He smiled self-righteously, and Nakhtmin granted him an admiring look. "The medicine killed Merwer. Only someone well-versed in the art of healing could have meddled with it."

Of course, he'd almost gotten on the wrong track. The culprit must have known what ingredients the remedy contained and have access to it. Had Merwer talked any other physicians at the House of Life into joining him in his endeavors? Then a realization hit him hard: Ouseret was a physician as well!

The priest's inquisitive gaze hadn't missed his confusion. "What's wrong? Your face looks ashen. Was the juice off? That sloppy little—"

"No, it's nothing," Nakhtmin croaked and gulped down more of the liquid. "It's just the heat. I'm not used to it any longer."

"Right, you're from the south, one of us, I saw that right away," the prophet said, as if that made them best friends. "Where from? No, let me guess, Abdju?"

While Nakhtmin's lips formed meaningless sentences, his thoughts circled around one thing only: Hori must not find out that he suspected his beloved. Not until he could be absolutely sure Ouseret was guilty of the crime her father had been convicted of. His friend would rather kill him than let him badmouth the sister of his heart. And they really didn't need another murder! Now he did not only have to prove Nehesy's but also Ouseret's innocence. Dear gods, let us find another viable suspect soon, no, the true killer!

Kawab's voice billowed past his ears without him catching a word until the priest shook him slightly. "What do you think? Tomorrow evening?"

"Huh? Sorry, my thoughts had wandered off to faraway places."

His host didn't appreciate that at all, and Nakhtmin cursed himself for not paying attention. However, Kawab quickly forced his features back into the usual obliging smile. "Dinner at my house. You, your wife and your friend will be my guests tomorrow, yes?"

That fully jerked him back to reality. "Tomorrow? Oh, I'm sorry, but we already have other plans." After all, Sanefer might invite them to his table, and according to the salesman the estate was located quite a bit outside the city. Most of all, though, he wanted to avoid spending more time with this annoying man.

He felt scrutinized with utmost attention. "Is that so?"

Since he hadn't lied, Nakhtmin was able to hold his gaze without trouble. "I'm afraid so."

"Too bad. Well, another occasion will certainly arise."

Nakhtmin suppressed a groan. "I'm sure of that. Now, however, I should go home before my wife starts worrying where I've disappeared to." He rose. "Thank you for your hospitality."

Kawab got up as well. "For nothing! I have to thank you. I'm very pleased to have met you. From Khent-min and now one of the big men in the royal residence!"

Nakhtmin forced a broad grin. "You're exaggerating, and it's not like you're an insignificant man in your position."

Under such mutual flattery, over and over again, they took leave until the gate to Kawab's estate finally closed behind him. What a relief!

An impatient Muti already awaited him in the entry hall. "Where've you been all this time? I thought we're going out tonight?"

Who'd been out and about all day with Ouseret and left him alone at home? However, he knew from experience that he'd better keep that to himself. "Our neighbor invited me to his place for a chat. I'll freshen up, then we can leave." Since Hapi buzzed around them, he didn't think it smart to share details of his encounter with Kawab right here and now.

Nakhtmin waved at Hori strolling down the stairs.

"I'll stay here," his friend announced. "Give the prophet my apologies, but he probably only invited me along out of courtesy since he'd mostly want to get to know the two of you."

Muti knitted her eyebrows. "Hori, son of Sobekemhat, what are you up to? Do you intend to visit Ouseret?"

Hori blushed—answer enough.

"An evening alone with you is the last thing Ouseret would want right now. You'll only scare her away if you pester her," she said sternly.

When Hapi left the room for a moment, Nakhtmin dangled the bait in front of his nose. "Besides, neighbor Kawab might have provided a new lead—straight to the Amun temple."

Intrigued, Hori yielded, and soon the three of them set out, bearing Ameny's presents.

Amunhotep's estate was also located at the riverbank, but farther south than the house of Ouseret's parents. A servant awaited them at the gate and led them through the garden designed in straight lines and distinct shapes. Nakhtmin immediately wondered whether the prophet was unmarried.

After a few steps, their host welcomed them. To Nakhtmin's surprise, the man was fairly old. He'd imagined Ameny's counterpart younger. After spending time with sleazy Kawab, Amunhotep's congenial demeanor was a relief. Or was he falling for a deception?

"Welcome! How nice that you could make time on such short notice."

"We have to thank you for the invitation," Hori said and introduced them.

"Ah, the daughter of my esteemed colleague!" A smile brightened the aged face. "I don't get to enjoy such pretty company during my meals very often these days."

Muti performed a graceful reverence. "Father always speaks so well of you."

"Oh, no formalities!" He took Muti's hand and raised her with the sprightly elegance of a young man.

Maybe old, but not infirm and certainly not senile, Nakhtmin added to his first impression. At a glance from Muti, he remembered the gifts. "Venerable Amunhotep, Ameny asked us to present you with this token of his esteem for you. There's also a message." He proffered the package wrapped in waxed cloth and sealed with Ameny's signet.

Their host's age-mottled hands revealed four papyrus scrolls. "Oh, that wonderful man! These are copies of the texts I wrote to him about only recently. They are lacking in our library." Mumbling, he read the letter from Ameny. His face had turned serious when he lowered the note and glanced at Hori's upper arm and the bracelet covering the ankh tattoo. The prophet also wore a bracelet in the same spot. "Please thank my much-valued colleague. According to his message, I can fully trust you." He sighed. "Well, maybe I should."

Amunhotep's words surprised Nakhtmin. Why should the prophet trust them, not the other way round? With an inviting gesture, their host ushered them into a gazebo where the food had been set up. During the meal, they mainly talked about court gossip, about which the old man seemed surprisingly well informed. Muti was in her element. However, as soon as the servants had removed the dishes and retreated, Amunhotep scrutinized them with a frown on his face. "What's the real reason for your journey to the Southern City?"

Nakhtmin caught Hori's uncertain look and sucked in his lower lip. Ameny seemed to trust this man, so maybe they should, too. He shrugged. "It's true, we don't seek recreation but a murderer."

Hori glared at him in horror.

He soothed him with a gesture. "It's no state secret after all."

Disappointment overshadowed the priestly features. "Oh, and I'd hoped... Then you aren't here on his majesty's request to inspect the situation in Waset?"

"No," Hori said, drawing out the short word. "Not directly."

What was that supposed to mean? "Do you think this could have anything to do with the other—"

Hori darted him a reproachful look that silenced him. No, they couldn't simply reveal the king's request to check out things.

"What is there to inspect in Waset?" Hori asked furtively.

Amunhotep cast an anxious glance around. His bald head shone in the light of the oil lamps dangling from the roof of the gazebo. "There's much despotism in this city. Didn't you notice all the soldiers in the streets?"

Baffled, Nakhtmin studied him. "Yes, there are quite a lot, but I thought the nomarchs of the south were entitled to keep their own troops to protect the borders to Kush?" Was there more to it? Fear crawled up his back.

The prophet nodded. "I believe Antef reinforces his garrison. I reported my worries to the king, but my message may have gotten lost on the way. Otherwise his majesty would have reacted already."

Nakhtmin didn't know what to say, and Hori also remained silent. Only Muti offered an explanation. "Maybe the nomarch needs more people to secure the roads to the oases."

Amunhotep cast her a look hard to interpret. "You may be right. Forgive an old man his childish worries. Most likely the king himself ordered the reinforcements." Leaning back, the prophet looked crestfallen.

Nakhtmin remembered Kawab's words insinuating that Merwer bribed the priests, particularly those of the Amun temple. That didn't sound convincing now that he'd met the man. The first prophet had the king's interests in mind and suspected the nomarch of foul intentions. Had Kawab lied? But for what reason? Still, sometimes lies lurked in friendly words, while a disgusting person like Kawab might speak the truth. Nakhtmin's friendship with hapless Wenen made for a good example. Although the young priest had harbored no evil intentions, he'd caused unfathomable suffering and death, and he'd lied. Did Amunhotep pretend to be concerned to sound them out? And on whose orders? They really needed to think twice whom to trust in this city.

"Maybe you can help us with something else," Hori was saying. "We are actually looking for the true killer of—"

"You'll only bore our venerable host with that," Nakhtmin interrupted before Hori could reveal the name. "It's just a quarrel between two peasants. What would Amunhotep know about such trifles?"

"Um." Hori's face showed how he felt about Nakhtmin's interference, but he said no more.

Amunhotep's disappointment fully surfaced now. "We haven't known each other for long, but I assure you of my good intentions. Ameny writes that the king listens to you. If that's true and the Two Lands are dear to your hearts, please tell the pharaoh—life, prosperity and health—what you've seen and experienced in Waset."

Nakhtmin felt ashamed for his rudeness and feared to have misjudged the old man. He opened his mouth to take the man into his confidence. That moment, Amunhotep grasped his wrist. "Leave the city while you can!"

He pulled out of the claw-like grip and shook off the sensation of dread. "Venerable prophet, I'll weigh your words in my heart. However, it's late already..."

Back on the street and out of the gatekeeper's earshot, Hori stepped in his way. "What was going on in there?"

Nakhtmin rubbed his neck. He felt anything but at ease. "I think I've made a mistake..."

"I'm inclined to agree with you!" his friend barked.

Muti intervened. "Let Nakhtmin explain why he acted so strangely. I'm sure he had a good reason. Right?"

Indignant, he glared at Hori. "Oh yes!" And then he relayed his conversation with Kawab. "So even if Ameny is friends with the man, I'm not sure he's trustworthy."

Hori shook his head. "Kawab has gummed up your wits with pomegranate juice!" he called. "Maybe Merwer only made donations so the gods would bless his endeavors. He certainly needed that. We could have asked the prophet but you prevented that, yokel that you are. Didn't you notice? Amunhotep is afraid!"

"Why should such a powerful man...?"

Muti interrupted him. "Well, what's done can't be undone. Maybe we'll get another chance to speak to the prophet and clarify things."

THE BEAUTIFUL SON

Day 8 of month Wepet-renpet in Akhet, the season of inundation

Hori was dying to set out for Sanefer's estate. If he knew his rival, he might be able to beat him, or so he hoped. He had to find a way to replace Sanefer's image in Ouseret's heart with his own.

Muti seemed excited and curious as well, only Nakhtmin was a little downcast since yesterday. Hori hadn't been able to find out if that was only due to his blundering at Amunhotep's place or if something else troubled him. Not even the prospect of getting a copy of the court transcript had cheered up his friend. Instead, he'd managed to drag down Hori's high spirits by pointing out that only a physician could have meddled with the medicine. A sunu or a sunut—male or female doctor? Hori didn't dare to ask that question.

Finally the sun god had passed the zenith, and they boarded a little boat made of bundled bulrush reeds. Nakhtmin had hired it in the morning. The owner, a sun-tanned fellow with the leathery skin of a fisherman, was willing to take them to their destination and back for a fee. Before they departed, the man put down the mast with the rolled up sail since the wind would blow in the opposite direction. Then he eased the boat into the strong current taking them north without effort.

"Almost high tide," Muti said in wonder since the peak of the water masses arrived several days later in the north.

The boatman nodded.

Nakhtmin murmured, "Caution! In this city even the reeds pass on what the wind whispers."

Hori cast him a surprised look. Something else must have occurred yesterday, something his friend didn't want to share with him—most likely at the obnoxious neighbor. When he prompted him, Nakhtmin only mumbled something that sounded like, "Best to avoid him."

Either way, Hori also deemed it prudent not to talk about the purpose of their visit in front of the fisherman. He might be doing business with Sanefer and warn him that his customers weren't what they pretended to be. And thus they talked very little. Fortunately, it didn't take long until their boat approached the eastern shore and the man tied it to a broad wooden jetty.

"That's almost a harbor!" Muti called.

"Looks like ships regularly unload their freight here," Hori agreed and pointed at the well-trodden path winding up to a gate. A large box-shaped building peeked over the top of the wall. "That must be Sanefer's storage hall." Hori thought the fisherman studied him with a wary look—or was he imagining things? He quickly added, "I guess he stores the ostrich feathers there. Can't wait to find out if they really are as splendid as his shopkeeper claimed."

Since Muti and Nakhtmin looked flabbergasted, he cast them a meaningful glance. From now on, they'd have to watch even more closely what they uttered.

As if to confirm his worries, the gate opened that moment, and a servant walked toward them. "Welcome to my master Sanefer's estate. You must be the noble folks from the royal residence."

Hori recovered from his surprise first. Sanefer had been notified of their visit, so no wonder that he expected them. "Right you are. Take us to your lord."

The man bowed slightly then waved them along. Behind the gate a vast park with lush vegetation expanded, maybe to hide the ugly bulky storage hall from the owner's eyes. The path meandered between shrubbery and tall trees, whose canopy of leaves softened Ra's rays to a twilight. Alas, it wasn't cool here. The air steamed with moisture. Pearls of sweat trickled down Nakhtmin's back, and wet spots showed on Muti's linen dress. Soon the path widened and, rounding a bend, they saw a gorgeous two-story house, much larger than that of Nehesy or Hori's home back in Itj-tawy. The bright whitewash hurt his eyes and measured up to the coating of palaces of the highest dignitaries in the residence. Hori pursed his lips for a soundless whistle. Maintaining such a stately mansion required a significant staff, so the owner had to be wealthy.

The late Merwer puzzled him more and more. Everyone sang his praise, a kind and obliging man, and still it seemed like he never kept his generous promises. People deemed him rich, but if they wanted to do business with him, they had to shoulder the full risk. If the trader lost more than he gained, how could he afford such an estate? He shrugged. Likely they'd heard less about the man's successes than his failures, because the latter caused people to lament their losses loudly. Merwer's content partners might prefer to revel in their profits without anyone knowing.

Enjoying a pleasant breeze, they walked toward the building, and Hori imagined Ouseret as the lady of this mansion. Like a queen, she'd walk through the rooms, while servants fanned her with fluffy ostrich feathers. In the evenings, when her husband returned home... Bile rose in Hori's throat. Indeed, compared to such luxury, his possessions were meager. Then he remembered something Nakhtmin once said to him when he was looking for a great present for Ouseret: "She doesn't look the type to adorn herself much."

No, the Ouseret he knew didn't care much for material prosperity. The medical toolkit he'd given her, though, really made her eyes light up. His heartbeat slowed. Well, Sanefer, what else do you have to offer?

That moment, a young man stepped from the house. That had to be him. His bright and spotless white shendyt was of the finest quality, however a bit too long to satisfy fashion demands in the residence. Hori's lips curled in contempt. Only men who wanted to look sharper than they actually were donned such clothes. Shoulders and chest were adorned with a wide collar, but Hori had to concede that his chest was broad and his shoulders looked strong. He gazed down at himself and wondered if his own body could bear comparison with his rival's. His belly had become a little flabby lately, unlike Sanefer's, which boasted clearly defined muscles. He obviously didn't leave physical work to his servants only. As they approached, Hori studied the face of Ouseret's fiancé: handsome, but so was his. At least he didn't need to fear comparison in that regard. Disappointed, he released the breath he'd been holding. Although he'd hoped to find the man revolting, he couldn't. Sanefer's smile appeared friendly and obliging. Spreading out his arms, he welcomed them. Hori ground his jaws in dismay.

Nakhtmin must have noticed since he whispered, "Did you think Ouseret's lover would be an ugly fat man with crooked teeth?"

No, of course not. What had she said? 'He was nice, and we liked each other.'

"Welcome to my modest home!" he called. "I'm Sanefer."

They introduced themselves, and the trader expressed his delight over such high and noble customers. Now a young woman stepped from the shadow of the house and joined them. "Ah, my sister Satnefert. These are the people from the royal residence interested in ostrich feathers."

The girl nodded, but kept her gaze lowered. Beside her radiant brother, she appeared homely and shy, but the not quite so beautiful daughter tried hard to play the mistress of the house. After she'd gently asked the servants to bring refreshments, she stayed close to Sanefer as if she needed him for support because she didn't believe herself to be in charge here. Where might their mother and Merwer's wife be? Oh, right. According to Ouseret, she was ill. Strange that Satnefert, coming from a good family and certainly eighteen years old or more, hadn't married yet.

Their host led them to wooden chairs and a table in the shade of a protruding sycamore. They settled down, and the servants brought jugs of juices and wine, plates with cool melon pieces and other fruit, a perfect afternoon snack that wouldn't make them sleepy.

"What brings two royal physicians to the Southern City?" Sanefer asked.

At a loss, Hori glanced at Nakhtmin, but his friend apparently hadn't expected being interrogated either.

Muti saved them. "Recuperation. Hori has been severely injured not long ago, and I've suffered from remittent fever. Thus the king granted the wish of his royal physicians for a vacation. May the dry climate speed up our recovery."

"Oh sure. Very generous of his majesty—life, prosperity and health." A hint of vexation crossed his face. "And now you wish the treasures of the south to enchant you. Have you visited the sacred sites of Waset already?"

Hori caught himself grinning and stopped. Their host had changed the subject from illness and injury so fast, it bordered on rudeness. The mother ailing for years, the father always lamenting over one affliction or another, no wonder other people's health didn't range among his favorite topics of conversation. He couldn't resist the temptation to release a slight groan. "Oh, my head's aching again. You know, since that blow to my head, I always feel queasy and it's like I've got a worm in my head. Pains, constant pains…"

Although Sanefer turned away, Hori caught a glimpse of weariness reflected in his features. In stark contrast, Nakhtmin stared at him in astonishment. "But Hori, you—" Then understanding dawned. "Um, should I get your medicine?"

Naturally, they didn't bring any, but Sanefer couldn't know that. Feebly, he shook his head. "Should pass soon. You know these fits come and go." Rather childish of him, but he thoroughly enjoyed annoying his rival. "We heard you've lost someone recently. Your father…" He let his voice trail off. However, he didn't wait for one of the siblings to answer but exclaimed, "Dear gods, I hope we didn't disturb you during the mourning period!"

Did Nakhtmin also notice the discomfort besetting Merwer's offspring? Yes, he scrutinized their expressions. Didn't look like the beautiful children liked to talk about that either. Out of grief or guilt? Hori couldn't tell.

Sanefer gave a contrived laugh. "No, no, mourning's over. Thank you for your compassion. Business must go on, right? Life doesn't wait for us."

Hm, didn't sound like he'd loved his father and not like someone so devoted to him that he broke his promise to Ouseret, because her father had been accused of the murder. Sanefer's display of cordiality appeared more and more like a mask to hide whatever might be lurking underneath. Well, he was a trader, but did his goods live up to the florid promises?

Satnefert gently placed her hand on her brother's. "That's what father always said," she whispered. Her eyes glistened with tears. Sanefer pulled her to him and kissed her forehead. Both suddenly seemed pensive, aggrieved by sorrow.

Hori despised himself for jumping to the conclusion they didn't miss and mourn their father. That moment, Sanefer lifted his head slightly to glance over his sister's head. Not a trace of dolefulness showed in his eyes. Or did Hori imagine all that? These speculations didn't get them anywhere. They had to separate the siblings! He cleared his throat. "I'm so sorry I ripped open the healing wounds of your loss again. Maybe we shouldn't do business today. Sometimes it helps to recall stories of beautiful moments in the life of a deceased. What was your father like? All over Waset, people call him an amiable man."

Different expressions conquered Muti's face in quick succession. The first scolded him, 'How could you? Shame on you!' The next showed cautious admiration. Hori decided to ignore the reproach and turned to the girl. "Would you like to stroll through the garden and tell me about him?"

She nodded numbly.

Nakhtmin's gaze followed Hori and Satnefert strolling between the bushes. His friend placed an arm around the girl, and she trustingly snuggled up against him. Incredible! He wanted to shake Hori. How could he exploit the girl's grief so ruthlessly? When he finally managed to tear his gaze from them, he realized Muti had usurped the brother. To Nakhtmin's chagrin, the fellow seemed quite enchanted by his pretty companion. Now, he too wrapped an arm around her! Shortly after, they disappeared out of sight. Only Muti's laughter occasionally drifted over to him. He was still torn between storming after them and letting Muti follow whatever strategy she had in mind when someone touched his arm. Looking up, he saw a woman.

"Can I get you something, my lord?"

He swallowed with difficulty. The exquisite beauty of the maid dried up his mouth. Dear gods, what temptation had Merwer invited into his house when he hired her! "What's your name?" he croaked.

"I'm called Nofru."

Beauty, of course. His gaze wandered over her enticing body, exposed more than covered by an almost transparent garment—who dressed a common servant in such fine linen?—and got stuck at her slightly chubby waist. Was she with child? "Keep me company since I've been abandoned," he demanded although he was very aware of the danger her presence posed. But then he'd resisted Muti's brazen friends, thus he felt confident he could handle her, too. After all, he loved his wife.

Lithely, she settled at his feet.

"Those two...they...um." Get a grip! She's just a maid. "I meant to say my friends are consoling your master and your mistress because of their tragic loss."

"Oh." Nofru sighed. Her hand wandered to her stomach as if on its own accord.

A typical gesture, Nakhtmin thought. She was really pregnant, and it looked like Merwer might be the father. Did his other children know? What would they think of him cheating on their mother? Albeit the trader wasn't made of rock. No wonder he gave in to such temptation, particularly if his wife hadn't been able to satisfy his desires for quite some time. Or had Nofru been lying with the young and handsome son of the family? That would explain why Sanefer had lost interest in marrying Ouseret and having her move in with him. Two such extraordinarily sensual women... Did the trader's son deserve so much luck? His thoughts hurtled like clouds in the storm. Perhaps Nofru would tell him whose child she carried. "You seem to mourn your master as well," he said.

She lowered her pretty head, so he couldn't read her face. "He was so amicable, so friendly and funny, everybody simply had to love him."

"Who'd treat a girl like you in any other way? I'm sure you've repaid him generously." Ugh, how mean of him to say that, but he had to find out more, and politeness wouldn't get him anywhere.

She batted her eyes at him. "What if...?" Her fingers stroked his calves.

Lo and behold, what a cunning minx. But she played the humble servant pretty well. He laughed. "In Merwer's place I'd have divorced my wife and married you." Forgive me, Muti!

The corners of her mouth twitched in an attempt to hide her contempt. "Merwer wasn't like that. You know, his wife is sick. And his business partners would never have approved of such selfish behavior. Only after...oh, nothing. Forget what I said."

No way! If only she'd finished the sentence, but he was pretty sure she meant to say, only after his wife died would marry her. Had he promise wedlock to the maid? Had she been sick and tired of waiting? Possibly, but Merwer's death wouldn't have gained her anything. Maybe she'd been targeting his son after her elderly lover's death. Mourning together could build a strong connection, and Sanefer might not know about her pregnancy. Nofru could have hoped to pass it off as his child. At least Merwer had acted decently toward his sick wife by not getting rid of her. Did that suffice to make him the wonderful fellow everyone claimed he was? Maybe, but he was only a man. Nofru may have seduced him on purpose. "Already forgotten." He grinned and pretended to pluck a memory from his heart and toss it over his shoulder. "It must have been quite a shock to you as well that your master had been poisoned. People say his doctor did it. For me that's really hard to believe because I too am a physician. We preserve lives and don't destroy them. Did you know that Nehesy fellow?"

She nodded. "He came and went all the time, he and his man-like daughter." At the mention of Ouseret, her nostrils flared in disgust. "However, I'd never have thought that he of all people..." She gazed north as if somebody there might have been more likely to do it.

Enthralled, he leaned forward. "Yes?"

Returning from wherever her thoughts had led her, she shrugged. "It's like you say, hard to imagine a doctor committing such a crime."

He couldn't let her off the hook so easily, thus he too glanced north. "Do you have neighbors here? I'm surprised Merwer settled so far from the city."

"Only peasants live here. The land belongs to Merwer—well, now to Sanefer. My master leased it from the pharaoh—life, prosperity and health—and split it up into smaller lots which he rented out to the peasants for a fee."

Oh, that's what Ouseret meant with farming. Many wealthy men did the same. They swept up the best land, and common people wanting to plant crops near a city had no choice but to lease from them at a higher rent than they would have paid the king. Pensive, Nakhtmin let his gaze wander. "Could one of the peasants have harbored a grudge against Merwer for depending on him?"

She jerked up. "Who told you that?"

Damn, he'd thought out loud! Now she'd clam up in distrust toward a far too nosy 'customer.' Now he could only hope she wouldn't tell her master! Her cry, however, had confirmed his suspicion. Merwer hadn't been popular with everyone, which would have been a miracle for a man making a living with risky enterprises. Since he'd already scared her, he might as well continue questioning her. "So Merwer did have a quarrel with one of his peasants?"

She snorted. "One?" Almost inaudibly, she murmured, "Ungrateful lot, dirty mud diggers."

Whoa, the girl really embraced her master's case! Did she expect it would be soon her case? "How many renters are there?"

"Three," she murmured. "Djehutinakht, Heny and Wahka are their names. This year they argued over the amount of rent."

"Hasn't that been settled in advance?" Nakhtmin asked and leaned closer to her although he was more interested in her words than her looks since the girl obviously bore a grudge against the peasants.

At long last, it spilled out of her. "My lord wanted to plant new grain. Everyone would've benefited, so fa—um...Wahka offered one of his two fields. The three of them also provided their jointly owned plow and ox for the undertaking, but the gods were against them. Cutting the furrows deeper than usual turned out rather challenging, the ox was injured and the plow damaged. To complete the disaster, the corn dried up before it could ripen."

Nakhtmin groaned. "The three families must be ruined." Then he wondered how she knew so much about this if she despised the peasants.

She cast him a wary look. "At least that's what they'd told my master day after day. They refused to pay the rent, claiming they'd starve if they did."

A gust of wind rustled the sycamore leaves and carried Muti's far off laughter to him. "And your master had a different view on things," he stated. "However, the law is on the peasants' side, I believe. If someone borrows something and damages it, they have to replace it. That's the custom."

For the first time she seemed uncertain. "Well, if you look at it that way..." Then she glared at him in defiance. "But didn't the land belong to my master? Didn't they rent it from him?"

Nakhtmin sighed. "He didn't own it, only leased it. There's a difference. And the ox...oh, never mind." He didn't feel like explaining legal matters particularly since he wasn't all too sure himself. In any case, as one of the peasants, he'd have been filled with bitterness toward Merwer as well. This didn't compare to surplus gold invested by a wealthy physician, this was about the very livelihood of three peasants and their families. Dear gods, this had to be the same grain Nehesy had paid for! He still wondered why Nofru showed so little sympathy although she probably came from a poor family as well.

Steps approached. Hori and Satnefert returned in amicable understanding. His friend must have turned his charm on full. The slightly reddened cheeks suited Sanefer's sister; she looked almost beautiful now. He smiled at her in appreciation. As though to defend her new possession, Nofru suddenly slipped her hand between his thighs and started massaging his penis before he could fend her off.

"I really can't leave my husband alone for a moment."

Nakhtmin flinched at the voice coming from the other side, pushed away Nofru's hand and turned. "Muti…"

ON THE WRONG TRACK?

Hori giggled. Always fun to watch how easy it was for Muti to make his friend feel embarrassed. He clicked his tongue in appreciation. "My dear Nakhtmin, how do you do it? The most beautiful women are at your feet."

That cracked up Muti as well, and Nakhtmin visibly relaxed. She said, "Should we take a look at the much-acclaimed storage hall now? That's why we came here after all."

Nakhtmin jumped up. "Yes, please!"

Satnefert mumbled an excuse and went into the house. Hori was glad to be rid of the girl. He'd learned a few things from her, but most of the time she'd spent singing the shopkeeper's praise. Now Hori knew the salesman was called Ini, and as the name promised, he really seemed a *gift* to Merwer's shy daughter. She'd spilled they could get married now that her father wasn't trying to betroth her to one of the rich, old courtiers. Despite her happiness in that regard, she seemed torn and really aggrieved by Merwer's death. Looked like Nakhtmin had been right about a child's love. How much would it affect him when his father died? These days he couldn't imagine feeling any grief since his heart knew him alive and stubborn as always. And where there was life, there was a chance. Only death ended everything, hindered all reconciliation. Suddenly, he had to swallow and blink away tears. The possibility of never detecting approval or affection in his father's eyes hit him with unexpected vehemence. "Yes, let's go," he said without much enthusiasm.

Large as it was, the storage hall turned out a gloomy, almost empty room with air slits high up in the walls allowing only a little sunlight to penetrate. Dust danced in the beams. Apart from the bales of ostrich feathers, Hori only saw some sacks of corn, gnawed by mice. The air smelled stale, a little musty, as if moisture rose from the river. Likely the air slits were too high up. He wouldn't want to store anything of value here.

Sanefer seemed a little embarrassed by the state of the hall. He profusely apologized and explained the death of his father had caused a standstill of business.

Doubts sneaked up on Hori. Shouldn't there be more goods here anyway? After all, the shop offered a considerable selection. Come to think of it, Ini had mostly a mingle-mangle of oddities on offer with some precious and rare pieces among them. Maybe a clearing sale of all that's left? But how did Sanefer want to make a living in the future if he didn't purchase more goods pretty fast? Ouseret said the young man had been working in his father's business already for some time, so the transition should have happened smoothly. The only new delivery since his father's death appeared to be the ostrich feathers, which Sanefer must have purchased on the Nile island Abu, the main trade hub for wares from the southern foreign lands like Kush. Quite strange...if Merwer's enterprises had really earned him so little, as his payment practice toward his creditors suggested, how could he maintain the large estate? Finding an answer to that question might lead them to someone wanting the man dead.

Mutnofret didn't show any surprise at the lack of goods but released a cry of joy when she saw the feathers, which jerked Hori out of his musings. "Oh look, aren't they amazingly downy?" She accepted an already assembled fan from Sanefer and gave it a try. "Just what I always wanted to have!" The way she batted her eyes would have brought stronger men than Nakhtmin to their knees.

Hori grinned. Muti played her part of an eager customer really well. Naturally, she already owned a similar fan. In visible unease, Nakhtmin already fondled his bag with tradeables. He haggled with Sanefer for a while, then they settled for a surprisingly small price. The trader's son wasn't really into it. Had he no clue about negotiations and the value of his goods or did he simply want to get rid of them as soon as possible? At least he got the gesturing of a market seller right. His bracelets jingled and rode up his arms. Hori spotted several light-colored scars on his wrist and the back of his hand. The latter were smaller and more inconspicuous. Grease burns, he guessed but refrained from offering medical advice on how to treat them. The skin had healed already, and he'd only upset Sanefer again if got started on health issues and cures once more. Besides, he wanted to get away. He could barely wait to hear what his friends had to report of their chats with the members of Merwer's household.

During the return trip, Hori could tell Nakhtmin was bursting with exciting news, but the fisher's presence prevented them from discussing matters. Now that Muti no longer had to pretend, she seemed withdrawn and pensive. Which of them had the more interesting story to relate, and what impression had beautiful Sanefer made on Nakhtmin's perceptive wife? He certainly couldn't make head nor tail of the man, even when he ignored his nagging jealousy. If only they'd rented a boat without a boatman, then they'd be able to talk freely! But none of them knew the shallows and currents in this area. The river's water was still green, but soon high tide would arrive and color it red. Back home, neither Nakhtmin nor he dared to brave the raging surge with their boats then. Here it would be pure madness to even consider it. The fisher had mounted the mast and set the sail, but they still moved much slower against the current than they had coming here. At a leisurely pace, they passed flooded fields.

"What kind of building is that?" Muti asked and pointed at an unusually high wall shimmering from behind palm trees. It looked like it had been built recently. "I already noticed it on our way there."

They all turned to the boatman for an answer. He spit out a leaf of reed he'd been chewing and shrugged. "Garrison," he growled.

So that's where the omnipresent militia came from. Of course they'd be stationed close to the city. However, it was strange that the stronghold was built to secure the road leading north. On the other hand, what did he know about such things?

On the riverbank, the palaces of the rich paraded past them. Some had seen better days and gave an impression of glory long gone, others appeared much newer. Something was wrong with this city, but he couldn't put a finger on it. When they finally reached the small jetty of Nehesy's estate, Hori felt so glad that he paid the fisherman far more than the agreed price.

The wiry man bowed reverentially. "Whenever you need a boat again..."

Deep in thought, Hori hurried off to the gate through which Muti had just disappeared, when he heard Nakhtmin say, "I'd like to use your services again tomorrow."

Pricking his ears, he turned around. "You would? What are you up to?" Tomorrow, the scribbler in the archive should have the copies of the trial records ready for him, and he was eager to get his hands on those.

Nakhtmin made a vague gesture. "I want to take a look around the fields here. Maybe I can figure out a way to make mine more productive."

Baffled, Hori blurted, "Since when…? Ouch!" That doofus had pinched him.

The fisher looked from one to the other then asked in confusion, "Will you need me tomorrow or not?"

"Yes," Nakhtmin confirmed with emphasis. "But in the morning, please, second hour."

When the man had left, Hori said, "What are you planning to do? And don't talk to me about farming fields—you don't have any!"

"I don't, but the deceased Merwer certainly had fields, and I'd like to inspect them," Nakhtmin replied mysteriously.

Hori couldn't imagine why this might be relevant for their case. "Do as you wish, but don't count on me. I'll fetch the copy of the court records from the archive."

They'd almost reached the house when Nakhtmin suggested, "How about we invite Ouseret over? What we've found out concerns her the most."

The sound of her name sped up Hori's heart. "No need to twist my arm. As you know, I cherish her company more than anyone else's." A glance at the sun told him they'd have to wait another hour for the evening meal to be ready. "Should we send Hapi over? I don't feel like going out again today."

"You remember the name of our servant!" his friend cried out in wonder.

Hori smiled with pride.

That moment Muti came outside and called, "Guess who's here?"

"Ouseret!" Nakhtmin shouted in surprise.

The unexpected sight of her left Hori dumbstruck. No time to prepare for meeting her! The smile froze on his lips, and since he didn't know what to do with his hands he clenched and unclenched them a few times. Why would he do that? He wasn't about to attack her!

She avoided his gaze, seeming even less approachable than usual. While Nakhtmin greeted her and Muti took her hands to lead her into the garden, Hori just stood there mute like an ushabti figure, as if he needed an order from the gods to shout, "Yes, here I am! What shall I do?"

"Listen, I—" Ouseret began, but Nakhtmin placed a finger to his lips and silenced her.

"Wait until Antef's people are gone," he whispered and she nodded.

To Nakhtmin's chagrin, Hereret and Hapi stayed until the evening to serve them and couldn't be convinced to leave earlier. That only increased his distrust toward them. What servant wouldn't happily accept finishing work early? As long as the two still fluttered around them, Hori and Muti shared nothing about today's outing. Naturally, he bit his tongue as well. Maybe the secrecy wasn't really necessary.

The nomarch couldn't possibly mind their looking into an old case. The next moment, Nakhtmin realized that they were basically questioning the integrity of the local court. Muti, Hori and he could afford to incense Antef since they'd be leaving soon, Ouseret, however, lived here. If her situation was difficult now, how much more complicated would it become if the nomarch held a grudge against her and rolled boulders, not just stones, in her way?

Ouseret barely contributed to their general chatter, didn't even ask what they'd found out during an unobserved moment. Nakhtmin felt new anger toward the stupid woman well up inside him. They did all this for her, but she didn't care if they put themselves in harm's way. Why did she even come here?

Hori licked the grease of a crisp roasted waterfowl from his fingers and burped slightly when Hereret brought the water bowl for them to wash their fingers. "That was nice, but now I'm full."

The women murmured their agreement.

While Muti finally ushered the servants off, Nakhtmin thought of another reason why nobody should learn about their investigation: People tended to speak less guardedly when they didn't know what you intended with your questions. If Nofru had known he was trying to expose a murderer in Sanefer's household, she'd probably have locked up. Instead, they had new suspects. The three peasants had reason to begrudge Merwer. When Muti sat down again, he was about to broach the subject, but Ouseret's deep voice sounded first.

"I wanted to apologize to you. I'm really sorry for my behavior yesterday. I...I felt embarrassed because you found me in such dire circumstances. None of you deserved my resentment, instead you have every right to be upset with me."

Hori, who'd been drinking every word from her lips like nectar, beamed with delight. Nakhtmin grinned, but raised his eyebrows in surprise when his friend grasped Ouseret's slender hand, and she didn't pull it away. Well, not straightaway. Maybe Hori's case wasn't lost yet?

"We need to apologize for showing up out of the blue, uninvited and unannounced," Muti said and stepped on his big toe under the table.

He suppressed a cry and wondered what he'd done to deserve that. "Thoughtless of us," he murmured his agreement. "But we mostly wanted to offer our help. There's no need to be ashamed when you suffer injustice by others. We've found out quite a few things." With a questioning look, he meant to prompt Hori to tell them what the pale sister told him. However, his friend stared at Ouseret like a cow and seemed to have swallowed his tongue. Nakhtmin sighed. Oh well, he'd go first then. "We've visited Sanefer's estate this afternoon."

A gust of wind brought a cooling breeze from the river, but Ouseret's cold look made him shiver even more.

"What did you do?" she squeezed out. "You shouldn't have gone there..." She rose. "Forget the whole matter! I will, too."

Nakhtmin didn't dare to reply. After a moment of speechlessness, Muti called, "How are we supposed to help if we don't even know the people involved?"

Ouseret couldn't hold her gaze and sank onto her seat again. "Stop it! Haven't I told you everything you need to know? You should—"

Nakhtmin was sick and tired of her behavior. "Not by a long shot! And how could you if you don't know everything either? Did you know that during the experiment with the new grain, for which your father paid, three peasants renting land from Merwer had also suffered losses? No? I didn't think so. One of them forfeited the harvest of one of his two fields. In addition, the jointly used plow was damaged and the ox injured."

At long last, Hori jerked out of his swooning trance. "Oh, that's why you want to go back there tomorrow. They really had good reason to take revenge. Each of them must have wished him evil." Now, he turned back to Ouseret, and to Nakhtmin's relief, his gaze stayed clear and focused. "I've talked to Merwer's daughter. Satnefert is in love with the salesman Ini. Did you know that?"

Ouseret pulled up her shoulders in discomfort and shied back a little from him. "Hm, I suspected as much, but that was only a passing fancy. As far as I know, she's been promised to someone else and has agreed to the marriage. Listen—"

Hori clicked his tongue. "Agreed? That's over now. Merwer's dead, and your friend Satnefert plans to move into Ini's house soon."

Whoa, Nakhtmin didn't think the shy girl had it in her to act against her father's will. So that was why the fellow desperately wanted more responsibility and a share in the profits, so he could offer his bride a nice home. Oh dear, what if Sanefer didn't want to keep his father's promise? Promises, promises…too many had been made and few kept. A thought sneaked through Nakhtmin's heart and vanished before he could grasp it.

"If she's so in love with Ini, why didn't she object to marrying someone else?" Muti wondered.

Nakhtmin cast her a loving look. His wife would never have accepted a man pushed on her as bridegroom, not by her father Ameny, whom she dearly loved, and not by anyone else. But Muti was Muti.

Hori explained, "You've met her, seen what she's like. Merwer must have talked her into it; he mostly wanted a rich and influential husband for her, someone with connections to the nomarch. Satnefert always only loved Ini, but her father wouldn't accept that." He paused and rubbed the root of his nose. Then he cast Ouseret a questioning look. "I believe the trader wasn't that rich if he needed the wealth of his future son-in-law. I have the feeling Merwer always took from others to finance his risky endeavors. If they succeeded, he got his share. If they failed, they did so at his investors' expense. Maybe he'd overdone it, duped the wrong person?"

Ouseret's eyes narrowed to slits. She looked like she wanted to jump at his throat. "I—"

"I know you liked the man," Nakhtmin tried to calm her. Always so cool-headed, Ouseret seemed blind to Merwer's flaws, the mistakes of her fatherly friend. "What we've found out so far casts a different light on Merwer's trade affairs, and his storage hall is pretty much empty."

Hori leaned forward. "Ah, you found that strange as well for a supposedly quite successful businessman?"

He nodded. "And he amused himself with his servant Nofru."

Ouseret gaped at him, but before she could say anything, Muti cut in, her voice sharp. "Well, he wasn't the only one, my husband didn't seem appalled by her either."

If only he hadn't broached that subject! But Nofru's position in Merwer's household might be important for their investigation. "I didn't want that! She simply..." He fell silent when he noticed Muti's mouth twitch with mischief. And Hori contributed a subdued cackle. *You just wait until you're married, my friend!* He mustered all his dignity. "If you don't want to hear what I've found out..."

"No, stop it, all of you. You don't understand...!" Ouseret's voice rang with despair. She grabbed his hand.

He ignored her. "As Ouseret informed us, Merwer's wife has been confined to her bed for a long time now. Her husband took in beautiful Nofru not only as his servant but as his lover. I believe she carries his child. And..." He paused for emphasis. "...he promised to marry her once his wife had passed on."

"And now you think she killed him because she grew impatient?" Muti quipped. She took the lantern and lit the torches mounted around the pergola. Night had fallen.

Ouseret's grasp around Nakhtmin's hand had tightened more and more, while he'd talked. He pulled away from her. "I got the impression Nofru now keeps Sanefer's bed linen warm." After a quick glance at the tall physician's stony face, he mumbled. "I'm sorry, I know he's only recently reneged his engagement to you."

Both women stared at him, and Muti called, "You think he left her? What a silly idea, my husband. Ouseret ended it. She banished Sanefer from her life."

Hori's features showed an amazing succession of emotions: Astonishment, joy, disbelief and finally happiness. Then he blurted, "Is that true, Ouseret? *You* ended the engagement?"

Nakhtmin had to avert his gaze lest he be blinded by the bright hope shining from Hori's eyes. As if that improved his chances with her. Hm, maybe it did? At least she couldn't have loved Sanefer much.

She nodded and pressed those luscious lips together. "Yes. After he gave testimony against my father in front of the vizier, I couldn't possibly move into his house."

A stupid grin on his face, Hori's head bobbed up and down in agreement like that of a curlew searching for worms. His friend probably meant to say he'd never betray her, but Nakhtmin could understand Sanefer, too. As a loving son, he wanted to see his father's killer punished, a wish that took first place in his heart. However, Ouseret would never be able to forgive him. Her feelings toward him hardened—likely against all men, which explained her negative reaction to Hori courting her. And now she'd learned her former fiancé was sleeping with another woman... And Muti had known which of them reneged on the engagement! His head jerked around to her. No, he could question her about that later. "Tell me, my darling wife, what did you find out today? I only heard you flirt and laugh with beautiful Sanefer."

One of her elegant eyebrows hiked up in mockery. "Oh my, with all the philandering going on I totally forgot to interrogate him! And I wasn't the only one either."

He wanted to retort, but Ouseret's reproachful stare reminded them how serious this matter was for her.

Muti sighed. "I actually did find out very little. Has he always been so reserved?"

Reserved? Nakhtmin suppressed a grin. In that case, Ouseret and Sanefer might have been a perfect match. Muti's face had turned as pensive as earlier on the boat. "What are you mulling over?"

With some reluctance, she continued, "Sanefer went on about how little value he attached to physicians, and I found that rather unusual since he'd wanted to marry you." She scrutinized Ouseret.

"My profession never mattered between us and he did show some interest in medicine, however, he had no patience for ailing people. Now, please stop the questions!" Scorn flared up in her eyes. "I told you to—"

Muti cut in. "He never mentioned you but said he was glad to escape these two…" She waved a hand at Hori and him. "…before they commenced talking about diseases again."

Believing that Nehesy had killed his father probably increased his dislike for physicians. Then Nakhtmin remembered what he'd meant to ask Ouseret the other day. "You did come to Itj-tawy to do research in the library of the House of Life there. Did you hope to find a natural cause that would explain Merwer's symptoms and death?"

Twice she rubbed her face with one hand, then her chagrined features turned expressionless again. "I know that it was silly of me. There's no such disease."

"No," he agreed. "Somebody must have poisoned Merwer with colocynth. If Nehesy didn't do it, who else knew what kind of medicine Merwer used to take, so he could make it look like your father's doing? Um…" Realizing what treacherous territory he'd entered, Nakhtmin paused. Ouseret belonged to that group of suspects. "I mean who knew the ingredients and could have obtained more? And who had access to his medicine?"

"You mean apart from my father and me?" Ouseret voiced his nightmarish suspicion nonchalantly, as if it didn't concern her. She huffed. "That's all well and good, you've done a lot. Thank you. But I don't want you to continue your investigation. Stop it!" She buried her head in her hands.

Was that a confession? Did Ouseret fear they'd expose her as the culprit and therefore wanted them to cease? But why would she have tried to find an illness matching Merwer's symptoms then? Of course! She wanted to free her father because he was innocent of the murder she had committed! Nakhtmin sneaked a glance at Hori, but he seemed surprisingly calm. He shook his head fervently, but did nothing to make him regret his words. Then it dawned on him that Hori must have thought along those lines as well. Without conviction, Nakhtmin said, "I don't regard you or Nehesy as suspects, which means there's no reason for us to stop. Let's consider things together. Who could have done it? Who knew what the remedy consisted of and how dangerous it was?"

Slowly she lifted her head and sighed. "All right, I'll tell you. My father had made this strong concoction for Merwer before. That was well known in the House of Life and certainly in his household as well. Each time, Father admonished his patient not to take more than the recommended dosage, and he probably instructed the persons tending to him and serving his food."

That could have been anyone in the house except maybe Merwer's wife. But who knew what the sick woman was really capable of? "His wife might have found out about his affair with the servant girl," he suggested.

"Who? Ankhes-Nit? No way! She's been unable to get out of bed for a long time now. Her mind has dimmed, she's hardly aware of what's going on around her, and it's probably a blessing for her under the circumstances. With regard to the colocynth, it grows at the river, as you know. Anyone could have plucked a fruit or two, and that's it!"

The plant wasn't that common in the south. Nakhtmin couldn't remember ever having seen any back home. One had to know where to find it. Was Ouseret trying to divert them away from her as a suspect? He had to swallow. That didn't look good...

All of a sudden, Hori jumped up. "Ha!"

They all stared at him in astonishment. "What do you mean 'ha'?" Nakhtmin asked.

"Ha, as in: Wouldn't Merwer have noticed if his medicine had become more and of a different consistency? Or did Nehesy provide the drug in pills?"

"No, he dissolved it in wine and honey so it turned into a syrup," Ouseret explained impatiently. "At the House of Life they use a powder made from the ground seeds of the fruit. That's more concentrated and not as bitter as the pulp. First he let the ground lotus flowers soak in wine, then sifted them and added incense and the colocynth seeds. In the end, he sweetened it with honey."

Nakhtmin sighed. The pulp of the fruit couldn't have been added then, unless someone served it to him in his meal. However, some powdered seeds could have been easily added without anyone noticing. Damn, it didn't get them anywhere if Ouseret only kept leading them back to the House of Life. Or did it? "Did any other physicians do business with Merwer?" he asked her.

After mulling over it, she shook her head reluctantly. "I don't think so. But then men wouldn't simply entrust a woman with such information." Her voice took on a strange note, as if someone squeezed her throat. "It's possible." After a while, she added, "But I don't think any of my colleagues are capable of such a crime."

Nakhtmin knew exactly what she meant. Someone directing all his efforts at curing others couldn't just turn into a killer.

A sob escaped Ouseret's mouth. "If I had the slightest idea who could have murdered him, don't you think I would have done something about it? You're looking at the wrong place! You are in the wrong place! Don't interfere, you'll only make things worse!" With that, she jumped up and ran off into the darkness.

Hori dashed after her, but soon returned breathing hard and limping. His knee was bleeding. "Gone. She knows her way around here, unlike me."

Nakhtmin darted him an unhappy glance. "We've thoroughly messed up."

Surprising Findings

The next day, Hori still found himself in a subdued mood. A while ago, he'd heard Nakhtmin and Muti leave the house, but he'd just turned over and slept on well into the morning. While eating his breakfast alone, nothing distracted him from brooding. Naturally, his thoughts mostly circled around the lady of his heart. He couldn't regard Ouseret's visit yesterday as the sign he'd hoped for, a sign of them getting closer to each other. She'd separated from Sanefer before she met him, so she didn't leave the fellow because of him. However, they weren't together any longer, and Ouseret had allowed him to hold her hand. For a moment, he cherished the memory.

No, he shouldn't fool himself. She'd fled from him, and he didn't understand why. How could his help make anything worse for her? Hori straightened his shoulders. Whether she wanted it or not, he'd keep investigating until her father had been cleared of all accusations, and the copy of the records would make for a good start to achieve that. With grim determination, he set out for the palace. Ouseret would appreciate his help some day.

This time, he found the archive right away and entered without knocking. However, the mat, on which the scribe had sat the other day, wasn't occupied, and he couldn't see anyone else around. "Hello? Is anyone here?" he called into the semi-darkness. There, steps. A sense of dread made his heart pound and his hands sweat. What foolishness! He was imagining shadows everywhere. When he could finally make out the face of the approaching archive clerk, he didn't recognize it. This wasn't Seni or the other fellow, but a stranger.

"What do you wish?" the lanky man asked.

He wiped his hands on his shendyt. "Hm, Seni…I wish to speak with Seni. Can you tell him that someone's waiting for him?"

Raising his arms in regret, the scribe snarled, "Unfortunately, Seni isn't here today. Can I help you?"

Hori's dread increased. "And the other man? I came here the day before yesterday, and a scribe was sitting up front." Maybe Seni had given his colleague the copy so he'd hand it over to Hori.

The clerk shook his head, causing the sinews in his throat to bend like reeds in the wind. "Both no longer work at the archive."

What? That couldn't be a coincidence! Had the men simply made off with his bribe? No, the collar wasn't valuable enough to give up a good position. His mouth felt parched. "Um, Seni promised me a copy of court records. Has he possibly left it here for me?"

The man's nose twitched like that of rabbit. "Has he now? Not that he was authorized to do such a thing for anyone asking."

Dear gods, don't make me do it all over again! "It's not for anyone asking but for the vizier of the Two Lands. If you were so kind as to take a look? The recordings of the last kenbet session. The transcript for the king's archive has been lost."

Eyebrows hiked up. "Hm, oh well." He disappeared into the adjoining room and produced rustling noises. Then steps sounded farther down the enfilade. Muffled voices. What took the man so long? Seni had found the document in the first room and pretty fast, too. The steps grew louder and sounded like more than one person. They halted, and someone seemed to sift through the shelves again. If only he could understand what the clerks were saying! At long last, two men returned to the antechamber and Hori stiffened. The archive worm had brought his superior along: fly frond in hand, badge of rank around the neck. Did he have to tell the whole story all over again? What if they demanded proof that Sobekemhat requested this duplicate? He suppressed a groan.

"Um-hrm." The newcomer cleared his throat ostentatiously. "I am Amunmose, head of the archive. You asked for the records of the last kenbet." Looking down his bird-of-prey nose, he scrutinized Hori. "Unfortunately, the file in question isn't on the premises." He made it sound like that was Hori's fault, like he was blaming the supplicant of theft.

Hori folded his arms over his chest. "Impossible. The day before yesterday, I saw the document. It was here. A clerk named Seni promised me a duplicate by today."

Amunmose's head jerked forward as if to skewer Hori with his nose. "Seni was not authorized to make any such promises. He no longer works for our master, the nomarch Antef. You should have placed your request with Antef. Only at his orders are we allowed to provide copies to you."

Despair welled up inside Hori. "Then I'll take that route." And by all the demons of the underworld, he'd do exactly that! The nomarch had welcomed them in a friendly manner and knew who they were. He'd surely concede.

The archive worm giggled but fought to suppress it and fell silent when Amunmose cast him a sharp look. In his response, the head of the archive made no secret of his satisfaction, "You don't understand. Even if you were the pharaoh—health, prosperity and life—I couldn't grant your wish. The file has disappeared. Whoever removed it neglected to leave a note of registration telling us where it has been taken."

Hori blinked until the words sank in, then he jerked up and wanted to go for the man's throat but restrained himself. "That can't be happening! I need this copy!"

"Maybe Seni...?" the worm whispered in Amunmose's direction.

Yes! That had to be the explanation. Seni would have taken the scroll when they fired him. He probably wanted to offer the original to Hori to make ends meet for a while. Cheered up, Hori turned to leave.

However, Amunmose thundered, "Impossible. All clerks are searched when they leave these rooms. Every day."

That dampened Hori's hopes but didn't destroy them completely. A corrupt official would know ways to smuggle out a document. He had to find Seni, then he'd get what he wanted. Hiding his confidence as much as possible, he took his leave.

Standing outside the palace, Hori wasn't sure what to do. How could he find the old hunchback in this large city? And Seni was a very common name. Then he remembered that the various crafts had their own quarters in Waset. Most likely public servants also lived close to each other. Indeed, he only needed to ask a few people to find himself in the respective area not too far from the palace. Since he'd slept in this morning, Ra's bark had already risen high into the sky. Atop the roof terraces surrounding the upper floors of the two-story adobe houses, women already prepared food, while their children frolicked in the alleys. A naked brat with her head shaved except for the lock of youth wanted to squeeze past him. It was a girl maybe six years of age. He grabbed her arm. "Caution! But say, do you know an archive scribe called Seni?" he asked.

She squealed and would have scurried off if he hadn't tightened his grip.

"Let my sister go!" a cracking voice sounded from behind him.

He turned around to an older boy, whose voice was already changing, grinned and released the little one. "You're a good older brother. I'm sure you can tell me in which house the archive scribe Seni lives."

"Rickety and bent like a zebu?"

He nodded happily. "You know him!"

"Over there, the house at the end of the street."

Hori thanked him and pulled out a honey cake wrapped in a lotus leaf he'd brought as his lunch. "Here you go, but share it with your sister."

Just a few steps and he reached Seni's house, which sat abandoned under the midday sun. The old man probably had no wife or daughter who'd take care of him. A hint of guilt made him hesitate. Was it his fault the scribe and his colleague had lost their employment? Well, it had been their decision to let him bribe them. He knocked reluctantly. Nobody answered, so he tried again, louder this time. Nothing. In his despair, he pressed an ear against the wood. It gave and opened with a scraping nose. Nobody here, but the door unlocked? How odd.

"Seni?" he called. "Are you home? It's me, Hori, son of the vizier. Seni?"

Still nothing. The house appeared uninhabited. His gazed brushed over the ladder to the upper floor. This time of day, the sleeping chamber would be unbearably hot. Hard to imagine an old man being there, and Hori hadn't seen him on the terrace either when he'd peered up from the street. Nobody reacted to his shouts, not a soul was to be found in this room nor in the adjoining pantry, except spiders, but at least the shelves and jugs were nicely filled. Seni wouldn't have left for good without taking all that with him. Well, Hori could wait. He settled on the bench in the main room and once again pondered over Ouseret's strange behavior. Now that he relaxed, hunger gnawed at him. Too bad that he'd given the boy his food. He traipsed back into the pantry and reached for a loaf of flatbread. Hard as a rock! It had to be a day old at least. He didn't want to scavenge Seni's other provisions but broke a piece off the bread and washed it down with water from one of the jugs. Where could the old man be? Maybe he'd already found a new position. Hori groaned. If so, he'd have to wait here until evening, which was the last thing he wanted. Suddenly, he laughed out loud and told himself, "Hori, you're such a doofus!"

Seni wouldn't carry the scroll with him, no matter where he'd gone. If he'd taken the document, it had to be inside the house. He dashed up the ladder, but halted on the top rung and sniffed. That smell he knew all too well, the scent of death. Anticipating what he'd find in Seni's sleeping chamber, he carefully opened the door, stirring up a cloud of flies. The old man lay on his cot, belly already swollen a little, looking like he'd died yesterday or the day before in his sleep. That's what his neighbors would think when they found him at some point. Hori, however, noticed the unnatural angle of his throat. Somebody had broken his neck. Seni had been murdered!

He stood petrified and felt the going of his heart all the way to his fingertips. Somehow he couldn't shake off the feeling that this had something to do with him. But why? How could he, after only a few days in Waset, have caused the killing of a this archive official? Sweat poured from all his pores and not just because of the heat, which was indeed hardly bearable. He had to pull himself together. As Nakhtmin liked to say, he wasn't the heart of the world. He took a deep breath—not through the nose though—and exhaled. Since his time in the weryt, he was used to the stench of corpses, but most were brought to the embalming compound before they'd decomposed so much.

He had to find the scroll!

Taking caution not to create a mess, he searched the chamber and the few pieces of furniture. In the end, he even felt under the sack of straw, on which the old man lay, although he was starting to feel a little queasy. Nothing. There weren't any more rooms, only the roof terrace to which a door in the staircase led. Hori didn't think it smart to stroll around on the roof of a murder victim, well visible to anyone looking his way. And Seni would certainly not have hidden it there. He went back down and thoroughly searched the pantry but didn't find the scroll. Either Seni hadn't stolen it from the archive or his killer had taken it with him after the deed. What for? Did someone object to Hori reading the records because they contained a clue pointing at the true murderer of Merwer? That seemed a little far-fetched. Too bad he'd never learned the name of the other scribe. Well, maybe he should be glad. If his colleague was dead like Seni... Hori cursed his guilelessness when coming here. The children would remember him, and he might end up at court, tried for murder, once again—an experience he did not want to repeat!

With a sensation of pure joy, Nakhtmin regarded Muti's relaxed features as she lazily lounged on the springy reeds of the boat, enjoying the morning sun shining on her. And he was finally alone with his dear one! Maybe they should have made this journey without Hori, but he had to admit his friend's investigation had distracted them from their grief more than any recreational vacation on their own could have done.

Muti blinked and smiled at him. "Isn't it beautiful on the river today? Look at the ibises diving for small fish!"

"Mh-hm," he droned. Behind them two dinghies seemed to race each other. One moment the left rower caught the better current and shot forward, the next moment, his competitor did. Nakhtmin mentally bet a copper deben on the boat with the high bow ending in the shape of a papyrus. Yes, he was certain that bark would pass the branch arching over the water first.

"Oh, look at the geese!" Muti called. "We don't have as many back home by far."

Sure enough, whole flocks of the giant birds floated on the waves or waddled through the mud on the riverbank. "The goose is holy to Amun," he explained. "And because the god emerged from the world egg of the great honker, his priests are not allowed to eat eggs. Maybe in and around Waset the birds must not be hunted." For a while he watched the animals then turned back to the boats. Oh no, they were hidden in a river bend. Ah, there was 'his' boat again and in the lead as he'd expected. Of course, now he couldn't tell if it had passed the branch first but he felt like a winner anyway.

"There's Sanefer's quay," Muti whispered and pointed at the small private harbor.

They'd not use that one today. The siblings would certainly find it strange if the couple from the residence returned so soon again. "Take us to the next spot downstream where we can alight," Nakhtmin told the fisher.

The taciturn man nodded, and soon the bottom of the boat skidded over mud next to a palm tree, whose almost horizontal trunk served them as pier. First, Nakhtmin climbed out of the rocking craft and onto the tree, then he helped Muti and smoothed his shendyt. Although they'd negotiated the terms with the fisher beforehand, he reminded him, "Wait here. We'll be gone for a while. Just like yesterday, we'll reward you well."

Without a word, the man tied the boat to a root, cast his line and got comfortable in the shade of doum palms.

They walked several yards over a harvested field to a path. The river had flooded almost all the farmland; soon the water would reach all the way up. Nakhtmin helped Muti over one of last year's irrigation ditches, now overgrown and only a muddy rivulet. After each flooding, the ditches had to be cut anew.

"What do you hope to learn from the peasants?" she asked.

Nakhtmin didn't really know. "I mostly want to get an impression of the people. All three lost a major part of their livelihood because of Merwer. Could one of them have been enraged enough to kill the trader? Since their land borders the man's estate, they might have been able to sneak into his house unobserved."

She snorted. "That is if they knew what remedy Merwer received from his doctor for his afflictions."

"Yes, that's the thing," he said. "I gave it some thought. Merwer was someone constantly talking about his ailments. I know such people, and they tend to tell you exactly what they've already been taking to cure them. It's like the story of the eloquent peasant; they talk and talk to get attention."

"And that makes you suspect one of the farmers might have thought…oh!" She squealed.

Nakhtmin flinched. "What's up?"

"Just look what grows and prospers there!"

He gazed in the direction she pointed out. "Colocynth!" Incredible! He hadn't thought they'd find the murder weapon right before their noses.

Once they'd reached the ground-covering plants, they quickly found two stems close to each other, which had been harvested recently. Since the fruit wasn't suitable to eat and even animals avoided it, this appeared highly suspicious to Nakhtmin. He cast his wife a meaningful look. "Where might the man be who farms this land?" he wondered pensively and shielded his eyes. "Oh, someone's over there between the bushes. Hiho, heeellooo!"

"Where?" Muti asked.

A crack and rustling noises drifted over to them from the very spot, but nobody was heading toward them; the sounds moved away. Nakhtmin bushwhacked through the shrubs, but found nobody. "Strange! I could have sworn…"

Muti giggled. "Maybe an animal?"

"Hey, I do know the difference between human and beast," he protested lamely. She was probably right. Who'd loiter in the bushes? From behind a knoll quite a bit farther north, a man came walking. Nakhtmin rubbed his eyes. "That can't be the same fellow unless he's got wings." He waved.

The peasant, judging by his unbleached shendyt, didn't return the gesture but kept stomping toward them. They'd better move away from the colocynth plants! If Merwer's overdose came from here, the tenant of the land didn't necessarily pluck the fruit himself, might not even know that someone took any, but he'd certainly wonder why strangers took an interest in this weed. Nakhtmin clutched Muti's hand and pulled her toward the man. They met on the path.

"This is my land," the farmer growled instead of greeting them. "What are you doing here?"

Nakhtmin put up a friendly smile against the man's indignant frown. "Forgive us for intruding. We are from the north and considering leasing land here. I'm Nakht and this is my wife Nofret." He'd only just thought of using false names. To avoid Sanefer learning about their snooping around and talking to his peasants, Muti and he weren't wearing any jewelry or signs of rank and had donned simple clothes, but they hadn't discussed aliases. To his relief, Muti only blinked once without giving away her surprise. "Before we make a decision, we thought we should find out what grows best in the south."

An expression hard to place conquered the coarse face of the peasant. "Hm, you can have my fields. Looks like I'll have to give up farming. I'm Wahka."

Give up? Now, that was interesting. "The land doesn't yield much? Hard to believe. Inundation will turn out perfect again, just like last year, not too high and not too low. Or is old age forcing you to retire?" Nakhtmin suppressed a grin because Wahka was a man in his best years. His strong body, however, appeared haggard like after a year of crop failure.

The peasant ignored his scoff. "Neither. I'm leasing the land from a trader and won't be able to pay the rent this year after I've sent the king his dues, so I'll lose my home."

"Oh no! I'm so sorry," Muti sang. "What happened to get you in such a predicament? Is something wrong with the land? Can it not support you?"

Wahka considered his reply, then snorted. "Well, no need for me to be secretive about it. Last year, the trader coaxed me into sowing grain from foreign lands on one of my fields. I shouldn't have listened to him and planted emmer wheat as usual. But the prospect of large returns made me deaf to the objections of my heart. As long as the water stood high, the foreign seeds prospered, soon after, the plants withered. I had to let my daughter, my only child, go off into service, so I'd be able to pay levy to the king. The tribute collectors of the pharaoh—life, prosperity and health—don't care what grows on the fields or doesn't, they take what's the king's." He kicked a dried lump of loam, and it crumbled.

Nakhtmin nodded his understanding. The taxes on field crops varied from year to year, depending on the level of inundation and the size of the land. Wahka had to pay for the field where nothing grew just like for the other one. That probably left him with enough to eat but no seeds for next year and no grain with which to pay the rent. "Doesn't the trader show mercy with you since he caused your predicament? That doesn't seem fair to me. Hm, maybe your neighbors can help you."

"Would be nice, but that's not going to happen," Wahka snarled. "They also trusted Merwer's golden tongue. You know, Heny, Djehutynakht and I have jointly purchased and used several things, among them an ox and a plow, and we helped each other with the sowing. For this new grain, we had to dig deeper furrows than usual until the plow was torn asunder. That made the ox trip and break its foreleg. We had to slaughter the beast. Unfortunately, that field was the first one we'd plowed, so we had to hoe the others by hand and stomp the seed into the ground ourselves. The effort that took cost us far too much time. The ground was already drying up. None of us brought in a full harvest."

Although Nakhtmin had heard parts of his story from Nofru before, he realized only now that Merwer's wonderful grain had destroyed the livelihood of all his renters. The girl had told him the three peasants had purchased the ox and bronze plow together as did many other small farmers since they couldn't afford such amenities otherwise. Farming never yielded riches, as the larger part of the harvest went to the king. In return, the pharaoh distributed grain to the people of the Two Lands in times of hunger. The three peasants must have hoped to improve their situation—maybe buy an additional ox—if they followed Merwer's suggestion. And now they looked at the shards of their destroyed livelihoods. "And the trader didn't lower the rent under the circumstances?"

"Our chance, our risk, he said."

Nakhtmin sensed Wahka's desperation and helplessness. What could a small farmer achieve against rich Merwer? He remembered all too well that a little nobody was nothing but fly droppings in the eyes of the Mighty.

Muti put Nakhtmin's scorn into words. "This trader isn't a decent man! It was his fault, so he should cover the damage."

Another mysterious expression slid across Wahka's face. "The gods have already punished Merwer. He died recently."

"And what are you going to do now?" Muti asked, radiating honest sympathy.

"Who knows? For a smart man there are always possibilities. Maybe I can convince the trader's heir…" His gaze turned far away.

This time, Nakhtmin believed he saw cunning in Wahka's face. What could he mean? Was there something he could use to put pressure on Sanefer—maybe he knew who'd plucked the colocynths? He cleared his throat. "Well, your fields don't seem suitable for our purposes. We'd rather not depend on a landlord like your former one. Nofret, we should farm the land of a temple domain instead. We'd have to pay additional tribute to the gods but at least everything would be in order."

"I wish you more luck than I had. Now I'd better prepare for the approaching high tide. Maybe I can at least grow enough vegetables so my wife and I won't starve."

"All the best to you," Muti said.

Deep in thought, they hiked along the path for a while before Nakhtmin realized they were heading for the large estate. "I guess it's hardly worth talking to the other two peasants. What do you think?"

His wife shook her head. "They'll tell us the same, but our friend over there would likely hear of our improper curiosity."

They climbed a hill and looked down onto the large house. Nakhtmin shielded his eyes and made out a figure in the garden, the maid Nofru if he wasn't mistaken. "We should return to the boat," he said. "If someone of Sanefer's household sees us, he'll realize there was something fishy about our visit yesterday."

"I wasn't intending to walk on," she retorted. "I just didn't want Wahka to see where we'd turn after leaving his property. Our coming here by boat might make him wary." Muti took a look around and grabbed his hand. "Now, he's got his back to us. Let's run."

Giggling, they bushwhacked through the shrubs just as he'd done earlier, chasing the mysterious sounds. What a relief that this investigation turned out so harmless that even Muti could join in and have some fun. This time, he didn't have to fear for her safety. Behind the bushes, the copse of palm trees rose. In their shade, they'd left the boatman.

Only a short time later, the taciturn man took them back to the Southern City. During the return trip, Muti remained silent and introverted. Likely, she was mulling over what they'd learned today. Nakhtmin's thoughts hurried ahead to Nehesy's estate. He couldn't wait to read the court records Hori had procured today. Lazy, he let his gaze wander over the water glittering in the sunshine. Not many boats were out and about during the midday heat. However, he spotted his friend the boatman with the papyrus bow. He waved at him. Although the single man on board stiffened, he didn't wave back but turned and shortened the sail to slow his speed. Nakhtmin called himself a fool. Just because he recognized the boat, its skipper didn't necessarily remember him, if he'd looked at him at all earlier. He probably thought him an imbecile greeting strangers. This could even be a different fellow. Numerous ships had a similarly carved bow.

The All-Knowing Nomarch

Day 9 of month Wepet-renpet in Akhet, the season of inundation

Hori hastened back to the estate, couldn't leave the officials' housings behind fast enough. The ground beneath his sandals seemed scorching hot, trying to burn him. Breathless, he reached the house and stormed inside, but his friends weren't there.

Hapi was refilling an oil lamp and looked up. Shaking his head in disapproval, he asked, "Would you like a refreshment, my lord? You look a little heated. Where've you been?"

Harsher than intended, he replied, "Water! Bring me water." The servant's question only increased his fear. What if the man was really reporting to the nomarch? What if Antef drew the right—or rather wrong—conclusions after he learned about Hori returning in such a wrought up state, once Seni's corpse was discovered. All of a sudden, he'd turned from hunter to hunted.

He quenched his thirst, then took to pacing in the shade of the large sycamore. After what felt like an eternity, Nakhtmin and Muti finally entered the garden through the gate leading to the river. Taking a breath of relief, he couldn't wait for Nakhtmin to talk him out of his worries and Muti to mock him gently. The couple seemed relaxed and content with themselves. Should he destroy that right away? He had to!

"We're back and bearing news. Where are the records?" Nakhtmin asked immediately and looked around as if Hori might have hidden them for him to search.

He squirmed. "I don't have them. It's a long story. You go first." Although he didn't expect groundbreaking revelations from them, he wanted to hear whatever they'd found out before his horrifying adventure diminished everything else.

"What's that supposed to mean, you don't have them?" Muti seemed to look straight into his heart; pearls of sweat trickled down his nose; he swallowed hard. Her expression turned frightened. "What happened?" she whispered.

The wings of his fear must have grazed them both since Nakhtmin paled now, too. Nothing for it but to spill it all. He made sure nobody was close enough to listen in on their conversation, then he relayed to them what happened. Oh, what an effort it took to rein in his emotions and thoughts, but he needed their unbiased view on the events.

When he finished, the two exchanged concerned looks. "That can't have been a coincidence," Nakhtmin called. "Somebody wanted to prevent you from looking at the transcript!"

To Hori's horror, his friend had jumped to the same conclusion as he had. He motioned for him to lower his voice, but Muti was the one to speak next. "The man's death might not necessarily have anything to do with you," she countered. "The nomarch's officers may have taken the scroll away from him before he even got the chance to copy it or smuggle it out of the archive."

Thanks! That was what he wanted to hear. He released the breath he'd been holding. "You're probably right. And someone so easy to bribe must have done that kind of thing before. Maybe a previous customer killed him. Or he was murdered for a completely different reason."

Pleased with his agreement, she nodded. "You might even be wrong about the murder. Seni could have died of natural causes."

He shook his head. "No, I'm pretty sure breaking your neck in your sleep is anything but natural." A new wave of dread washed over him. "The collar I gave him as payment, it wasn't among his belongings either."

Nakhtmin placed a hand on his shoulder. "Man, you're sweating profusely. Calm down! Someone may have broken into Seni's house to rob him. He might not have expected the homeowner to be there since he wouldn't have known the man had lost his position."

"Yes. Yes..." In that case, however, the file would still be in the archive, which it wasn't. Or had Amunmose lied to prevent Hori from requesting Antef's permission to inspect the records? But why would the head of the archive do that? There was only one way to find out whether the papyrus had really disappeared: ask Antef for it, except that increased the chance of vizier Sobekemhat finding out about Hori's request. His father wouldn't hesitate to make clear the king's duplicate had not been lost. Oh well, worse things could happen. That would take time, and he'd be back home by then to be harangued by his father—as usual. If only he'd thought of reading the records while still in the residence!

"Did you notify anyone of Seni's death?" Muti inquired. "An awful thought to imagine his decaying corpse lying there and possibly ruining his chances for an afterlife."

He snapped at her, "No! How'd that have looked? First I ask for the man's house, then I report him dead? Yes, it troubles me, too. After all, I know best how..." He fell silent because Nakhtmin rolled his eyes—as always when Hori mentioned the weryt but wouldn't really tell anything. "Did *you* at least find out something helpful?" he asked with little hope. The peasants depending on Merwer didn't seem likely poisoners.

His friend surprised him with an abundance of insights giving him much food for thought. While listening to Nakhtmin's report, the sense of dread caused by Seni's death never quite left him though.

"It's possible the peasant, in his justifiable anger, managed to administer the colocynth to the trader and thus kill him," his friend finished.

Hori shook his head. Could it be that easy—Merwer's death simply the consequence of an argument between landlord and tenant? In that case, Seni's murder really was unrelated to their investigation. However, if the peasant was as innocent as Nehesy, someone else had been pulling the strings. Someone powerful enough to fire two archive clerks and ruthless enough to commit another murder to cover up the first. Groaning, he gave up his pacing and settled next to his friends. "I'm afraid, we'll have to check out Wahka again," he murmured. But how to do that without tipping off the peasant? They had to prove Wahka's guilt or innocence without leaving a doubt. Could the common man even have done it? "Let's assume you're right. Wouldn't someone have seen the peasant sneak onto the premises and meddle with Merwer's medicine?"

In silence they mulled over the question, then Muti said, "Wahka might not have needed to do that. What if he had an accomplice inside Merwer's household. He provided the fruit, but someone else administered it to Merwer. Someone he'd been used to accepting food from. We are looking for a woman!"

Hori cursed himself a fool because he hadn't thought of that himself. Nakhtmin groaned. "Of course!"

Muti looked very content with their reaction. "Then let's talk this through. Wahka realized Merwer would not treat him fairly and there was no other way to get justice. He and his two fellow peasants were ruined by the wonderful grain."

"Hold on," Hori interrupted. "The accident with the plow could've happened just as well if they'd planted their fields as always. That was simply unfortunate." Although he didn't want to justify Merwer's behavior, they needed to stick as close to the truth as possible.

Muti's mouth opened, but before she could say anything, Nakhtmin bent forward and interjected, "I wouldn't be so sure of that. Wahka told us they'd needed to cut the furrows deeper than usual for Merwer's grain to prosper."

While Hori again reminded him to keep his voice down, scorn sparked in Muti's eyes. "Now, if my noble lords are done, I'll continue. The peasants regarded themselves as ruined, and Merwer refused any kind of compensation. Wahka—"

Noticing a pattern, Hori cut in. "Again people invest their possessions to make one of Merwer's grand schemes possible! Whether gold or oxen, loss is loss. By now I'm really convinced the man was doing that on purpose. If he succeeded, he yielded nice profits. If he failed, it didn't affect him. That's one way to become rich."

"But then we don't even know if he really was so rich when he died. I'm thinking of the almost empty storage..." Nakhtmin's voice trailed off.

Muti jumped up and stomped a foot down. "What's wrong with you? You keep interrupting me as if my words were nothing but chaff in the wind." Her vehement motion must have startled a bird in the oleander bush. Cracking and rustling drifted over from there.

At her outburst, Hori too had flinched with guilt. Now he assured her, "Quite the contrary. Your words gave my thoughts wings, but you're right, that was very rude of me. Please go on, I'm curious what else you have to say."

She took a deep breath and continued, "Perhaps Wahka went to Merwer's house to complain, and thus one of the servants learned about the matter. One of the women, who also held a grudge against Merwer, may have recognized this as her chance for revenge. She convinced Wahka to bring her two fruits of the colocynth—hold on!" She paused, then cursed. "The woman would have needed to know about the plants growing on Wahka's land and the ingredients of Merwer's remedy. Well, according to Ouseret, Nehesy had given specific instructions with regard to the dosage, right?"

After her fit of rage, Nakhtmin seemed uncertain if he was allowed to say something. He only nodded, his lips pressed together.

"With such a strong and possibly dangerous drug, Nehesy would certainly have done that," Hori agreed. "But you're right. Whoever asked Wahka for the fruit must have known where they grew and what they were. I'm not sure if the daughter of a noble family like Satnefert would know much about plants. We should check into that. The same goes for the bedridden mother if we don't want to exclude her altogether."

Darting her husband an ominous sideways glance, Muti said, "That brings us to Nofru. As Merwer's lover and maid, she likely served him his meals."

"Um..." Nakhtmin started then fell silent again.

Hori grinned. With regard to beautiful Nofru, his friend should keep his mouth shut if he valued marital bliss. How skillfully the girl had ensnared him. He jumped in for Nakhtmin and said, "If she was Merwer's lover and is carrying his child, she lost everything when her master died."

Muti pulled up her shoulders. "Perhaps she was tired of waiting. She might have hoped to find a younger and more attractive husband in Sanefer. It's possible Merwer's son got her hopes up. Sanefer is a hard man to read."

Hori pricked his ears. "What do you mean? You've talked to him for a longer time but hardly told us anything about your conversation."

"Because we only exchanged chitchat. The weather in Waset and in the residence, the city of the river. Stuff like that. Oh, I only realize now that he asked quite a few questions about the new leadership of the Amun temple in Itj-tawy. That did surprise me, particularly since he made it sound like he'd been there. He mentioned the obelisk in the courtyard..."

That was really odd since this part of the temple was reserved for priests. How could Sanefer know about it? Hori sifted through his memory. No, not even the tip of the obelisk could be seen from outside the temple compound surrounded by a high wall. Muti naturally heard about it from her father who'd recently been appointed first prophet of Amun. But why would a trader's son take an interest in a change of power in that temple? Sanefer didn't seem consecrated although it was possible, of course. Maybe he was a wab priest like Nakhtmin and he were, then chose a different career instead of serving the gods. In that case, he'd be allowed to enter the temple.

Nakhtmin cleared his throat and murmured, "Sanefer's sister could have done it, too. As far as we know, she had a good reason to want her father out of the way. Her unfulfilled love for the salesman could have driven her to do it. However, she didn't strike me as capable of such a crime..." He darted Hori a questioning look.

He shook his head. "No, her grief for her father seems real to me, the way she slinks around all downcast. She'd probably have yielded to her father's wish and married the rich official." A man in a high office, unpaid bills, an empty storage hall... An idea formed in Hori's heart. "That marriage might have solely been arranged because of the wealth her future husband called his own. It sure looks like Merwer had been in trouble. With several failures in a row, his web of promises may have broken down. Satnefert might have felt obliged to help father and brother out. Just think about it for a moment. His peasants weren't able to pay the rent, how could he have maintained his estate, for which he owed the king levy." And Satnefert's ominous fiancé would have had connections to the nomarch's palace. Again, Antef wiggled his way into Hori's considerations, and his unease returned. Although the ruler of the Waset nome hadn't given them any reason to distrust him, Hori feared him and his power, ever-present in the shape of his armed soldiers.

That moment Muti lifted her head and looked around. "Do you know where our servants might be? I haven't seen them since our return, and I could use a bite to eat."

Hori's heart picked up its pace. "That's really peculiar. Normally they skulk around us all the time." Still, neither Hapi nor Hereret had come to ask if they needed anything. When his searching gaze brushed over the nearby bushes, a rustling ensued. It sounded like someone crept around there. Eavesdropping? He waited a moment then decided to take a look. Nobody there, probably just a bird.

"Perhaps they are sleeping through the hot hours," Nakhtmin suggested.

In that case, they should have prepared a meal and left it for them to eat whenever they returned. As if on cue, steps approached a little later. The maid came down the path from the house, her gaze lowered. "Forgive me, I didn't notice you'd returned."

Hori was far too happy about the bread, cool drinks and fruits she carried to scold her. As she bent down, papyrus rustled. He noticed a scroll stuck in her belt and narrowed his eyes in distrust. "What do you have there?" Could the girl read?

She blushed. "A messenger sent by the nomarch brought this an hour ago." She pulled out the note.

"And why do you only bring it now?" After all, he'd encountered Hapi when he'd returned. He'd have told her. They might not have noticed Muti and Nakhtmin's return but couldn't have missed his. Hori took the message, unrolled and skimmed it before reading aloud, "*To the royal physicians Hori and Nakhtmin as well as the lady Mutnofret, greetings. For too long, I had to forgo your company. I'm inviting you to dinner at the palace. Come at the seventh hour. Signed, Antef, nomarch.* Hm." Pensive, he lowered the note. Forgo their company—as if they were best friends when they barely knew the man.

"On top of everything else," Nakhtmin sighed. "I hope he won't keep us long."

Hori rather feared the powerful man asking unpleasant questions like what he'd wanted at the archive. Despite the friendly tone of the invite, the sense of dread returned with full force.

Unlike Muti, who grew up in a house where the powerful and mighty were regular guests, Nakhtmin didn't feel at ease during social gatherings since he never quite knew how to behave. "Festive attire?" he asked his wife while bending over his chest of clothes.

She shook her head. "Antef's message sounded more like an informal affair with just a few people there."

How could she tell from the few words? But he trusted her judgment, and a little later, Hori's appearance confirmed it. He too hadn't dressed up much.

The palace wasn't far from their estate, so they walked through alleys buzzing with people heading home in the early evening hour. At the gate of the former royal residence, a servant holding a torch awaited them and led them through the dark, deserted corridors. Their flapping steps echoed from the walls. Nakhtmin sensed Hori's restlessness. If only he knew what troubled him. He'd probably not told them everything so as not to worry Muti too much. What he had told them was frightening enough. He could only hope the death of the archive scribe had nothing to do with their investigation. Or else their search for Merwer's murderer might turn out dangerous after all...

This time, they walked past the banquet hall, where Antef had hosted them before, and penetrated the labyrinth of palace corridors much farther. Nakhtmin couldn't shake off the feeling they were walking straight into a trap. Would they ever be able to find the way back? He chided himself a fool. Why shouldn't a servant lead them to the exit? Hori's almost tangible trepidation must have rubbed off on him. However, their current guide had an eerie air about him, the way he walked ahead in the flickering light of the torch, not speaking a word. At long last, he stopped at a door.

Muti passed his bent back first, then Hori and finally Nakhtmin. Behind him, the door closed with a dull thud. He peered over his shoulder, but the servant hadn't followed them inside. Nakhtmin almost expected to hear the scraping noise of a bar. Suspicious, he eyed his surroundings. As far as he could see in the scarce light of three oil lamps, the room was large but barely furnished. Food was arranged on a low table, but nobody sat on the cushions scattered around it. They were alone.

Nakhtmin glanced at Hori. "What's going on here?" he whispered.

His friend shrugged.

"We're right on time," Muti said. "Our host lacks politeness."

For a while, they stood around waiting, and Nakhtmin wondered if they shouldn't just sit down when a different door opened and revealed Antef.

He studied them from the shade of the doorframe—only his eyes glittered in the dark—before he entered the room and put on an apologetic expression. "Excuse my delay. I had to take care of an urgent administrative issue. Please sit down." His hands motioned toward the table as he headed to it energetically.

This time, Nakhtmin scrutinized the man more thoroughly. His body showed no trace of slackness, which was quite unusual for a high official. Djehutihotep had been a great contrast.

"Thank you for accepting my invitation on such short notice and welcome to my personal chambers." Antef's bushy eyebrows wiggled up and down as he talked.

Hori jerked out of his torpor. "We have to thank you," he said, smooth-tongued. "To what do we owe the honor?" He settled on a cushion next to Antef and held up a supporting hand to Muti so she could lower herself without endangering her tight-fitting dress.

Nakhtmin cursed himself for his oversight. That should have been his task! Already he'd disgraced himself; he was and would always be a country yokel.

The nomarch looked up and gave a thin smile. "I like to know who comes and goes in my lands, and we've hardly gotten to know each other. It's just a simple meal of the kind I eat every day. Help yourselves."

Nakhtmin didn't hesitate. At least his hands had something to do now. During the meal, they only talked about meaningless things, so he had time to think about Antef's words and demeanor. Why had the nomarch seemed so friendly and frank when they first met? Today he made a very different impression on him: inscrutable, restrained, dangerous. Antef's behavior, even his appearing late, seemed well calculated, yes, like a performance serving only one purpose, to let them know he had ears and eyes everywhere. Or was he imagining things because Hori's fears were contagious? The absence of servants only increased his discomfort. Without witnesses around, Antef could simply let his guests disappear without a trace, if he felt inclined to do so. Nakhtmin rolled the bite he'd just taken around in his mouth. Bitter? No, fortunately not.

"I hear you've already visited the House of Life." The nomarch paused until they all looked at him.

Hori's forehead creased, and Nakhtmin felt affirmed in his belief Antef kept them under close watch. He sensed his facial muscles turning into a grimace and pulled himself together.

A hint of satisfaction lit up the noble face, the left eyebrow hiked up. "Are you thinking about moving here?" His laugh sounded forced and it probably was supposed to.

Right, Antef left nothing to chance. Nakhtmin swallowed hard. What else could he mean but to insinuate that he knew they'd inquired about purchasing land today? No, he couldn't have found out about that—or could he?

Hori shook his head thoughtfully. "No, my noble lord. Principal Bakenamun simply showed me around since I was curious to see if your House of Life was different from ours. One can always learn from others. However, our royal master expects us back at the residence soon."

A gust of wind blew through the ventilation slits under the ceiling and made the flame of the oil lamp flicker. In the unsteady play of light and dark, Antef's face alternated between a demoniacal and a cunning expression.

"Oh, I'd assumed..." Antef left the rest of the sentence unfinished.

A drop of sweat ran down Nakhtmin's back although he shivered suddenly. He glanced at Muti.

She displayed her loveliest smile. "Dear Antef!" Her voice rang with generations of highest dignitaries. "We'd love to accept your invitation to stay in the Southern City forever, but it's impossible, unfortunately. Hori and Nakhtmin are not only physicians of the pharaoh—life, prosperity and health—but also two of his closest advisers he wouldn't want to miss."

Nakhtmin was glad not to have anything in his mouth that moment or he'd definitely have choked. Hiding his mouth behind a hand, he faked a cough so Antef wouldn't see the astonishment on his face. However, his precaution hadn't been necessary. For once, the nomarch openly showed his feelings if only for a short moment: anger, scorn and a hint of admiration for Muti.

"I hope we won't do anything during our stay here that infringes upon your customs. If so, please tell us so we know better in the future," she continued. "In the south people live in a different way than we are used to. And you have many things here that are hard for us to get, ivory for example."

"Is that so?" The nomarch stared at Muti as if he thought she must have lost her mind.

She released a ringing laugh. "As a child I believed ivory was some kind of wood which grew on the Nile island Abu. I always wanted a comb made of ivory. Now I finally own one. I'm sure you have an excellent connection to the nomarch there?"

What was she up to? Ivory? They'd purchased ostrich feathers as a specialty here! Nakhtmin noticed Hori opening his mouth to say something, but then he apparently changed his mind.

Antef agreed and furrowed his brow so his bushy eyebrows met each other. He obviously had no clue either, where Muti was going with her ramblings.

"Oh, it must be wonderful to rule there! Gold from Nubia, ebony from the lands beyond the Nile, everything gets there first. And those large animals with the long necks—what are they called again?" She cast Antef a questioning look.

"Ostriches," murmured the nomarch absent-mindedly.

She giggled. "No, I don't mean birds, but four-legged beasts. Giraffes, that's their name. Have you ever seen stranger creatures? What made you think of ostriches? By the way, do you know Sanefer?"

"Nat...um...what? No. Who's that?"

"Just wondering since you said you know everyone in your domain," Muti said nonchalantly.

Nakhtmin broke out in a sweat. What dangerous game was his darling playing? By now, he had an idea what she was up to, but Antef wouldn't let her fool him and go unpunished. He feared for her safety if she continued on this path. Or was it too late already? He placed a hand on her forearm. "You're babbling, my dear, and our host must have had a long, hard day. I'm sure ruling over a nome is almost as exhausting as governing the Two Lands. And you wouldn't bore the king with such a trifle, would you?" Glad to have drawn Antef's attention away from her, he suffered her angry gaze without moving a muscle in his face.

A deep crease showed over the noble nose. "I don't think the two can be compared, and your wife certainly didn't bore me." His appraising gaze flicked to Muti and back to him. Then he rose. "It's late and we should retire. Be careful with your further endeavors, the river is treacherous this time of year." With these words, he disappeared through the same door he'd used to enter.

Nakhtmin's tension eased, but now he trembled. Antef's last words had amounted to a poorly veiled threat! And he shouldn't even have known about their boat trips!

On their way home, nobody talked.

UNEXPECTED ENCOUNTER

Day 10 of month Wepet-renpet in Akhet, the season of inundation. Decade day

Fear held Hori's heart in a firm grip and wouldn't let him sleep. During the lonely dark hours of the night, he intently listened for any noises. Would they come to lock him up? Accuse him of Seni's murder? But nothing happened. At some point, he couldn't bear the silence any longer and got up.

To his surprise, he encountered the maid in the corridor leading to his room. What was Hereret doing in the house at such an early hour? Antef's people having keys to the estate was alarming. They could come and go as they pleased. Hori suddenly perceived their presence as a gag keeping him from speaking his mind and even from thinking straight. She was definitely spying on them for her master, reporting everything his guests from the royal residence did and said. Hm, there was a bolt on the inside of the gate…

She also seemed surprised to see him. "Should I set up the morning meal, master?" she asked.

"Yes, do that." An idea germinated in his heart. "Oh, and we won't need your services afterward again, Hereret."

"Y-you're letting me go?" she stammered in visible horror.

He smiled in an appeasing manner. "Only for today. Is Hapi here as well? Oh good. Let him know as well that you can both have the day off. After all it's decade day."

She nodded subserviently, but didn't look happy at all. Hori could well imagine why.

Later, he personally made sure the two really left the premises and then barred the gate. At least this once he wanted to talk to his friends without fear of being overheard. He settled down and helped himself to bread, milk and fruit.

He'd just finished when a pandiculating Nakhtmin appeared at the edge of the roof terrace and blinked down at Hori. "Ah, breakfast! We'll join you in a moment."

While his friends ate, Hori paced. "Antef knows about my connection to Seni! I can feel that he knows everything."

Nakhtmin groaned. "I'll crick my neck trying to look at you. Sit and calm down. If he'd wanted to arrest you, he'd have done so yesterday."

Hori halted. "That's true, but all his insinuations."

Nakhtmin's face darkened. "Yes, I heard those, too. Still, he said nothing that would allow us to feel certain how much he actually knows."

"You're wrong, my husband!" Muti had remained unusually silent since their return although she'd acted so boldly toward the nomarch.

Hori admired her courage, but in Nakhtmin's place, he'd have gone mad with worry for her last night. "You mean because he lied about Sanefer? Yes, very clever of you to confuse him with the ivory then ask about the trader. He recovered his wits quickly though, but not fast enough. He knows Sanefer and probably quite well, too. I just wonder…why did he feel the need to lie?"

She made a dismissive gesture. "I don't mean that. The ostriches gave him away. I made it sound like I purchased an ivory comb from Sanefer. My reasoning was, if he knew what we really bought, that would baffle him and make him wonder why I was lying about ostrich feathers. When I asked him about the long-necked animals, he named the animal he was mulling over in his heart, an ostrich. If he hadn't known about the feathers, he'd never have thought of birds when I asked about long-necked animals."

"So that's what you were up to!" Nakhtmin called.

Hori granted her an appreciative glance. "Brilliant! Not even we saw through your game."

Visibly content with their admiration, Muti continued, "Now we know Sanefer told the nomarch about our visit and what we purchased. What I don't understand is why such trivia should be of interest to the man."

Hori chewed his lower lip. Antef and Sanefer…was their relationship, no matter the nature, relevant to their murder investigation? What role did the death of the archive clerk play? He failed to weave all the threads into a pattern. If only Ouseret weren't so secretive and told them all she knew. Was she even worth their efforts? They faced danger for her, and she brushed them off. However, the very idea he might never see her again hurt so much, he couldn't breathe. The next moment, shame filled him. First and foremost, they should serve Maat and restore justice. This wasn't about Ouseret and his pining for her! "We have to go back to Sanefer!" he called.

Nakhtmin snorted. "Well said, and which pretext are we going to use this time?"

Right, they couldn't just drop by. His estate was quite out of the way, not a place to casually stroll past.

Nakhtmin grimaced. "I'd rather not go there by boat again."

Hori darted him a baffled look. What was that all about?

Muti mocked, "Suddenly afraid of water, are you?"

His face turned a shade darker. "Didn't you notice Antef threatening us?"

"N-no…" Hori mumbled and tried to recall Antef's words and what might have given his friend that idea. Then it dawned on him. "He warned us of the treacherous current. Is that what you mean?" At Nakhtmin's eager nodding, he almost burst out laughing, but then he remembered in what context the words had been uttered and how Antef had emphasized them. He broke out in a cold sweat. "So he knows we've hired a boat. Nakhtmin, what's wrong with you?" His friend had turned ashen.

"The dinghy with the papyrus bow!" he exclaimed and jumped up. "When Muti and I went to see the peasants I noticed a boat that was following us. The bow ended in a papyrus shape. And I'm sure I saw the same boat behind us during the return trip."

Mutnofret tried to calm her husband. "There are dozens of such water craft. And if it was the same boat, it might have returned by pure chance just when we did."

Hori shook his head. "No, I think Nakhtmin's right. Antef left little doubt that we've been watched, whatever we did, wherever we went." But why had he wanted them to know? Suspicion had turned into certainty. Of course! "He wants to discourage us snooping around some more," he called out. Dear gods, he could only hope none of his spies saw him enter Seni's house! But if Antef had wanted to prosecute him for murder, he'd already have him arrested. He took a deep breath.

Muti pursed her lips. "That's my impression, too, but why would he want to prevent us from disclosing who really killed Merwer?"

"Maybe he wants to protect the true murderer!" Nakhtmin blurted. "That's why we weren't supposed to find out that he knows Sanefer."

"Slow down. You think Sanefer killed his father?" Hori considered the possibility then shook his head. "I can't think of a reason why he should have done it."

"I can't believe you of all people are saying that," Muti scoffed. "Who whines all day long that he wants Ouseret? If Sanefer loved her like you do, killing his father might have looked like the only way to set up his own household and finally make her his."

Hori's cheeks burned. As so often, she was spot on. But something didn't quite fit. When he managed to sort it out, he snapped his fingers. "Impossible! If he loved her so much, he'd never have let Nehesy take the blame. Ouseret told us how convincingly he spoke against her father at the trial. He can't possibly have expected her to forgive him that." And last, but not least, where was the splendid Sanefer today? Certainly not trying to win back her favor. Besides, the pretty boy hadn't seemed lovesick at all. He'd been very controlled, making it impossible to tell what was really going on with him. And Ouseret? Why was she so withdrawn? As if she felt ashamed of her engagement to Sanefer. Maybe she'd surrendered to his advances. Oh, he couldn't think about that! What troubling images. Sweat-glistening bodies entwined in lust, moaning—and it wasn't him joining with Ouseret but that merchant. Bile rose in Hori's throat.

"Well, you could pretend that you wanted to invest in Sanefer's business," Muti interrupted his torturous thoughts.

Nakhtmin gaped at her, and the horrible visions in Hori's heart dissolved. That really made for the perfect excuse to visit the trader again! He pecked a surprised Muti's cheek. "Beautiful and smart! Nakhtmin is one lucky fellow. That's how we'll play it."

"We should've hired a palanquin," Nakhtmin grumbled. In this heat, the straps of his sandals chafed the skin between his big toes and the next ones. He definitely wasn't used to walking long distances on foot any longer, and it had been foolish of him to wear the new sandals. And Muti? Her shoulders seemed to sag with exhaustion when she should be taking things easy. And what kind of impression would it make on Sanefer if they arrived all hot and dusty?

Hori stopped abruptly and spun around. He'd been doing that regularly since they'd set out, so he could spot anyone following them. After passing the garrison, the street along the river was deserted. Someone trailing them would have to noisily plow through the reeds to avoid being seen. At least they encountered no more soldiers here. Hori and he had exchanged worried glances at the sight of the many armed men swarming into the city. Today was the tenth day of the week, decade day. The men would want to have some fun in Waset. Nevertheless, Hori and he had tried to draw as little attention as possible.

Hori trudged on again. "A palanquin would have been far too conspicuous," he repeated his argument against such a comfortable means of transportation. "And we couldn't have looked behind us."

Nakhtmin wondered what his friend meant to do against a spy if he spotted one. Knock him out, shake him off? That seemed as silly as the fear he'd felt the evening before. In the glaring light of the sun god, followers lurking in the shadows seemed so unreal. Antef probably thought he'd scared them enough to give up on the hunt for the murderer.

"As long as we're cautious, the nomarch can't do anything against us," Hori murmured.

That moment Nakhtmin realized what troubled his friend. He feared an ambush and cudgels flying at them from behind. Would the nomarch go as far as having them killed on the road? An attack on the river would have been far easier to disguise as an accident. Tragic but not unusual. Nakhtmin swatted at a fly buzzing around his nose. Though a diligent administrator of the nome, Antef was a dangerous man. What was he hiding from them? Muti shrieked beside him. A sound that chilled him to the bones. Was it happening now? She staggered and he barely managed to catch her in time. "What ails you?" he asked.

"Sprained my ankle. I overlooked a stone. No reason to get all agitated." A hand on his shoulder for support, she limped into the shade.

Relieved, he released the breath he'd been holding and almost laughed at his irrational anxiety. However, they still had quite a distance to walk, and now this!

Hori stepped closer and felt her ankle. "Tut, it's swelling. You should cool your foot and not put any weight on it."

Nakhtmin was beside himself. "Just great. Didn't I say we should hire a palanquin?" Muti looked exhausted, at the end of her strength, and they were already a fair distance from the city with nowhere a farmhouse or any sign of human life in sight.

"Nakhtmin!" Mutnofret's voice lashed out at him like a whip. "Your whining doesn't help anyone. Let's think about how to proceed from here."

He swallowed the rest of his lament and brooded in silence.

"Shall I carry you?" Hori offered and made a few steps along the path, which was ascending a little from here on.

She gave him an amused look. "You wouldn't get far."

Nakhtmin lowered himself into the dust beside her and put her foot in his lap. "Does that hurt?" he asked fingering her ankle.

Although she shook her head, she twitched in sudden pain and pressed her lips together.

"There's nothing here to cool the foot except the river. You'd ruin your dress. Hm, we could take turns carrying you," he suggested although he knew they'd be completely exhausted soon. "Hori...Hori?" Where had he disappeared? He detected him on the top of the hill, gazing in all directions. Then his body stiffened, and he came running toward them. "There's a bunch of people with a donkey heading in our direction!" he called to them.

The gods must have sent them. Nakhtmin took a breath of relief and stood next to his friend.

The arrivals turned out to be a peasant family who'd apparently laden all their belongings onto the pack animal. It wasn't much though. When the man introduced himself as Heny, Nakhtmin had to suppress a gasp. One of Merwer's three tenants! He scrutinized him with curiosity. What had caused the man to take his family and all they owned to Waset?

While Hori explained their predicament and begged Heny to lend them the donkey, Nakhtmin leaned close to his wife and whispered, "Wahka's neighbor."

She nodded and answered in a low voice, "They are leaving the land. Their situation must have changed for the worse since we talked to Wahka yesterday."

Heny's two children cast Muti and him curious glances; their mother, however, looked withdrawn and downcast. No wonder, since they'd lost their home and were heading into an uncertain future. Under her threadbare dress, bones protruded. He turned his attention to the two men. Heny held his arms crossed in front of his chest and his lips pressed together. His whole body denied their request.

"...only to the next estate where we should be able to borrow a palanquin or a pack animal. I understand that we'd be holding you back, but we can't continue without you," Hori said.

Having lost everything, this peasant wouldn't trust them nor feel the urge to help noble folks. Nakhtmin pitied him and even more his children. What would happen with them now? Could the family find work at one of the temple farms? That would provide them with a roof over their heads but little more. They'd lose the freedom to go where they wanted, would need the overseer's permission. And everything their work yielded would belong to the temple. They'd have no opportunity to put something away. He joined Hori and Heny. "I'll give you a generous reward for your troubles."

The peasant's nostrils flared in contempt. He'd probably heard similar things from Merwer a few times too often.

Nakhtmin quickly unfastened his collar of carnelian beads with golden links and held it out to Heny. The man's eyes grew wide. What was dangling before him would keep him and his family above water for quite some time, even allow him a new beginning somewhere else—or as Sanefer's tenant. Nakhtmin was well aware that he offered him far too much and groaned inwardly, already mourning the loss of such a precious thing. At the same time, he felt the need to make up for these people's misery. What did Hori call it? Balancing the scales of Maat.

"Husband," the farmer's wife whispered almost inaudibly. When Heny didn't react, she tore the jewelry from Nakhtmin's fingers and said with determination, "We're happy to help you." Casting a reproachful glance at her husband, she stuffed the collar into one of the bundles and started to tear jugs and baskets from the supporting frame on the donkey's back.

Heny's arms still hung limp by his sides. He neither helped nor hindered her. "And what's going to happen to our things?" he mumbled with chagrin.

"The children and I will wait here for your return," his wife hissed. "We're in no hurry after all."

Mutnofret perched on the donkey's back like a queen, while the peasant led it on a short rope, stomping ahead and keeping his head down. After a while, Nakhtmin couldn't bear the man's peevish silence any longer. He left Hori's side and caught up with him. "I really am grateful for your help. Without you, we'd have been at a loss," he flattered. "My wife has just recovered from a fever and is still weak."

From the corner of his eye, he saw Heny's eyebrows hike up—in astonishment or mockery? "Wealthy as you are, you should have hired a palanquin," he grumbled, leaving little doubt what he thought of the intelligence of rich town folks.

"It was my fancy," Muti called from the donkey's back. "I overrated my strength. Traveling on the river, the distance didn't seem so long at all."

The peasant snorted. "Actually, where are you heading? There's nothing around here." He darted Nakhtmin a skeptical look.

He broke out in a sweat, not wanting to mention Sanefer's name since Heny likely held a grudge against him. Maybe he'd push Muti off the donkey and abandon them if he learned about it. After all, his wife had already pocketed the precious collar.

"We're on our way to a trader," Hori called and hastened to them. "He sold us ostrich feathers the other day, and now we want to buy more as presents for our mothers. We're only here for a short stay, on vacation."

Heny's face darkened. "You shouldn't trust that dealer."

"Huh?" Nakhtmin uttered. "He seemed very friendly to me."

"Ha!" the farmer snorted, waking from his lethargy. "Honey on their tongues, that's what they've got, the people living in that mansion over there." He pointed at the estate already coming into view. "Well, maybe the son is more honest than his father had been," he quickly added when he noticed their curious looks.

"Sure sounds like you have quite a story to tell," Muti murmured in sympathy. "How come you packed all your belongings and left your home?"

The distrust immediately returned to Heny's face. "How do you know we left our home?"

"We may do imprudent things at time, but we're no fools," she simply said. "Why else would you have packed all that stuff on a donkey?"

Chagrined, Heny stared at the white walls shimmering in the sunlight. "The trader who used to live in that house was my landlord, and he ruined us with his schemes."

To their left, a rock formation protruded into the street and narrowed their path. They couldn't walk next to each other any longer, so Nakhtmin fell back and walked beside the donkey's belly.

"Us?" Muti asked casually. "You and your family, you mean?"

"Yes, and two more peasant families. All his tenants. And now, Wahka is dead."

Horrified, Nakhtmin couldn't believe it. Only yesterday they'd talked to the man, and now he was dead? Without thinking, he blurted, "How? How did he die?"

"What's the life and death of a farmer to you, lord? He broke his neck, his daughter says. She found him." Heny spit out in contempt. "Not that she'd been visiting him a lot, now she can hope to make her way to a higher state in life."

Wahka's daughter? Nakhtmin recalled what the man had told them. Right, he'd mentioned a daughter he'd had to send off to work as a maid, his only child. But what did Heny mean by a 'higher state'? Or had he misunderstood?

Hori breathed heavily, pushed past Nakhtmin and grabbed Heny's shoulder to make him turn around. "A broken neck, you said? An accident?"

Nakhtmin swallowed hard. The archive scribe had died in the same way. Did Hori suspect a connection? Did he think Wahka might have been killed as well?

Heny shrugged his bony shoulders. "Haven't seen his body and didn't ask his daughter. But Wahka wanted to complain to the new master about the rent." He scratched his neck. "I'd rather stay alive and leave without complaining." He trotted on, but Hori stayed back, looking deep in thought when Nakhtmin passed him.

He shivered despite the heat of the day. Shouldn't they turn back to the city? But how could the deaths be connected? What had the archive clerk and the peasant in common except…? It must have to do with Merwer's death! He blurted, "Are you insinuating that Sanefer killed your friend?"

When Heny stopped abruptly, Nakhtmin almost bumped into him. Slowly, the farmer turned around and looked him in the eyes. "I wouldn't put it beyond the young master. But who'd listen to someone like me?"

"We do. We listen to you!" Hori called from the end of their little caravan.

Nakhtmin nodded fervently and sent his friend a questioning look. Should they reveal everything to the man? At a slight nod in response, he cleared his throat. "Well, you should know that we came to Waset to find out the truth about the death of the trader Merwer," he confessed.

Heny sneered at him as if he thought him an imbecile. "His murderer has been arrested and convicted awhile ago. What did you have to do with Merwer? He wasn't any better than his son."

"We're friends of Ouseret," Muti announced. "She's the daughter of the physician who's been convicted of the murder—unjustly as we believe. Ouseret has already tried to clear him of the charge, in vain. Now we're trying to find out something that proves Nehesy's innocence. You knew both men. Do you think Sanefer capable of killing his father?"

Heny's doubtful glance wandered from her face to Hori's then rested on Nakhtmin. At long last, he sighed and nodded. "I know Ouseret. She once treated my son when a snake bit him. A good woman and physician. I never understood why she even bothered with Sanefer. Yes, I think him capable of such a crime, but he couldn't have done it. He wasn't around when it happened."

"What do you mean?" Muti called. "That he wasn't in the house when Merwer died?"

Heny looked up at her, blinking against the bright sun. "I mean he wasn't even in the Southern City. He was accompanying a shipload of his father's goods to the north and had already departed before Merwer became so sick that he couldn't leave his bed anymore. Sanefer didn't return until after he'd died."

"By Seth's testicles!" Hori exclaimed, putting Nakhtmin's thoughts into words. They'd just lost their best suspect.

Morosely, he kicked a stone into the water. If they had to eliminate Sanefer from their list of possible perpetrators, what about the other two deaths? Where was the connection if Antef wasn't trying to protect a guilty Sanefer? In the light of this revelation, he had to acquit the nomarch of ordering Seni and Wahka's deaths. He apparently had no reason to do so. Or could he be trying to protect someone else belonging to the household—at all cost? Not likely. Maybe Seni actually died because of a personal quarrel, and Wahka's death was indeed an accident. With some relief, he took a deep breath. He didn't feel comfortable dragging Muti into such a dangerous investigation.

"Do you have any idea who else might have killed him?" Hori asked. His voice rang with desperation.

Good question. There weren't many people left, mainly the two women, Satnef-ert and Nofru. Although the daughter might have had a reason to kill her father out of love for the shopkeeper, she was such a timid girl Nakhtmin couldn't imagine her committing such a crime. Albeit he wouldn't put it beyond the cunning serv-ant, except she had nothing to gain by his death. Hoping for new insights, he looked to Heny.

Unfortunately, the man shook his head. "I've rarely been at my landlord's house, usually only once a year when the rent was due."

Out of the blue, Muti asked, "Do you know about colocynths growing on Wah-ka's land?"

"Sorry, can't help you there. I'd have weeded out the stuff right away, but I don't care what my neighbors do. How do you know what grows there?" Heny directed a questioning look up at her.

"We…um…" Unsure, she glanced at Nakhtmin.

"We walked around Wahka's land yesterday," he confessed. "We wanted to question him and noticed a spot where the plants prosper, and from at least two of them, fruits have recently been harvested. You are aware that Merwer had been poisoned with colocynth?"

The farmer nodded. "I attended the trial, like half the people in Waset." Then re-alization dawned on his face, and he turned angry. "Are you trying to say my friend Wahka killed his landlord? He'd never have done that, although we tenants all had good reasons to wish him evil."

"No, no!" Nakhtmin hurried to placate him. "How could Wahka have adminis-tered the poison to him? We discarded that idea right away. But he might have known who in the great house plucked the fruit. And that might have been the rea-son…"

Hori interjected, "That's a load of nonsense! How could any of the women have broken the peasant's neck? That would have taken a strong man. Damn, we know less than on the first day we set foot on the pier of the Southern City!"

Of course, that wasn't true, but Nakhtmin understood his friend's reaction. He decided to keep his thoughts about Wahka's death—murder or accident—to him-self for now. Heny already seemed confused by their jumping from one topic to the next. "Let's move on," he suggested. "Or it will get too late to call on Sanefer. Heny, if you wait at the gate and accompany us to Waset afterward, I'll be happy to help you and your family with a fresh start."

A grateful smile crossed the man's haggard face. "I'll be here."

SHE IS GONE

Deep in thought, Hori couldn't appreciate the landscape to the left and right of their path. If they had to discard Sanefer and the women, there was nobody left in the trader's household who could have broken Wahka's and possibly Seni's neck. But what about Ini the salesman? He was strong enough and didn't have to look after the shop on a decade day, so he could have come here. But the killing of Merwer? It wasn't impossible but highly unlikely that Ini knew what the remedy consisted of and how dangerous an overdose was. And he couldn't have easily obtained colocynth seeds. Hori plodded the last steps to the gate of the estate, staring at the donkey's backside and the twitching tail lashing out at annoying flies, when a thought struck him. What if Sanefer had killed the peasant? He might not have murdered his father but possibly the scribe and Wahka.

"Here we are," Heny said. He stepped from one foot to the other in discomfort and looked like he wanted to melt into the shadow of the wall.

Nakhtmin helped his wife dismount the donkey, but Hori mulled over their guide's strange behavior. It looked like the peasant and Sanefer had parted in disagreement. Or Heny had left his land without informing his landlord and without paying the overdue rent. Probably the latter. Heny had talked about Sanefer with less contempt than about his deceased father. To refuse him his rightful rent must be troublesome for the peasant. "We won't tell your former landlord that we've met you and you're waiting here," he assured the man.

In visible surprise, Heny's eyes widened, but he quickly lowered his gaze again. "Thank you," he mumbled and retreated until he and the donkey disappeared from sight behind a projection of the wall.

Nakhtmin also seemed surprised by Hori's comment but didn't say anything. Instead, he pounded on the gate.

A servant opened and eyed them with suspicion. "Yes?" Since he probably always served at the gate, he couldn't have seen them during their last visit when they'd arrived by boat.

"We are business friends of your master," Hori announced flamboyantly. A self-confident demeanor intimidated most people and made them do your bidding. "Take us to him."

Nakhtmin lifted his injured wife onto his arms. "My wife sprained her ankle," he explained to the baffled man.

Following the servant down the path to the house, Hori remembered Ouseret's contradictory behavior. Why didn't she tell them what happened between her and the trader's son? He decided to draw Sanefer into a conversation himself today, the man who'd once enjoyed Ouseret's favor. Oh, he'd better not think along such lines. Those troubling images returned. Why Sanefer and not him? Why did she shun his courting as if she were shy or prudish? Ouseret mystified him. Whenever he thought he held the key to her heart in his hands, he realized it didn't fit.

They met Sanefer in the garden where he chatted with his sister. Although they'd come here to talk with him, he was surprised the man could afford such leisure. Didn't he have work to do? Considering the empty storage hall, he'd have expected him to be trying frantically to get back into business. Ah, no, not on dec-ade day. He wanted to slap his forehead. Even servants living in the household would get some time off if not the whole day. Nevertheless, Sanefer needed an income. And then there was the death of his tenant. Even if he hadn't noticed He-ny leaving his land, the man should be trying to replace Wahka as soon as possi-ble, or the two fields would lie idle this year. Come to think of it, that should make Sanefer even more interested in their pretend wish to invest in his business.

Glancing at the unexpected guests, Sanefer lifted his eyebrows in an unspoken question and rose. Smoothing his face and his shendyt, he came toward them. "The physicians from the residence again." His gaze stuck to Nakhtmin carrying Muti. "What happened?"

Nakhtmin told him about the little accident and set his wife down with great care. Leaning against him, she stood on one foot and swayed a little.

Hori couldn't shake off the feeling they were anything but welcome. With great reluctance, it seemed, Sanefer finally offered them to sit down. Satnefert jumped up and provided a cushion for Muti. Then she clapped, and a servant appeared. "Bring our guests refreshments," she ordered.

They settled in the shade of a large sycamore.

"Where's your maid today?" Nakhtmin asked and looked around for beautiful Nofru. "Does she have the day off?"

"She's in mourning. Her father died today," Satnefert explained.

From the corner of his eye, Hori observed her brother slightly shaking his head as if he disapproved of them learning about it. Hold on—that peasant, Wahka, he'd been found dead today. Could he have been Nofru's father? Hori caught Nakhtmin's gaze. His friend apparently thought the same thing. And the colocynth grew on Wahka's land which made the pretty young woman a prime suspect. Maybe she did have a reason to kill her master and lover…

"What brings you here?" Sanefer asked rather brusquely.

So unfriendly today? Did the man suspect their reason to visit him the other day had been a pretext? Before he could come to a conclusion, Nakhtmin already dove into a cumbersome explanation of what they'd come up with beforehand. When he uttered the wish to invest in Sanefer's business, their host's face became even stonier.

"I do not intend to continue in the way my father used to do business," he said. "I want to become independent of investors and specialize in trading with goods from the north. Therefore…" He looked about to get up.

Hori noticed the spotty scars on his hands and forearms again. Although they'd healed well, they should annoy a vain young man like the young trader.

"That's a shame," Nakhtmin said. "I'd hoped to increase my wealth with your help. Oh well, I'll try my luck with dealers back in the north."

Hori suppressed a groan. Had they come all this way, only to be kicked out again right away? Nakhtmin shouldn't give up so quickly. No help from Muti to-day either. Pale and weak, she just sat there looking exhausted. Hori made a last desperate attempt to extend their stay by asking, "Should I make an ointment for your scars? They could become almost invisible."

Sanefer's nostrils flared, while he tried to hide the spots by crossing his arms in front of his chest. "We haven't had the best experiences with doctors recently," he squeezed out.

His sister looked embarrassed by his rude behavior. "That's a very kind offer," she mumbled shyly.

At long last, the servant arrived with mugs and a jar, to which pearls of condensed water clung. Judging by Sanefer's expression, he'd have loved to refuse them the drink. So that was how the beautiful son looked when he dropped the mask of courtesy. Now, Hori really thought him capable of committing the cold-blooded murders of Wahka and Seni. And if he'd done that, he might have killed his father as well. But he'd been away when his old man died. Was that true or had he only pretended to accompany a shipment? Yes, he could have left the ship and returned early. All of a sudden, Hori couldn't wait to get away from here.

Under Sanefer's impatient gaze, they gulped down their drinks and took leave from the siblings. Hori was eager to present his new theory to his friends, but on the way to the gate, he realized what was wrong with it. The nomarch didn't fit the bill. How could Sanefer have convinced Antef to threaten them? The powerful man wouldn't allow anyone to force his hand. Was the young dealer so important to him? Confused, Hori wiped the sweat from his forehead. Such a conspiracy seemed rather unlikely. Sanefer probably didn't have anything to do with the threats. Muti's little trap with the long-necked animal might have prompted the response 'ostrich' by pure chance. But Nofru! She must have had her pretty hand in this. As Wahka's daughter, she'd known where to find the colocynth and had access. Besides, she was most likely the one to bring Merwer his medicine. Nothing easier than adding the powder when nobody was watching. What did they know about Nofru's feelings? Maybe she hadn't shared Merwer's bed voluntarily. Nofru and Sanefer as accomplices in his murder? Possible…

As long as they could be seen from the estate, they hurried in silent understanding along the dusty path as if the devourer were chasing after them. Hori didn't want anyone in the house to see them with the peasant. The same wish probably drove Heny and Nakhtmin to haste. When they reached Heny's family, the last stretch back to the city turned out more challenging since they had to take their possessions along as well. Muti found herself squeezed in between jugs and baskets on the donkey's back, but not everything fit. Nakhtmin, Hori and Heny packed the rest on their backs. It didn't take long for Hori's shoulders to ache under the weight of a grain sack that pushed the pearls on his collar into his neck. In envy, he glanced over to Nakhtmin plodding ahead of him and no longer wearing a collar. He'd love to take his off too. Even Nakhtmin's whining earlier that they should have rented a palanquin wanted to sneak onto his tongue, but he restrained himself.

By the time they finally arrived home, Hori had reached the end of his tether. He leaned against the wall next to the gate and let the little caravan pass, Nakhtmin and Heny with the donkey, then Heny's wife and the two children, before he stepped through and barred the gate. Now, servants taking care of them would have been nice, but no, he'd had to give the domestics a day off. So he had to wash himself as well as possible before he could don fresh clothes.

He found Nakhtmin still in his bed chamber tending to Muti, so he went down to the garden. Heny's children played at the water basin, squealing with joy, while their parents unloaded the donkey.

At his approach, Heny looked up. "Where can we put the animal, lord?"

Abashed, Hori scratched his neck. "There's a shed that way. I'd guess a goat had been kept there once. Maybe that would do? Otherwise you'll just have to tie up your donkey somewhere and let it graze."

"And where can we...?" Heny's wife lowered her gaze. The noble house probably rendered her speechless.

Hori led her around the building to an unused staff annex and pulled the knob. The wood had gone out of shape a little, but with some force the door opened. A wave of stale air hit him. Strange how quickly that could happen. This part of the house shouldn't have been empty for long. The nomarch's servants preferred the more comfortable accommodations at the palace for good reason. "You can put all your things in here. Any provisions you might just as well put in the pantry if you like." Less danger of mice getting to them there. "You can use any of the rooms here and sleep where you like—or on the roof, like we do."

She smiled in gratitude, hurried out and soon hauled the first sack along the path. Cursing to himself, Hori helped.

Nakhtmin rounded the corner. "What ruckus is this? Muti has just fallen asleep! Oh." Grasping the situation, he gave them a hand carrying in the rest of the things. "How do you feel about hiring Heny and his wife as servants?" he asked afterward.

Hori recognized the advantage of such an arrangement right away, and the farmer woman's eyes lit up. "Wonderful idea! There comes Heny, let's hear what he has to say."

The couple happily agreed to take on the position. The woman immediately hurried into the kitchen, while Heny summoned his offspring to help getting two chambers ready.

Hori gave a slight laugh. "Thus we're rid of the nomarch's spies. Antef won't be happy when we send back his people tomorrow. Without admitting openly why he wants them here, he can't really object. Boy, you look dusty like the desert god incarnate. Let me be your servant for now. Off to the bath with you!"

A little later, they slouched on a bench along one wall of the house, legs stretched out. Sipping beer, they enjoyed the last rays of the sinking sun, while enticing cooking smells caressed their noses. Hori was wondering if he should share his thoughts with Nakhtmin right away or wait for Muti when his friend said, "Well, we've found out quite a few things today, and there's someone who should give us answers." He cast a questioning look at Hori, but he had nothing to add to that. "I better go get Ouseret."

Oh, he meant *her*! Hori sat up straight and felt new energy flow through his limbs. "I can do that!"

Nakhtmin snorted and grabbed hold of his shendyt. "As much as I'd like to leave that to you—you know how she shies from you. I'm starving though. Oh well, go tell Muti and help her if necessary. You'll wait for us with the meal, right?"

The slapping of his sandals on the dusty street sounded overly loud in Nakhtmin's ears. At this time of day, when Nut, the goddess of the sky, had already swallowed the solar disk and darkness lay over the Two Lands like a veil, barely anyone was out and about. Most inhabitants of Waset already sat on the roofs of their houses, preparing for the night, maybe unrolling their bulrush mats. Nakhtmin's left side hurt with stinging pain. Gasping, he leaned against a wall to catch his breath. Onward! He had to move on, although he dreaded the moment when he'd have to break the bad news to Hori. Gradually, his body recovered from the fast run, and he continued at a slower pace. They wouldn't be able to do anything tonight anyway. Finally reaching the estate in the Street of Palm Fronds, he hesitated a moment before he walked through the gate.

He found his friend still sitting on the bench, his knees pulled up, his gaze longingly fixed to the path where he expected to see Ouseret approach. Only the torch flame dancing in the light breeze kept him company. Either Muti was still sleeping or did so again, which was good. She desperately needed the rest.

As soon as Hori realized that he returned alone, his features darkened. "Where is she?"

Nakhtmin swallowed hard. "Gone," he squeezed out. There was no way to tell him more gently. "Meseh and his wife were quite surprised when I appeared. Ouseret had told them she'd spend the day with us. Obviously a lie so the good folks wouldn't worry." What had Ouseret really been doing today and why hadn't she returned home yet?

Devastated by his words, Hori blurted, "She hasn't been here either. I don't think we missed her. She never wanted to come here. I'll tell you what happened: She fled from me again! Wanted a head start to make sure we can't follow her." He buried his face in the folds of his shendyt. Muffled sounds spoke of his misery.

Nakhtmin desperately wished Hori was right about the reason for Ouseret's disappearance, but he couldn't believe it. He wrapped an arm around his friend's twitching shoulders. "Why should she run from you? You've shown a lot of self-restraint and didn't press her."

Sniffling, Hori lifted his head a little. "Yes, I did, right?" After a short pause, he added, "No flight?" The short glimmer of hope died instantly. "Then something must have happened to her!"

"That's what I fear. I think she wanted to do some investigating herself." Nakhtmin ground his teeth. That foolhardy woman had kept more than a little knowledge relevant to solve the mystery to herself. How had she put it? 'You're looking in the wrong place.' By now, she probably knew exactly where Merwer's murderer was to be found. Why, oh why didn't she trust them? She was certainly strong and tall enough to kill the scribe and the peasant by breaking their necks. He sighed. Could he tell Hori these tormenting thoughts? "Maybe she's staying with friends," he said lamely.

Hori glared at him. "Stop talking such nonsense!"

He ducked and chided himself a fool. Ouseret wasn't exactly the social type. Whatever happened to her, it didn't help if he tried to spare Hori. Nakhtmin sighed. "In the best case, she nosed around where she shouldn't have, and that's why someone's detaining her." Two faces appeared before his inner eye: Sanefer's and Antef's. Was he being unfair to them? They still had no idea if the deaths were related.

"What if she's also…" Hori's voice cracked.

Sympathy filled Nakhtmin's heart. Far worse fantasies must torture his friend. He'd found Seni's corpse and knew what the men they tried to unmask were capable of. "I think her body would've been found already if she were also…dead," Nakhtmin tried to console him. After all, the other victims hadn't been hidden either. He glanced at the table where the evening meal awaited them. "Let's eat or I'll starve to death!"

After a few bites, Hori slammed his fish back onto the plate. "I wish I'd shaken that unbearable Sanefer until he spilled everything!" He jumped up and paced. "Just to think Ouseret might have already been his prisoner, while we sat there sipping juice!"

His mouth full, Nakhtmin mumbled, "That'd ecshplain why he wanted to get rid of us sho fasht." He swallowed. "I don't believe his tale of a new business model. I think he didn't want us to take another look into the storage hall."

Hori interrupted his restless march to grab Nakhtmin's arm. "Because he's holding Ouseret prisoner there?"

"Possibly. Maybe Heny knows something, heard or saw something?" He shook off his friend's grip. "Where do you want to go? Oh no, let the man sleep!" Nakhtmin couldn't imagine how uprooted the peasant must feel. At least he had a roof over his head, and that had to be more than he could have hoped for when they'd set out in the morning. Fortunately, the man stayed here! Heny would have noticed the comings and goings at his landlord's mansion, the relationships between the people living there, Nofru…

As if Hori had guessed his thoughts, he cried, "We definitely need to question him about Merwer's lover!"

"Yes." A crooked smile sneaked onto Nakhtmin's face as he conjured up the girl's beautiful features. Nofru was a temptation a man could hardly resist for long. What whim of the gods had placed such a delicate creature into that brute of a man's cradle! On their return trip, Heny had confirmed that Nofru really was Wahka's daughter. The familial connection between the two seemed very suspicious to Nakhtmin. Who, if not someone growing up there, would have known of the colocynths? "I wonder why Merwer's wife tolerated her presence. She must have realized what was going on."

Hori waved dismissively. "Forget Nofru!"

Nakhtmin wanted to protest that Hori had brought up the girl himself but let it go. He was all too familiar with these leaps of thought and didn't feel like quarreling.

His friend continued, "It's far more important to find out where Ouseret is. I bet Sanefer is keeping her somewhere, that dog!" He held up his nose toward the gate in the wall, like a jackal on a scent.

He couldn't possibly want to…

Yes, Hori set off and called over his shoulder, "I'll sneak onto the premises, and then we'll see what Sanefer's hiding." He strode into the darkness.

A protesting bird fluttered up. Hori might wake the whole neighborhood with his shouting. "Hey, stop right there and come back!" Nakhtmin called in a subdued voice. He ran after his friend and grabbed him. "How do you think you can get onto the premises at night without a boat? The gate is certainly barred and the wall's too high to climb over."

Hori jerked free. "I have to find her. Tomorrow might be too late!"

"Hush!" Again, Nakhtmin grabbed Hori's wrist and frantically tried to think of how he could change his friend's mind. Climbing over the walls would be pure madness. And they couldn't even be sure the trader had taken Ouseret. Right, that should work! "Wait! Sanefer didn't kill his father. That much we know. So Ouseret had no reason to accuse him. She might be kept somewhere else. Do you really want to break into Sanefer's place? If someone catches you, you're doomed!" To his relief, Hori stopped trying to shake him off, so he added, "Besides, she said we were looking in the wrong place when we told her about our visit with Sanefer. Remember? Why then should she hope to find clues there?" With gentle force he pulled Hori back to the table.

In the light of the torch, he saw the agitation in his friend's face until Hori admitted with a sigh, "Oh, by Seth's testicles, you're right."

"I wish I weren't," Nakhtmin grumbled.

"Why's that?"

"Because that means we have to catch someone unknown to us, or the nomarch has her." And Antef certainly had the means to make unwanted persons vanish from the face of the earth. He shuddered. "Maybe someone at the House of Life knows where she might be."

SCARS

Once again, Hori entered the courtyard of the Amun temple, this time with Nakhtmin by his side. His friend gaped in wonder since he hadn't been here before. Although Hori had suggested taking this route to the House of Life, impatience drove him on. "This way."

To his relief, Nakhtmin tore his gaze from the gorgeous murals and followed him through the second pylon. At the sight of the Sed festival chapel of Senusret I, Nakhtmin sighed with longing. "So beautiful!"

"Yes. Through here."

A little later, they entered the shadowy corridors of the House of Life and ran into the principal, Bakenamun. After a short moment of confusion, he recognized Hori. "Ah, the royal physician! Then this must be your colleague?" He scrutinized Nakhtmin with undisguised curiosity.

Hori introduced his friend then said, "We need to prepare medication for Nakhtmin's ailing wife. Joint pains, you know. The affliction keeps returning, but we hadn't expected it to rear its ugly head in this warm and dry climate." Since at least one of Muti's joints ached, this wasn't much of a lie.

Bakenamun looked baffled. "At such a young age? How pitiable, pitiable. Take what you need of our stocks. Please follow me, I'll take you to the herbal storage."

Behind the man's broad back, Nakhtmin winked at him. They'd come up with this pretext during breakfast. Now they could inquire about Ouseret. Besides, they'd find out how easy it was to get one's hands on powdered colocynth seeds. After all, they didn't know for sure if the plants on Wahka's land had served as murder weapons.

"Has physician Ouseret shown up here in the meantime?" Hori asked full of hope.

Bakenamun slowed his pace. He looked over his right shoulder. "Oh, I heard she's back in Waset, but so far she hasn't come here yet." The tone of his voice suggested that Ouseret wouldn't be welcome at 'his' House of Life either, but it was hard to tell whether that was because of her father or her lengthy absence.

Hori felt like deflated bellows. A tiny hope, the only one he had left to cling to—that Ouseret might have suspected one of her colleagues and confronted him—had just evaporated. Where else could she be except in Antef's custody or Sanefer's house? Again, he heard her cry, 'You're looking in the wrong place!' Not at Sanefer's then, which only left the nomarch, and Nakhtmin would finally agree.

He'd have loved to storm the palace first thing in the morning, but his upper arms still hurt where Nakhtmin's firm grip had bruised them. His friend had shaken him and shouted, "Antef can't have committed the murders, not alone anyway! Where'd he have obtained the powder that killed Merwer? If Ouseret had been looking for the perpetrator or rather his helper, she'd have gone to the House of Life, wouldn't she? Besides, Antef might not have had anything to do with it."

Now this lead also turned into a dead end, and he wanted to scream!

Nakhtmin likewise pulled a long face. "Too bad. She's become a good friend of my wife, and I'd have loved to invite her over to keep her company."

Bakenamun released a snorting sound. "If I were in your place, I'd watch more carefully with whom my wife associates. We're here, here we are."

Since Hori knew the place already, he wouldn't have needed a guide, but to simply help himself to the provisions in a foreign House of Life without asking would have been rude. "Thank you, venerable Bakenamun. We won't keep you any longer."

The head of physicians grunted something like, "Anytime" and waddled off.

Nakhtmin opened the door and released a cloud of intense herbal scent into the corridor. Hori noticed the massive bronze lock. A middle-aged man pounded something in a mortar and looked up as they entered. His face showed astonishment then curiosity, but he continued his work unperturbed. Hori remembered the same man standing at the table and working away when he first visited the place, albeit Bakenamun had only allowed him a quick glance into the room back then. Actually, no, he'd urged the principal to move on—in his impatience to see Ouseret again.

"Who are you, and what do you want?" the man asked without looking up again.

"We're physicians from the royal residence. Bakenamun gave us permission to mix a remedy," Nakhtmin explained.

A smile conjured a wreath of wrinkles around the man's eyes. "I've heard about you! I'm Neferhotep and in charge of medicinal herbs. Tell me what you need and I'll prepare it for you."

Baffled, Hori stared at Neferhotep then Nakhtmin. "Doesn't every physician make his own remedies here?"

The smile deepened. "I know that in other Houses of Life along the Nile that's the case. However, Bakenamun introduced this method here. It saves time, and there's less waste. It's been a success, oh yes, a success."

Nakhtmin murmured, "How convenient! But if we suggested that to Imhotepankh…"

Thoughts tumbled around in Hori's heart, and he could no longer listen to what his friend was saying. If Neferhotep prepared all the cures, even those leaving the House of Life, Nehesy's medicine couldn't have been spiked with an overdose of the poison here. Unless someone managed to snatch some of the powder, while Neferhotep had been absent, then added it to Merwer's remedy later. His gaze dropped to the key on Neferhotep's belt. Likely the man always locked the door whenever he left the room. Still, someone might have sneaked in at a moment of distraction… Strange that this fact hadn't done anything to exonerate Nehesy. Of course, he could have made the powder himself. Hori had never used colocynth so far, but it wasn't difficult, only time-consuming since the seeds had to dry for a few days, like those he saw on a kiln across the room.

Neferhotep kept pounding away. Spellbound, Hori stared at the doctor's hand. Spotty scars marred his wrist and the back of his hand. Just like the ones on Sanefer's skin! "Those are burn marks, right?" he asked with feigned nonchalance and pointed at the man's hand.

"What?" Neferhotep seemed confused, then he laughed. "Oh that! No, that's what happens when you don't pay attention. Happened to me while shredding colocynth. The juice of the fruit burns the skin as you certainly know."

Hori suppressed a groan. Of course! They'd learned that during their studies: Never handle colocynth with bare hands. Instead, carefully scrape out the seeds with a knife. Back home, physicians also tended to protect their skin with a thick slathering of goose fat. So he'd never seen such scars before. Neferhotep's long experience had probably made him careless. Hori conjured up all he remembered from his times as a student: The juice caused blisters on the skin, very similar to those of burns. And they left such characteristic scars? Marks like the ones on Sanefer's hands. Sanefer who hadn't been home when his father died... Agitated, he grabbed Nakhtmin's arm. "He did it after all!" he hissed.

His friend didn't catch on, but Hori's cry drew Neferhotep's attention. "Who did what?"

Damn, he needed a deflection. "Oh, nothing, I've just been thinking aloud, pardon me. What a coincidence. We need medicine containing colocynth." He listed all the ingredients.

Neferhotep's eyebrows hiked up into a frown. "For joint pain, ey? Just be careful! It's not been long since a patient took too much of it." He emptied the mortar into an earthen jug and thoroughly cleaned the tools. "Didn't turn out well, not well at all," he mumbled while sifting through the shelves.

"Oh yes, I know exactly what dosage to use," Nakhtmin hurried to say. "As long as you stick to the amounts Hori specified, nothing can happen."

The man's back stiffened. Slowly, Neferhotep turned around to them. "What are you trying to say?" His eyes narrowed to slits. "Are you insinuating that I made the medicine to strong?"

Hori held his breath and fervently shook his head.

His friend's face flushed. "I...no! May the gods prevent my doing so! No! I'm certain you perform your work with utmost diligence."

"Indeed I do!" Neferhotep confirmed, hands on his hips. "Indeed!" Snorting and grunting, he continued with the preparation, moving very slowly and deliberately, asking Nakhtmin to confirm the amount of each ingredient. "It's up to you, doctor, not to poison your patients," he said with emphasis, while he wrote the name of the medicine onto the little clay jar before handing it over.

They thanked him and fled Neferhotep's realm.

"Phew!" Nakhtmin uttered as soon as the door closed behind them.

"Oh come on, that was great!" Hori exclaimed. "We should have come here much earlier to investigate... I've been such a doofus! We could have proven Sanefer's guilt much earlier!"

"Huh? Calm down. Someone might come along any time or listen in on us from behind a door. Wait until we're outside...or even better until we're home."

Despite his impatience, Hori bit his tongue. He'd have loved to run to the Medjay to tell the royal law officers straight away. However, his friend was right. Who could they trust here? And they still hadn't gotten any closer to Ouseret. Where was she, and more importantly, in whose hands was she? Ones marred by colocynth juice? One thing had become obvious now: They had been looking in the right place!

Suddenly, Nakhtmin grabbed his wrist. "I fear for Muti. Let's go and fast, too."

When they stormed through the garden toward Mutnofret, she looked up and smiled. Nakhtmin tried not to show his relief. He didn't want to upset her, neither with his worry about her nor with the actual danger they might be in. While Hori released an excited stream of words, he remained silent, only gazed at her. The finely curved lips, which so often curled in mockery, the beautiful velvety eyes... Losing her would be unbearable.

Those eyes now sparked with amusement. "Can you tell your friend he'll swallow his tongue if he doesn't slow down? I don't understand a word. What's he talking about, scars?"

Hori paused in astonishment then began all over, this time more coherently, and ended with the words, "Sanefer must have scraped the colocynth seeds from the fruit growing on Wahka's land and ground them into the powder that killed his father. No doubt about it!"

Nakhtmin chided himself for a yokel because he only now saw the connection. He'd barely paid attention to Sanefer's scars, while Hori naturally noticed his rival's physical imperfection.

Muti pursed her lips. "That might be the case, but he can't have administered it to him personally since he hadn't been there, right?"

"Yes, he needed an accomplice." Nakhtmin mulled over it and finally everything made sense. "Nofru! She probably grew tired of waiting for Merwer's wife to die, particularly since she's with child. What if Sanefer promised to marry her?"

"Hm, but how could he convince her that he'd keep his promise when he was still engaged to Ouseret?" Muti asked.

Nakhtmin could think of several possibilities and almost heard the young man purr, 'I never loved her. Her father will have to take the fall for the deed, then I can renege on my promise...'

Hori scoffed. "Men can convince a woman in love of pretty much anything."

"Oh, is that so? And all women are stupid enough to go for it? Don't let Ouseret hear what you think of her!" Muti interjected.

"I..."

For a while Nakhtmin gloated over Hori's distress then he took mercy on him. "I don't think Nofru was in love with Sanefer or his father. I got to know the minx a little. She knows which tree grows the juiciest fruit and lies down under exactly that one. For her employer's peasants, she held only contempt although she was the daughter of one of them. I believe her beauty spoiled her heart. She thinks herself above her humble origins and strives for a higher state in life—something she feels entitled to. Didn't Heny say something along those lines? She hopes to become the mistress of the household." He paused and stroked Muti's hand. "Maybe her pregnancy made her fear Merwer's wife would kick her out. She might have perceived a necessity to act soon."

"How does that help us find Ouseret?" Hori grumbled, still sulking. Then with more vehemence, he continued, "If Sanefer is the killer, he has abducted her. But certain folks..." His reproachful gaze lingered on Nakhtmin. "...prevented me from going there last night to check out his estate. If she's still there, and something happens to her because I didn't—"

"By the gods, stop it!" Nakhtmin shouted.

"Right," Muti called. "Spreading blame helps neither us nor her. There's one thing, though. I can't fathom why she still defended Sanefer if she already suspected him to be the true culprit."

Yes, that puzzled him, too. Whenever Ouseret had spoken about Sanefer, her tone had been matter of fact, close to disinterested. She never tried to disguise his possible guilt or hint at it. Passion only surfaced when she talked about her father. A thought flared up in Nakhtmin's heart, and he choked on his own saliva. As soon as the coughing fit ebbed, he croaked, "What if she isn't trying to cover things up for Sanefer?" Muti and Hori both looked at him, one questioning, the other hopeful. All of a sudden Nakhtmin's idea didn't make so much sense anymore. "I...um...what if she's protecting her father?" he stammered the rest of the sentence.

"What?" both cried in unison.

Hori jumped up, crossed his arms and glared at him with scorn flashing from his yes. "Are you saying that Nehesy did it after all?"

His friend had completely misunderstood! "No, that's not what I meant," Nakhtmin retorted quickly to calm him down. "Sanefer may have threatened that something could happen to her father in the stone pits if she pointed a finger at him. However, I don't know...It was just an idea, and now it doesn't make an awful lot of sense to me any more either."

"Ha!" Hori scoffed. "Next time, think first—"

"No, wait!" Muti gracefully inclined her head to one side as she always did when she mulled over something. "Not Sanefer but Antef! Where has Nehesy been banished? To Kheny in the Ta-Seti nome, right? The quarries belong to the nomarchs' domains, and they are also responsible for guarding the prisoners. If someone could make sure Nehesy had an accident there, then it's the ruler of Ta-Seti. He also wields the power to make Nehesy's life there a little more pleasant, more survivable."

Nakhtmin thought about it. "Yes, that's a possibility. Sarenput is the ruler of the Land of the Bow; he plays a central role in trading much-coveted goods from foreign countries farther south: ivory, ebony and...ostrich feathers! Would Antef entertain good relations with his colleague in the south? Definitely!" The excitement made his palms sweat. "Could trade be the link between Merwer, Antef and Sarenput? But why did Merwer have to make way for his son?"

Hori's eyes widened, and he slammed his right fist into his left palm. "Of course! For whatever reason, Merwer must have become an obstacle for the two powerful men, so they must have convinced, hired or forced Sanefer to kill his own father! A conspiracy! Could Antef also have lost investments in Merwer's businesses?"

That moment, steps approached from the house, and they all fell silent. Nakhtmin recognized Heny's broad-shouldered frame. "What's up?" he asked.

The former peasant cleared his throat in discomfort. "There's a messenger from the palace. He demands an explanation why you sent away the servants."

Now that on top of everything else! Nakhtmin had completely forgotten about it. When the two servants came to the estate in the morning, Hori had paid what they owed them and dismissed them regardless of their protests. Naturally, they hadn't expected Antef to simply accept that, but he'd preferred to push the matter aside.

Hori nodded at Heny. "I'll take care of it." Together, they walked toward the gate of the estate and soon disappeared from Nakhtmin's view. He sat next to Muti. "Isn't all this a bit much for you, darling?"

She furrowed her brow. "What? No, I love to solve mysteries, and you know that. It was so boring while you and Hori were gone. However, if Antef is really the one behind the murder of Merwer—"

"And that of the archive scribe Seni and the farmer Wahka," he added.

"Right. Then why should the man stop at a royal physician?"

Horrified, Nakhtmin stared at her for a long moment then he laughed. "No, he'd never dare! What could possibly happen to Hori? It's only a messenger, and Heny is with him. Don't worry, he'll be back soon."

"Yes." Her smile made his heart beat faster and aroused different desires in him. Her fingers played with the physician's amulet on his chest then circled his nipples. "Finally I've got you to myself."

He wrapped his arms around her and pressed his lips on hers. How long it had been! He wanted her so much. When she closed her fingers around his erection, he stopped thinking.

"My lord? Master?"

Slowly, Nakhtmin came to his senses. A dense canopy arched over him—he must have fallen asleep! Muti lay in his arms, dozing as well. Dear gods, the sun was setting already! Gently, he disentangled himself from his wife and wrapped the shendyt around his waist. Nakhtmin looked up at a knowing smile, which quickly gave way to a worried expression. He took Heny aside lest they wake Muti. "What is it this time?" Probably the evening meal, but that didn't warrant disturbing them.

"The other master still hasn't returned from the palace."

Horror chased away all drowsiness. "Hori accompanied the messenger to the palace?"

Looking miserable, Heny nodded. "The man insisted, at the nomarch's orders. He was supposed to bring you and the lady as well, but we assured him you weren't here."

How hard could his heart pound without jumping out of his chest? "And why didn't you tell me earlier?" he barked.

Heny seemed to shrink under his stare. "Master, he interrogated me, asked where I come from, where I'm heading, threatened if I told you anything... Then he ordered me to send you to the palace as soon as you returned. But you were sleeping, and I... Oh, I'm so scared!" Sudden scorn flared up in his face. "I wish I'd never met you! We've already packed and loaded everything onto the donkey. My family's waiting at the gate for me. You mighty folks have to settle your quarrels among yourselves!" With that he turned away and marched into the growing darkness.

Nakhtmin stood petrified with fear. Hori had been gone for hours, and that boded ill. Should he go to the palace and place himself at the mercy of Antef? Never! Damn Heny, why hadn't he warned them earlier! Instead, he'd packed up to take his own family to safety.

Limping steps behind him. Slender fingers clasped his hand. "I heard everything," Muti whispered. "We have to leave as well! It's only a question of time until Antef will send his soldiers, and then we're doomed."

Nakhtmin kissed the parting of her hair smelling of grass and flowers, so innocent. Why hadn't they been arrested already? Antef must have believed the lie that they were gone for the day. Since they hadn't shown up at the palace yet, the nomarch's minions likely awaited them somewhere on the street. They'd be asked politely to follow them to the palace just like they'd done with Hori. Most likely Antef expected them to follow his 'invitation' without a moment's hesitation since he couldn't know what they'd found out in the meantime. "Oh, Hori!" he groaned. "He blindly stumbled into the trap."

She shook her head, which tickled his arm. "Not blind—except maybe with love. He hoped to find Ouseret, and now both are detained. Oh Nakhtmin, where can we turn for help? If they don't find us here, they'll check all the guest houses next."

He squeezed her hand. Good question. Where could they hide? They didn't know anyone here except... "Let's go to Meseh! Hopefully he can put us up. I doubt anyone will come looking for us there." He paused and listened. The wind carried bits of conversation over the wall. Neighbors or... "Do you think you can walk?"

Her fingers squeezed back, and she nodded. "I should be fine if you support me. Let's get out of here! We can put on the simple clothes we were wearing the other day. Everything else we'll just leave here."

Nakhtmin first went to the big gate of the premises and barred it as silently as possible so that Antef's militia couldn't just enter unhindered. Muti waited for him in the garden. Now she took his arm and limped into the house by his side. They didn't light any lamps since their shine might be noticed on the other side of the wall. Instead, they felt their way in the dark. Wrapped in the coarse shendyt, Nakhtmin grabbed only his small bundle with precious little things to trade. Then he helped Muti out of the house and down the short path to the wicket leading to the waterfront. "We'll have to wade through water for a little bit," he told her and sent a prayer to Hapi, the Nile god. "Do you feel up to that?"

CAUGHT

The palace's antechamber bustled with people coming and going. Hori cast a questioning glance at the messenger.

He only shrugged his shoulders. "The yearly tributes arrived today. They are all sitting in there at a large banquet."

Indeed, Hori heard laughter and a buzz of voices filter into the atrium. Strange that Antef would summon him on such a day because of some trivia. However, it also calmed him. The big man would have better things to do than deal with him. To his surprise, the servant neither took him into the large reception hall nor toward Antef's private chambers but chose the corridor to their left where Muti, Nakhtmin and he had spent their first night in Waset. Since the sun had already passed its highest point, only faint light shafted through the slits in the wall. Why didn't his companion get a lamp or a torch? They walked past door after door and headed straight for the end wall of the corridor, where two armed guards stood. Before Hori could wonder if further hallways forked off there, he detected the hole in the ground, a gaping maw into the underworld. No, *no*! He spun around and ran—directly into the arms of two more soldiers following them. He screamed in fury and lashed out, but his fists didn't connect. They clutched his arms and dragged him to the abyss despite his resistance. A calloused hand covered his mouth and muffled his screams. Then he dropped step after step into the vault.

Rough hands shoved Hori through a door that was slammed shut behind him. A bolt scraped. He was a prisoner! Locked up under the nomarch's palace. Without a torch, it was pitch dark in here, and all sounds echoed overly loud in his ears, even the steps of the departing men. Now the trapdoor at the end of the corridor crashed down. Silence. What was that? A rustling noise.

"Who are you?" A woman's voice. One he knew very well.

His heart leapt. "Ouseret! It's me, Hori!" He padded in her direction with utmost relief to have found her—alive! He almost tripped over her legs.

She snapped at him, "Stay away from me, you triple-horned oxen! Yokel! Lovesick imbecile! Of course, you couldn't leave things alone. Now my father is doomed, and it's all your fault!"

"Huh?" Each of her words hurt like a stroke with the rod, but he didn't understand anything anymore. And he was getting tired of her hostility and accusations. His jaw muscles cramped. Maybe Nakhtmin was right, and Ouseret wasn't the woman for him, for no man. "You know, it's really your fault. I have no clue what you're talking about, because you never tell the whole truth. Instead, you want me to guess whatever you keep to yourself and fulfill your wishes although unknown to me. I'm not a magician, only a man who wants to help you. A man who…" He let his voice trail off. A moment of silence engulfed them. No, he wouldn't tell her again what she knew already, that he loved her more than anything else in the world. In contrast to her, he'd always been open with her. Why couldn't she be like other women? A woman who sank into his arms to find solace and support. Then she'd likely not interest him much, he admitted to himself. After all, the high-hanging grapes were the sweetest.

When she finally replied, she sounded baffled. "I really should have told you everything, particularly after I'd been warned."

His head jerked up. "What? What was that?"

"Soon after my first visit with you." She sighed. "Come, sit with me. Here's some straw."

He padded on until he heard crackling noises under his sandals, then he squatted and lowered himself. Ouseret's body, so close to his, radiated warmth, but the wall felt cold against his back. He fingered it. Natural rock? The air was stale, there seemed to be no ventilation. "Hm, I've never seen an underground chamber before except in tombs. Is this a secret prison?"

She gave a snort. "Oh yes, Antef's Chamber of Silence. Until yesterday, I'd also only heard rumors about it and didn't believe it really existed."

At least she talked to him in a normal tone for once. The warm timbre of her voice sent a pleasant shiver down his back despite their predicament. "I don't assume there's another way out of here except for the door over there?"

"No, and the bolt is made of thick wood."

Hori felt for her hand. She didn't withdraw it. Not right away. He took that as a good sign. "What do you think Antef is planning to do with us?"

He felt her shrug. "He'd have released me once you'd returned to Itj-tawy. He knows I won't make a move against him as long as he has my father at his mercy. But you simply couldn't give up. Oh well, too late now."

Back to the residence and the king? That moment Hori realized the nomarch couldn't let him go now, under no circumstances. Even worse, by simply following the messenger to the palace, he'd probably forfeited not only his own life but Ouseret's as well. "He will kill us." How could he say the unfathomable and stay so calm?

"Yes."

The word pierced his heart like an arrow and stuck, quivering. He couldn't let that happen! They could do to him whatever they wanted, but not to Ouseret! He jumped up, walked over to the door and rattled it in vain. It barely moved. "Hello! Hey, anybody out there?" He pounded against the wood until his fists ached.

"Hori, Hori. It's useless. Nobody can hear you."

Gasping, he stopped.

"That's why it's called Chamber of Silence. As soon as the trapdoor's closed, no one hears our screams."

Oh yes, the trapdoor! Truly a maw into the underworld. Disheartened, he dragged himself back and settled on the straw beside her. "He can't do this," he blurted. "People will be looking for us." A sudden glimmer of hope struck him. "Nakhtmin knows where I am!"

A sympathetic smile in her voice, she said, "For whom do you think the door will open next?"

The thought alone made his heart race. Not his friends! But of course, Antef had to detain Nakhtmin and Muti as well. He could no longer risk letting them travel back to the royal residence, neither Hori, nor Nakhtmin, nor Muti, because they'd tell the pharaoh what happened here. And he couldn't do anything to warn his friends, was powerless! "I simply don't understand," he groaned. "Why? What's Antef got to do with it all? By now we're pretty certain that Sanefer killed his father, there are sure signs." Although it might no longer make a difference, he wanted to find out the truth.

He could hear her inhale deeply and release the air. "Then he really did it? I had my suspicions, but he was traveling. How could he do it?"

"Nofru. We believe he enlisted her services. Why the girl went along with it, we have no idea, but she knew where colocynths grew on her father's land." He paused. "You suspected him? Was that the reason why you broke up with him?"

A wild scream erupted from her chest. "*He* did it? And he accuses Father?" Only with effort did she seem to regain control. "No, we'd separated before, before I had any idea… Oh, that dog! To think that he knew Father was innocent! Aaah!" After a pause, she continued more calmly. "Back then he showed me a different side of his character. One unknown to me until then, but that's probably his true face. It hadn't affected him the least bit when I reneged on the engagement."

Hori glanced in her direction. "No? Hm, I should have thought of that. At first, I figured he killed Merwer so he could finally marry you." Perhaps she'd now tell him a little more about what happened between her and the young trader.

Judging by the noises, she'd pulled up her knees and wrapped her arms around them. Hori leaned against her ever so slightly, which confirmed his impression.

"Our relationship was never like that, never *passionate*," she said, her voice ringing with sarcasm.

He shook his head in disbelief. How could a man not be crazy for her? In Sanefer's place, Hori would have done anything to finally make her his. Even killed his father? He tried to imagine that, but no. Although he felt no love for the old man, life was holy. Ending one with force meant eternal damnation. Maat would turn her back on him. He wanted to ask her why she even got engaged to that idiot but feared she might clam up again. "How's the nomarch involved in all this?"

She sighed. "If only I knew! But he has to be, right? Or else we wouldn't be here. Besides, a few days ago, a palace messenger took me aside at the market and threatened me. He said if my friends and I won't stop investigating Merwer's death, my father would have to bear the brunt of it. He was rather specific, too: less food and work in the stone pits. It seems like he's currently allowed to tend to the injuries of the other quarrymen, but that can change at any time. Oh Hori! He wouldn't last long. Father isn't young anymore."

She grabbed his hand, which sent a delicious shudder through him. How much he'd love to wrap her in his arms… Patience! "Hm. That means Antef also knows of Sanefer's guilt and wants to cover up what happened." The vanished records, the threats directed at them… But why? How could the nomarch be involved in the affairs of the trader? "Is it possible that Merwer also lost gold Antef had supplied to finance one of his endeavors? But why would he use Sanefer to commit the crime and why in such a manner?"

"No idea, but let's go back a step for a moment. You didn't tell me why you're so sure Sanefer did it. Not that I doubt your word…"

"Because of the scars." He practically sensed her disbelieving gaze on him and gave a slight laugh. "I noticed scars on Sanefer's hands, like burn marks. You certainly know Neferhotep at the House of Life, right? He has very similar ones, and I asked him how he obtained them. Squirts from colocynth juice caused them."

She released a drawn out "Aaaah. I should have realized! It was I who tended to his blisters when they were fresh. I'm such a stupid cow! He claimed he burnt himself. And you come to the conclusion that he prepared the poison that killed his father? It's possible. Fully aware that Merwer's next fit would only be days away, he prepared everything and instructed Nofru. Then he set out on business so not even the slightest suspicion could fall on him. Very cold-hearted. Still, that fits with how I see him these days. I believe he is a calculating man to the core."

Hori's heart beat faster. He was rid of his rival, now he only needed her to warm up to him. Too bad he was locked up here as well, or he could come to her rescue. Maybe if he got her father released… He told himself to stop dreaming. All he could do was unveil the truth even if nobody but Ouseret would hear it. He cleared his throat. "What do you really know about the relationships between the members of Merwer's household? You kept a lot to yourself." He failed to keep all reproach from his voice.

"You mean Nofru's position?" she asked after a short pause.

"Nofru, Satnefert, Merwer's wife, each of them might be relevant to understand what happened and why. To clear your father of all charges, we'll need more than a few scars."

She snorted in contempt. "You're delusional! Whatever we find out, we'll take to our graves. This is our grave!" Her voice cracked as if she was holding back tears.

Gently he placed an arm around her hard and tense shoulders, then quickly withdrew it. "Oh well, solving the mystery makes for a good pastime. Besides…I…" Oh dear, he'd sound really tacky, but he had to say it. "I'm serving Maat, and just maybe…um…it'll help balancing the scales of world order?"

He felt her stare at him. Any moment now, she'd burst out laughing, laughing at him. Her breath gently caressed his cheek. "Yes. It might help condemn the villain at the Judgment of the Dead—if not in this life. Once his name has been said aloud, the culprit won't be able to make excuses when he's facing Anubis."

Happy because she understood, Hori smiled. The magic of the spoken word…

Muti's arm wrapped around his shoulder, Nakhtmin fought his way through the waterfront mud. Fortunately, they lived in a house at the corner, so it wasn't that far to the access road leading to the Street of Palm Fronds. Nakhtmin certainly appreciated it since Muti put more and more weight on him while he struggled to keep his balance on the slippery ground. On top of that, crocodiles might be lurking just below the water's surface! He kept one hand on the wall along the river, and when he felt the corner, he peered around it. Over his shoulder, he said, "I can't see anyone. That means there's no spy here either." His heart beat slower now, but the danger wasn't over yet.

"What are we going to do if they see us emerging from the alley?" Muti whispered. "No gate opens to this street. We'll draw attention."

He shared her concern. By now, a round moon had risen and shed pale light that allowed them to see and be seen. "Let's hope we're mistaken and nobody is waiting to catch us. Not yet anyway. Come on."

They reached firm ground and wiped their muddy feet on dry grass. Nakhtmin held Muti until she'd slipped into her sandals; he only needed the wall for support. Her face glowed pale in the livid light and looked tense. "Are you in great pain?" he asked in alarm.

"I can do it," she murmured. "Have to."

The Street of Palm Fronds was only a few steps away now. While she waited, leaning against the wall, he sneaked up to the intersection. After a quick glance around the corner, he jerked back his head and returned to her. "Two men," he whispered. "They are loitering at the wall across the street. One of them is looking our way, the other in the opposite direction."

In a subdued voice, Muti released a very unladylike curse, "May Sekhmet's arrows let their testicles rot off in an agonizing way! What are we going to do now? Can we escape them if we run?"

Considering Muti's sprained ankle, he shook his head. "Not likely. Perhaps they'll become less alert or even fall asleep if we wait. Let's sit down. For now we're trapped here."

They settled with their backs against the wall. "Maybe they'll return to the palace once they realize that we won't come home tonight," Muti said.

"Maybe." More likely at least one of them would keep watch, or they'd break open the gate and search the premises. Then they'd notice the unbarred gate to the river and... "Ameny's going to kill me if something happens to you," he groaned and buried his face in his hands.

"I'll kill you if you start whining now!" she hissed. "So far, nothing's lost. Listen, what's that?"

He craned his neck and pricked his ears. Steps in the Street of Palm Fronds? Were the men leaving? He rose and crept to the intersection again. The noises came from the left not right. A palanquin approached—the nomarch's minions watched it with keen interest. Nakhtmin dashed back to Muti barely visible in the shade of the wall.

"A palanquin! They'll search it for sure. That'll keep them distracted. We probably won't get a better chance!"

With an effort, Muti struggled to her feet. The injured ankle didn't seem to bear her weight well. Damn! He simply lifted her into his arms and soon wheezed like a hippopotamus. This might work for a short stretch, but to cross the moonlit crossroad, they'd have to be fast and silent. He gently let down his beloved. "Lie down flat on the ground lest they see you." The voices of the palanquin carriers grew louder. Soon their chance would have slipped by. They couldn't do it, not both of them together. But he could! And leave Muti behind? He had no choice. "Listen...you have to wait here, while I try to get across. Then I'll circle around the block and approach the thugs from the other side so they'll see and follow me. Thus I'll draw them away from you. While they'll search for me downstream, I come back and take you across the street. Then we can make our way to Meseh. Hm, do you think you can stand waiting here all by yourself...? Oh, let's forget about it."

She clutched his hand. "It's our only chance. Do it. I'm sure it'll work."

Her determined voice drowned out his concerns. "All right, I'll do it. Just stay here and lie still."

Reluctantly, he tore himself away from her. Bent low, he crept back to the corner, keeping close to the wall and its shadow, then crouched so he could sprint across as swiftly as possible. The palanquin hadn't passed yet. The wait became torture. Finally the four carriers, two up front and two at the back, trotted past, bearing the gently rocking structure made for two people, the curtains drawn. Perfect! Antef's thugs for hire would expect him and Muti to sit inside. A torch bearer walked ahead to illuminate the way. When he passed, he seemed to look straight at him. Nakhtmin lowered his head, while his ears rushed. Had the man detected him? No, the carriers up front now marched by without anyone making a fuss. The men in the back paid no attention to him either. His racing heart slowed somewhat.

About thirty steps down the street, they were stopped. A babble of voices drifted over to Nakhtmin.

"What's going on?"

"On the nomarch's orders!"

"Who are you?"

Nakhtmin recognized the mewling tone of his nosy neighbor, the Khonsu priest. What was his name? Oh, right, Kawab. His bald head shimmered in the moonlight when he leaned out of palanquin. Damn, one of the palace minions moved to that side and looked straight in Nakhtmin's direction. He'd never get across the street unseen. Ah, now the noble lord deemed to alight. As the alley was so narrow, they moved to the front of the group where the torch bearer stood waiting. They turned their backs on him. Now or never. Every muscle in Nakhtmin's body tensed as he sprinted off, trying to move as silently as possible. Had he been fast enough that no one spotted him? He couldn't afford to stop and check but ran down the street. Only when he reached the next turnoff did he pause to catch his breath and look back. Nobody was following him. Leaning against the wall, he gasped for air. He had to move on! Soon he reached the next intersection. Turning toward the river now, he'd get to the Street of Palm Fronds again where those thugs lurked, but approach them from the opposite direction. Dear gods, it was pure madness to offer himself as bait! Nevertheless, he placed one foot in front of the other without haste now. He had to appear untroubled. The walls lining the alley offered no protection against curious looks. Doubts gnawed at Nakhtmin. He wasn't a great runner, and if they caught him...Muti was helpless without him. They *must not* apprehend him! Even before he reached the turnoff to the Street of Palm Fronds, he heard Kawab's penetrating voice first, then the others as well.

"...did seem a little dubious to me. Very tight-lipped, that physician."

"Did you see him anywhere today?" That would be one of the spies.

"Good man, I'm just now returning from the banquet at the palace. How should I have encountered the wanted man? Or do you think his excellency would have placed you here if he were entertaining the villain?"

Nakhtmin didn't dare to move. They were far too close! Antef's people must have moved on toward Kawab's estate. If he showed his face now, he'd barely get a head start, and this alley offered hardly any shadows in which he could hide. He hurried back to the street running in parallel and dashed around the corner as if the devourer herself were chasing him. For his plan to work, he had to get to the next crossroad at least. If he remembered correctly, the priest's house was located between the alley he'd just fled from and the next one, but closer to this one here. If the spies accompanied Kawab to his gate but no farther, the distance should suffice to give him a reasonable head start.

Traipsing through the night, he realized how quiet everything was with occasional noises drifting over the high walls to him. The crossroad came up. He turned into it and noticed only the walls to his left were well maintained. On the opposite side, the plaster flaked and peeled off everywhere, and gaps showed in the capstones. He recalled the deserted houses—over there had to be one of them. Did that provide a possibility to shake off his pursuers later?

He discovered a gate, but it hung crooked on its hinges. With some effort, he managed to push it open far enough to squeeze through. One step into the untended overgrown garden, he got caught in a thorn bush. The cloth of his shendyt tore when he disentangled himself. Least of his worries right now. At a loss, he stared at the plant. There was no getting through here, and with some bad luck, he might get himself trapped. He squatted and discovered a sort of tunnel winding through the shrubs. Maybe animals or playing children had formed it. Nakhtmin thought of snakes lurking there and closed his eyes. He had to risk it. On all fours, he worked his way through the vegetation. To his relief, it thinned out soon. Where once flowers must have bloomed, the lack of watering had left only barren earth around the disintegrating walls of the former house. With joy, he detected another gate leading to the Street of Palm Fronds. This one also opened with some force. He left it ajar, so he could slip through later. Yes, with an easily reachable escape route, he felt much better about his endeavor.

He crawled back to the other gate, stepped into the alley and continued to the intersection. Peering around the corner, he saw the palanquin disappear behind the wall of Kawab's estate, while the priest still stood chatting with the minions. Nakhtmin took a deep breath and strode toward the three men.

Kawab spotted him first and shrieked, "There, that's the man you want! Grab him!"

Nakhtmin swung around and dashed off. Fortunately, he was far enough ahead to slip through the half open door onto the overgrown premises before his pursuers had turned into the alley. With caution, he closed the gate and went down on his knees. Crawling through the tunnel, he heard the sandals of the spies slap over the dusty road. They came closer, very close, and moved past. He was grinning to himself because his plan had worked so well. They'd search for him anywhere but here. Still, he'd have to run a considerable stretch on the open road to reach Muti and take her to safety—before the minions decided to return to their posts.

He brushed earth and twigs from his shendyt while walking toward the main gate, but before he stepped through, he made sure the street was deserted. To his relief, the nasty priest had disappeared as well. He wouldn't have put it beyond the man to wait for the soldiers to return with Nakhtmin as their prisoner. Something to tell his friends about. However, Kawab had either joined the hunt for him or had retreated behind the walls of his estate. Nevertheless, Nakhtmin kept to the shadows on his way back to where he'd left Muti.

She was gone!

Nakhtmin's legs gave. They must have found his darling! Likely Kawab was holding her so he could deliver her to Antef personally. Oh no! He sobbed in agony and staggered back to the intersection, no longer caring if they arrested him. Without her, his life was meaningless!

"Sh-shhh!" A hissing noise from the other side of the street.

He lifted his head and saw a figure peering at him from behind a projection in the wall. Muti? His lips formed the word, but his tongue refused to do its duty as he hurried to her. Only when he really stood before her, he cried, "Muti!"

She placed a hand over his mouth. "Are you insane to crow like that? I thought I better limp over while they are chasing you."

Shouts from the other end of the alley announced the minion's approach. He'd never expected them to search in that direction as well. Squeezing into the nook with Muti, he realized they still faced the same predicament only in a different location. How could they get to Meseh with Muti's injured foot? The spies hurried past, didn't look back, and soon after, everything turned quiet again. He dared a peek and cast a longing glance at the silvery band of the river.

"A boat!" Muti said the moment he thought it.

"Why didn't we think of that earlier!" he hissed. "I'm sure we'll find a craft we can borrow. Just borrow—after all, we're no thieves. Come on, let's make a move while the coast is clear. You'll hide, and I'll procure a boat."

FLEE!

Day 12 of month Wepet-renpet in Akhet, the season of inundation

Kheper approached with a metal tool in his hand. Hori wanted to scream, but lying on the cold stone of a worktable in the weryt, he couldn't move a finger or his tongue to stop his friend, who now pointed the awl at his nostril. Of course! The embalmer was about to push it into his skull to remove the useless gray stuff in his head. Hori relaxed. As long as the man didn't remove any vital organs, he should be fine. Phew!

He blinked and the world around him turned all black. Where had Kheper gone? His mouth felt parched like the western desert. Someone breathed next to him, and he finally managed to shake off the dream. Ouseret! He'd imagined his first night with her quite different. Water! No, there was nothing except a bucket for their excrement, likely not for their convenience but to make things easier for the people who'd have to clean up after them. Bitterness flooded Hori's heart and joined the gnawing self-reproach and the raging scorn for Antef. How could he have been so stupid to walk into this trap?

Beside him, Ouseret stirred. "Good morning."

He snorted. "Is it morning? Might as well be the dark of night." Still, she was probably right. It felt like a new day. "Did you ever get anything to drink since they locked you up in here?" he asked.

"Yes, and food." Her tone turned accusatory. "That's likely over now."

She might be right again. Luckily, it was fairly cool down here. However, if the nomarch meant to let them die of thirst, he wouldn't have to wait long. Horrified, he realized nobody would take care of his body, no preparation for eternity! A grave without name, eternal oblivion. He recalled the black abyss the first prophet of Anubis had opened in the grave of Osiris, the screams of the damned… His own soul would separate into ka, ba and shadow after his death… If the necessary rituals weren't performed, ka and ba were lost, but his shadow, the dark part of him, would stay with all its dismal memories and roam this world—and one day it might encounter Antef or Sanefer. That prospect offered little consolation. No wonder he'd dreamed of Kheper. Why had they even bothered to incarcerate him? That only made sense if… "Maybe they will bring us something. Antef might still want to talk to me when he's got the peace of mind," he said. Yesterday's banquet might not have left him time for interrogations.

She remained silent for a while then mumbled, "Because he didn't have you slain the moment they caught you? Maybe. He did briefly question me, but I hardly know anything. Well, let's wait and see…"

Hori laughed but ended up sobbing. "What else can we do?" He felt his way to the bucket and relieved himself. Next to it stood a container with sand to spread over it and reduce the stench. A small wooden shovel stuck in the box. Pensive, he weighed it in his hand. Light weight and without sharp edges, it wouldn't do as a weapon, but the box might! "When you got food, how many people came in here?" he asked, while an idea formed in his heart.

"One. Why?"

Hori rose, found his way to the door and fingered it. No slits though which one might push something, not even at the bottom. "And the man has to unbar the door and come in?"

"Yes, of course. I don't understand the purpose of your questions."

"Let me mull it over." The trapdoor was separate from the nomarch's private rooms and from the administrative area, far from all visitors coming and going. "Do you know what part of the palace we're in and who uses it?"

She stepped next to him; he sensed the heat she emanated and deeply inhaled her feminine scent. If only she'd... He pulled himself together.

"I think this wing remains unused most of the time."

"Why's that?"

She stepped away audibly. The straw rustled, then she said, "As far as I know, Antef accommodates guests there, delegations from the south or north."

Then last night several emissaries would have slept in that wing. Tributaries from all over the Waset nome. And he'd been dragged down here while the guests feasted with Antef. "So the corridor is rarely used, right?"

"Yes, but I don't understand why you'd want to know that."

In growing excitement, he walked over and settled beside her. "Listen...I think I have an idea how we can escape."

She released a contemptuous snort. "Oh, sure!"

Sulking, he almost kept his mouth shut, but it couldn't work without her participation. "Why don't you let me explain first and scoff later? The guests of yesterday's banquet are prone to leave some time in the morning. Only afterward, someone will come to us."

After a moment's consideration, she said, "You're right, Antef wouldn't risk someone noticing the trapdoor. It's usually covered."

He grinned. "So, when the guard comes in to bring us food and drink, we have to act fast. While he still has his hands full, you throw sand in his face. The stinging pain will make him close his eyes, and I'll hit him over the head with the sandbox. Of course, we pour the sand out first. The box should be heavy enough, and it has sharp edges. That should knock him out."

She grasped his wrist in excitement. "It might actually work!" A chuckle escaped her throat. "You might not be such a dumb yokel after all."

"Many thanks." Unfortunately, she couldn't see him push out his lower lip, but he felt more delighted than insulted anyway. "Of course, there could be a second man waiting upstairs. Once we've disabled the first, I can take it up with the next one." He felt very heroic.

"That's why you asked where we were!"

"Yes, we can only escape if nobody sees us climb through the trapdoor or overpower a second guard. In broad daylight, they'd raise an alarm right away, and Antef would catch us faster than we'd appreciate. When the first guard goes down, we can't hesitate or we'll raise suspicion."

"And what if two men come down here? Antef might want to question you right away, right here."

That would spoil their plan, but he didn't think that likely to happen. "Well, we'll find out. If the gods are on our side, one guard will come and there won't be anyone upstairs." Her sneering laugh dampened his hopes, but he added, "Well, at least we've got a plan."

Her warm hand felt for his and squeezed it. "Yes, and that's a lot."

It seemed to take forever until sounds filtered into their cell. The noise of footsteps on stone grew louder, leaving no doubt that someone was coming their way. He broke into a sweat. The first attempt had to work since they wouldn't get a second chance. He lifted the box, a solid piece of workmanship and quite heavy even without the sand. "Get ready," he whispered to Ouseret and took his position beside the door.

He could hear her walk over to the mound of sand and fill the little shovel. "Ready."

The steps sounded very close now. Hori shook his head since his ears rushed and wouldn't allow him to discern if one or two people approached. No talking, so hopefully... The bolt scrunched, and the next moment blinding light flooded through the crack. Of course, the man needed to illuminate his path through the underworld. Used to pitch black darkness, Hori barely managed to discern the guard was alone and carried a tray with both hands, bread and a jug on top. Then he scrunched his eyes shut. The next moment he heard a scream. Something cluttered to the ground and shattered. He blinked when water splashed his feet. It had worked so far. The man couldn't see because of the sand Ouseret had thrown at him! Hori leapt forward and slammed the box down on him. The guard staggered, lashed out in all directions and hit Hori's nose. First, he sensed blood tickle his upper lip, then a wave of pain crashed over him. He swayed, almost fell, but fought back the pain, huffing and puffing bubbles of blood. Once again, he swung the box at his opponent's head, and the man finally collapsed. "Now!" he called to Ouseret and allowed the pain back. Clenching his fists, he let the receding wave wash over him. When he managed to open his eyes again, Ouseret had grabbed the torch from a wall mount.

She stared at him. "You're bleeding!"

"It's nothing," he mumbled. "Let me go ahead."

Her slender body blocked his way. "If anyone sees you like this, they'll know something's wrong." She handed him the torch. "Hold this." Then she bent over and tore a strip of cloth from the seam of her dress and dipped it into the puddle on the floor. Cautiously, she dabbed at the blood on his lips and felt his nasal bone. What a soft touch she had. He moaned in happiness, and like an echo, the man on the floor groaned.

"Not broken," she stated.

"And it basically has stopped bleeding."

The guard stirred.

"Quick, we need to get out of here," Hori hissed and shoved Ouseret into the corridor. Then he shut and bolted the door. Relief seized him. At least that fellow couldn't harm them anymore. Of course, that left the question what awaited them upstairs. "I'll go ahead, you take the torch." Then realization hit him: he was unarmed! In his agony he hadn't thought of searching the unconscious man for weapons. And in their haste, he'd even left behind the box. Go back in there? Muffled shouts filtering through the door discouraged that approach. Too late. He was a dumb yokel after all. Better not to mention any of that to Ouseret.

The corridor was only a few feet long, and Hori saw no other chambers, only rough projections in the wall where they might once have tried to dig more cells into the rock but failed. Brushing his fingers over it confirmed his assessment: The rock crumbled in places. Was this dungeon built in ancient times? No, somehow it fit better with Antef's viciousness. He reached the stairs and took one step after the other until he could peek through the opening. Wary, he glanced over the edge and the folded bulrush mat, which would normally cover the door. Only a few shafts of light illuminated the corridor. In the patchwork of light and dark, he discerned an armed man leaning against a wall at some distance and looking the other way. Oh, damn! It would have been far too easy, of course, if they'd simply been able to walk out of here unhindered. And to top it off, the fellow had to stand so far away. How could he possibly get to him and overpower him without a weapon? He had to surprise him! He pulled in his head and stepped down to Ouseret. "Hand me the torch," he commanded. "Hide in the nook beside the stairs. When I tell you to run, you dash up and run for your life. Don't stop to wait for me."

"But…"

Hori shook his head. "At least one of us has to escape and find Nakhtmin and Muti and inform the king. Do what I say!"

He waited until she'd merged with the shadows, then he held the torch out of the opening and waved it, while keeping his head down. "Hey, I need a hand!" he called in a low voice.

Nothing. He peered over the edge once more. The guard hadn't heard him. Hori ducked again and shouted louder, while waving the torch.

This time he heard steps and something like a suppressed curse, followed by, "What is it now?"

Hori pulled down the torch and extinguished it on the wall. Darkness, almost as dense as in their cell, surrounded them, and that was good. When he deemed the man close enough, he held out his hand. "Help me up," he said.

The next moment, he felt a hand grab his, and Hori yanked, yanked hard.

About to lose his footing, the guard screamed. Hori's other hand clamped around his wrist, and he put all his weight in the final pull. The man came tumbling down. Hori squeezed against the wall, but the stairway was narrow. The guard flailed, trying to get a hold, and grasped Hori's ankle. No, no! The foot slipped out under him. All he could do was flip around, throw himself onto the steps and slide down on his belly. Ouch. He kicked at his opponent in despair, but the grip on his ankle didn't ease up until they hit bottom. At least, he landed softly on the stubborn fellow. Unfortunately, the fall hadn't harmed but enraged the guard—his hands immediately clamped around Hori's throat and squeezed.

"Now!" Hori managed to croak just in time, then tried to pull away those suffocating hands. He sensed the air move as Ouseret leapt over them. At least she'd make it to safety. The much stronger soldier pulled him over as if he weighed nothing then rolled on top of him. In the twilight filtering down through the hatch, Hori saw his eyes glow with triumph. The eyes! Hori lifted his arms to jam his thumbs into the sockets, but the guard realized what he was up to, straightened and pulled back his head—out of reach. Frantic, Hori felt around for something to use as a weapon, but he only fingered gravelly dust. What worked once might work again. He thrust the crumbs at his attacker, but he was already too weak. Without leaving any impact, the stone fragments trickled down on him. That was it. He was done. His limbs when limp.

That moment the grip around his throat loosened. He breathed precious air and new courage. However, he'd barely moved to fight back when the brute clamped both his wrists in one paw and slammed his right fist into Hori's face.

All went amazingly well. After a short search, Nakhtmin found an abandoned fishing boat among the reeds. The flood must have washed it up here. Not only did it look undamaged, but two paddles lay inside! Then luck fled him. The strong current made it impossible for him to row back to Muti. Of course, high tide had to arrive just now. His untrained arms couldn't beat it. At least he managed to get back ashore, so he pulled the craft along as he stalked through the mud. At long last, he recognized the access road, where Muti awaited him, pulled the boat a bit up the riverbank and helped her climb in. Oh boy, they caused quite some noise! Fortunately, the spies were either still searching for him or deaf, since nobody came running.

Despite the intimidating current, he dared to sit in the boat with Muti. He had to take his wife to safety—this close to their house, Antef's men could detect them anytime. As soon as he pushed away from the bank with one oar, he lost control. They flowed with the current and passed the basket makers' district before he could hold onto an overarching branch. His arms felt like they wanted to jump from their joints, but he somehow managed to maneuver the craft ashore.

"Phew, I thought we'd swoosh all the way to the Great Green." Muti sighed in relief.

"Just what we'd need!" He rubbed his sweaty neck. At least they should be safe for now, but they couldn't just stay here. Again, he waded through the mud, this time pulling the boat with Muti in it. If only he could shake off the fear Antef's soldiers might detect them any moment…

Breathless, Nakhtmin stomped along the wall of a large estate. The sludge tugged on his feet as if it wanted to grasp and swallow him. And the nomarch's men came ever closer. He heard their shouts. The river suddenly narrowed to a tunnel-like alley. He ran on and on, but stayed in place. Someone grabbed his shoulder. Nakhtmin screamed in terror.

"It's only me, Meseh," a voice said.

Nakhtmin jerked up and realized he'd gotten entangled in the folds of the linen sheet he'd used as a blanket; it practically entwined him. "A bad dream," he gasped.

"That's what I thought. You should get up." The basket maker cast a worried glance around.

Nakhtmin squinted against the light of the new day and saw first movement on the roofs around them. A suckling cried a few houses away and thus encouraged another child to join in.

"I'll be right down," he promised the old man and peeled off his bindings. Was Muti up already? With her injured foot she hadn't been able to climb up here, but slept on the bed downstairs, which the couple used during the cold season—or when the Resetyu, the southern winds, carried desert sand. Muti had declined his company since it would be stuffy enough for her alone in the chamber.

The basket maker's wife clambered up the ladder, bringing food from the pantry. When she saw him crouch there, she urged, "Hurry up!" Then she lit the fire in the cooking pit.

Her unease transferred to him. He really shouldn't be seen here. A stranger raised questions in a tight neighborhood like this. When they'd knocked at the elderly couple's door last night, they had only given them shelter after voicing serious concerns. They were already worried enough about Ouseret, whom they regarded as their foster child, and the fate of her friends from the residence was of less importance to them. Nakhtmin broke into a sweat, recalling the moment he'd stood at their door, Muti in his arms, fearing that they'd turn them away... He tried to shake off the nightmarish impressions that had followed him into his dreams.

He snatched his shendyt, which had dried overnight, and climbed down the ladder to find his darling awake but unable to get up. Dejected, he embraced her and wiped sweaty strands of hair from her face. "Let me take a look."

As far as he could see in the dim light, the ankle had swollen some more. Nakhtmin suppressed a curse. No wonder, though, after yesterday's exertions. Meseh brought him an oil lamp. In its shine, he could clearly see the violet discoloration. The strain of their flight had made it worse. She needed rest, but they weren't safe here. The Southern City was like a well-sealed jug, and Antef controlled the plug with his soldiers. With longing, he thought of the royal speedboats but doubted even those experienced boatmen would dare to brave the river at high tide. Even if they did, he couldn't request them without Antef learning about it. How could he get his palsied wife out of town? And then there was Hori. Could he simply abandon him? He groaned.

"What ails you, my husband?" Muti asked.

Through the hatch leading up to the roof, cooking smells drifted into the room and enticed Nakhtmin's nose. Meseh's wife descended and placed a bowl with bread, onions and fried fish between him and Muti before she climbed up again. In dismay, he glanced at the food. "We can't stay here, but I don't know where we can go or how we'd get there."

She bent forward and took his hand. "First you need to eat, then we'll figure out something."

If only he could share her confidence.

A little later, Meseh's wife left the house to sell her wares at the market. Nakhtmin understood that their sticking to everyday routine was essential so as not to raise suspicion, but when Meseh also readied himself to leave, dread filled him. Of course, the old folks couldn't offer them much in the way of protection, but still...

"I only need to cut new rush and will be back before the sun reaches its highest point. Bolt the door behind me and don't open it to anyone," the basket maker admonished them.

The small, little-aired room heated up fast. Sweat trickling down his back, Nakhtmin glanced up to the hatch in the roof with longing. No, too dangerous! Even down here, they barely dared to speak in normal voices. But then, what could they say to each other? They were stuck, and thus only the noises of the waking city filled the small house. Suddenly, a strange sound came from the door. Every muscle in his body tensed, a pulsating rush filled his ears. He must have imagined it. No, there it was again, a gentle knocking. Holding his breath, he looked at Muti. The thin wood of the door wouldn't keep out a man determined to enter.

"Who?" she mouthed.

He shrugged and gestured for her to lie down, then he spread the sheet over her. In the gloom, she probably wouldn't be detected right away. And what about him?

Now the person outside pulled on the door, but too gently for the bar to yield. Whoever was out there knew someone had to be at home—only the houses of the rich had locks, common folks could only afford bolts. Dear gods, the intruder would break down the door pretty soon. Frantic, he looked around but spotted no other nook or cranny he could slip into. So he grabbed a wooden stool and positioned himself next to the door, which would cover him when the fellow stormed in. With some luck, he'd be able to overpower him. At least if it was only one man... A thought crossed his mind: Wouldn't the nomarch's soldiers shout and demand access? He pressed his ear against the door and listened to the faint attempts of the stranger. The heavy pounding of his heart drowned out everything else, but then he thought he heard a name: Ouseret!

"Ouseret, is that you?" he asked, voice quivering, and heard Muti rustle the sheet.

Silence on the other side, then, "Yes! In the name of merciful Isis, open up!"

He pulled back the bar. As soon as the crack was large enough, the tall physician squeezed in, shut and bolted the door again. She'd come alone.

Muti pushed the sheet from her face and sat up. "Ouseret! Thank you, dear gods!"

"What are you two doing here?" she blurted.

Nakhtmin's joy over seeing her alive and kicking waned. "What's that supposed to mean? Where've you been all this time makes for a much better question. And where's Hori?"

"Hush, keep your voice down! Nobody must know that I'm here. Where's Meseh?"

Nakhtmin had to muster all his self-control or he'd have shaken her. Couldn't this foolhardy woman give him a proper reply at least this once? While Muti answered her question, he paced the room like a caged lion. Then he barked at her, "And now you'll tell us if you know anything about Hori!"

Regret showed in her face, or maybe it was only the gloom causing such an impression. "I'm afraid he didn't make it."

Fear clutched his heart. "Didn't make what? By Seth's testicles, tell us what's going on!"

She sat next to Muti on the bed and sagged. Faltering words trickled from her mouth. "The nomarch's soldiers intercepted me on the way to my parents' house and took me to the palace. That was yesterday—no, the day before. In a small chamber, Antef questioned me. He wanted to hear what you know and to whom you've passed on your knowledge."

"I hope you didn't tell him anything!" Muti interrupted before Nakhtmin could.

The usual contemptuous snort preceded her response. "What could I have told him? I hardly know anything. That was a little...dissatisfying for him, I believe.

He wasn't happy at all, so he sent me to the Chamber of Silence—that's a dungeon under the palace—as bait he said. And his first fish soon bit: Hori. But we broke out this morning." She described her adventurous escape, sneaking through the palace then the city, always in fear someone might recognize and stop her. "Hori was still fighting the second guard, who must have overpowered him," she ended miserably.

"And you simply left him there?" Nakhtmin called. "The man who loves you! I...you..." His indignation robbed him of words.

"Please, quiet down!" Muti admonished him.

The corners of Ouseret's mouth quivered and pulled down, but no tears welled up in her eyes. "That's what he wanted me to do. He said, 'Run and don't look back, one of us has to make it!' His words. Don't you think that if I'd seen a chance at all, I'd..." Her voice cracked, and she turned away.

His wife wrapped an arm around her and pulled her close. "You did well." Over her shoulder she cast an indignant look at Nakhtmin that said something like, 'See what you've done now!'

However, he felt far too outraged by Ouseret's cowardice to care.

Muti said, "At least now we know where he is."

"If he is still there and alive," Ouseret murmured. "Antef won't appreciate my escaping. He'll apply all his forces to catch us. And then he'll remove all our traces from the face of the earth." The words hung heavy in the stale air. Her head jerked around and she scrutinized him. "Why are you here?"

Muti relayed their adventure, and she nodded. "Smart of you."

He groaned. Unfathomable what would have happened if they hadn't escaped Antef's people last night. His Muti in a dark dungeon, awaiting certain death... With her injured ankle, flight would have been impossible. He too would have had to decide: Leave her behind and hope to rescue her later or die with her. The lump in his throat ached and made his voice sound dull. "I'm sorry, Ouseret. Can't have been easy for you to leave Hori behind."

She looked at him. "No, but it was our only chance. I hold him in high esteem for sacrificing himself for me..." She swallowed several times. "Oh, dear gods! Please protect him!"

"As long as we don't know better, he's still alive," Muti said with determination.

Her confidence instilled courage in him. "Yes, you're right. We have to do something. How can we save him?"

Ouseret laughed out, but it wasn't a happy sound. "Do you by any chance have an army hidden somewhere? We could use it to storm the palace. No matter where Hori is now, they're certainly guarding him well. Hm, Antef seems to think that you're spying for the king."

Nakhtmin rubbed his face in disbelief and settled next to the women on the bed. "How could he possibly think that? We just wanted to disclose the truth about Merwer's death!" Sudden hope filled him. "And when Hori explains that to him..."

Muti issued a noise somewhere between a sob and a laugh. "Oh dear, my husband is such a yokel!" With pity in her eyes, she stroked his cheek. "No, I take that back. You are simply a good person."

Should he feel insulted or flattered?

"Antef can't afford to let even one of us survive," Ouseret summarized the abominable truth. "Even if he believes Hori that your intentions were harmless, he now has to fear the pharaoh will hold him accountable for imprisoning us. And believe me, the last thing we want here in the south is the king poking his nose in our affairs."

It felt like she'd sparked a light in the darkness of his heart. Nakhtmin jumped up. "That's what it's all about, right? The affairs of the south."

She stared at him and knitted her eyebrows. "Possibly."

Before he could spin his thoughts any further, a knock at the door jarred him. But this time it was the sequence he'd agreed on with Meseh. Nakhtmin pulled back the bolt.

The basket maker entered and flinched at the presence of a third person in the room. Then he recognized Ouseret and embraced her with subdued cheer. "Oh, the wife will be so happy to see you, my girl!"

Nakhtmin wondered what name Meseh's wife actually had, but that wasn't important now. "Does Antef know where you've been staying since your return from the residence?"

Looking miserable, Ouseret nodded, and Nakhtmin hissed a curse he couldn't suppress. The nomarch would come looking for the escapee here first—and catch him and Muti as little extras. They had to leave as soon as possible!

WHERE TO NOW?

Day 12 of month Wepet-renpet in Akhet, the season of inundation

Agony. Hori remembered being in such a state before. Back then, long, slender fingers had taken care of him. "Ouseret…" Why couldn't he open his eyes?

"Oh, our guest is honoring us with his presence," a male voice scoffed.

Each tone sent waves of pain through Hori's skull. Instinctively, he squeezed his eyes shut, but that only increased his suffering. He wanted to touch his face, but his arms were tied. He could only lift them a little. And the memories returned with force. The Chamber of Silence, Ouseret! Had she managed to escape? Again he tried to open his eyes—in vain. "Who's there?" he squeezed out.

Somebody laughed, and it didn't sound nice at all. The same voice as before proclaimed, "You're in my power, and now you'll tell me everything you know, spy!"

Hori groaned. "Antef?" The nomarch not feeling the need to stay in the background boded ill for him even if there had been little doubt left about the man's evil intentions. "I'm no spy." His mouth was parched. Words didn't come easy. "Water, please."

Unintelligible whispers were followed by, "Give him something to drink. After all, we want to loosen his tongue."

Hori heard footsteps, then someone lifted his head a little and held a mug to his lips. Greedy, he drank. Much better. Where was he? No longer in the cell, since he lay on something soft. A cushioned cot? Then he had to be up in the palace somewhere, likely in one of the guestrooms in the wing with the trapdoor. Did they mean to torture him? Then his screams could be heard, but they might simply take him back down into the Chamber of Silence—what mockery that name was! Damn, he'd witnessed how blows with a stick had made the most obdurate villain talk. He wouldn't be able to bear the pain for long. Maybe he should simply tell Antef everything, the whole truth. But somehow he didn't believe the nomarch would care to hear about his unfulfilled love for Ouseret and his efforts to find Merwer's killer. This was about something else. What did Antef hope to learn from him? Perhaps if he pretended that he could and would find out anything for him… However, only the powerful man himself could tell Hori what he wanted to learn. He had to get Antef talking.

He drained the mug and licked his chapped lips. "Ask and I will answer," he said and blinked despite the pain. For a moment, he saw some light. Then he hadn't gone blind. His lids must have swollen after the battering he'd received.

Antef's voice sounded closer now. "So that's how you want to play the game? Oh well, fine with me, but be warned. If you lie or hesitate, you'll regret it. Did the king send you because of Merwer's death?"

The king? Why should his majesty care about the demise of a man in far-off Waset? "We did come here because of Merwer's death," he replied truthfully if a little on the evasive side.

Antef pulled up a chair and sat. Hori could sense the man bending over him, which raised the hair on his arms.

"Did his majesty send you and your physician friend to Waset to take Merwer's place?"

"Huh?" Hori croaked in confusion. The nomarch knew they were doctors and not traders.

"Don't take me for a fool!" Antef's voice remained level, which only made it sound more threatening. "I want to know if you were supposed to spy on me. Now that the pharaoh's man at my court has been…withdrawn, his majesty must be eager to install a new source of information, or two. After what lady Mutnofret boasted the other day, I had to assume that would be you and your colleague."

Merwer had been a spy in Senusret's employ? Hori's thoughts chased each other. If only his head wouldn't hurt so much! He recalled the king's request to keep their eyes peeled and their ears pricked during their travels in the southern nomes. Yes, his majesty had been concerned and apparently for a good reason. They'd experienced Djehutihotep's self-importance in Khemenu. Here in Waset, the nomarch acted less conspicuously and had fooled them. Antef was obviously the worst of the whole bunch! No wonder the king kept informers in distant parts of the Two Lands. Antef had probably seen through Merwer's cover a long time ago but didn't do anything against him. Thus, he could keep an eye on the king's man. After his death, someone he didn't know about yet would have to take Merwer's place. That was why Antef believed they were spying for Senusret. What a ridiculous idea! But why did he have Merwer killed if that only brought disadvantages and uncertainty? And why had Sanefer agreed to do it for him, son against father? He had to find out more!

"No spies!" he asserted. "We…we were supposed to find out if Merwer really died because of Nehesy's medicine. The king…he didn't quite trust the verdict, and we are excellent physicians…"

Antef blew air through his nose then clicked his tongue. "Imagine that. No spies, but the king has gotten wind of our dung heap. Hmmm."

A chair creaked. Hori's hand was grabbed and a finger pulled back to the point it hurt. "Did Merwer manage to send another message to the king before he died? Talk!"

Hori gasped. "Stop! You don't need to hurt me!" The grip eased. "No, no message. His majesty was…" Oh dear, he'd better consider carefully what tale he concocted! "He was suspicious because of the timing of the man's death. Therefore the investigation. Merwer had announced important information to come soon." His hand was released.

"Oh," the nomarch uttered.

Apparently Hori had guessed right. Antef was planning something, and Merwer had found out about it. However, before he could inform the king, the nomarch had taken care he kept such knowledge to himself. It had to be something so egregious, the pharaoh was not to learn about it at all cost. Therefore, Merwer's death wasn't supposed to look like an 'accident' since that would have raised suspicion. And a scapegoat needed to be arrested—Nehesy!

Hold on…there was something else…but what? Oh, right: *another* message— apparently the trader had already sent one, which never reached Itj-tawy. Antef had intercepted it, maybe exchanged it with one of harmless content? How? How had Merwer sent his messages? Realization hit him: via his trading ships! And those were accompanied by Sanefer, the man who killed his father. Antef had ordered Merwer's death, but the execution of the murder bore Sanefer's signature. It was carried out in a way that gave no cause for king or kenbet to suspect the contracted killer nor the one who'd hired him. "Sanefer is *your* spy!"

The man beside him chortled. "Congratulations! I overrated your reasoning power if you haven't figured that out any earlier than just now."

Unfortunately, Hori had to agree. One of the reasons for realigning his business: While Merwer had spent his time in Waset, Sanefer naturally had to be in the north if he wanted to be of use to his master. The murder had never been about love or profits, but treason. Betrayal of the ruler of the Two Lands! "And why wasn't I allowed to read the records of the kenbet? Why did the scribe Seni have to die?" he inquired.

"Don't pretend you didn't know I sent the king a modified copy!" Antef yelled, and his voice echoed painfully in Hori's head. "Why else would you have requested to see the original, ey?"

He groaned. "I never saw the duplicate. Only wanted to find out...ugh, my head hurts! I only wanted to find out who testified against Nehesy and what statements they made."

Antef gave a soft laugh. "Then the old hunchback died for nothing. Oh well, he was just a flyspeck."

Hori clenched his fists. If only he could lay his hands on the bastard! "Why modify the transcript?" he babbled to keep Antef talking.

"Oh well, you might as well die knowing everything. Sanefer, that idiot, let slip that he was in Abu when he received news of his father's death. That might have baffled the king since Sanefer had orders to take Merwer's message straight to the north, not head south first. I'd sent him there to inform nomarch Sarenput that our secret was safe and we could proceed as planned."

Secret? Plan? Slowly a picture formed. Merwer had sent his son to the king with an urgent message. But Sanefer gave the letter to Antef; together they'd changed it into a harmless report. Whatever Antef was up to, Sarenput of Ta-Seti was his accomplice, and he needed to learn that Merwer no longer posed a danger. While the ship set out on a slow journey north, Sanefer rushed south and informed Sarenput, well aware that his father might already lie on his deathbed. And a notice of his demise actually caught up with him in Abu. The young trader boarded a faster ship going north and arrived together with his freight at the royal residence, the falsified message in his pack. And then Sanefer slipped up in front of the kenbet. However, nobody noticed, since the judges present didn't know where Sanefer was supposed to go. Only the king could have suspected foul play. Oh, Antef had resumed talking. "Sorry, what was that?"

"Where are your friends right now, you imbecile?" the nomarch barked.

Terror struck Hori. Nakhtmin. And Muti. He must not betray them! Actually, he didn't really know where they might be now. Certainly not at the estate, which Antef would have searched thoroughly already. They must have managed to escape. Oh, that was an excellent idea! He suppressed a smile and said, "They departed yesterday early in the morning, heading for the residence."

"What?" The chair toppled over.

Rough hands grabbed Hori's shoulders and shook him. He whimpered in pain and felt nauseous. At the last moment he turned his head toward Antef and threw up.

"Damn, what a disgusting mess!" The nomarch jumped back, and the hands released Hori.

He fought against the grin pulling on the corners of his mouth despite it all. At least he'd gotten a tiny revenge. The wretched dog must have stormed from the room. Hori heard him give his men orders at quite some distance. A little later, someone removed the ties from his hands and legs. He was lifted onto a stretcher and carried into another room, where he was fettered to another cot before the idea to attempt escape even entered his heart. However, he was in no condition to run and fight. Although it was probably not meant as a courtesy to him, he appreciated that they didn't leave him lying in his vomit. The noble ruler certainly wouldn't want to befoul his sandals when he tormented him again. Befoul sandals, how fitting! Hori snorted a desperate laugh.

The door slammed shut. They must have left him alone. After initial relief, despair seized him. What would happen next? Where were Nakhtmin and Muti? If only they'd given him more to drink. Pain raged in his skull, and the rest of his body had taken quite a few blows as well. The brute down in the dungeon must have been outraged because he'd gulled him.

He tore at his fetters, but they didn't yield. His last hope lay with his friends and Ouseret. Could they rescue him? He groaned. Even if they'd escaped Antef's soldiers, it would take them days to reach the residence. And here in Waset, he couldn't expect any help. Dear gods, oh Maat! Please let at least my friends get away, he pleaded in silence.

"We don't want to endanger you and your wife," Nakhtmin assured the concerned-looking basket maker. "However, I don't know where we can turn. Do you know someone willing to help us?"

Meseh scratched his scalp. "The roads leading north and south are blocked. I couldn't even get to my usual spot at the river, where I like to cut the bulrush. And the nomarch commands many armed men. If he doesn't find you here, he'll have them search one house after the other."

No need to spell it out for Nakhtmin. They probably wouldn't find even one cranny in all of Waset where they'd be safe. And it was too late for them to get out of the city. He groaned. "We somehow need to inform Senusret about what's going on here."

Ouseret snorted. "What good will that do? The king is far away, and before a message reaches—"

"Pigeons!" Muti exclaimed.

Just as baffled as the others, Nakhtmin stared at her, then he remembered. "Of course, the pigeons! Except…how do we get our hands on one?" He thought of the birds at the Amun temple in Itj-tawy and Ameny…

"Amunhotep!" Muti and he called in unison.

Ouseret placed her hands on her hips. "Can someone explain to me what you're talking about?"

Muti grinned. "All the large temples of the Two Lands keep pigeons—or rather exchange pigeons."

Ouseret shrugged. "So what?"

"The sender marks it with his color, then releases the bird. These animals always fly back to the loft where they hatched. Let's say we release a pigeon originating from Itj-tawy, but carrying the color of Waset, the king will know that the Amun temple of the Southern City needs his immediate attention and he'll send someone."

Nakhtmin watched Ouseret's features as she worked out the complicated system. She nodded. "It's a shame though that we can't tell the pharaoh what exactly is going on here. What if he thinks it's about some minor issue and only sends one man?"

Good point. Nakhtmin groaned. For them to free Hori and get out of Waset, the king would have to mobilize an army. Would he do that just because a pigeon arrived? Maybe two or three in quick succession…? They were running out of time. "We can think about that later. First, we have to get out of here. Will Amunhotep give us shelter?" Remembering his churlish behavior toward the old man, hot shame filled him.

"We should have confided in him right away." Muti sounded calm, but he sensed the reproach acutely.

"Yes, I messed up there. We don't have a choice now; Amunhotep is our only hope for refuge."

"And not the worst," Ouseret agreed. "Even Antef respects the high priest. He won't dare to have his house stormed. Not so soon anyway."

Nakhtmin breathed a little easier. Now he only had to find a way to get Muti out of here unnoticed, hide with the two women for a few hours until Amunhotep would return home from the temple then convince the old man to give them shelter.

How did she do that? Gracefully, Ouseret walked ahead of him, balancing a jug on her head and only supporting it with one hand. The other held the front handle of a large basket, in which Muti was hiding. Nakhtmin wore a fishing net around his shoulders that covered the lower half of his face. Apart from that, he only had to carry the back end of the wicker chest but found it hard to keep up with Ouseret.

All of a sudden, her back went rigid, and she turned her head slightly. "Two soldiers are heading our way."

Nakhtmin started although he'd anticipated such an encounter. "Don't look directly at them." He peered around Ouseret and saw the fellows approach. They chatted away and didn't pay much attention to their surroundings. Nakhtmin released the breath he'd been holding. Apparently, they weren't part of a search team, or Antef was in no hurry to scour the city for them. After all, he knew they couldn't go anywhere. Now the two men pushed past Ouseret and forced her as well as Nakhtmin to step aside. One of them even jostled him. His heart wanted to jump out of his throat, but the soldiers didn't seem surprised to see a fisherman at high tide. If someone did question him, he'd claim he wanted to mend the net. At least these minions moved on without bothering them. Didn't bear thinking what would've happened if they'd wanted to take a look inside the basket!

Nakhtmin couldn't thank Meseh enough for the things he'd provided for them to use as camouflage—particularly for Muti. The old man had to borrow the large basket from a colleague, though, because he usually didn't make such big containers. And the netting he got from a fisherman he was friends with and for whose boathouse they were heading now. When the skewed shed built of cane near the waterfront came into view, Nakhtmin noticed with relief they weren't far from Amunhotep's estate. Hopefully, they could hide there until nightfall without being bothered by anyone. Cautious, he set down his end of the basket and took the jug from Ouseret. They'd certainly appreciate the water it contained. Nakhtmin opened the door and peered inside. A fishing boat used up almost all the space, but that was to be expected. At least they could get comfortable in the dinghy made of papyrus bundles. The whole wall facing the river also served as a gate and could be opened to launch the boat with ease. At the moment, the gate was barred from inside.

Together they pushed the chest inside, and he closed the door to the street. Ouseret lifted the basket's lid.

In the sparse light, Nakhtmin saw the sweaty face of his wife. "You can come out now, darling. We are safe here."

They helped her since she'd gone all stiff from cowering inside for so long. The women climbed into the boat, while he unbolted the large gate and opened it a crack.

Muti lifted her head. "Why are you doing that?"

"As an escape route if danger threatens from the street." The same moment he realized his mistake. Muti couldn't take flight. They'd have to push the boat into the water and trust the river god would show mercy.

"At least we're getting some fresh air," Ouseret's deep voice rang from the gloom.

It really was fairly stuffy in here. He ladled water from the jug and handed it to Muti.

"Thanks. Why don't you drill a spy hole into the wall or door to the street?" she suggested.

"Right, one of us should keep watch at all times," Ouseret agreed. "You'll take the first shift."

Sighing, Nakhtmin accepted his lot. Fortunately, the wickerwork was so brittle he found it easy to make a small opening with his fingers. After a while, he glanced back at the women and found them fast asleep. Just great! The day turned out a long and boring one for him. Far too often, he dozed off while standing there, but the rustle of the reed roof woke him every time. Hardly anyone milled about the path to the river, probably a good sign. Occasionally, he heard a dog bark or a child scream farther away, while nothing hinted at soldiers bothering the inhabitants of Waset.

"Antef will likely wait until dusk," Ouseret suddenly said.

Nakhtmin flinched. It had been silent for so long. "Why do you think so?"

"Because everyone's at home then."

"Hm." Could be.

"My guess is that his men have surrounded the city so that nobody can slip out. Thus he can search house after house without hurry."

"You're worried about Meseh."

"Of course." The white of her eyes glowed when she looked at him.

Even now, she seemed far too composed. This mysterious woman puzzled Nakhtmin once again. Hard to imagine that she'd ever give in to desire. Poor Hori. Oh, but his friend might soon be a dead man and melting Ouseret's heart the least of his worries. How could he save Hori? A thought formed in his mind.

"Why are you grinning?" Ouseret asked.

"Nothing. I'll tell you later." Actually, the idea was so ingenious he could hardly wait to get to Amunhotep.

At long last, dusk encroached on the river. The netting wrapped over his shoulders, Nakhtmin strolled casually down the waterfront promenade. Only his sweaty hands betrayed his fear someone might see and recognize him. And he worried about Muti, whom he'd left behind in Ouseret's care. Two women up against the nomarch's militia...

The path led into the street where Amunhotep's estate was located. Now, Nakhtmin wasn't alone anymore. Craftsmen headed for their quarters, and the palanquins of the rich rocked toward the large houses at the river. He let the net slide to the ground and pushed it under a bush. Hopefully nobody would steal it and rob the fisherman of his means to make a living. But if he showed up in such a disguise, Amunhotep's servant would likely send him away. He smoothed his shendyt—which looked anything but impressive—and ran his fingers through the strands of his wig. Well, that was all he could do. Hopefully, Amunhotep's doorman wouldn't require a lengthy explanation. He sent a prayer to all gods known to him then knocked on the prophet's door.

It opened right away. A servant cast him a suspicious look, but then he recognized Nakhtmin. "You were the guest of my master a few days ago."

Relief flooded him. He'd have loved to dash past the man and get off the street, but he pulled himself together. "That's right. Today, I come without invitation but on urgent business."

With an inviting gesture, the servant stepped aside. "The venerable Amunhotep is at home."

AN UNEXPECTED ALLY

Day 12 of month Wepet-renpet in Akhet, the season of inundation

"...worse injuries than we thought...hours unconscious—"

Hori couldn't hear more before the man talking moved away from the door. Antef gave orders but he didn't understand them. In any case, it had been a smart idea to feign unconsciousness as soon as the guards' steps had announced their approach. And he had indeed dozed off again and again—what else could he do? Now, he felt much better. Only a few hours had passed since Antef interrogated him. The door closed. Alone again, he blinked open his right eye, but his sight remained hazy. As if the gods meant to make up for his loss of sight, he heard very acutely. A fly buzzed in through one of the ventilation slits and settled on Hori's nose. Instinctively, he wanted to chase it away, but his ties prevented it. Wrinkling his nose didn't impress the annoying insect at all, instead the slight move caused him new pain. "Oh, you know that I'm defenseless, don't you?" he whispered.

As if to mock him, the tiny feet scurried all over the landscape of his face. He thought he could even feel the greedy palp tasting the liquid oozing from his lids and shivered. Many inhabitants of the Two Lands suffered from eye diseases often ending in blindness—caused by flies. The black lining usually offered protection, but nobody had been so accommodating as to take care of his makeup. In agony, he turned his head and tried to shake off the beast, but it stuck to his skin like syrup. Still struggling, he heard noises outside. Somebody was coming! If only he could keep acting unconscious! That moment, the fly took off. Thank you, gods! This time, they didn't just glance into the room; steps approached his cot.

"Take care of his injuries but don't untie him!" a gruff voice ordered from the hallway. "The man's dangerous." The door closed.

Hori kept pretending to sleep.

"I'm Ipuwer, your doctor." The voice sounded young and pleasant. "Can you hear me?"

Better not take a risk.

The physician snorted. "Oh well, then I'll just keep talking. Oh boy, they really worked you over." He bent close to Hori's ear. "You're Ouseret's friend, right?"

Unable to resist, he whispered back, "Yes." The next moment, he cursed himself. Just because the physician acted trustworthy, that didn't imply he meant well. But he couldn't have kept up the act once the man touched his wounds anyway.

Ipuwer gave a slight laugh. "I'm glad to finally meet you."

Had Ouseret told this fellow about him? Hope flooded him. "Have you seen Ouseret? Was she able to get away?"

"Get away? I don't understand...Was she here as well?"

Hori uttered a curse. Could this be a particularly clever method to sound him out? But to what avail? The nomarch knew of Ouseret's escape. Really a friend? He didn't have much to lose. "Listen, Antef keeps me prisoner. If you care about Ouseret, help me get out of here. Otherwise just tend to my wounds and leave me alone."

Silence, then Ipuwer said, "You've picked a powerful enemy in Antef."

As if he hadn't figured that out already! "Then you are going to help me?"

"I...um...I'll take care of your injuries. Not many people in Waset dare to defy him, and those who do regret it pretty soon."

Oh, so Antef had made it a habit to make unwanted individuals disappear, and everyone knew about it. Ipuwer was a damn coward! Hori suppressed the tears of disappointment welling up in him. What kind of a friend was he? Likely, his interest in Ouseret was mostly stirred by his loins, while he wouldn't risk his own wellbeing for her. He blinked but couldn't see much. How he'd love to beat up the man!

"Whoa, stop fidgeting and let me see," he physician discouraged his efforts. Soon cooling pads lay on both lids, and Ipuwer's skilled fingers turned to his nose. "No fracture. Do you feel pain anywhere else?"

"Ribs," Hori squeezed out between clenched teeth. "And I'm thirsty."

The doctor felt his chest. "Yes, some nice bruises but nothing serious. Hm..." He paused before continuing, "I'll tell the nomarch several of your ribs are fractured and your condition is serious."

How would such a lie help him?

Before he could ask, Ipuwer explained, "He won't have you guarded so closely if he thinks you incapacitated."

"Thanks," Hori mumbled, still confused. Because of the fetters, he really couldn't move, and as long as he couldn't see, an escape was out of the question. "Do you know where Ouseret might be now? Antef had us both arrested, but she managed to get away this morning."

Instead of a reply, he heard the man handle something. Water being poured into a mug. "Can you lift your head a little? Yes, that works."

Hori gulped greedily. This might be his last drink for a long time. Fortunately, Antef still hoped to get information from him or else they'd simply have let him die.

Again that subdued laugh. "According to rumor, Antef's personal guards marched north in haste this morning. The nomarch seems to believe she's already half way to the royal residence. Is that so?"

Hori relaxed. Then Antef had fallen for his ruse when he claimed Nakhtmin and Muti had fled north. Now he could only hope that it was not true since in that case, he'd have sent soldiers after them. No, Nakhtmin wouldn't abandon him. But where could Ouseret be hiding? She was at home here; she'd now hiding places... Oh, no! He'd forgotten all about Muti's sprained ankle, and his friends didn't know their way around Waset. "Have you heard anything about my companions?" he asked, ignoring Ipuwer's question. He couldn't really trust him yet.

"You mean the other physician and the daughter of the Amun prophet? No."

He took a breath of relief. If Antef had caught them, Hori would probably have noticed some ruckus, unless there were more secret prisons. All of a sudden, he felt an urge. "Um, I need to piss."

Ipuwer giggled. "Well, I'm not supposed to untie you, but I doubt you can hit the chamber pot lying on your back. Hold on." he loosened the ties of one hand and one leg, then he rolled him onto his side.

Hori groaned although the pain was bearable. While passing his water, he wondered again whether he could trust the physician. Did he have a choice? He wasn't exactly looking at an abundance of candidates vying for the position as his ally.

"What's your relationship to Ouseret?" he asked. "At the House of Life, she didn't seem very popular, and she never mentioned you."

Ipuwer didn't say anything but set down the chamber pot. Hori wished he could read the man's face.

"We studied together, graduated the same year," the young doctor finally said. "As the only woman in class, it hadn't been easy for her."

Studying together could foster close relationships—but also hostility as he knew all too well. "You mean they didn't respect her?"

The scraping noise sounded as if Ipuwer scratched his neck. "You could say that…" He paused and sighed. When he continued, determination rang in his voice, and Hori knew he wouldn't try to deceive him. "No, far worse! You know her, she's a desirable woman—and she wasn't engaged yet. They…they…"

"They what? Come on, spit it out."

Now, pain carried in Ipuwer's voice. "One day, three other students lured Ouseret into one of the treatment rooms. By pure chance, I walked past the closed door and heard her scream." He gave an embarrassed laugh. "I realized those weren't cries of agony but cries for help. I barged in. Two were holding her and the third…"

Hori groaned in anguish.

Ipuwer swallowed audibly. "I was too late. No idea for how long they'd been at it already."

Horrifying images tormented Hori. Had one after the other taken his darling? No wonder, she shied from every touch! "But she's so strong!" Not only physically, but in her soul. Rape was an abominable crime and for good reason punished by death. The victims often suffered their whole life. Ouseret had never appeared like a victim to him, though.

"Oh, she found a way to take revenge," Ipuwer said and giggled. "She couldn't press charges since the three were sons of Antef's closest friends. Instead, she secretly administered castor oil to them—on the day we had to take our exams."

Hori burst out laughing. "No way! She didn't!"

"Sure did. You should have seen those bastards when their intestines started gurgling. Every one of them soiled himself in front of the examiners because they didn't dare to run to the privy."

Which would have equaled failing the test. Hori giggled when he thought of who they'd been. "The sons of flunkies would have flunked the exam. I'd have loved to see that," he gasped. "And then? They must have guessed who got them in trouble."

"Sure." Ipuwer sounded smug. "And one of them was stupid enough to complain to Bakenamun."

"Oh. And?"

"Well, he had to explain why he suspected Ouseret—and so he confessed his own crime. Probably thought nothing would befall him."

Hori took a sharp breath. "By Sekhmet! What happened then?"

"The venerable principal of physicians consulted the first prophet of Amun and the head of the House of Life, and they agreed to ban all three from the temple. Forever."

"Phew." Not exactly the punishment they'd deserved but a harsh one. "Antef didn't object?"

"Not even he would interfere with affairs of the Amun temple. Not yet anyway. And it really did Ouseret well, particularly since she didn't have to see the villains every day. But she isn't the same, it changed her. She actually never wanted to get married, but soon after the rape, Nehesy announced the engagement of his daughter to that trader's son. Well, at least that spared her further unwanted attention."

Then her betrothal mostly served to protect her? Ouseret must have wanted him to believe she'd loved Sanefer and likely lain with him. What had she said? 'Our relationship was never like that, never passionate.' No, not likely.

"If only she hadn't acted so haughtily. I heard the three talk about her before it happened. That she wasn't really a woman, and someone should check... Albeit I never thought they'd dare. Nothing but the twaddle of spoiled young men..."

Hori clenched his fists, wanted to demand their names, but what good would that do? Then he felt like shaking Ipuwer. He could have prevented it! However, the fellow already blamed himself enough, and at least he'd been a friend to Ouseret during that difficult time. Couldn't have been easy, and Hori wouldn't have wanted to trade places with him back then. He recalled his encounters with Ouseret. So often, she'd shied from him, a courtier's son just like her three tormentors. What could she expect from him? He concentrated on Ipuwer again.

"...to me. She said she was pregnant and asked for my help."

"Dear gods, as if she didn't have enough problems already!" Although usually the very idea of an abortion made him feel sick, he understood why Ouseret wanted it. Giving birth to the child of one of her rapists, and not even knowing whose it was—unthinkable! "Did you do it?"

"How could I have refused? She'd never have confided in anyone else, and I knew she'd have done it herself, without supervision. You know how proud she is."

Oh yes, and it seemed like a miracle after all she'd been through. What a pity that she picked Antef's spy as her protector, probably just because he didn't desire her. Genuine feelings for her wouldn't have allowed him to make Nehesy take the fall for the murder of Merwer. Hori took a deep breath. "Thanks for telling me." She'd never have entrusted him with the awful story. "And thanks for having been her friend. Do you know Meseh, the basket maker?"

"A little. I know that she was staying at his house. You think she's there?"

"No, definitely not." He paused. Could he risk getting the old man and his wife in danger? If Ouseret trusted Ipuwer, he should too. "However, he might know where she went. Should you meet her there, please tell her to find my friends and in—" No, he couldn't ask her to do that. She was wanted, too, and in contrast to Muti and Nakhtmin, people knew her. "No, please, I need *you* to look for my friends. They must be hiding somewhere, but Antef's—"

The door was opened. "Hey, what's taking so long? You're supposed to fix him up and not stay by his side until he's fully recovered!"

"Almost done," Ipuwer called. The door slammed shut, and he bent closer. "Listen, I'll see what I can do for your friends. And for you. I'll only wrap the ties loosely around your limbs. Here."

Hori felt something hard and metallic against his forearm and hastened to shove it under his body. A scalpel? "Thanks," he whispered. "Don't worry, I won't try anything until I can see. But it'll feel nice to be able to walk around during the night."

"I'll come back tomorrow," the physician promised.

Restless, Nakhtmin paced behind the gate and listened to the noises of the night while still hoping for the best. Finally, he heard the scurrying feet of the returning palanquin bearers. One shout, and the gatekeeper opened. Sighing with relief, Nakhtmin saw Muti's face poke out between the drawn curtains. They were safe!

Now he could finally accept Amunhotep's friendly offer to wash the sweat of a long day from his body. The cold water was a pleasure! Wrapped in fresh linen, he joined their host. "How can I thank you? You're putting yourself in harm's way by giving us shelter. I…I'm ashamed of my earlier distrust toward you. Please accept my apologies." Besides regret, Nakhtmin also felt anger at himself. They'd have been spared quite some troubles if he'd trusted the first prophet right away!

The left corner of Amunhotep's mouth pulled into a smug smile. "You are forgiven. You didn't know Ameny once was my favorite student and has been my closest friend for years now."

"But I *should* have known—because of the present." Nakhtmin sighed. At least the old man didn't hold it against him. "We don't want to endanger you and yours in any way, but—"

The first prophet placed a hand on his forearm. "I'm old. Too old to be afraid of that nomarch any longer. Don't you worry. How can I help you?"

The prophet was amazing! Nakhtmin grinned with joy, dropped all formalities and politeness. "First off, are all your servants trustworthy? I mean…" Now he did feel uneasy after all. "Could one of them be tempted to tell Antef about us staying at your place?" He scrutinized the girl serving her master and his unannounced guests the meal.

Amunhotep smiled with understanding. "You can trust them under all circumstances, because I do so, too."

That had to suffice. Now the two women emerged from the house, Muti leaning on one of Amunhotep's walking sticks, and joined them.

After the meal, Nakhtmin sat back to savor the feeling of a full stomach and smiled at his wife. "Better?"

"Much better. And now we should tell Amunhotep what this is all about."

Nakhtmin nodded and started his report with why they'd wanted to investigate Merwer's death.

Amunhotep soon interrupted him. "I knew Merwer. His death must have been a hard blow for his majesty. You're acting on his orders?"

He stared at the priest. "His ma—? What do you mean? No!"

Amunhotep seemed just as confused. "Why then an investigation?"

Ouseret explained in her deep voice, "Because my father was his physician and got convicted for the murder. However, he didn't do it."

"We act of our own accord to help Ouseret," Muti confirmed. "But tell us, wise Amunhotep, what do you know about Merwer? Enlighten us."

The old man shook his head in disbelief. "Well then…now that Merwer's dead, it won't hurt if I tell you he was the king's informer in the Southern City."

"His spy!" Nakhtmin blurted and finally saw things fall into place. "And I suspected he'd bribed you and other priests!" A new wave of shame overpowered him. How could he have believed such a thing? "That priest of Khonsu, Kawab, hinted at corruption. But I have no idea what the payments may have been for. Did they even exist?"

"Oh, they existed. Kawab! Spittle licking creature of his master Antef! I should have expected him to snoop around behind our backs. The gold came from the pharaoh's coffers, intended to assure the loyalty of the militia leaders to the ruler of the Two Lands and that of the minor nomarchs in the area. It was less conspicuous to distribute the funds via the temple and our domains. Merwer couldn't be exposed. I'm afraid our efforts were in vain, though, or Antef's coffers were deeper than those of the king. And judging by what you've told me, the nomarch had seen through Merwer's activities. Shortly before his death, Merwer found out the mightiest men in the south, Antef of Waset and Sarenput of Ta-Seti were conspiring. Secret garrisons in secluded spots throughout the nomes, new recruits… They mean to usurp the whole south and then challenge the king. They've probably achieved their first goal already if the scarce reports from our sister temples are accurate, and the latter should be imminent. It's become difficult to receive or send messages. Apparently, Merwer didn't manage to send his warning to the residence before his demise, or it was intercepted."

In Nakhtmin's heart thoughts swirled. Amunhotep talked of insurrection and high treason! What had he gotten his wife into? He cast a desperate glance at Muti. Damn Hori, damn Ouseret! It couldn't be true, must not! Then he realized why it was impossible. He bent forward. "But Merwer's son killed him, not Antef. The scars on Sanefer's hands are sure signs," he exclaimed in relief. No conspiracy at the highest level.

Amunhotep granted him a sympathetic smile. "Just what I feared. I warned Merwer his son might have changed allegiances. He's been at the palace a little too frequently, undertook secret trips south when he should have accompanied his father's freight. That confirms my suspicion. Merwer's message never reached his majesty."

Nakhtmin moaned and his gaze traveled to Ouseret, who just sat there calm and composed. How could she? "Your fiancé!" he exclaimed. "And you didn't notice anything?" To his satisfaction, she paled.

"We were never really close," she blurted. "Didn't I tell you that he only recently showed me his true face?"

Muti also stared at her with reproach. "No, you didn't exactly put it that way. In general, you shared very little with us, considering that you supposedly care so much about your father."

Before Ouseret could retort, the prophet raised his hands in an appeasing gesture. "Now that Sanefer's crimes are evident, the important question is what we should do with our knowledge." He shook his aged head dejectedly. "When the rent collectors of our temple returned from the countryside, they told me Antef's soldiers have encircled the city. Nobody can leave. I'm afraid the revolt against the north is imminent. The renegade nomarchs will take advantage of the high tide, the king's ignorance and their military superiority. And we can't warn his majesty!"

Nakhtmin decided this was the right time to present his idea. "Maybe we can."

Both women stared at him. "The pigeons?" Ouseret asked.

"Yes, the pigeons. You tie colored ribbons around their legs, right?" Amunhotep couldn't do more than nod, because Nakhtmin rushed on in his growing excitement. "We could add a slip of papyrus with a message to the cloth strip. It would have to be short and explicit. The king would learn what's going on here. He could send his troops south!" Out of breath, he paused.

Understanding conquered Amunhotep's features. "Of course! Why didn't anybody think of this earlier?"

Muti took Nakhtmin's hand and squeezed. "That, my husband, is truly a smart idea!"

Nakhtmin beamed. "You think so? Yes, you might be right."

Ouseret nodded gravely. "I don't know if that will save Hori, but at least we can help preserve the unity of the Two Lands."

FOR BETTER OR WORSE

Day 13 of month Wepet-renpet in Akhet, the season of inundation

"I've brought you something to eat," Ipuwer announced the next morning. "How are you?"

Hori grinned. "Weak with hunger, otherwise much better." At night he'd untied his bonds and tested the firmness of his limbs. Another day's rest and he could attempt an escape, provided he managed to open his eyes by then. "Would you please take off the bandages?"

Soon after, Hori blinked. The right eye opened a crack, he could see! A little blurred, but his vision should clear. Gradually, the features of his doctor emerged from the fog: a chubby young man whose broad face showed an almost as broad grin. Hey, this was the same fellow who'd tipped him off at the House of Life where to find Ouseret. How lucky that Antef chose him of all physicians!

"And?"

"Your treatment worked wonders, thank you. Thank you for everything! Hold on." Light filtered through the left lid, but the swelling was still more prominent. At least he could see something. "Oh, it's so nice not be blind any longer."

"You certainly seem more sprightly." Ipuwer paused a moment. "You'd best not let anyone but me realize you're on the mend. On my way to see you, Antef asked when he can pump you for information again. I won't be able to put him off much longer."

"Goats' droppings! Then I must do it tonight. Do you think you can convince him to wait until tomorrow?"

Deep furrows creased Ipuwer's brow. "I'll try, but the nomarch is agitated. Something's going on. His men are scouring the city, presumably for Ouseret and your friends."

Antef must have seen through his subterfuge by now, no longer believing Nakhtmin and Muti had left the Southern City. Hori didn't care to imagine how the nomarch would make him suffer for his lie and a day's fruitless search outside of Waset. Hopefully, Hori's alleged broken ribs would spare him blows with the rod, but there were less damaging ways to make someone talk. Though pretty harmless, getting his finger bent had hurt immensely. In his mind, Hori heard bones break and joints snap out of their sockets, and he grimaced. He had to elude Antef's vengeance before any such thing happened to him. If only he knew what the nomarch was planning. "Do you have any idea what this is all about?"

Ipuwer shrugged his shoulders. "I have no answer for you, but I'm sure nothing good will come of it." He turned his head toward the door, but all was quiet there. "Lately, more and more soldiers have come into the city. Antef checks everyone arriving as if he fears an enemy's invasion."

An invasion or evasion? Whatever the nomarch was up to must be big and directed against the pharaoh. Hori swallowed. Like pretty much everybody, he knew the story of the murder of King Amenemhet, founder of this dynasty. Antef couldn't possibly strive to harm the divine person of the pharaoh! Hori's belly growled.

Without a word, Ipuwer took half a flat bread from his bag as well as two small onions wrapped in lettuce leaves.

"Thank you." He devoured the food.

Ipuwer carefully collected the crumbs and hid them in the bag. "We don't want anyone to wonder where those came from."

Hori untied the remaining fetter on his leg and squatted on the chamber pot. "Hm, it's getting pretty full," he said in embarrassment then shrugged. "Oh well, it'll have to do until night comes. Then I'm out of here." He placed a piece of cloth over the pot to contain the stench somewhat.

"Talking of which…" Ipuwer walked over to the door and listened. "All quiet out there. You're lucky these rooms can't be locked from outside." They both gazed at the bolt on the inside. "However, there's always a guard close to the door and a second one keeps watch at the beginning of the corridor. Probably so that nobody ventures in here. I have no idea what it's like at night, though."

"At least one of them will keep watch, I assume."

"Yes, that's what I fear as well, although they think you injured and bound."

"I'm just glad they didn't take me down into the dungeon. From there an escape would be impossible." Normally, perpetrators were kept at the Medjay's office until their trial, but he hadn't committed any crime. Antef wouldn't want to risk Hori telling one of the lawmen what he knew since he couldn't be sure of their loyalty. He stretched out on the cot and let his new friend tie him up again on the side facing the door. On the wall side, he could easily slip out of the loosely wrapped fetters. That only left the guards as obstacles. Overpowering one, maybe two men… He wished he had more than a small scalpel. "What about the palace gates?" Did he hear steps in the corridor? He stared at the door.

Ipuwer must have heard the noises as well and quickly placed pads with fresh ointment on Hori's eyes. Then he wrapped a linen bandage around his head. "The palace gates?" he hissed. "Locked on the inside and guarded. I doubt you'd be able to move the massive wooden bar on your own."

Hori recalled the gigantic double gate. Even if he succeeded, he'd probably make a lot of noise in the process.

A knock at the door.

"Almost done!" the physician called and in a low tone added, "Listen, I've heard about a small gate in the wing where the clerks have their offices, close to the palace archive."

"Oh, I know where that is!" Hori said.

Before Ipuwer opened the door, he whispered, "Good luck!"

As soon as he'd left, Hori realized he should have warned the fellow. He too might be in danger after Hori's escape. Hopefully, Ipuwer was well aware of that!

To his relief, Hori remained untroubled for the rest of the day. Ipuwer must have warned Antef in a very convincing manner what consequences an intense interrogation might have. Hori spent most of the time in light slumber. Only when he thought it had to be well after midnight, the time when people were soundest asleep, did he get to work. He quickly removed the fetters then took off the bandage around his head. Since his eyes were used to the darkness, it didn't take long for him to make out the contours of furniture in the faint moonlight. He reached under the straw sack and retrieved the bronze blade.

With utmost caution, he opened the door a crack and peered into the corridor il-luminated by a torch. Nearby, a man was leaning against the wall, snoring. Hori's right hand clutched the scalpel, then he hesitated. Would Maat approve of him killing his guard? He had to disable the man fast and without a noise. A stab to the heart…? But his victim was helpless. No, he couldn't bring himself to perform such an atrocity. His gaze wandered through the room, and he spotted a dark shape on the little table. A vase? He lifted the object. Yes, an ornamental vase of alabas-ter or some other stone—heavy but not too unwieldy. Hori calculated the risk. If he hit the guard with that, the man might collapse and lie unconscious without anyone hearing anything—in the best case scenario. Of course, such a blow to the head could kill, but likely the man would survive. With less luck, he might not hit the guard right and would be doomed. However, the man was asleep. Hori could take his time and aim well. Better than the knife.

He slipped through the door and approached the armed sleepyhead. In time with his breathing, something blinked on the man's belt—a dagger! And a spear leaned against the wall, better weapons than the tiny knife. He felt much safer already. Still, his hands were slippery with sweat when he lifted the vase. What if he simp-ly crept past the man? Too risky. If he made the faintest noise, Hori would have to take on a trained soldier, who'd raise an alarm. One step and the next. He felt the man's regular breath brush over his shoulder. Now!

With a dull noise, the stone vase crashed onto his victim's head. Noiselessly, the man slid down the wall. He was still breathing! Thank you, gods! Hopefully, he'd be out for a while. With trembling fingers, Hori pulled the dagger from the belt and grabbed the spear. Then he closed the door to his former prison so as not to announce his flight.

His bare feet made no noise on the floor. Reaching the end of the corridor, he peered into the large antechamber of the palace, through which he'd passed a few times now. Nobody in sight. He took a deep breath of relief. The passages to other corridors gaped like dark mouths. Hori picked the one to the administrative wing. After a few steps, almost complete darkness enveloped him. Fortunately, he re-membered the way from previous visits. With all the doors and turnoffs, he'd have gotten lost otherwise. Nevertheless, the walk to the archive seemed to take far too long. There, a gate in the end wall of the corridor! Ipuwer must have meant this one. He fingered the wood and found a bar. Maat was on his side! If there'd been a lock… He pushed it back and slipped into the mild night air tasting sweet as hon-ey.

But where was he? Looked like a park, hopefully not one belonging to the pal-ace with a wall surrounding it. Not far into the garden, he hit a high wall and wanted to weep. Why had Ipuwer talked of a side gate if it was a dead end? Or had Hori picked the wrong one? Despairing, he walked along the wall, first heading left. No crevice or projection offered him a way up, not even a tree with sturdy branches to carry his weight stood close. Arms raised, he jumped up. His fingers clawed at the top and slipped; his bruised ribs sent waves of pain through his body. No way could he climb over. He walked in the opposite direction. Behind a bush, he made out a door in the wall and felt a bar. "Oh sweet Isis!"

With a scraping noise, the gate gave way. He stood in a street unknown to him. Or maybe he'd been here before but didn't recognize it in the dark. To his left rose the wall in the back of the palace compound. Houses of medium height lined the other side. Nehesy's former estate lay in the opposite direction. To get there, he'd have to walk around half the palace, pass the double gate and cross the open square in front of it. He clutched the spear harder. What if guards stood outside the gate? About to set off, he realized his stupidity. Why should he go to the estate? There'd be nobody but Antef's people awaiting the return of his friends. Where should he go then? Damn, the street leading north passed the garrison, and more troops were likely stationed south of Waset. The nomarch had the city surrounded with soldiers preventing anyone from getting in or out. He may have escaped imminent danger but was still on Antef's turf. Well, he certainly couldn't stay here. Hori trotted off to the right. Soon he passed a well that seemed familiar. Right, this was the quarter for palace officials, where he'd discovered the dead scribe Seni. The corpse must have been found and removed by now. The house would be deserted…

His hand already on Seni's door, he changed his mind. Here he'd be just as imprisoned as in the palace, only without an Ipuwer to bring him food and drink. After his getaway, Antef's people would scour Waset again. He needed a safe place and help! Damn, he should have asked Ipuwer where he lived. No, not a smart idea. Very soon, he'd make Antef's list of unwanted people. Where might Nakhtmin and Muti have turned for shelter? They knew just as few people as he did. Sudden realization hit him: the basket maker! Meseh might at least know where Ouseret was or could help him somehow. He directed his steps toward the river. Basket makers needed water to keep the reeds pliable. Meseh definitely had to live near the waterfront. He'd find the quarter.

Barely a sound but Hori's slapping feet could be heard. The whole city lay in deep slumber. Occasionally, a child's crying and a mother's mumbled words of endearment reached his ears, and one time the patter of someone passing water. At long last, his ears picked up the gentle murmur of the river and the wind rustling the reeds. He turned into a street running in parallel to the Nile. Right area, but in which of the many houses might Meseh live? This time of night he couldn't ask anyone. Only Maat could help him now. He sent a prayer to the goddess of a just world order and walked on. A little while later, he discovered a turned-over bulrush boat. Its owner must have dragged it higher up the riverbank because of the rising water. Though it didn't offer the same kind of protection as Meseh's house, it could pass for shelter. He pulled up the side and slid into the dark cavity. Here he'd be safe until a new day dawned.

It was almost dark when Amunhotep returned home from his duties at the temple. Nakhtmin took a breath of relief. Finally! This day seemed to have had twice the amount of hours as a normal one. Since he'd gotten up, he'd been on constant alert. Even behind the high walls, he could sometimes hear the barked commands of Antef's soldiers. It was only a matter of time until they no longer shied from searching this estate as well. He hurried to the old man. "Are the birds on their way?" They'd decided it would be safer to send two birds, just in case one of them didn't make it to the residence.

Amunhotep nodded. He looked exhausted. "With Amun's help, the king might already hold the message in his hands."

He sighed as he recalled the words he'd hastily scribbled on the strips of papyrus. Were they explicit enough? They had to be!

To the king of Upper and Lower Egypt from Nakhtmin, his majesty's physician. The south is in dire straits. Antef's troops are marching north. Upheaval threatens.

However, with the river being unnavigable, it might take days if not weeks until the king arrived in Waset. Unfortunately, he couldn't fly like his divine effigy, the Horus falcon. By then, Antef would have found and killed them, all of them. Uneasy, he scratched his cheek. "We can't put you in danger any longer by taking shelter here, venerable prophet".

A tired smile deepened the creases around Amunhotep's eyes. "Your concern does you credit. Albeit I will not tolerate you leaving. You wouldn't get far beyond these walls. Today, they searched the House of Life but didn't dare to enter the temple. Not even Antef would order such a sacrilege. Therefore, I'm convinced I'll be safe as well, particularly since nobody knows of our acquaintance."

Nakhtmin snorted. "I hope you're right." With unease, he remembered that Hapi knew of Amunhotep's invitation the other day.

"Let's seek the company of the charming ladies. At my age, there's not much occasion to savor the sight of two such beautiful faces."

How could the prophet stay so calm? Still worried, Nakhtmin followed their host anyway. Only now did he realize how hungry he was. All day long, he hadn't been able to eat anything.

During the meal, their mood was subdued. Ouseret pushed the roasted goat meat around in her bowl. At one point, she lifted her head and said, "I'm worried about my friends, the basket makers. If the nomarch can't get to us, he might try to loosen their tongues. They know that we're here…"

Muti grabbed her hand. "They won't betray us, will they?"

Ouseret's eyes glistened in the lamp light. "Everyone talks when the pain becomes unbearable. And I don't want…" Her voice cracked.

Her showing feelings touched Nakhtmin against his will. He still held a grudge because she cared so little about Hori's fate. Apparently, she was capable of empathy—if not for everyone.

"Some time tomorrow, I'll send one of my people there. Meseh's the man's name, right?" the prophet asked.

Ouseret nodded. "His house is the third in the Street of Bulrushes. However…venerable prophet, I'd sleep far easier if you didn't wait too long with sending one of your servants."

A mild smile crossed Amunhotep's face. "Then at dawn it will be. May they find shelter here as well, and thus our fate becomes theirs, for better or worse."

"Thank you," Ouseret stammered.

"Take care," Nakhtmin cautioned. "Nobody should find out that he's your servant."

Under the table, Muti kicked his shin and glared at him. "I'm sure our host knows how to handle the situation, my husband." She didn't cope well with the uncertainty either; all day she'd been unusually irritable.

In the dark purple light preceding dawn, Nakhtmin watched Amunhotep's servant, dressed in a simple shendyt, slip through the gate and hoped all would go well.

Ra sent his divine rays over the eastern horizon and began his daily journey over the firmament. Time passed. It wasn't really that far to the basket maker's quarter. Maybe Amunhotep's servant couldn't locate the house. Restless, Nakhtmin took to pacing behind the gate. When would the man finally come back? The prophet had already set out for the temple. Ouseret kept Muti company at the already cleared table in the gazebo. Nakhtmin's worries increased. What if the servant had been intercepted and recognized as belonging to Amunhotep's household? Only the usual noises reached his ears from the other side of the wall, the occasional chatter of passers-by. The soldiers hadn't yet resumed their search of the area. Surely, they'd be roaming the streets anyway.

Ouseret came to him. "Still nothing?"

Nakhtmin wished she'd worry about Hori just as much, but he too feared the worst might have happened. He shook his head. "If only I could go there myself," he blurted.

She bit her lower lip. "I wish I'd told you everything right away, about the threat and—" She paused.

Was there something else? Dear gods, couldn't she be frank and honest for once?

A little later, she lamented, "Now all my friends are in danger!"

"Who are you talking about?" Were there more than the old couple?

Ouseret grimaced. "Well, you, Muti, Hori…"

"Oh, right." So she did care about them after all. That moment he noticed noises at the gate, barely audible, close to furtive. Had to be them! He signaled for the keeper to pull back the bolt.

The gate swung open. However, not three but five people entered. Nakhtmin recognized the basket makers and the servant, but the chubby young man was a stranger to him. Maybe the couple's son?

Cheering, Ouseret greeted him as Ipuwer and embraced him together with the old folks.

A large basket rested on the fifth person's shoulder and hid his face. Only when the gate was barred behind them did he set it down.

Nakhtmin gasped. "By the devourer!"

Ouseret looked up and cried out. The man's face was swollen and discolored from fierce blows, but it still looked very familiar. At long last, his heart dared to jubilate. "Hori! It's Hori!" He dashed to his friend and pulled him into his arms.

"Nakhtmin! Have mercy. My ribs." Hori gasped, and Nakhtmin released him.

"…early in the morning, I wanted to ask for the way to Meseh's house, but then I encountered Ipuwer, who was also heading there," Hori finished telling them about his escape.

They all sat around the table. Nakhtmin had barely dared to breathe, while Hori talked—what an adventure!

"I thank the gods that we sent for you this early!" Ouseret's voice sounded even darker than usual. "The way you look, people will remember you when Antef's soldiers describe you. Did really nobody see you?"

Hori shook his head. "The basket hid the worst bruises, and the other side of my face was covered by my arm."

"Lady, I took great care," the servant assured her. "I waited until the streets were void of people. On the way back, we had to evade several patrols. Nobody noticed us."

Nakhtmin patted his back in appreciation. "Well done. Hm, I hope Amunhotep won't mind sheltering Ipuwer as well."

Indignant, Hori exclaimed, "Without his help, I couldn't have escaped, and Antef will soon find out who loosened my fetters—if he doesn't know already. Ipuwer would have to suffer the consequences of my escape."

"Nobody leaves!" Ouseret said. "This is the only safe place for us. If the prophet won't grant you shelter, I'll leave the protection of these walls together with you."

Meseh's wife patted Ouseret's hand "You're a good child." She still seemed to have trouble accepting where she was. With her chapped hands, she felt the fine linen hanging from the gazebo's roof to keep out insects. Then she sighed. "I'm glad you and your friends are safe here, but we have to go back, have to work. How'd we make a living otherwise?"

"That shall never concern you again." Muti's voice rang with conviction.

Nakhtmin displayed a crooked grin since he suspected who'd have to make sure of that. But he could afford to compensate the couple—if they ever made it out of the Southern City. If not... Well in that case, he probably needn't worry about anything any longer. "So be it."

FRIGHTFUL WAITING

Four days had passed since Hori's escape, and he gradually felt a little safer. The first prophet's estate was like an island surrounded by soaring waves. However, quite a lot of people had found refuge on that island: the basket makers, Ipuwer, Nakhtmin, Muti and himself. The swelling of his face had diminished, and according to Nakhtmin, he looked almost human again.

He found his friend at the water basin in Amunhotep's garden and joined him. "Hey, why are you standing around here all by yourself?" Muti and Ouseret enjoyed a game of Senet not far from them.

Nakhtmin granted him a crooked smile. "I'm mulling things over. There's too much I still don't understand. For example, who killed Seni and the peasant?"

"Is that relevant?"

"Is it irrelevant?" Nakhtmin retorted.

Hori shrugged his shoulders. "We'll likely never find out—one of the nomarch's cronies would be my guess. A soldier he trusts, maybe even the man who'd followed you by boat."

"Why not Sanefer? After all, Wahka was his neighbor."

Hori didn't have to think about it. "Sanefer's a coward. He had his father poisoned and made sure he was far away when it happened. To kill a man face to face with your own hands is something completely different. And a neck doesn't break easily—that requires skill. Something else points at Antef's spy: He knew exactly where we went and who we talked to, while Sanefer didn't."

"Antef might have told him—hey, don't get all worked up, I believe you. We know why they killed the scribe. It's incredible. We only realized something smelled fishy and suspected Antef's involvement because of that murder."

Hori laughed. "Yes, and since I hadn't read the king's transcript, I'd never have noticed the deviations." No, it wasn't funny. A man was killed—for nothing!

"Did you find out why the peasant had to die?"

He shook his head. "It may have sufficed that you and Muti talked to him."

"Yes." Nakhtmin drew out the word. "And Wahka was Nofru's father. Perhaps he knew or guessed that his daughter killed Merwer with poisonous plants growing on his land. He might even have appreciated it after all the trouble with the trader. Maybe he even suspected Sanefer's involvement. When we met him, he seemed like a man who knew something and hoped to benefit from it."

Hori nodded. "If Wahka wanted to extort something from him, Sanefer would have informed Antef."

"Maybe we'll never know, but I think that's pretty close to how it must have happened. Still, there's more we haven't figured out yet. So, Sanefer is Antef's informer, spy, whatever, and Merwer did the same for the king."

Growing impatient, Hori swatted at a fly. "What's not to understand?"

"Well, those strange enterprises of Merwer. Of course, he needed a cover to settle here, but why the shady commercial operations?"

"Oh well, good question." Hori hadn't considered this although Merwer's activities had initially been at the center of their investigation. As soon as he'd learned for whom the man actually worked, he'd never thought about it again. "Since the king funded his undertakings, he didn't need to seek profits. So why solicit investments?"

"Hm, Amunhotep mentioned Merwer using the priesthood, loyal to the king, to inconspicuously distribute gold to certain people whose allegiance the pharaoh needed to ensure. Maybe the supposed profits of Merwer's endeavors served a similar purpose: bribery."

"And after some of these fellows bragged about their luck, others approached the trader to gain nice returns of their investments as well, people that weren't worth bribing? Maybe ..." Not very convincing, Hori thought.

"In the meantime, I've come to think Merwer might actually not have been a kind person," Nakhtmin said. "Just because he was the king's man, doesn't mean he walked in the light of Maat. All those promises he made to all kinds of people, the shopkeeper Ini, Nehesy, Ouseret, Sanefer, Nofru, his wife, his tenants and who knows who else."

Yes, that was really strange. Why make all the promises when he should have known he wouldn't be able to keep most of them and perhaps didn't even intend to do so? "He told everyone what they wanted to hear," he mused. "A compulsive liar hoping to please everyone?" Had the long time of living under cover made him that way? For many years he'd acted the trader when he really spied for the king. Merwer must already have been employed by the previous pharaoh, Senusret's father. "Just put yourself in Merwer's place. You're an important trusted agent for the king but can't tell anyone what a significant role you're really playing. Yes, you shrug, but Merwer wanted attention, needed it. I believe he'd have loved to shout at everyone: 'Look at me, how important I am!' But he couldn't do that. Thus he started to make himself look more important in his cover role by taking business risks he couldn't finance himself." Maybe the man even embezzled funds from the king? The whole truth about Merwer's shenanigans had been buried with him.

Nakhtmin inclined his head. "Mh, maybe he did strive for attention. Ouseret said most of Merwer's ailments were figments of his imagination except for the chronic joint pains. Do you remember the widow of scribe Bahotep?"

"Oh yes, of course I do!"

"She only came to the House of Life every day because she was lonely and needed someone to talk to. Merwer may have wanted to prove himself a particularly shrewd businessman. That ploy with the miracle grain..." Nakhtmin chortled. "Maybe he'd have loved to become a peasant. And besides the king, Sanefer was the only one aware of his real profession. Hey, look who's coming!"

Hori peered in the indicated direction. "Amunhotep! At this time of day?" He headed toward him. "What's going on out there?"

Amunhotep gasped as if he'd been running. "They are searching the premises of the priesthood!"

Horrified, he swayed. At the mercy of the treacherous nomarch again? The other refugees who'd found shelter in Amunhotep's house approached as well.

"What will happen now?" – "Where can we go?" – "What shall we do?"

Amunhotep knew nothing specific but guessed the soldiers worked their way up from the lower ranks of priests to the top. Hori's heart pounded. Nothing! They could do nothing but wait. Persevering behind the walls, they soon heard men stomping down the street and occasionally the bursting of wood when a door was kicked in. Every noise made Hori flinch. Hours passed, and the soldiers ravaged places all around them. By Seth, they just sat around like timid fledglings in their nest. Soon the villains would break this gate too… With growing dread, they waited and waited. Not much longer, and he'd be willing to place his and his friends' fate at the mercy of the river god. Horns blew! Hori lifted his head. "Did you hear that?"

"What does it mean?" Nakhtmin asked.

More horns sounded. "They're summoning the soldiers!" Ipuwer called. "By Amun, they are leaving the area!"

Hori couldn't believe it. "Would someone climb that tree and peer over the wall, please?"

Ipuwer interlaced his fingers and helped Nakhtmin up onto the first branch. He sat in the treetop for a long time and let his gaze sweep the roofs, while Hori walked back and forth underneath.

Finally, his friend dropped from one of the low branches near him. "It's true! The search parties are retreating."

Wild hope filled Hori's heart. "The king?"

Ouseret snorted. "Not likely."

"I'll return to the temple. My absence during the evening ritual would be far too conspicuous, and I'm sure I'll find out more there." Amunhotep mounted his palanquin and soon disappeared though the gate.

"South of Khemenu already? How's that possible?" Muti later asked in disbelief. "And how did Antef find out that the king is marching toward Waset?"

"The high tide hasn't arrived in the north yet. His majesty must have rushed ahead with an advance party and possibly even a major part of the royal army by boat," Amunhotep mused and seemed much younger. "This is so exciting! If the most important nomarchs of the south are Antef's allies, as we assume, then Djehutihotep from Khemenu must have informed him about the pharaoh's approach. In any case, Antef has concentrated his troops and is sending them against his majesty's army."

Hori rejoiced. They'd be saved!

Nakhtmin however pointed out, "What if Djehutihotep's soldiers attack the royal army from behind?"

Amunhotep grinned like a mischievous boy. "You know our king! Do you really think he wouldn't have taken that possibility into consideration?"

Hori sure hoped he did.

Day 23 of month Wepet-renpet in Akhet, the season of inundation

"Careful!" Nakhtmin barked because he almost tripped over Hori's feet when his friend sat down and stretched out his legs. They were all on edge. He sighed and settled next to Hori. "Being locked in here and not knowing what's going on outside is awful."

"Could be worse, believe me."

Well, he was probably right. At least the news of the king's victory had reached them already. "Damn Antef supporters, I hadn't imagined they'd put up such resistance," he blurted.

According to Amunhotep, survivors of the battle had been streaming into the city since yesterday, chased by the king's soldiers. And the civilian inhabitants of Waset were gearing up to fight off the royal troops. Fierce street combat ensued. Jeers and war cries, cracking wood, busted walls, the sound of metal hitting metal, screams of agony—they heard the ruckus and quivered. The priest's servants had reenforced the gate. Occasionally, someone rattled it. How long could it keep them out?

"Why does that surprise you? In the Waset nome, only those who enjoy Antef's favor prospered. Now, not only the soldiers have to fear being held accountable by the king. And don't forget, while we know Senusret, he's a stranger to the people here, so they fear him."

"Hm, that may be. I was under the impression many inhabitants wished to shake off Antef's yoke."

Ipuwer joined them. "That's the case," he said and bit into a piece of melon, squirting juice. "But they haven't risked any form of disobedience for a long time now."

"I hope they find their courage before everything's over," Nakhtmin growled. He simply wanted to go home and take his wife to safety. However, Antef wasn't defeated yet...

Day 26 of month Wepet-renpet in Akhet, the season of inundation

Hori yawned and stretched his limbs. What a gorgeous morning! It was over. The time of fear lasting twelve endless days had come to an end. Yesterday, with the last rays of the sun, his majesty had led his army into Waset—to the cheers of the finally pacified inhabitants. He too had jubilated until his throat became sore, and not only to greet the king but in joy over being able to leave the estate for the first time again.

"Hurry up!" Nakhtmin called. "The pharaoh awaits our report."

Was it so late already? He hastened to the bathroom to wash, then donned his best shendyt before he joined his friend. "What about Amunhotep?"

"I guess he'll head straight from the temple to the palace if his majesty wants to speak with him again." Senusret had conferred with the royalists among Waset's elite until late into the night.

When the gate opened, Hori stared in astonishment at the havoc exposed by daylight. Stones thrown from the roofs lay scattered on the street. Some of them had ended lives as the blood splatter on the white walls testified. The nearer they came to the palace, the worse it got: torn down walls, busted doors, even blackened ruins still smoking after the blazes illuminated the sky until yesterday. Hard to believe they were no longer in danger here. The armed men they encountered were the king's soldiers.

"I wonder if Antef has been arrested by now."

Hori shrugged. "No idea." He pointed at the large double gate. "We'll get the answer there." Uneasy, he entered the palace. The wing with the guest accommodations and the trapdoor leading to the Chamber of Silence bustled with people. Senusret's men used the rooms. Hori averted his gaze and walked on.

Two guards crossed their spears and blocked their way. "What do you want?" one of them barked.

"Physicians Nakhtmin and Hori at the behest of his majesty," he said with more self-confidence than he actually felt. By the gods, if he never had anything to do with soldiers again, he wouldn't mind at all.

The other fellow nodded at his comrade and let them pass. A servant accompanied them. The king received them in the same room where Antef had recently threatened them. Everything looked the same, only the man whose charisma outshone everyone else present was a different one. They dropped to their knees.

"Leave us alone," Senusret commanded. His features looked more tense than ever.

Hori recognized the scribe Thotnakht as well as the royal servant Atef and nodded at both while they retreated. At the king's inviting gesture, they settled on cushions on the ground.

The ruler of the Two Lands sat likewise. "Well, it doesn't happen very often that two physicians send a pharaoh on a war," he began. "Particularly not when they are supposed to undertake a recreational journey."

Nakhtmin swallowed audibly, and Hori quickly squeezed his hand to calm him. The king's foul temper wasn't directed at them, but he still felt the need to justify their actions. "Your majesty, you asked us to keep our eyes open with regard to the nomarchs. And in doing so, we looked into nefarious abysses."

The pharaoh snorted. "Indeed. Tell me!"

Hori broke into a sweat. This monarch seemed a different man than the one he'd almost have called a friend back home. Although he was only a little older than Hori, Senusret radiated unyielding relentlessness. He didn't know how to start.

Nakhtmin jumped in. "Hori wished to look into a death that occurred some time ago in Waset."

He nodded hastily. "Yes, your majesty. I had reason to believe an innocent man had been convicted for the murder of the trader Merwer. I only meant to balance the scales of Maat, but I had no idea…your majesty?"

The king stared at him aghast. "Why did you concern yourself with this particular death?"

Hori's face burned, and Nakhtmin took over once more. "The accused is a physician named Nehesy and the father of a friend. She swore her father was innocent, and we found the circumstances of the speedy trial odd."

"I personally sent vizier Sobekemhat to chair the trial because I had my suspicions." The royal hand beckoned them to continue.

So that was why his father had attended! The pharaoh should have picked a different man, but it was too late now. And he didn't want to badmouth his old man in front of Senusret.

"Now we know Merwer had been your informer, but at first it looked like a banal family dispute." Nakhtmin elaborated on what they'd found out during the first days in Waset.

Hori took over. "By the way, Antef's men had been watching us from the first moment on, but we only noticed later. Unfortunately, two innocent people had to die because they'd talked to us. Merwer's tenant Wahka probably wanted to use his knowledge to extort benefits for keeping silent, so Antef had him eliminated. Then there was an archive scribe who'd promised me a copy of the trial records. He didn't get around to it before his demise." He avoided the king's piercing gaze. "So we figured Antef had to be involved although we were convinced that Merwer's son had planned and prepared the poisoning of his father."

"Sanefer?" The kings brow furrowed. "I know the young man. He occasionally brought me Merwer's messages. You must be talking about a different son."

Hori shook his head. "Apparently, Sanefer had been in Antef's services for quite awhile now. The nomarch had already found out that Merwer was your spy, so he used Sanefer to monitor and if necessary modify or lose messages to you. He didn't want to raise suspicion. Your transcript of the trial has also been forged, your majesty, because Sanefer testified that he'd received news of his father's death while he was in Abu when he should have been on his way north."

The king buried his face in his hands and groaned. "Reading this would indeed have alerted me. As it was, I didn't find any reason to question Nehesy's guilt."

Nakhtmin leaned forward. "Let's talk about the time before the murder. Since they controlled the flow of information between you and your informer, Antef and his allies among the southern nomarchs, mainly Sarenput, were able to recruit plenty of soldiers and conspire against you with the goal to usurp sole power over the south. Merwer, ignorant of his son's defection, must have recently discovered their plans. I assume he meant to travel to the residence himself to warn you. However, he knew the chronic joint pains would return this summer, so he asked Sanefer to go in his place."

The king interrupted. "The young man really did show up at the residence several weeks ago. That was before—" The corners of Senusret's mouth drooped, his gaze hazed over with grief. Hori guessed what he was thinking about, the death of his heir. The moment passed and he continued, "He had nothing of significance to report."

Hori nodded. "Naturally, that was a lie. Now Antef couldn't let Merwer live since his original message would have prompted a reaction from you. The trader would have known something was wrong if nobody up north was concerned about the intrigues of the nomarchs here. Sanefer was to take care of it."

Senusret refilled his mug then held the jug midair. "If I'm not mistaken, Merwer died while his son was far away. I'm sorry to say, but that disqualifies him as a suspect."

Nakhtmin seemed to shrivel under the king's reproachful stare. "He prepared the poison. His servant Nofru administered it to Merwer. On his order...um..." He fell silent.

"Exactly," Hori confirmed. "A poison of ground colocynth seeds killed the trader. As I said, Merwer fell sick every summer, and he always took the same medication, a strong drug that contains, among other things, colocynth. Sanefer knew that, prepared some additional powder himself and gave it to the maid before he departed. The girl would take care of her master, bring him his food—and his medicine. She only needed to add some of the powder when nobody watched her."

Brow creased, the king scrutinized him. "That sounds...complicated! Why did the servant do it? Was there a love angle to it?"

Hori gave a crooked smile. As if either of them was capable of such a feeling. "We believe Sanefer promised to marry Nofru to make her heed his wishes. The girl is truly a beauty and with child, either Merwer's or Sanefer's. She may have wanted to save herself from dismissal and poverty," Hori explained. "Additionally, Antef and Sanefer needed someone outside of his household to take the fall for the murder. Physician Nehesy was the perfect candidate, therefore the poisoning with something contained in the remedy. It was supposed to look like an overdose, accidental or not didn't matter. Nehesy certainly had reasons to resent his patient." He took a sip to moisten his throat.

Senusret closed his eyes and grumbled, "I read about that in the transcript. When one of my…um…people dies, I always take a close look. But there was nothing to confirm my fear the murder might have been politically motivated."

"Yes, unfortunately, my father believed the lying witnesses and convicted Nehesy. The physician suffers in the quarries of Kheny, your majesty, an innocent man! Antef must have rejoiced." He didn't dare to voice more criticism of his father. Sobekemhat shouldn't lose favor with the king because of him.

The pharaoh groaned. "What an intricate conspiracy! Quick now, I want to hear the rest as well. Today I'll lead my army south to regain control all the way to the Ta-Seti nome." He bared his teeth. "May Monthu help me catch Antef and Sarenput!"

Hori froze. "Antef escaped?"

"With his last followers, he left on the road leading south, likely heading to his co-conspirator. They'll confront us somewhere between here and Abu with their remaining forces. Fortunately, I have already obliterated the major part of their army."

"A great victory, your majesty! We missed most of it…you got here fast." Nakhtmin gave a shy smile.

Senusret leaned forward. "Thanks to your idea with the pigeon message, as Amunhotep tells me. I'll never forget."

Nakhtmin blushed.

"Well, I'll simply take the time to tell you how my majesty fared. As soon as I'd received the news, I concentrated my available forces. Fortunately, the garrisons around Itj-tawy were fully manned. They rowed for all their worth until we hit the precursors of the red flood just after Khemenu that same evening. From there on, we continued on foot with an enforced rearguard. After all, I didn't know how far north the treason had spread. Thank the gods! As soon as Ra's rays kissed the horizon the next morning, we were attacked from behind."

"The people of the Hare nome!" Hori exclaimed.

His majesty nodded. "They were as exhausted as we were but less well prepared, and we defeated them with ease. Three days later, my scouts reported the approach of a large contingent under the flag of the Waset nome. Antef was marching against us."

Hori recalled the moment they'd heard the horn signals summoning the search parties. Had the king moved slower…

"We threw ourselves at the enemy, and when they saw my majesty, their limbs turned to water."

Nakhtmin chuckled, and Hori joined in. "Really?"

For the first time since they got here, Senusret smiled. "That's how the battle will be depicted in the murals of the Amun temple in Waset, so it has to be true." His face turned serious again.

Hori shuddered. More likely, it had been an ugly carnage, followed by a fierce chase. And then the battle had continued within Waset for days until the last resistance expired and the city was taken.

His thoughts wandered to Ouseret. It had been so strange to see her again at Amunhotep's house, now that he knew... Of course, he hadn't mentioned anything, but she seemed to notice that he acted differently toward her. Or had Ipuwer confessed his indiscretion to her? Gorgeous Ouseret. Defamed, disdained, defiled. Hard to believe, but he loved her even more than before. To his own surprise, his heart felt content, just knowing she was safe.

After a knock at the door, Atef peered in. "Your majesty, everything's ready." The king nodded. "I'm coming."

Day 29 of month Wepet-renpet in Akhet, the season of inundation

Nakhtmin handed his friend the papyrus. "Read for yourself, his majesty commands us to join the army surgeons. Today."

Hori furrowed his brow. "Sounds like a bloody battle if he summons even us."

Nakhtmin looked to Muti who was able to walk again and now strolled through the garden with Amunhotep by her side. He didn't want to leave her alone, not here, although she should be safe in the prophet's house. Still, in this city one never knew who was a friend and who an enemy. Antef's surviving followers may have sworn to take revenge.

Ouseret came to them. "What do you have there?" When Hori gave her the message, her lips tightened to a thin line. "You'll have to leave."

"Well, you, too, I guess. It says every available physician is needed. Hey, Ipuwer, that includes you as well!"

The chubby young man came running, but Nakhtmin paid more attention to Ouseret's expression of disbelief. "I? I should go into battle?" she stammered.

Hori shrugged his shoulders. "Don't you think you can do it?"

Nakhtmin also thought he hadn't heard right. For days now, his friend had acted very differently toward the woman. A night spent together in a dungeon seemed to have had quite an effect. Or had something else happened? Hori certainly didn't urge her any longer. Although he obviously still liked Ouseret a lot, he didn't try to force her love.

She placed her hands on her hips. "Whether I can...? Of course! I can barely wait." Excitement shone from her eyes.

Nakhtmin hadn't seen her so lively in a long time. Ouseret smiled at Hori as if she suddenly saw him in a different light, no longer regarding him as an annoying insect. Hey, did he just witness a seed of affection germinate? Hori didn't even seem to notice. He discussed with Ipuwer what kind of equipment they needed. Nakhtmin grinned. That might turn out interesting.

He walked over to Muti and interlaced his fingers with hers. "My love, we have to leave, Hori, Ouseret, Ipuwer and I. The king needs our services. Amunhotep, can you take care of her?"

159

The prophet nodded, but Muti looked at him in horror. "You want to leave me here all alone?"

'Here you are safe,' he wanted to reply but he couldn't really believe that either. Muti had also changed. Where was the briskness he cherished, where her cheekiness? "Beloved heart..." He pulled her into his arms. She'd been through a lot, and their planned recreation had turned into war. His majesty demanded too much!

Hearing footsteps getting closer, he looked up. "I won't come along," he announced to Hori. "Tell his majesty I'm indispensable here."

Muti clutched him tighter, and he stroked her quivering shoulders.

Hori's gaze communicated understanding. "Of course. Take good care of her!"

"You take care, too! Come back in one piece."

OUSERET

In the light of numerous oil lamps hanging from the branches of a withered acacia, Hori had been working for hours without a break. Right now, he was finishing the amputation of a hand. He'd stopped counting how many men he'd treated. Friend or fiend, he didn't know. This second battle must have been truly a massacre; the king's superior forces had cut down the already weakened enemy.

The place reeked of blood and excrement, and the screams of the injured filled the night air. The next wounded had a blood-soaked shendyt wrapped around his middle. Hori removed it, and whitely, intestines bulged from a gaping abdominal cut. Irritated, he looked around. Why had nobody separated this man? He was beyond all help. While he marveled over how much the cut resembled that of an embalmer's, the man took his last breath. Hori wiped the sweat from his forehead. His gaze met Ouseret's. "Look here!" he called and pointed at the entrails.

She approached. "What's that?"

"The gut," he explained. "One of the metu, which transports excrement."

Curious she bent over the wound. "Fascinating!" Her fingers gently pushed the loop aside.

In silence, he watched her hand dig deeper into the hidden world of visceral organs. He wasn't allowed to say anything; this was actually knowledge only embalmers were privy to. However, it made him happy to share some of it with her.

Two bearers came to them. "He's a goner," one said.

Cursing they heaved the corpse onto the stretcher, and Hori looked at the next patient. A dislocated shoulder. "That's a case for two pairs of hands," he said and stepped behind the man's head to push down his upper body, while Ouseret pulled the arm and eased it back into the joint. In silence, they worked side by side for the rest of the night.

At dawn, their work was done for now. The king came and walked down the rows of wounded, his face fierce. Then he thanked the physicians for their efforts.

Every bone in Hori's body ached, but he felt strangely awake and exhilarated. He grinned without knowing why. The crust of dry blood on his face cracked. Then she stood before him, the face smeared and still so beautiful. She wrapped her arms around his neck and pressed her lips on his. First they felt hard, tight, then they softened and parted. He pulled her against him. She tasted of blood, sweat and tears. Exactly like that. His Ouseret.

Later, when they'd washed and eaten, he asked in wonder, "Why?"

She snuggled up against him, and said in a coarse voice, "Because you finally see me as a physician."

"But I always have," he said. "First, you were my doctor."

She shook her head. "Sure, tell that to a crocodile, Hori! First, you wanted to get a leg over me."

"Oh." Unfortunately, she was right. And then he'd fallen so madly in love with her, he always saw her as the woman he desired. Still, she'd wronged him. "I never doubted your skills."

She sat up and pulled back enough to behold him. Her face looked very serious. "It's just that foremost I'm a physician. All men only look at me as a woman."

"I can't blame them," he mumbled and dodged her blow.

"They don't have confidence in me, and they don't respect me. If an ailing man is given the choice between me and a male doctor, who do you think he'll choose?"

His fingers moved toward her thigh. "I know who I'd prefer." This time the blow landed. "Ouch!"

"How many men do you think offered marriage to me, so they could 'provide' for me—meaning I should give up my profession?"

Oh dear, he'd thought along such lines, hadn't he? Well, at least he'd meant to protect her. "I'd never ask you to do that."

She withdrew from him. "A long time ago, I swore to myself I'd never marry, but you men folk couldn't let that happen either." She looked straight at him. "You know, right?"

His cheeks burned, and he felt ashamed to be a man, but he held her gaze. "Ipuwer told me."

She nodded. "The engagement with Sanefer had never been real. My father had arranged that with Merwer, so I'd be safe."

"If only you'd told us earlier," he said. "We wasted so much time because we assumed a love story lay at the heart of Merwer's death." He paused. "But when you separated from him, it did hurt you."

"What makes you think that?" she cried out in indignation.

He rubbed the root of his nose. "Well, Meseh. He said you'd bawled your eyes out because of him."

She looked baffled then laughed. "Oh, Hori, son of the triple-cursed So-bekemhat, that wasn't because of Sanefer! I'd returned to Waset and found my childhood home locked and sealed. And I'd failed to clear my father, and then you…"

"Me?"

"Yes, you. I had to tear my budding feelings for you out of my heart. Loving the son of the man who'd sentenced my father—unfathomable! And you had to think me an awful person the way I'd behaved."

Hori couldn't get enough. Ouseret had already loved him back then? She'd certainly managed to hide it well.

A crooked grin sneaked onto her face. "And then you showed up here, and my fortifications threatened to crumble."

He understood that but not why she'd kept her personal background to herself. So he asked, "Was it because of the rape? Did you think we'd appreciate you less?"

The corners of her mouth drooped. "I felt ashamed." Her gaze met his and saw the unspoken question in them. "No, not because of the rape! Because of…what happened afterward…"

"The little revenge you took on those villains? Oh Ouseret, my Ouseret! You had every right to do that and more! They got less than they deserved if you ask me."

She shook her head, tears in her eyes.

What a yokel he was! "The abor—"

She put a finger to his lips and sighed. "So Ipuwer told you that as well. Of course I'm ashamed! I'm a physician. Life is sacred."

Hori embraced her and let her cry. "It's a scandal that a woman can only find security in the Two Lands as a wife but not when she works in a profession." He stroked her back. "His majesty should do something about that. Darling, I'm so incredibly sorry. Listen, we don't have to marry. I could simply call you to my house as my phy—" Her lips sealed his mouth.

Later she said, "Hori, son of Sobekemhat. Do you want to be my husband?"

He stared at her in disbelief.

Her mouth twitched with suppressed hilarity. "I don't mind if you want to keep working as a doctor."

Grinning, he threw his head back. "Really?"

Above them, vultures circled majestically. If his heart were a bird, it would soar and chirp like a lark.

Day 3 of month Tekh in Akhet, the season of inundation

Holding Muti's hand, Nakhtmin and she joined the masses heading to the square in front of the palace. The once again victorious king had returned to the Southern City. "I hope they caught the two treacherous nomarchs," Muti said.

Many people had already gathered in the open space, and from all sides newcomers squeezed the crowd tighter. The throng jostled and shoved. Nakhtmin studied the faces around him. Not all the inhabitants of Waset looked relieved to have shaken off Antef's yoke. Many people must have benefited from the man's reign and now blamed the pharaoh from far north for the killings in the city. Others appeared like they felt liberated, but they all seemed uncertain. Something new awaited them, and they still had to find out if it was good or bad.

Murmurs rose from numerous throats, people looked up. Nakhtmin followed suit. The king, no longer wearing the blue crown of war but the double crown of Upper and Lower Egypt, signifying peace, had appeared on the palace terrace, crook and flail crossed before his chest. How majestic he looked! Beside him, several men stepped up to the railing. Nakhtmin only recognized some. Hori wasn't among them. He and the other physicians remained with the wounded. "Can you understand what he's saying?"

Muti shook her head. "Wait!"

When Senusret paused, a man at the edge of the platform repeated the words of the ruler of the Two Lands, shouting at the top of his lungs, "Inhabitants of Waset! Your nomarch dared to rebel against the reign of the strong bull of Kemet, chosen by the gods. He has been arrested and will be judged by the big kenbet in the royal residence to receive his just punishment."

Nakhtmin took a deep breath. Antef no longer posed a danger. Muti squeezed his hand, likely feeling the same sense of relief.

"Until his majesty has decided who will lead the insurgent southern nomes, a military administration will be established. Every inhabitant has to follow their instructions. In the name of the king of Upper and Lower Egypt, of the bee and the sedge…"

Nakhtmin tired of listening to the many names and titles. The pharaoh had thrown a lot at the rebels. He deprived the mighty families of the south of their power. He wondered if Sarenput of Ta-Seti had also been arrested. At a leisurely pace, he strolled back to the first prophet's house with Muti. On a whim, he changed directions and headed to the Street of Palm Fronds.

"What do you want here?" Muti asked and stopped. "I certainly won't go back in there."

Concerned, he scrutinized her. "Our time there wasn't too bad. But I just want to see how my friend Kawab is faring."

"Kawab?"

"The slimy prophet of Khonsu who wanted to deliver me to Antef. I guess he's facing some hardships now. I just want to make sure he's aware of that."

She still balked. "Nakhtmin...it's not like you to be so...vengeful."

"Really?" Yes, she was right, of course, but Kawab had done something unforgivable, he'd endangered Muti. "That dog almost caught me the night of our escape, and what would have happened to you then?" He tightened his grip. "Come on, I promise you'll enjoy it, too."

Kawab displayed his usual affability as he welcomed them. Didn't he know Nakhtmin had recognized him that night, or did he simply not care?

"I'm so glad to finally meet your esteemed wife, so glad! Exciting times have arrived since we last saw each other. Exciting." He led them to the cushions in the garden and invited them to sit. A moment later, the same servant as the other day approached with a tray of refreshments.

Nakhtmin grinned. "That's true. I just told my wife how much we owe you. Oh, no, thank you, I don't want anything."

Kawab furrowed his brow. "Me?" An uncertain smile crossed his face. "Well, then I'm sure you'll tell the king as well, put in a good word for me, hehe?" He rolled a dried date between his fingers before shoving it into his mouth.

Nakhtmin glanced at Muti and saw mischief in her eyes.

"My *dear* Kawab," she said with emphasis. "I'll be happy to report to the king that you were one of the nomarch's minions. And wasn't it you who betrayed Nakhtmin to Antef's men waiting here to arrest us? Yes, his majesty should be interested to hear all that. I'm sure you'll get your reward. But now you have to excuse us. The first prophet Amunhotep awaits us."

Nakhtmin admired the graceful elegance of her moves as she rose from the cushion. He took her hand and waved nonchalantly at the speechless prophet.

Day 4 of month Tekh in Akhet, the season of inundation

"There! The stone pits of Kheny!" Ouseret squeezed Hori's upper arm.

To hide his concern, Hori kissed her forehead, heated by the sun. He could only hope they weren't too late. Antef might have sent orders to the prison guards, withdrawing Nehesy's privileges if nothing worse. Was it selfish of him to wish his finally found happiness not be overshadowed by grief? To both sides of the Nile, sandstone cliffs rose and constricted the riverbed. Their path meandered up a steep slope and then through a gorge that couldn't have been formed by the hands of men. Ahead, at its narrowest point, a gate blocked their way. Hori appreciated their companions, ten soldiers under the command of an officer. He was even happier to carry a letter bearing the king's seal with orders to release Nehesy.

Their escort was part of the troops heading for Abu to arrest Ankhu, the heir of Sarenput. His father had died in the battle, but his son probably wouldn't show more loyalty to the pharaoh. While the major part of the king's men marched on south, they'd followed the path through the gorge. He heard a peculiar sound that grew louder the closer they got to the gate. Only when he stood right in front of it, did he recognize the beating of numerous stone hammers on bronze chisels.

The guards looked at the message with expressionless faces. He almost laughed when it dawned on him why. These fellows couldn't read, wouldn't even recognize the king's seal! In contrast, the insignia of rank on the officer's chest did warrant their respect and they opened the gate.

A terraced ravine opened up before Hori. Men scurried about in its walls like ants. They carried rubble in baskets to an edge, where they let it patter down. Clouds of dust rose. Using ropes, several men dragged a large boulder on a wooden sled down a ramp. Two more ran ahead and moistened the slideway so the skids found little resistance. This reminded Hori of the gigantic statue of Djehutihotep, and he could hardly believe it had been moved in the same way. What would happen to the workers if the sled suddenly slid faster than they could run? He noticed Ouseret's worry-stricken face and draped an arm around her shoulder.

The supervisor sitting in the shade of a trellis detected them and hurried over, shading his eyes with one hand. "Greetings," he started then stared at Ouseret as if he'd never seen a woman before. "What brings you to the quarries of Kheny?"

Hori handed him the royal note.

This one could read. His eyebrows hiked up in astonishment, then drew together. "His *majesty* wishes the release of the prisoner? I'd prefer orders from my master Sarenput." His voice had a cunning note. Apparently, he hadn't been informed of the change in power.

Hori was happy to enlighten the man and to his satisfaction saw him pale.

"Of course, I'll have Nehesy fetched right away. Minmesu!" A guard scurried to them and received his orders.

A crash sounding as if the slope burst made their ears ring. Startled, Ouseret clutched him. The idea someone might throw boulders at them flared up in Hori's heart. Debris tumbled down the wall to his left.

The supervisor seemed to enjoy their fear. "That was just a loosened block. We force wooden wedges in crevices and pour water over them so they swell. At some point, the rock gives, and we have a nice new block for the buildings praising the gods and the...um...king—life, prosperity and health."

Hori snorted and wanted to retort, but Ouseret yelled, "That's him! Father, Father!" She let go of him and ran toward the two men. The next moment she threw herself into the arms of the figure shuffling alongside Minmesu.

Day 7 of month Tekh in Akhet, the season of inundation

"My goodness, I'd started to worry his majesty might have pressed you into his army!" Nakhtmin said and patted Hori's brown back. Of course, Senusret had told him which mission kept his friend away. He released Hori and eyed the older man next to Ouseret with curiosity. "You must be Nehesy! It's nice to see you well and free."

"I can't thank you enough for what you've done," Ouseret said. To Nakhtmin's surprise, she hugged him and Muti. "Without your help, Antef's infamous actions would never have come to light. My father is free, and so am I."

Nakhtmin cast a puzzled look over his shoulder at Hori. She was a different woman! His friend beamed at him. Could it be…?

"Please accept my thanks as well." Nehesy said quietly and sounded tired. Had he always been so short or had captivity shrunken the man? All things considered, he must have been lucky to be allowed to tend to the injuries of his fellow prisoners. Hm, was it possible that a bad conscience had prompted Antef to grant innocent Nehesy such a privilege?

Later, when they sat together under the roof of Amunhotep's gazebo, Ouseret's father spoke in a faltering voice about his time of suffering. "…and then, a few days ago, I had to join the others in the wall and haul rocks."

Nakhtmin's gaze met Hori's. His friend said, "On Antef's orders. Revenge for Ouseret's getaway." The tall physician snuggled up against him.

Nakhtmin rubbed his eyes. To see her so trusting and comfortable seemed absurd. Nehesy also studied them with a puzzled look on his face. Then he murmured, "Hard to believe that he's the son of Sobekemhat."

Hori flinched slightly.

Better to change the subject, Nakhtmin decided. "Um, yes. By the way, the Medjay caught Sanefer and brought him back to Waset. In the end, he abandoned his lord Antef and tried to flee to the north. The lawmen found Nofru still at the estate. That lout left her, just like his mother and sister, at the pharaoh's mercy."

"I hope they won't be too hard on the girl," Muti said.

Nakhtmin detected tears in her eyes. "She killed Merwer, and not by accident. I doubt she can expect mercy."

"But she's with child!"

Oh, that bothered her! "Darling, the king certainly won't have her executed before she's given birth."

"The poor mite!" Now she wept without restraint, and he knew that she cried for her own child.

Day 10 of month Tekh in Akhet, the season of inundation

Sanefer's speedily arranged trial—his majesty felt a strong urge to return home— drew a large crowd of spectators, some of whom had even traveled quite a distance. Hori was glad that he would be called as a witness to give testimony. He wanted to see the man atone for the suffering he'd caused. At long last, the accused had to take responsibility for his crimes at the big kenbet with the king as supreme judge. However, Nofru's trial came first. He glanced back at Ouseret, whose face he'd made out in the back of the hall. As a witness, he stood next to Nakhtmin in the first row.

Amunhotep and other prophets, whom Hori didn't know, flanked Senusret. Hori nodded at the old man, but he didn't notice, because that moment Nofru was dragged into the hall and drew the gazes of the judges. Her belly now protruded significantly, but her beauty radiated more than ever. Murmurs rose among the spectators showing their indignation at the rude handling of her. The Medjay forced her onto her knees, and in such a humble pose, she had to answer the questions.

"Nofru, daughter of Wahka. Swear the oath!"

Hori recognized the voice of Thotnakht, the royal scribe, drifting from the shadows behind his lord.

In a bored voice, Nofru rattled off the vow to speak the truth and listed the punishments threatening those who didn't keep their oath.

"You were a maid in Merwer's house?" the scribe inquired.

Nofru lifted her chin in defiance and darted the pharaoh a challenging look. "Yes."

Apparently, her extraordinary beauty affected the ruler of the Two Lands since he smiled at her. Hori held his breath. The little slut flirted with the king, wanted to seduce him! Unfathomable! Coquettishly, she inclined her head and played with her shiny black hair.

Senusret signaled to Thotnakht and took over the questioning. "While you were working at Merwer's house, your master took you to bed with him?"

The girl, certain of her success, took on the pose of an innocent victim and placed her hand over her heart. "Oh, your majesty, how could I have refused him? He threatened to chase my father from his land."

Amunhotep whispered loud enough that even Hori could hear it, "The peasant Wahka was one of Merwer's tenants."

"Ah," the king uttered. "So you carry the child of your master?"

Nofru nodded and feigned embarrassment.

"Then you were something like his second wife?"

Her shoulders hiked up and sank. "Yes, one might say so. He promised to marry me as soon as his wife..." Senusret's brows knitted, so she quickly threw in, "Oh, no, I'd never have done anything to my mistress..."

"Fine. I understand your mistress is well. Nobody blames you in that regard."

She relaxed again.

The king continued in a voice soft as a feather, "So you were promised to him, albeit when his son Sanefer asked you to get colo—" He frowned. Thotnakht leaned forward and whispered into his ear.

"Colocynth for him so you two could poison your future husband Merwer, you didn't hesitate?"

Inwardly, Hori grinned. The pharaoh was aiming for spouse murder. That was a heinous crime, to be punished by death. The king—far from being enchanted by her—had lured her into a trap.

She noticed her mistake and tried to undo it with another one. "My lord, have mercy! Sanefer seduced me! I couldn't think straight, my heart was in a turmoil!"

"So you also confess to adultery?"

Now her sentence might even include the destruction of her body by fire. Hori doubted that she could really be considered Merwer's wife if that were her only crime, but the threat worked.

She screeched. "No! I... It wasn't like that! They forced me, used me, first the father then the son!"

Amunhotep said, "Child, admit your guilt and we will refrain from sentencing you to the worst punishment: eternal damnation."

Nofru sagged and relinquished all pride. In a faltering voice, she told them how she'd grown tired of waiting for Merwer's wife to die. Instead, she turned to the son. How could she have taken care of her child without husband? Sanefer however only used her to help him poison the sick man while he was gone. Why he wanted him dead she didn't know. She'd hoped to become the mistress of the household after the young man had broken up with that 'horrible female physician.'

"What do you know about the murder of your own father, the peasant Wahka? Was that Sanefer's doing?" Amunhotep inquired.

"Nothing, I swear I know nothing about it! I thought an accident… You say it was murder? Dear gods, what have I done? What have I done?" She burst into tears.

Hori believed her, and apparently the judges did so, too. They retreated for deliberation without calling witnesses since the girl had confessed.

When they returned after a short time, Amunhotep smiled benignly. "The kenbet is inclined to believe you, Nofru, daughter of Wahka. His majesty, in his wisdom, decreed to spare you the burning of your body. As soon as you have given birth, you will be staked."

The room went dead silent, only from Nofru's throat erupted a barely human sound. She was still screaming when the Medjay dragged her out. Hori could hear her until two other guards brought Sanefer before the judges and closed the door. He remembered Muti's tears for the young woman. Did she really deserve such a harsh sentence, being skewered with a stake that only pierced her intestines but not a vital organ? She'd suffer agony for a long time before death finally relieved her. Then he remembered the pains Merwer must have endured. His agony would have lasted days, and she'd watched him suffer. Only now that her own life was at stake, did she show remorse. Yes, Nofru deserved what she had coming.

Sanefer had sworn the oath, and Thotnakht asked the first questions. The trader remained silent but stared at his persecutor with defiance.

Impatient, Senusret signaled for one of the Medjay to beat him—in vain. The accused kept silent.

The judges whispered to each other, then Thotnakht called, "Hori, son of Sobekemhat."

He approached Sanefer and stood beside him, with only one lawman between them. Sanefer bared his teeth and spit on the floor in contempt.

Hori didn't care. He spoke the vow in a clear voice, while a sense of helping Maat along to victory filled him. Without hesitation, he relayed what Nakhtmin and he had found out but omitted Antef's involvement in the crime. The king had asked them to do so because he didn't want the public to know that he used spies. Hori understood. It would have been a sign of weakness at a time when the pharaoh needed to demonstrate strength in the south. That was one of the reasons why Antef's trial would be held in Itj-tawy in seclusion. There they'd be able to tell everything.

At Hori's beckoning, the Medjay forced up Sanefer's arms so that everyone could see the scars that gave away the young trader.

Nakhtmin's testimony was much shorter since he didn't have much to add and mostly confirmed Hori's statement.

"Sanefer, son of Merwer. Do you want to say anything in your defense that could mitigate your sentence?" Thotnakht's voice boomed.

The accused lifted his head and scrutinized the judges with a provocative gaze. "You believe you know everything. But it was really her!" He turned around, searched the crowd, spotted Ouseret and pointed at her. "This physician, Nehesy's daughter, told me how I could kill my father without anyone finding out!"

Hori's heart skipped a beat. He stared at her in disbelief. She shook her head ever so slightly. No, she'd never have done something like that! His heart pounded against his ribs. What was Sanefer up to? Did he mean to drag his former fiancée—now Hori's—into the abyss with him out of sheer malice and in revenge? Because Nakhtmin and he had started snooping around on behalf of her?

At a gesture from his majesty, the Medjay cleared a path through the gibbering crowd, which was withdrawing from Ouseret as if she had a contagious disease, but forming a circle around her. Before the lawmen could reach her, Ouseret stepped forward of her own accord, her pose truly regal. Hori felt incredibly proud of her although he feared for her more than ever.

She stood where Nakhtmin had just given his testimony. In the sudden silence, everyone could hear her swear the oath.

"Ouseret, daughter of Nehesy, you heard the defendant Sanefer accuse you. What do you have to say?"

Hori wished Amunhotep would question her, not Thotnakht. The scribe's distrust carried in his voice.

She jutted her chin and looked into the eyes of every judge, one after the other. "I am a physician. My father Nehesy is a physician, and Merwer, the deceased, had been his patient for a long time. The truth is: I was engaged to Sanefer. The truth is: he asked me about the medicine my father made for his father. The truth is: Sanefer knew from Nehesy and me how dangerous the ingredient colocynth is. Another truth is that every physician in the Two Lands warns his patients when they need to take such a strong drug." She looked at Hori, who nodded and stepped up to her.

"That's correct." Her smile sent warmth into his icy limbs.

The king leaned forward and asked in a mild tone, "Why was there a deadly poison in this remedy? The royal physician Nakhtmin should explain."

His friend stepped up next to him. "Your Majesty, venerable judges. Some herbs heal in small doses but kill in high doses. Just like an excess of food isn't salubrious. Everyone here knows that human beings need to eat to survive, but if they eat too much, they throw up to get rid of it."

To Hori's joy, the judges nodded. Nakhtmin had chosen a great comparison.

His friend continued, "In a small dosage, the colocynth is used as a laxative and to ease joint pains. If one uses too much, the excrement turns bloody, cramps ensue that might lead to death like in Merwer's case. Every physician would strongly advise against taking more than the prescribed amount."

"Thank you, Nakhtmin. That was an explanation easy to follow." The king motioned for him to step back.

"But she told me everything, how to dry the seeds and grind them! It's her fault!" Sanefer shouted and charged at the judges' bench as if he wanted to strangle the king.

The Medjay caught him quickly and cudgeled him until he collapsed into a whimpering heap.

Hori reached for Ouseret's hand and squeezed it, but she didn't really need his support. "Sanefer asked me one day if the ingredient of his father's medication was the juice of the fruit. That prompted me to explain that we grind the dried seeds into powder, that was all. A seemingly harmless question—who wouldn't have answered it? I believed he was interested in my work, we meant to get married after all," she said almost cheerfully.

The judges whispered again then nodded. "You can leave the hall as a free and spotless woman, physician Ouseret. We believe you, among other things, because you were the one to set a new investigation in motion, which disclosed the truth."

Hori took a breath of relief and watched as she strode through the crowd and out the door. Almost reverentially the throng had parted for her this time. She probably would have been allowed to keep listening, but perhaps she'd had enough. How had she put it? After all, we meant to get married—no matter if it had all been fake, there had been a connection.

At last, Nofru's confession was read again since it incriminated Sanefer, and the trial ended. The verdict was patricide, the sentence death at the stake and burning of the corpse. Sanefer listened to the verdict without a sound as if it didn't concern him. However, he wouldn't be able to ignore the horrible agony and slow death, he'd feel them like any human being would.

The spectators streamed out of the hall, content that Maat had been served. Hori left the courthouse as one of the last. His gaze caught on the beautiful woman in the shade of a palm tree, waiting for him. He forgot all about Sanefer. "Ouseret!" he called, and she threw herself into his arms.

It felt good to serve Maat!

APPENDIX ~ EGYPTIAN DEITIES

Amun – *the hidden one.* Originally the local god of Waset (Thebes), he gained importance when the city became the capital of the 11th dynasty. First, he was the god of wind and fertility, displayed as a human with a feather crown. Since the ram was his holy animal, he was also depicted as a ram-headed god. Later the deity merged with other gods of the Egyptian pantheon (syncretism). As Amun-Ra, he incorporated the characteristics of Amun, Ra and Min.

Anubis – *the crown prince.* Jackal-headed god performing the rituals for the dead. He has special significance at the Judgment of the Dead when the hearts of the deceased were placed on scales and weighed against the feather of goddess Maat. This procedure assumes good deeds make the heart lighter, while bad deeds literally burden it. The dead recite all the things they did not do in their lifetime, for example lying, stealing, killing. If the scales tipped to the side of the heart, it was fed to the devourer. Since the Egyptians thought mind and memory resided in the heart, this meant a second and ultimate death. If the deceased passed the test, they were granted eternal life in the underworld.

Great Honker – in Egyptian onomatopoetically called *Gengen wer.* God in the shape of a goose whose egg symbolizes life and creation. One of the Egyptian creation myths claims Amun lay the world egg in the shape of a goose. Another one states Amun stepped from the egg.

Hapi – divine Nile flood, Nile god. He didn't have his own cult but was worshipped together with other gods.

Horus – *the distant one, who is above.* Falcon-headed god of the sky, mythical son of Isis, who conceived him when she transformed into a sparrow hawk and mated with the mummy of her husband Osiris. Horus was one of the most important deities of the Egyptian pantheon and strongly associated with the kingdom.

Isis – *seat, throne.* Mother of Horus and sister as well as wife of Osiris. She was patroness of mothers and lovers and depicted in human form with a throne on her head.

Khonsu – *traveler (of the sky).* The lunar deity was thought to be the son of Amun and Mut, forming the divine triad of Waset, his main cult site. Khonsu is usually depicted as a mummy wearing the lock of youth and a crescent on his head.

Maat – *justice, truth, world order.* Maat is a concept rather than a goddess. The word's meaning is a mix of justice, order and truth and signifies the ideal course of the world, where the sun rises every day anew and people treat each other fairly. The feather was her symbol, which she wore on her head when depicted as a human-shaped goddess.

Min – God of procreation and fertility, who was always depicted in human shape with an erect penis. He was also called Min-Kamutef, bull of his mother, which refers to the insemination of his divine mother. Min is father and son at the same time; he can create himself.

Monthu – Falcon-headed god. Originally, he was the main god of Waset (Thebes) before Amun surpassed him in significance. As the god of war and protector of weapons he was particularly worshiped in the 11th dynasty, which also influenced the names of pharaohs.

Nut – Goddess of the sky. Egyptians imagined Nut arching her body over the earth represented by the god Geb. Every evening, she swallowed the sun, which then traveled through her body to be reborn from her womb in the morning.

Osiris – *seat of the eye.* The god of the dead, depicted as a mummy with a feather crown. According to legend, Osiris was murdered by his brother Seth, who begrudged him his throne as ruler of the world. Additionally, he chopped up the corpse and spread the parts all over the earth. Osiris's sister and wife Isis succeeded in finding all parts and reassembled them. She reanimated the corpse and conceived their son Horus. From then on, Osiris ruled over the underworld and was depicted as a mummy. Abydos (Abdju) was the sacred place of this deity, and pharaohs as well as common people wanted to be buried there—if only in the form of a cenotaph, an additional, empty tomb. The myth of Isis and Osiris meant a lot to Egyptians.

Ra – or Re. Sun god and father of all gods. The cult of the god, worshiped in On (Heliopolis), was strongly associated with the kingdom. The solar disk adorns this human-shaped god.

Sekhmet – *the powerful.* The lion-headed goddess was responsible for war, diseases and epidemics but also for healing.

Seth – *creator of confusion.* God with the head of a fabulous creature, brother of Osiris. He's regarded as the god of the desert and all foreign lands, of evil and violence, but also as patron of the oases, god of metals and god of the dead, who picks up the deceased.

Thot – God of the moon, magic and knowledge. The Egyptians believed Thot had brought them scripture. He was depicted as ibis or baboon.

Appendix ~ Places and Regions

Abydos (Abdju) – The city of Osiris, the god of the dead, was located on the western shore of the Nile, about 100 miles north of ancient Thebes. In addition to the pharaohs of the first dynasties, many Egyptians arranged for their burial there or at least had a stele, a stone slab with inscriptions or reliefs, set up to become part of the resurrection ritual of god Osiris.

Abu – The Nile island Elephantine. Already populated in predynastic times, there were sacred sites like those of Satet and Khnum. The temple of Satet features the oldest nilometer to measure the water level. The island was a main trading spot for goods from the bordering southern countries like ivory, ostrich feathers, gold and more.

Biau – Sinai peninsula where the pharaohs had turquoise and copper mined.

Khemenu – the town of the eight, Hermopolis Magna, near the modern town El-Ashmunein, was the capital of the Hare nome and the main cult site of the god Thoth.

Khent-min – Today Akhmim, was about 125 miles north of Thebes and the main cult site of the god Min.

Kheny – at today's Gebel el-Silsila north of Aswan was a sandstone quarry in pharaonic times.

Itj-tawy – *encompassing the Two Lands* – Amenemhet I erected the city between the delta and Upper Egypt. The exact location is still unknown, but most likely it was close to the necropolis El-Lisht, where the first two kings of the 12th dynasty were entombed.

Kemet – *the black*. That's what Egyptians called their country.

Kush – or Nubia, the land south of Egypt (today Sudan). The territory starting at the first cataract (granite barriers in the Nile) was called Kush. Because of its rich gold deposits, the pharaohs undertook many expeditions and military campaigns into the southern neighbor's country.

Sekhet-hemat – *salt field*. Today the wadi Natrun, a group of oases west of the delta with extensive salt fields, which were already exploited in the time of pharaohs.

Ta-Seti – The land of the bow was the most southern nome of Egypt. Because of its location at the border, it was of great significance for the defense of the country, and the capital Abu was a hub of trade.

Waset – also Southern City. Ancient name of Thebes, today Karnak/Luxor. The capital of the 4th Upper Egyptian nome gained major importance when it became capital of the Two Lands during several periods of the Middle and New Kingdom.

Appendix ~ Glossary

Ba – The ba is also called the excursion soul or free soul of the Egyptians. It's the part of the soul depicted as a bird with a human head. During life, it's confined to the body, but when death occurs, it can separate from the body and fly around. However, it stays connected to the body and unites with it from time to time. The Egyptians believed the ba could be caught, injured and even killed.

Balance of the Two Lands – The place where the Nile branches out into the delta, the border between Upper and Lower Egypt.

Bones of the gods – Silver was rare in ancient Egypt since it had to be imported from faraway places. Because of its bright shine, it was called bones of the gods, while gold was referred to as skin of the gods.

Deben – Ancient Egyptian weight unit, its value varying in the Middle Kingdom. A copper deben was twice as heavy as one of gold. Besides barter trade, these pieces of precious metal served as a means of payment and for determining the value of goods. Deben were shaped in bars or rings, which allowed one to break off smaller bits.

Decade day – Tenth day of the week. Egyptian months consisted of thirty days split into three weeks of ten days each. On the last day of the week people had off from work. Additionally, work ceased on important religious holidays.

Eye of Horus, Udjat eye – Symbol of the god Horus. In their fight over the throne of Osiris, Seth ripped out his nephew Horus's left eye. The god Thot healed it, and since then it symbolizes medicine. In addition, mathematical fractions were based on the proportions of the eye, and these ratios were used for dosing the ingredients of remedies. Painted onto the hull of a boat, the eye was supposed to protect against dangers lurking in the water.

Going of the heart – Egyptian expression for the pulse, which they believed was caused by air and the life energy of a human being.

Great House – In ancient Egyptian, pr-aa referred to the seat of the king. In Greek times, the term became synonymous to the king, who from then on was called pharaoh.

Hem-netjer/hemu-netjer – Priest/priests. This group of priests ranged above the wabu and was divided in orders of initiation. From the highest order of priests, the hemu-netjer-tepi, the prophets of the gods, were selected.

Honey disease – honey urine, diabetes.

House of Life – One might call it a kind of university, where the higher professions like scribes, physicians, artists and priests were educated. It also provided rooms to cure the sick as a sort of walk-in clinic.

Inundation – The Egyptians counted years by inundations since the Nile floods were a yearly recurring event and therefore offered a fixed time frame. To specify a particular year, the regency of the king was given (year 3 of Amenemhat).

Iteru – Egyptian measure of length equal to about 6.5 miles.

Ka – A part of the soul. The ka leaves the body of the dying and continues to exist independently. As a double of the deceased, it serves as its guardian spirit. It inhabits a statue erected specifically for it in the tomb of the dead and feeds on the sacrifices placed before the statue.

Kenbet – Board of judges, which consists of dignitaries with jurisdiction over property claims and crimes. Besides these local courts, there was the Great Kenbet with the vizier and the pharaoh as chairmen.

Lock of youth – In the Old Kingdom an iconographic mark of the king's children. In later times, the lock of youth was also worn by the children of noble families. While the rest of the head was shaved, one braided curl hung from one side to the shoulder. Since the Horus child is also depicted in this way, it can be assumed these children were equated with the divine child. When they reached adulthood (at the age of 13 in ancient Egypt), the hair was shaved off. From the earliest dynasties on, noble Egyptians covered their heads with wigs. In the course of time, fashion changed and so did the headdress made of real hair or plant fibers. Certain professions wore a specific type of hairstyle, which made them recognizable. Wearing a wig was a status symbol, but originally the custom likely had hygienic reasons.

Medjay – Law enforcement, mercenary soldiers from Kush or the desert tribes.

Metu – *Vessels*. The Egyptians believed the body to contain tubes, the metu, which transported blood, water and air from the heart, the central organ, to all other organs. They imagined it in analogy to the Nile with its web of channels to water the fields. The metu were also responsible for the disposal of excrement: mucus, feces, semen, urine. It was important for those canals to not clog up and form a 'sand bank' so that all juices could flow unhindered. This is why Egyptians had regular enemas to cleanse the metu. At the same time, floodings of the organs, for example with blood, were deemed unhealthy.

Middle Kingdom – After the First Intermediate Period, the family of the nomarchs of Waset asserted itself under the rule of Mentuhotep II and unified the torn country. During the Middle Kingdom, Egyptian culture blossomed. Most works of literature which survived were written in that period.

Necropolis – City of the dead.

Nome – Administrative division in ancient Egypt. There were 22 nomes in Upper Egypt and 20 in Lower Egypt, which were ruled by nomarchs. Their borders probably derived from former tribal territories of prehistoric times.

Nomarch – The nomarchs were responsible for law enforcement and tax collection in their nomes but in a fairly autonomous way. In the course of history, whenever the central power weakened, some nomarchs expanded their fiefdoms and tried to usurp power.

Pectoral – large amulet covering the major part of the chest.

Pylon – Large gateway made of stone, built in front of temples.

Resetyu – Southern winds. Old name for the Khamsin, a hot and dry desert wind carrying sand and dust.

Sedge and the Bee – (Nesw Bity) Part of a pharaoh's title. The bee symbolized Lower Egypt, the sedge Upper Egypt. A pharaoh had five different names in total.

The nesw bity name was the throne name a pharaoh chose in addition to his birth name. Another name, the nebty name (the two mistresses) also showed the dualistic attitude of the Egyptians: the vulture goddess Nekhbet represents Upper Egypt and the snake goddess Wadjet Lower Egypt. Both animals adorned the pharaoh's crown to protect the king. Additionally, the king chose a Horus name and Golden name.

Shut – Shadow. Each living being casts a shadow, and thus it is proof of a physical existence. The Egyptians believed it also contained part of a human existence. After death the shadow disengaged from the body, but usually returned to it. If the mummy was destroyed or the body never mummified, the shadow strayed freely and could cause harm to the living.

Senet – A board game depicted in numerous murals since the first dynasties. Two players tried to place their pawns on a certain field on a board of thirty squares. The Romans adopted the game. It might be a precursor of backgammon.

Strong bull – The king was often equated with a bull since the animal represented virility, power and strength.

Sunu/Sunut – Male/female physician. Even women could become doctors but seldom trained in that profession.

Sycamore – also called sycamore fig or mulberry fig. With its protruding canopy, the tree made for an ideal shade dispenser in Egypt, where few deciduous trees prospered. Many parts of the sycamore were used as food or cures, and in Mennefer (Memphis) a holy sycamore was worshiped as embodiment of the goddess Hathor.

The Two Lands – Upper and Lower Egypt. Even in prehistoric times, the fertile Nile valley had been a place for different cultures to settle. The population of the marshy delta had been a different one than that of Upper Egypt. The mythical king Menes, however, managed to unite the two kingdoms. For Egyptians, this event retained immense significance throughout history. Their language reflects the duality in many ways as a consequence of previous individuality. Particularly in imagery, the unification was symbolically reenacted over and over again.

Ushabti – *Answerer*. Figurines in human shape made of clay, wax, wood or stone, often varnished or painted green with inscriptions and the name of the deceased they were to represent. They were placed into the graves since Egyptians believed the heavenly fields needed to be farmed, and the gods might call the transfigured to any other tasks. Should this happen, the answerer figurines were supposed to jump up and shout, "Here I am and will go wherever you order me!" Then they'd take care of any work deemed too menial for dignitaries.

Wab priest – The wab priests were the largest group within the priesthood of a temple. They ranked below the prophets in the temple hierarchy and took care of a major part of the daily offering services.

Weryt – Embalming hall. What the weryt looked like or how its interior was made up is fairly unknown. In Memphis, an embalming hall for Apis bulls was discovered, and it can be assumed the weryt for humans was designed in a similar fashion.

CALENDAR

Early on, Egyptians had a fairly exact calendar based on the annual Nile floodings. Additionally, they observed the course of the stars. When the morning star Sirius, Sothis in Egyptian, rose with the sun, the Nile floodings were about to begin. This marked the start of the year. The Sothis year and the solar year diverge slightly. Every 126 years—approximately—a one-day difference needs to be figured in.

One peculiarity is that the first month of inundation started earlier in the south than in the north, because the floods arrived there about two weeks later. I've used the later dates in this novel, because Itj-tawy was located quite far north.

Egyptians knew three seasons with four months of approximately 30 days each.

Akhet (inundation)

Wepet-renpet – June 19

Tekh – July 19

Menkhet – August 18

Hut-heru – September 17

Peret (emergence/winter)

Ka-her-ka – October 17

Shef-bedet – November 16

Rekeh wer – December 16

Rekeh nedjes – January 15

Shemu (harvest/summer)

Renutet – February 14

Khonsu – March 16

Khenti-khet – April 15

Ipet-hemet – May 15

Heriu-renpet – *between the years*, the five leap days, June 14 to 18.

The day was divided into 24 hours, with 12 attributed to the night and 12 to the day. The day began at sunrise and ended with sunset. This close to the equator the hours of daylight varied far less than farther north or south. A week encompassed ten days, the year consisted of 36 weeks, plus five leap days called Heriu-renpet. In early times, these were regarded as dominated by demons, later they were dedicated to the gods. These leap days came right before the new year.

Julius Caesar adopted this very exact calendar, and it formed the basis for the Julian calendar. Thus our calculation of time, to a large extent, goes back to the calendar of ancient Egypt.

POSTSCRIPT

Dear readers,

As always, I tried to melt fiction and history into an authentic story. Where sources of information were scarce, my imagination jumped in and developed scenarios that might have been possible. In the following, I'll explain where I took the liberty to modify things or make them up.

Senusret III is one of the great pharaohs of the middle kingdom who pushed the borders of the country far south during his reign. However, when he ascended the throne, the nomarchs had great power in his country. For generations, dynasties of the important families ruled their areas in almost complete sovereignty. The nomarchs also assumed the positions of mayors and prophets of the important gods and concentrated other offices in their hands—and the title nomarch, Haty-a, was the only hereditary one in Egypt. This led to a decentralization and loss of power for the king. Precariously, the major part of the military forces was under the command of nomarchs and organized in militia units.

The statue of Djehutihotep, a historical character, really existed. The nomarch had its transportation painted on the wall of his tomb. This scene symbolizes the presumptuousness of these feudal lords.

We don't know what actually happened back then—there are no records or other sources, but fact is: The rule of the nomarchs abruptly ended with Senusret's reign. No more grand tombs were cut into the rocks, and the title nomarch ceased to exist. The king installed merited military or administrative officers to govern the nomes. I developed the fictitious scenario of an attempted coup spreading from the two most powerful southern nomes Waset and Ta-Seti.

We know that Amenemhet I did employ informers since his reign as founder of a new dynasty was controversial. Although I found nothing about Senusret III using informers as well, it seems very likely that he did.

Money and monetary compensation did not yet exist in ancient Egypt, only barter trade. Pieces of copper and gold with a specific weight served as a precursor of actual currency, mostly to fix the price of a product. Direct exchange of goods was also common: bread for milk, linen for bronze blades and so on. Salaries were paid in natural produce, likewise rent and taxes. Since all the land belonged to the king, anybody who wanted to farm land or settle on it had to pay rent to the pharaoh. The same applied to what grew on the land. The king's tax collectors took almost all the surplus harvest, however, they distributed it among the people either as salary for state employed workers or to everyone in need during famines. A peasant's lot was hard though. In the season of inundation, when the fields were flooded, they had to work on the royal construction sites, for which they were paid with natural produce. Then there were the temple domains. The king allowed the temples to farm the land so they could maintain the buildings and support the priests.

Foreign trade was also under the control of the king. Thus no mercantile community developed as we know it, instead people organized the transport of wares. Since this concept is rather strange to modern readers, I decided to turn Merwer into more of a conventional merchant. At the time, his miracle grain, rice, was still unknown in the Middle East, but may have reached Egypt via the trade routes from Asia. Of course, an attempt to plant rice like wheat or barley could only fail.

Pigeons were already used in ancient Egypt to carry messages, however probably no written ones. I invented the concept of colored ribbons. Naturally, from there it would be only a small step to add a letter—and how else could the king have saved my heroes just in time?

I hope you enjoyed reading this novel. Of course, I'd love to get feedback and reviews.

Kathrin Brückmann
Berlin, July 2016

Also by Kathrin Brückmann

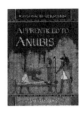

Apprenticed to Anubis: In Maat's Service 1

Hori and his fellow students celebrate their graduation from medical school. In a bar brawl, he accidentally kills the vizier's eldest son. For punishment, the king renders an unusual verdict: life in the service of the dead at the weryt, the walled-off embalming compound.

At the same time, young ladies at the pharaoh's court drop dead without obvious cause. When the corpses are brought to the weryt, Hori, now trained in embalming and organ removal, discovers the girls were murdered. Only he can't leave the place without turning his life sentence into a death sentence—or can he? An adventurous investigation unfolds.

Shadows of the Damned: In Maat's Service 2

Hori and Nakhtmin have barely adjusted to their new duties as the pharaoh's palace physicians when Hori is summoned to the secret embalming compound. A heart has been found there, which doesn't belong to any of the corpses; a heinous crime must have been committed, which robs the dead of any chance for an afterlife.

While clueless Nakhtmin begrudges his friend for simply disappearing and makes new acquaintances, Hori finds out far more than he bargained for and unwittingly puts his own life on the line. The surplus heart isn't the only thing off kilter at the weryt: the very secrets of the necropolis are in danger!

Of course, Nakhtmin soon gets dragged into the eerie investigation although he should rather take care of his pregnant wife. However, the shadows of the damned are encroaching...

Read more about it at http://hori-nakhtmin.jimdo.com/

Made in the USA
Middletown, DE
21 February 2019